Inherent Cost

Alicia Cameron

ForbiddenFiction
www.forbiddenfiction.com

an imprint of

Fantastic Fiction Publishing
www.fantasticfictionpublishing.com

INHERENT COST
A Forbidden Fiction book

Fantastic Fiction Publishing
Hayward, California

© Alicia Cameron, 2016

CREDITS
Editor: Rylan Hunter and James L. Wolf
Cover Design: Siolnatine
Cover Art: Adapted by Siolnatine from photo by Pressmaster at Dreamstime
Map: Siolnatine
Production Editor: Erika L Firanc
Proofreading: JhP323

SKU: AC2-000206-02 FFP
ISBN: 978-1-62234-296-9

Published in the United States of America

"My orders take precedence

over the orders of a complete stranger," Jere said bluntly. "My slave knows better than to answer questions about my personal life. I'm assuming you didn't ask him a question about the clinic hours, or a medical treatment, or anything of the sort."

The man looked surprised, and Wren sensed that he was backing off with his gift. The nervousness and compelling need to disclose information dissipated quickly from Wren's mind.

"You're very prepared," the man admitted. "I didn't expect you to have such strict rules for your slaves, nor did I expect such a distinct separation between your work and personal life; after all, your home and clinic are combined."

"I find that boundaries are remarkably important in a situation like this," Jere pointed out, glaring. "I didn't choose the structure of my property, but then, you wouldn't know that because you're not from around here, are you? Why are you in my clinic taking time away from legitimately ill people?"

The man pulled out a business card, handing it to Jere. "I'm with the State Slave Inspection Agency, a division of the Slave Control, Regulation, and Enforcement. There was a concern submitted about one of your slaves, as well as your abilities as a slaveowner, and the agency is doing a pre-screening to determine whether we will consider a full audit or not."

Also recommended...

You may also enjoy these other ForbiddenFiction works:

Subjection by Alicia Cameron
In a harsh, unyielding world where slaves are treated as less than animals, Sascha struggles to come to terms with everything he knows being ripped away from him, but a life of success could never prepare him for his life as one of the Demoted. Sinking lower and lower, Sascha begins to lose hope, but the whim of a mysterious, wealthy man has the potential to change all that.

When Cashiel sees Sascha, a young man who reminds him of the very history he is trying to escape, he makes an impulsive decision that he may regret. The slave could expose everything, or he could be the most valuable asset that Cashiel has ever acquired.
http://forbiddenfiction.com/story/AC2-1.000202

Counsel of the Wicked by Elizabeth Schechter
Matthias has spent his whole life on the edge of a very small world. The bastard child of a fallen woman, his magical talents as still unseen, he's known nothing but judgment and hatred from the harsh, religious people of his enclave—except for Balthazar, the son and heir of the High Elder, Balthazar shows Matthias kindness, love... and desire. When the High Elder discovers what his son has been doing, Matthias is arrested and sent to an isolated prison known simply as "The School". There, and in the wastelands beyond, Matthias learns the secrets behind the hypocrisies of the Council of Elders, and discovers his true heritage, true power, and true love.
http://forbiddenfiction.com/story/ES1-1.000222

DISCLAIMER

This book is a work of fiction which contains explicit erotic content; it is intended for mature readers. Do not read this if it's not legal for you. All the characters, locations and events herein are fictional. While elements of existing locations or historical characters or events may be used fictitiously, any resemblance to actual people, places or events is coincidental.

This story depicts fictional BDSM; it is not intended to be used as an instruction manual. It contains descriptions of erotic acts that may be immoral, illegal, or unsafe. The characters are not models for the Safe, Sane and Consensual forms embraced by most current practitioners of BDSM. The author takes license with the use of BDSM for dramatic effect. Do not take the events in this story as proof of the plausibility or safety of any particular practice.

To my favorite person:
Keep doing exactly what you want to do,
when you want to do it,
how you want it done.

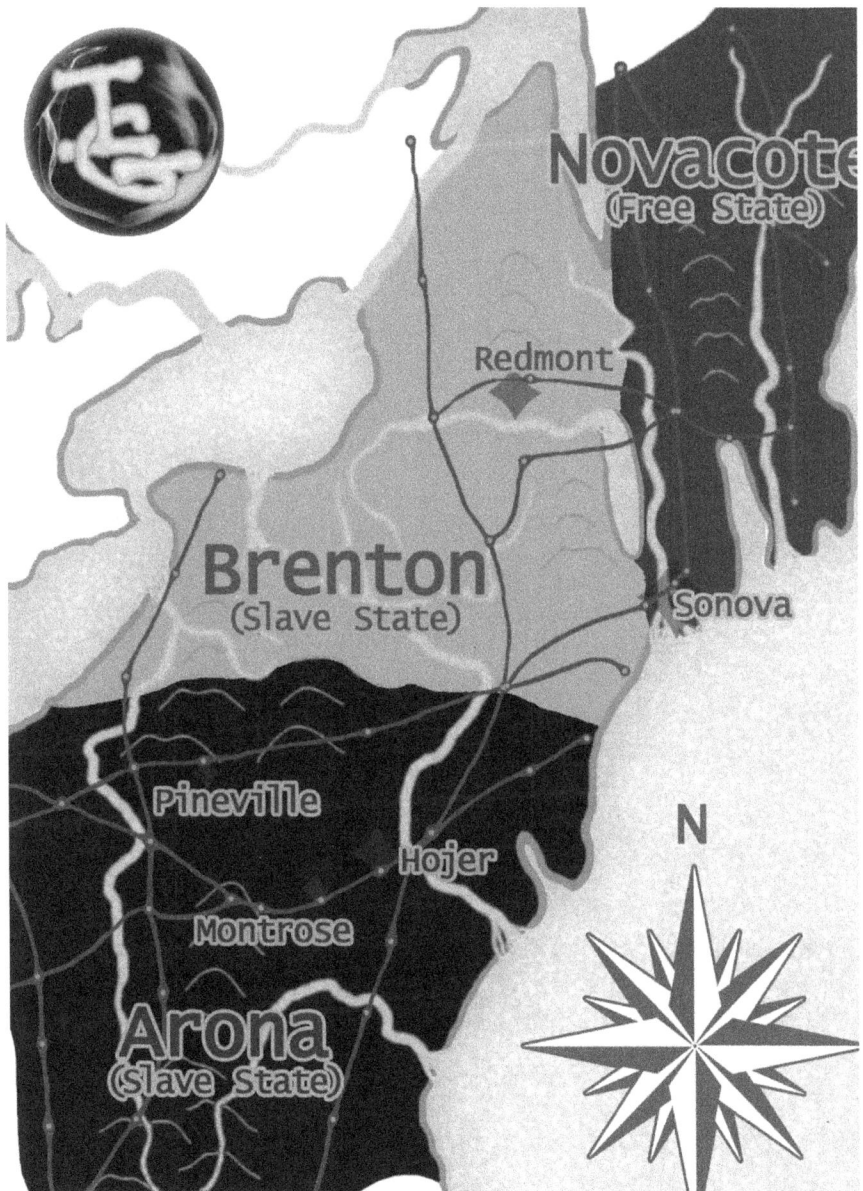

Contents

Chapter 1

Anniversary

"Where did you hear about this place?" Wren asked, settling happily into the speed train seat next to his lover. They had gotten a private car, hidden from prying eyes, allowing them to talk freely. "I couldn't imagine anything of the sort ever existing in Hojer."

They were headed to a new restaurant a few towns away. A gimmick; it allowed masters and spoiled slaves to eat together, curled up on a comfortable chair for two, instead of strictly relegating slaves to the floor. While it wasn't exactly the same as going out as equals, Wren knew it was likely the best way that he and his master would ever celebrate any anniversary.

"Paltrek," Jere admitted, smiling.

"Of course, he'd know of a place like this," Wren said, laughing. Jere's friend Paltrek was always up-to-date about everything that occurred in the slave state, and didn't mind the clear distinctions between free and slave. Like Wren, Paltrek had grown up in a slave state, accepting the way things were as a matter of course.

Jere, on the other hand, had fought social conventions as hard as he could from the moment he arrived in Hojer just over two years ago. Taking the role as the town's doctor, he had been confused and desperate for guidance. Fortunately, Wren had provided that, gently instructing his master on how to best fit into the strange culture of Arona—a slave state. In just a matter of months, their relationship progressed from a tense situation between slave and master, to a tentative companionship, then to a loving relationship that grew over time. Wren had always been there to help Jere figure out the intricacies of slavery, and Jere had been there to support Wren through

1

anything he needed, whether it was the challenges of trying to have a real relationship, or the difficulties of overcoming the horrors he had experienced at the hands of his previous master and trainers.

"He said it started as a pet-friendly restaurant, you know, actual animals, but I guess it got a little messy and the state health agency shut it down. They gutted it and started over with pets that wouldn't have accidents."

Wren laughed, cuddling close to his master, although Jere was so much more than that. He was Wren's other half: his boyfriend, his partner, whatever they wanted to call it. Wren knew that allowing slaves to dine with their masters was just an excuse for a new restaurant to make more money, but he appreciated the gesture. Jere longed to leave the state and free Wren, but it simply wasn't allowed. The best Jere could do was treat him well at home, keep him out of the public eye, and spoil him as much as possible. Wren was happy to go along with those plans.

"I'm excited to see what it's like," Wren decided. "Thank you for taking me."

"Of course," Jere replied, smiling as he leaned over, pressing his lips against Wren's.

Wren didn't hesitate to return the affection. He was glad that they had gotten a private car, because he wasted no time climbing on top of Jere, pinning him against the back of the seat and holding him down, kissing him roughly. Jere returned the favor by wrapping his legs around Wren, pulling him close. The rocking of the speed train only added to the excitement, moving them quickly enough that the landscape outside of the window blurred before their eyes. The speed trains had replaced most other major forms of transportation decades ago, running on a mix of mind gifts and solar energy. Both were far more sustainable after the resource crisis that occurred after The Fall. They weren't always reliable, but they were the best way to get around.

Wren wasn't about to actually fuck his master on a speed train, but he had no problem turning him on and teasing him. Like most people, Wren had a special ability, a speed gift, which he used to work his hand down Jere's pants quickly, grabbing his cock and jerking him as Jere gasped with excitement.

"Want me to make you come right here?" he teased, pleased when Jere gasped and nodded.

Smiling, Wren kept going, intent on his task until a sudden bump interrupted his pattern. Jere caught him before he fell to the floor, and Wren held on tightly.

"What the hell was that?" The speed trains were usually smooth.

"Probably just debris on the tracks," Jere assured him. "It's been storming again. Maybe a tree branch or something."

Wren nodded, pleased when the ride became smooth again. He leaned forward, pressing against Jere and making use of his second gift. Firesetting could be used for far more than just igniting things; Wren had learned how to control it with enough accuracy to heat even the most delicate parts of his and his lover's body. He warmed them both; the speed train wasn't cold, but he knew Jere enjoyed the effects of his gift.

For so many years, he'd had to hide his firesetting gift. Most people developed their gift around the time they reached puberty — and only one. Wren had developed a second one not long after, and he had been hiding it ever since. Nobody but Jere and Jere's mother had any clue about it, and he liked it that way. It wasn't safe for anyone else to know. It didn't matter that he could use it to influence temperature in all sorts of directions. All anyone would see was a dangerous slave who also had a mental gift; a rare anomaly that would put him at risk of government seizure and experimentation. The fact that Jere not only appreciated it, but also encouraged it, made Wren love him even more.

Jere responded to the gift with excitement. Some days, it seemed like even the slightest hint of heat had Jere asking for more, craving Wren's touch, begging to be fucked. The gift that Wren had been so afraid of for so many years was turning out to be one of the best sex toys either of them had ever encountered. As Wren kept the heat consistent, he leaned forward to kiss Jere again, forcing his tongue between Jere's lips roughly and quickly. Jere yielded to him, letting out a little moan of excitement. Within minutes, Jere was thrusting into Wren's hand again, kissing him eagerly.

Then the speed train let out a loud, metallic screech and everything went dark.

Wren blinked, shaking his head and sending glass flying. He was disoriented for a moment, trying to understand how they were lying in the dirt, and why there were massive piles of metal everywhere, blocking the light that managed to shine through the cloud of smoke and dust.

He reached out through the mind connection that he and Jere shared, feeling around until he felt the familiar psychic presence of the man he loved. Jere wasn't responsive, but he was alive, and he was close. Wren looked around, seeing a familiar arm poking out from beneath what appeared to be the side panel of the speed train. Without a second thought, he tore the sheet of metal off of his lover, gasping in horror when he saw the deep gash across Jere's head. Clearing away some more debris, Wren pulled him into his arms, making sure he was still breathing.

"Jere," he whispered, pulling him close. "Don't leave me. I need you, baby. Please wake up."

Wren's world was focused on Jere, but the screaming and shouting around him filtered in as a team of medics arrived, sent in on another speed train that ran on parallel tracks. Wren fastened Jere's pants and checked him for any other injuries, anything that he could address with the limited medical skills he had picked up from assisting Jere over the past few years in the clinic. Jere was a healer, gifted with the ability to cure illnesses and repair injuries with a touch and a bit of psychic energy. Now, he lay there helpless, motionless, blood pouring from the cut. All Wren could do was apply pressure to the head wound and wait for more help. He tried not to notice it, but the warm blood that ran between his fingers forced him to wonder just how long Jere had before the worst happened.

It seemed like it took forever, but someone finally came. Wren had rarely been happier to see strange free people.

"Please, sir, my master needs help!" he called, the moment one of the medics came close enough to hear.

The medic came over quickly, glanced at the head wound, and called for a team of slaves with a stretcher to come and collect Jere, taking him back to the train the medics had arrived on. Wren let him go reluctantly, following alongside the stretcher until a hand on his arm stopped him.

"You'll need to come with us," another medic said. "No room in the train for slaves."

Wren wanted to fight, but he knew better. The medic obviously had a psychic gift; he had picked up on Wren's lack of one in an instant. Wren was better dressed and far more privileged than the other slaves, but his physical gift stood out to those with the abilities to detect it. Trying to follow Jere would only delay his treatment; worse, it could get Wren into trouble. For a slave, "trouble" could mean anything from beating, to imprisonment, to re-training. In any case, it would mean more separation from Jere.

Wren nodded, following compliantly. He felt tears forming as he watched Jere being carried away and placed into the speed train with the other injured free people. He would have done almost anything to go with him. For a moment, the thought of revealing his firesetting gift and pretending he was a free person crossed his mind. He crushed those thoughts back inside, afraid to even think such a thing. Revealing his second gift would mark him as different, dangerous. It would be even worse than being left alone. As the people just kept being piled onto the speed train, his hopes of joining them were crushed. As he watched, the train zoomed away from him and into the distance.

The medic who caught Wren led him to where a variety of other slaves were gathered, most just scared and shaken up. Once the medic left, he glanced at another slave. "What's going on?"

"Speed train derailed," he explained, shrugging. "Slave train was all right, but they won't let us continue if our masters have been taken to one of the hospitals. Looks like you were in the passenger cars."

Wren was confused for a moment before taking notice of his own status. He was covered in blood, mostly Jere's, but as he paid more attention, he realized that some of it was his own. He had a few scratches here and there, including a big cut stretching from just below his neck down and across his chest. As he became aware of his own injuries, he realized that he was sore and aching now that the adrenaline was dying down. He pressed his hand against his chest and yelped in pain, startled by how much it hurt. The same pieces of speed train that knocked Jere unconscious must have landed on him as well. From the sharp pain, Wren guessed that he had at least a few cracked ribs.

"Where are they taking us?" he asked his fellow slave.

He shrugged again. "You should see a vet," he advised. "I think the rest of us are being boarded at the vet clinic, anyway."

Wren felt a cold chill pass through him at the idea of being treated in an animal clinic. Human healers and animal healers had entirely different gifts and training; only the desire to separate free from slave brought humans to a veterinary clinic. Again, Wren knew better than to protest. He hid his disgust and his fear, nodding. Jere would come for him just as soon as he was healed.

They waited for what seemed like hours as speed trains arrived, the smaller, faster ones that were reserved for emergencies. The free people who weren't injured were the next to go, and then the injured slaves. Wren was among this third group, herded into the small train car next to a few other slaves who had suffered injuries on the ride.

The ride wasn't long; all too soon, Wren was being led into a veterinary clinic. He tensed as he heard screaming from inside, mixing with the howls of dogs and screeches of cats as well as other noises he couldn't and didn't want to identify. The entryway was crowded and fairly clean, giving Wren hope that his experience would at least be tolerable. As a vet tech guided him into a back room, he tried not to gag at the smell that threatened to overwhelm him. The stench of animals, waste, and disinfectant blended together, but the smell of waste far overpowered everything else. The clinic was obviously overcrowded with the victims of the speed train crash.

The vet glanced at him in the hallway, not even bothering with an exam room for her initial assessment. She flicked a flashlight at his eyes and reached out her hand toward him, likely attempting to do a wellness check, or whatever passed for a wellness check from an animal healer.

Wren pulled back, ducking her hand. A healer's touch could bring pain as quickly as healing, and one who was trained on animals was likely to do more harm than good. Worse, a psychic healing connection could reveal his firesetting gift. "Please, ma'am, my master won't want someone else treating me."

The vet glared at him and Wren tensed as the tech's hand tightened on his arm. Wren felt the panic rising through his body and he forced himself to tamp down his firesetting gift, keeping his temperature from rising out of control.

"I mean no disrespect, ma'am," Wren said, hoping to appease her. "My master is a healer and he's very possessive. He'll be furious if anyone else tries to heal me. He will not authorize this treatment and he certainly won't pay for it."

The vet scowled. "I still need to make sure it's stabilized," she said, glancing past Wren.

Wren flinched as he felt another set of hands grabbing him. Two techs held him tight and he knew that he couldn't resist them.

Without wasting any more time, the vet reached out, grabbing Wren by the back of the neck. The second he felt her hand, he felt a shock of pain. The psychic healing connection that Jere could initiate so smoothly and painlessly was being forced by this vet, and Wren felt like knives were being stabbed into his brain. It had been like this ever since Wren first got his speed gift; at least, until he met Jere. He had almost forgotten the agony that a subpar healer could cause.

"Quit fighting it!" the vet snapped, giving Wren a shake.

He couldn't help fighting it. His firesetting gift was too dangerous, too close to the surface. For years, he had hid it. He had hid it from his trainers at the training facility, and he'd hid it from his previous master, crushing it inside of himself even when he was burned and the gift could have protected him. He felt the vet forcing her way inside of his mind and psychic energy and he fought to make his speed gift more prominent, to shut down, to do anything to evade her. Still, she made her way in, filling Wren with the sickening sense of someone else's psychic presence. Wren blurred his thoughts, blurred his emotions, and tried to keep her as far away as possible, no matter the pain it caused him.

But the firesetting gift had become a part of him.

Months of using his gift with Jere's protection and encouragement had weakened his ability to hide it. The psychic connection with the vet was fuzzy, like looking through a dirty window, but he could feel his temperature heating up and he could feel her confusion. As she probed his energy to assess his health, the fire inside of him grew more intense and he began to struggle. He had to get away; no injury was worth revealing this gift.

Without a plan, he launched at the vet, thrashing and screaming, not caring that he was acting like an animal. His speed gift gave him an advantage, allowing him to pull free from the grasp of the vet techs and out of the reach of the vet. He felt her trying to strengthen her psychic hold on him by initiating a paralyzing mind-bind, but her skills were weak and Wren had far more psychic ability than she expected. He jerked away and tried to run, only to find himself in a room full of cages. He had no idea where he was going or what to do when he was out; his only goal was to escape.

The goal was quickly defeated as a strong, harsh blast of cold water sprayed him and the cages, knocking him aside and slamming him against the back wall. Wren gasped and gagged as the water bruised him and choked him, and it took him a minute to cover his face with his arms, crying out in pain as the movement jarred the injury that he had gotten on the speed train. A part of him was relieved that the cold water quelled the firesetting gift.

Once he was subdued, the torrent of water stopped, and the vet glared at him angrily. She strode over and grabbed his leg, not initiating a connection with him again, but threatening to. "Try that again and I'll put you down."

Wren went still, fully aware that a healer of any sort could end life as quickly as they could save it. As a slave, he knew the vet was well within her rights not just to make the threat, but also to enforce it. Jere could sue her, but it wouldn't bring Wren back from the dead. Wren would be lucky to escape without being beaten.

"Get some restraints," the vet ordered. "Sharp ones. I want him completely subdued for the rest of his stay. He's got some cracked ribs and cuts, but he's stable. Put him in a holding kennel and let him suffer every time he takes a breath."

"Yes, Dr. Barrett." The tech complied with a smile.

Wren waited, passive and quiet, until she returned. The vet kept her hand around Wren's leg, holding him with the threat of her power as the tech opened the door to a cage.

"Give me your hands," she ordered, and when Wren complied,

she jerked one closer and slapped a restraint around it.

As the tech tightened the restraint, Wren whimpered, but stayed still. The restraints were lined with sharp spikes; any movement cut into his skin. Once they were fastened to both of his hands, the tech took one and handed the other through the bars of the cage to the vet. As Wren was pulled back, he felt the sharp metal stabbing into his wrists, overshadowed by pain in his ribs that left him breathless and whimpering. They ignored his cries and secured his arms to either side of the cage, making it impossible to move or escape. Once he was secured, they slammed the door, forcing him to curl his legs up, and latched it from the outside. They moved on to the next patient without a word.

The cage was small, obviously not made for humans, and Wren wondered if the clinic was overcrowded or if he was just here for punishment. A few moments passed and the pain in his body became tolerable as he realized that other slaves were housed in similar conditions. Below him was an unconscious slave, stuffed inside in a position nearly as uncomfortable as the one Wren was forced into. The clinic was packed, noisy, and the stench of bodily fluids was everywhere. As Wren glanced around, he realized that many of the slaves had been forced to relieve themselves inside of the cages, or as far outside of them as they could manage. He never thought he would be reduced to this again.

As he sat there, crouched over miserably, he tried to feel the mind connection with Jere. It was weak but still present. Wren was relieved to realize that Jere was not only alive, but that he hadn't been taken too far away. The mind connection didn't work well over long distances. With any luck, Jere was in the same town, maybe one or two towns away at most. Once he was healed and regained consciousness, he would come for Wren.

Wren waited for hours, aching, wet, and scared. He tried to sleep and make time go by faster. He startled when he felt the psychic jerk of the mind connection between him and Jere go dark.

Without thought, Wren turned and heaved, throwing up in the corner of the cage. Sudden breaking of a mind connection was always unpleasant, but Wren was more horrified by thinking about why it was broken. The logical part of his mind knew it was likely related to the healing process that some stranger was performing on Jere, but there was another explanation that was far more threatening.

If Jere were dead, the mind connection would be dark forever.

He didn't know what would happen to him if Jere were dead, and he didn't want to find out.

Chapter 2
Retrieval

Jere awoke to a pounding headache and a sense of confusion.

"Where the hell am I?" he mumbled, looking around. He quickly realized he was in some sort of hospital or clinic, the white walls and smell of antiseptic familiar to his senses.

As he realized where he was, his next concern was the emptiness he felt inside his head. For years, he had been accompanied by Wren, joining him in his thoughts, his emotions, and his psychic abilities. Now that he was left alone, he had only his own fear to focus on.

Jere jumped to his feet, unnerved by the realization that he had been healed, that someone had used the very gift on him that he used every day on others. The last memory he had was being on the speed train with Wren, and then everything was blank. He was thankful to whoever had healed him; if he had been knocked unconscious, he was sure something had gone wrong. He had no idea what that something would have been. More importantly, he had no idea where Wren was, or if he was even alive. The mind connection might have broken due to whatever injuries he sustained, or it might have been broken for a far worse reason.

He spied a slave carrying some medical supplies. "Where am I?" he demanded, frantic. "Where is my slave? Is he here?"

The slave pulled away from him, frightened. "I'm not sure, sir. I'm sorry... can I get the doctor for you?"

Jere scowled. He didn't want to take his rage out on this slave, but was furious and worried about Wren. "Find me my clothes!" he snapped instead.

"Yes, sir," the slave agreed, setting down the tray of supplies and pulling out a bag with Jere's clothes in it. "They've got blood on them, sir."

Jere didn't respond, he just grabbed them and started changing. He had to find Wren, and he wasn't about to do it wearing nothing but a hospital gown.

The slave slipped out of the room while Jere was changing, a move Jere couldn't really fault him for. He stormed around the clinic area until he found a doctor. "Where is my slave?" he asked, no more polite than he had been with the slave.

"Any property that survived the accident would have been taken to see Dr. Karmin Barrett at the local veterinary clinic," the doctor informed him. "I can get you directions if you'd like."

Jere felt his anger growing. "What in the hell is he doing at a goddamned vet's office? And what... wait, what accident?"

The doctor shook his head. "Your speed train derailed. You suffered significant head trauma; it's no wonder you don't remember it. I don't know about your slave. I wasn't on the train. I just got a bunch of wounded passengers dragged to my door and you were one of them. You've been completely healed, but your energy might be a little depleted. You should take it easy for a few days—"

"I'll settle my account and take those directions, please," Jere cut him off. "I'm sorry. I'm a little agitated."

The doctor didn't respond; he just gave Jere the bill, the directions, and a form to free the clinic of any liability that might occur. Within minutes, Jere was making his way through the unfamiliar streets, intent on finding the veterinary clinic where he hoped he would find Wren. The alternative was too horrific to think about.

Fortunately, the clinic wasn't far. Jere longed for a speed gift, or even one of the terrifying, polluting cars that were popular before The Fall. Human-drawn carts and bicycles were becoming popular in the cities, but in rural areas, communities were close enough that most people just walked—or ran. Jere was out of breath by the time he arrived, exhausted from his already poor health and anxious to find Wren. He didn't bother checking in at the reception area, he just pushed through the doors that led to the back room. Jere searched through the psychic energy he could feel, relieved when he felt Wren's presence. It was strong and steady, if terrified. Jere wasn't sure whether to be relieved that he was alive or furious that someone had scared him. He followed Wren's presence until he arrived in a back room, ignoring the protests of the veterinary staff who tried to block him.

When he pushed through the door, he was struck with the overwhelming stench of bodily fluids. Both animal and human, the odor reached Jere's nose quickly and he tried not to gag. He covered his nose with his bloodstained shirt and pushed forward, relieved when he finally saw Wren.

His partner was alive, but he was caged and chained like an animal, locked inside of a cage barely large enough *for* an animal. He was injured. Jere didn't need to use his healing gift to notice it, Wren was covered with blood, whimpering in pain and trembling with fear. Jere wasn't usually a violent man, but he had to hold himself back from grabbing every free person in the building and stopping their hearts.

Jere whirled on the vet tech who was trying to pull him out of the holding room. "Get him out of there now!"

"Sir, he should probably be treated by the vet," the tech suggested. "He's been restrained for his own safety. He's quite volatile and badly injured—"

"That didn't seem to matter until I showed up with money, did it?" Jere snapped. "I'm a fucking healer. A human healer, not some inadequate animal healer. Get him out of there!"

"Let me just grab the paperwork."

Jere didn't bother to follow, he just grabbed the first chair he saw and turned toward the row of cages, intent on battering them apart.

"Jere!" Wren hissed, growing pale at Jere's fury. "They're animal cages. There's a latch at the top—don't go breaking things!"

Jere paused, his rage calmed somewhat by hearing Wren's voice. He set the chair down and made his way over to the cages. He opened the door quickly, then glanced at the restraints encircling Wren's wrists. Little drops of blood were dripping from them, and he felt the rage returning. He knew Wren hadn't been any sort of threat, and even if he was, there was no need for this sort of treatment. There was no need for his lover to be in a vet clinic in the first place.

"Just get them off, please," Wren requested, looking desperately into Jere's eyes. "I want to go home."

Jere nodded, reaching in and examining the restraints. The buckle needed to go tighter before it would come off, and he knew it would hurt Wren. He calmed himself slightly and placed his hand on Wren's cheek.

"Let me make it stop hurting," he said quietly. "And I can fix the mind connection while I'm at it."

Wren nodded, giving him a weak smile.

In seconds, Jere had pushed his way past Wren's psychic defenses. The old connection lit up in response, bringing them back together instantly. Jere was flooded with the panic and terror that Wren felt, and he tried not to let too many of his own emotions spill over. Wren would know that Jere wasn't angry with him, but that much rage would be intimidating for anyone. As Jere worked to dull Wren's pain, he felt Wren turn his head slightly. The kiss that Wren placed on his hand steadied him as it always did. Jere would heal Wren properly, but he was already feeling dizzy and weak from his injuries. Blocking the pain as much as possible, he pulled the buckles to release the restraints. Jere was pleased when his lover was free and in his arms again. He eased Wren out of the cage, glancing over the injuries that he had sustained. He felt renewed anger when he realized that none of those injuries had been treated, not even with a simple painkiller.

"I take it you're the boy's master?" a voice asked behind them.

Jere turned, one arm still wrapped tightly around Wren, the other out and ready to harm. The woman speaking—whom Jere assumed was the vet—didn't even flinch.

"Yes, and we'll be leaving," Jere informed her curtly. "I don't want to be in this place another minute. What you did to my property? It should be criminal!"

"He's the one who resisted treatment," the vet informed him. "Said his master was a healer and wouldn't let anyone else work on him. Put up a hell of a fight when I tried."

"Bullshit. You tortured him."

"I assessed his health," the vet replied. "At the risk of danger to myself. For a slave with a speed gift, he has quite a strong psychic presence. He was able to break away from the healing connection with ease. Fortunately, we were still able to keep him safe while you were away."

"You can't even clean the shit off your floors," Jere replied, utterly disgusted. He had worked in emergency departments before, real ones where they treated humans like humans. These sorts of conditions would never have been tolerated. "I wouldn't bring a dog here to be put to sleep."

"All the same, we still have a fee for boarding and stabilizing your property," the vet informed him, shoving a statement into his hand. "And we need you to sign a release indicating that we didn't provide services because of your request."

Jere glared at her, ready to fight until he felt Wren squeezing his hand.

"*Please, Jere. It's not worth it. Just take me home.*" The psychic connection they shared allowed them to have private conversations despite being around other people.

Jere nodded, signing the release and digging some money out of his pocket. The offending pile of shit was still lying on the floor, and before he had a chance to think about it, Jere threw the money and the release form down on top of it, grinding it in with his heel.

He turned, pulling Wren along with him. As they left, Jere felt a little pang of guilt as one of the vet's slaves was ordered to retrieve and wash the money.

He kept a tight hold on Wren as they walked away from the vet clinic.

"*Was that really necessary?*" Wren asked.

"*Probably not,*" Jere admitted. "*I was just so fucking angry. How dare they put you in a place like that! In a cage with those fucking things on you!*"

"*I'm fine, Jere,*" Wren reassured him. "*I'm just glad you're okay. The last I saw you, you were unconscious, bleeding out from that head wound. I'm glad someone got you healed.*"

"*Didn't spare you the courtesy,*" Jere muttered, furious. "*How dare they take you to a fucking vet clinic!*"

15

"*It's protocol in most places,*" Wren reminded him. "*Not all healers will see slaves, and I'm sure the medical clinic was busy. A lot of people were hurt.*"

Jere was silent. He hated this place, hated any place that had slaves. He had done everything he could to protect Wren and it still wasn't enough. He spotted a sign for an hourly hotel and pulled Wren along with him.

"*Let's get you healed and rest a little,*" he suggested. "*Then I'll figure out when the next speed train can take us home.*"

Wren just nodded. Jere paid for the room, ignoring the concerned look on the attendant's face just as he had ignored the people they passed on the street. With the amount of blood on them both, they made quite a scene. Once they reached their room, he pulled Wren into his arms properly, holding him tight.

"Let's sit," Jere suggested. "I can heal you."

Wren sat, but held Jere back at arm's length. "You need to take care of yourself first," he insisted. "Get something to eat, drink some water. You're pale and shaking."

"You're in pain!" Jere protested. "You should have been healed hours ago!"

Wren nodded. "Yes, and we'll both have bigger problems if you push yourself too far. I want to go home, Jere, not sit here and wait for you to regain consciousness again."

Jere flushed, embarrassed. He knew it wasn't his fault, but he felt responsible for what had happened to Wren. "Okay," he agreed.

Reluctantly, Jere left Wren in the rented room and made his way to the business next door, buying some sandwiches and water and bringing them back to the room. When he returned, Wren was showering with his clothes on, washing himself and the clothing at rapid speed. Jere sat and started eating dutifully; he had no appetite, but he needed the energy to heal Wren. As he watched, Wren finished showering, stripped off the clothes, and warmed them between his hands. Jere watched in amazement as steam came off the garments; in seconds, they were dry. Wren turned around with a tired smile on his face.

"Want me to do yours, too?" he asked.

Jere shook his head. "Save your energy," he advised. "I'm a doctor; I'm used to having blood on me."

Wren nodded, dropping down on the bed. "I wasn't hurt too badly," he said quietly. "I could probably wait until we get home...."

It was painfully obvious that Wren was lying. The slightest movements made him wince, and he was breathing as shallowly as possible. There was no way Jere was letting his lover suffer from those injuries until they went home. "I'll finish eating and then I'll at least start on healing you. Maybe it won't be perfect, but it will be a start. You'll be out of pain, and you won't risk bleeding all over your freshly cleaned clothes."

Wren nodded, leaning against Jere. They were quiet as Jere finished eating and ran his hands over Wren's body, figuring out where he was injured and what to heal first. Jere barely noticed when he entered into Wren's mind; they were close enough that it was as familiar as his own by now. He focused first on stopping the pain; Wren's collarbone had been severely bruised and a few of his ribs had been cracked. He felt Wren breathe a little easier once he blocked the pain, then he started to mend the bones, knowing it would take far too much energy to heal them completely. As it was, he could set them, start the healing, and finish when they got home. Wren lay pliant next to him, and when Jere couldn't push himself any further, he stopped, keeping his hands on Wren's body.

"Feeling better?" he asked, even though he knew Wren was.

"Much," Wren agreed, sitting up to kiss him. "Thank you."

Jere shook his head. "I should never have left you like that. This was supposed to be a nice day out, something fun. Instead... I don't want to think of what they might have done to you there."

Wren gave him a curious look. "I'm sorry, did you arrange for the speed train to derail? Or pull the roof of it onto your face? It was an accident, Jere. It's a risk we take every time we go out. I'm aware of it, even if you seem surprised. That's just how it is."

Jere shook his head. "It shouldn't be. I want you to be safe, even if I'm not there to protect you. There has to be something I can do."

Wren smiled, pulling Jere's arms around him. "I'm with you. I'd really like to never end up in a place like that again. But you came. That's all that matters."

It was halfway through the next day by the time another speed train arrived and brought them home. Jere was still exhausted; he had slept some, but any recovery he made was immediately funneled into healing Wren. He couldn't shake the feeling of guilt, just like he couldn't stop planning ways to keep him safe in the future.

Growing up in a free state, where there were barely even any mentions of slaves, Jere had only been minimally aware that slaves were even a possibility in the modern world. In his mind, such things were relegated to the most backwards, barbaric places in the world, surely no place that he would ever visit. He had never expected to own one of his own.

Or two of his own, as it was.

They arrived home to find the house quiet and seemingly empty. Jere looked around for a moment, wondering where his other slave was.

Isis came out after a few minutes, the not-so-secretly relieved smile on her face showing as she realized she hadn't been abandoned. Her paranoia had faded considerably over the year since Jere bought her, signing over a small sum of money for the girl who was about to be sent to die at a workhouse. She had been beaten, starved, and was nearly insane back then. Over the past year, she had healed both physically and mentally, slowly opening up and starting to trust first Jere, then Wren. She took pride in her appearance now, arranging her long, dark curls in different styles, and selecting clothes that brought out her green eyes and olive skin tone, what little bit of skin she allowed to show, anyway. She had made remarkable progress.

"The mind connection went dead," she said, shaken. "And then, you guys didn't come home... is that blood?"

Jere just nodded. "Yes. Our train derailed. Are you okay?"

Isis nodded. "I hid," she admitted. "I'm glad you're back. Are you both all right?"

Jere shrugged. "I got good treatment."

"I got to spend a few hours in a vet clinic for the first time," Wren informed her, his tone conveying his disapproval. "But Jere came and got me."

Isis shuddered. "Sorry. I've been there. Those places are awful."

"So I noticed," Wren agreed. "They had staff at the training facility, and once my last master bought me, when he bothered to heal me at all, he healed me himself. I think I'd rather be left to die than have a vet treat me again."

Isis nodded.

"It won't happen again," Jere promised, his tone fierce. He just wished he knew how to keep that promise.

"Jere, you got some messages at the clinic while you were out. A lot of people wondered where you were. And some creepy guy in a suit came in looking for you. He wasn't sick or anything, and he kept trying to ask me questions, but all he'd say was that he wanted to talk to you."

Jere raised an eyebrow. He had left Isis there to clean and organize while they were out; he hadn't expected her to go above and beyond. "You actually talked to people?"

She shrugged. "You forgot to lock the door. I made sure not to be rude when I answered, even that one guy. I told him that you didn't want me talking to people, and that I had work to do in the back. Behind a locked door."

Jere grinned, imagining how that must have gone. She could be abrasive at times. "Did you write down what they wanted?"

Isis rolled her eyes. "Yeah, because I'd forget so quickly."

Isis had a memory gift that went beyond photographic. She remembered everything she had ever seen or heard from the time that the first signs of her gift started to show. It had resulted in her being taken as a slave when she was a mere seven years old instead of the traditional age of thirteen. Isis had been valuable as a spy, too young to even read the letters she memorized for her masters. As she grew older, her behavior became uncontrollable, and so did the harsh treatment she received. For years, she'd experienced nothing but torture and abuse. She had only been fifteen when Jere had bought her, but she had seen far more of the world and its cruelties than either of the men who had adopted her. As she slowly became acclimated to her new home, she was learning how to use her gift far more effectively to help manage things in the clinic, where she doubled as a note-taker and assistant.

"You want me to write it down so *you* don't forget?" she asked Jere, teasing him.

"Yes, please," he admitted. He knew his memory was nowhere near as good as hers.

"All right," she agreed. "You can get details or anything when we do the energy thing."

Jere nodded. Siphoning psychic energy, or the "energy thing," as Isis called it, was an uncomfortable but useful process; connecting to someone else's psychic energy source was intimate, and thoughts and emotions and memories got all tangled up in the psychic web. Jere's medical ethics made him recoil from the very idea, but when he had agreed to treat the slave population in Hojer, he had found himself with few other alternatives.

"Speaking of energy, you should get some rest," Wren hinted. "You're back to work tomorrow and I'm sure it will be busy."

Jere shrugged. "I'm all right," he protested, knowing he was as exhausted as Wren said.

Wren leaned over and gave him a light kiss on the cheek. "You're half-dead. You're covered in blood. You're slower than I am. Go get in the shower, and then I'll come and make sure you're clean."

"Gross," Isis commented, heading toward her bedroom. At sixteen, she was well aware of what couples did in bed at night, and as a slave she had experienced far too much of the sort against her will in the past. Now she was happily enjoying a second childhood, and had no interest in anything sexual.

"You're just jealous of all the fun we have," Wren teased.

"Ew!"

Isis made a face at them as she left. As patient and compassionate as Jere was with Isis, she and Wren had developed a far different relationship. He teased her and didn't tolerate any of her bullshit tantrums. Isis went along with it and appreciated his no-nonsense manner. Wren had even compared her, rather begrudgingly, to his own little brother, the one he hadn't seen in years. Isis hadn't stopped smiling for days after that comment.

Jere laughed and headed to the shower as Wren had ordered. He was relieved to know that the man he loved and the girl they had both grown to care for so deeply were safe. His little family depended on him.

Chapter 3
Working Order

Wren took a few moments to tidy up, not because anything was actually dirty, but because it was one of the few things that he could do to calm himself without seeming too obvious. For Jere, the incident today must have seemed isolated, a problem that he could solve quickly by being strong and threatening, tearing into the vet like she would simply dissolve into thin air once he left.

It had been nice to watch, in a way. Jere was sexy when he got that protective, and a part of Wren rejoiced that his lover would take so many risks for him.

But as much as Jere was being valiant, Wren knew that an overprotective master could come off as entitled, too involved with something that was considered property. Challenging the way that society in a slave state worked could bring criticism and judgment; worse, it could draw attention to their unconventional lifestyle. These risks weighed on Wren's mind as he polished the counters, trying to push away the feelings that his master had crossed a line.

Even with the time Wren took to calm down, Jere still had yet to get into the shower by the time Wren joined him. Jere was standing in the bathroom that connected to the master bedroom, examining the freshly healed skin on his forehead. The healer hadn't left a scar, but the skin was new and pink. Wren came up behind him, catching his eye in the mirror, and turning him around forcefully. He drew Jere into a deep kiss that left them both breathless. He clutched at Jere's back, half-tempted to rip his shirt off of him, but deciding that he should show at least a little bit of restraint.

Besides, having a speed gift made undressing his lover all that much faster and easier.

Within seconds, Jere was wearing nothing but a smile as he stood in front of Wren.

"I'm so glad you're okay," Jere said.

Wren smiled. Even after all this time, it was strange that someone cared so much about him. "Go shower. When you're finished, I can make sure that everything is in working order."

Blushing, Jere complied. While he did, Wren rearranged the closets, trying to distract himself. Everything seemed fine when Jere was with him, but when he was alone, he couldn't help but think of the accident, the awful vet clinic. Jere was pissing off a lot of people lately, and Wren had to wonder when it would all fly back and hit them in the face. Worse, when Wren was alone, he couldn't ward off the anxiety that he had felt since he had struggled and nearly failed to hide his firesetting gift. Maybe they were both getting too comfortable.

In just a few moments, he heard the water turning off. Jere stepped out of the bathroom, still damp, and made his way over to Wren. "Ready to test me out?"

"Perfect timing," Wren agreed, motioning for him to come closer.

Jere stepped forward, pressing his naked body against Wren's clothed one. He rubbed up against Wren and leaned in to kiss him again.

Wren smiled, snaking his hand down to grab at Jere's cock, stroking it as he whispered into his ear. He felt his temperature rising along with his cock. Just thinking about what he wanted to do with Jere turned him on. Knowing that he could let his gift out freely made it that much more exciting.

Jere reached down to unfasten Wren's pants, making quick work of the fastening. Wren shuddered as he felt his fly undone and his skin exposed to the air. It had been so difficult to let his guard down when he and Jere first started to explore each other's bodies, but now he felt certain that he could trust Jere to do just about anything and make it feel good.

Jere worked his hands inside of Wren's pants, sliding them down a few inches and pulling out his cock, which was already growing thick and hard. He stroked it gently, and then moved his hands back up under Wren's shirt.

Wren let out a sigh as Jere touched him. This man made him feel better than anything else in the world; he had for so long, and Wren didn't think he could ever possibly tire of it. Jere touched him in exactly the right way, at exactly the right time, and he knew Wren's body better than Wren did.

After planting another kiss on Wren's lips, Jere smiled and dropped to his knees, his face just inches away from Wren's cock.

"Is this the kind of examination that you wanted?" Jere teased, looking up at Wren without a trace of shame. "I took a good blow to the head. Medical advice says we should definitely check my gag reflex, swallowing abilities... make sure my tongue works...."

Wren smiled, trying to hold back a laugh. Jere leaned in, letting the tip of his tongue brush against the head of Wren's cock.

"And later, we can make sure everything else works."

Even more turned on by the warm breath as Jere spoke, Wren felt himself growing full of need. He reached out, running his hands through Jere's hair lovingly, then jerking him down, pleased when Jere responded enthusiastically. Wren held him down, forcing Jere to take him deep for a few seconds, before relaxing his grip and letting him do as he pleased.

When Jere sucked his cock, when Wren was rough with him, it was more than just the physical sensation. It somehow seemed to put things back in order, like they were meant to be. Wren hated being a slave, and he hated anything that reminded him of it. Reversing their roles in bed made interruptions like the vet clinic easier to tolerate.

The fact that Jere didn't so much as question any of it made it that much easier.

It wasn't long before Wren stopped thinking about slavery and roles and ways to overcome them—Jere had his mouth wrapped around Wren's cock, one hand clutching his ass, and the other playing with his balls, and Wren didn't want to think about anything else at all. He relaxed quickly, the familiar hands and mouth doing their work, and he thought about how much he loved Jere, and how perfect everything was.

Jere worked him expertly, starting slow and taking his time, moving his lips and tongue over Wren's cock like it was his favorite thing in the world. From what he told Wren on many occasions, it *was* one of his favorite things in the world, so it was a rather apt comparison.

Slowly, he built up speed and excitement, and when Wren started to thrust, Jere obligingly took the length of his cock deep into his mouth, swallowing him down and making a little humming noise that Wren could feel vibrating through his whole body.

Wren reached out, grabbing a fistful of Jere's hair and pulled him close, thrusting into his mouth while still keeping a tight grip. Jere's response was to suck more eagerly and to reach around, wrapping his arms around Wren's legs to steady himself as Wren fucked deep into his mouth, over and over again.

"You feel so good," Wren told him, happy to help keep the pace up by pounding into Jere's face with his hips.

"*Are you finding me in full working order?*" Jere teased, taking advantage of the mind connection. "*We have to try this sometime when you're sitting at the front desk of the clinic. So fucking hot.*"

During the day, Wren probably wouldn't agree, since there was important work to focus on. Right now, it sounded amazing, and the idea of Jere taking care of him while he pretended to work was too enticing not to think about. If it weren't for the difficulty of getting dressed and walking through the house, he would suggest that they do it now, but it seemed like entirely too much work. Besides, the idea alone was enough fodder for Wren's imagination, enough so that he realized he hadn't even replied. "Okay," he managed, after a while. He was too caught up in the blowjob to think of anything else. "We should try it tomorrow. Or later tonight."

He let Jere continue to suck him for a while, loving the lazy pace, and then he decided it was time to move on. He wanted more, and he knew Jere would only be too happy to give it to him.

On impulse, he pulled Jere up by his hair, pleased when he saw the big smile that the move inspired in Jere. Wren pulled him closer, forcing Jere to bend down a little bit so his ear was at the same level as Wren's mouth. Wren could have stood on his tiptoes to reach, but it was better to make Jere bend for him.

"I want to fuck you," Wren revealed, sensing through the connection as well as through Jere's body language that Jere was in total agreement.

"Yes, please," Jere agreed, pressing his body against Wren's. "How do you want me, love?"

Wren smiled. He loved when Jere offered himself up like this. "Bent over the edge of the bed," he decided. It wasn't the most intimate position, but he wasn't feeling particularly intimate tonight, he was feeling rather predatory, and this only accentuated that feeling.

Jere smiled, gave Wren's cock one more sensual stroke, and then positioned himself as requested, searching around under the covers for the lube. They had started celebrating their anniversary before they even left home the other day, and Jere had insisted that cleaning up would have been a waste of time that they could otherwise spend touching each other. He handed the lube to Wren when he found it.

"Messy," Wren teased, taking the lube and giving Jere's ass a playful smack.

"I think we both liked the results of our messes," Jere pointed out, shaking his ass a little bit as he smiled back at Wren.

"I think you're absolutely right," Wren agreed. He worked quickly with the lube, stretching and teasing Jere to the point of moaning in just a few minutes. He paused, considering the fact that he was still fully clothed, and then decided that he kind of liked it that way.

"Look at you, all spread and waiting for me," he teased, one hand pressing down on Jere's back as the other reached around to grab at Jere's cock. "All hot and hard for me already."

"You make me hot," Jere mumbled, thrusting into Wren's hand. "Make me hotter?"

Wren happily complied. He knew just how much Jere loved feeling his heat, no matter how much of a threat it was. While he kept it private, he had started using it so often in bed that it was feeling natural. Maybe it made it harder to tamp it down when he needed to, but the benefits of adding it to their sex life were amazing.

Tonight, he started with the hand that was stroking Jere's cock, expertly controlling the temperature until it went up higher and higher, enough that he could feel Jere squirming.

"Trying to get away, or to get closer?" Wren asked.

"Both?" Jere replied. "It feels good. And it hurts."

Wren just smiled. He knew that Jere liked both of those things, and he loved giving them to him. He was getting quite skilled at the hurting part. He had been trained for years to make his masters feel good, but hurting someone had terrified him the first few times. The way Jere coaxed, begged, and came harder than ever when they played like that assured Wren he was on the right path. Lately, Wren had taken on quite the ambition of his own.

"Can you take a little heat elsewhere?" Wren asked, wiggling the fingers that were buried deep in Jere's ass.

"Fuck yes," Jere replied, an excited shudder going through his body. "Please?"

Wren laughed, working the heat on his other hand as well, and feeling quite proud as Jere squirmed and moaned for him. He loved that sound, and he loved knowing he was the one doing it.

"That is so amazing," Jere mumbled, his body rocking almost in time with his words. "Get me all warmed up and then fuck me?"

Wren fully supported the plan. He toyed with Jere for a few more minutes, working him up and warming him up until Jere was rocking hard and heavy against his hand, begging Wren to fuck him already. Wren drew it out just a little longer, pushing Jere closer to the point of desperation, and then he granted Jere's wishes, replacing his fingers with his cock and slipping into Jere without missing a beat.

It was strange, feeling his cock entering a space that he had just warmed above usual body temperature, if only by a few degrees. In theory, Wren could warm any part of his own body, but he hadn't yet been able to master the trick of making his cock generate heat. At least, not more than it did naturally.

Still, Jere was quite warmed from Wren's earlier play, and Wren was filled with excitement as he worked himself completely into Jere, easing out only slightly before pounding back in and making them both gasp at the impact. Wren kept one hand on Jere's cock, noticing how hard and ready he was, and his other hand was up near Jere's face, bracing against the mattress so Wren could get a good grip, stabilizing himself as he thrust into Jere faster and faster.

Without warning, Wren felt a tongue and teeth on his wrist, and he opened his eyes to see that Jere had taken an interest in the hand that he had there. As he continued fucking him, he raised his hand off the mattress, stroking his fingers lightly across Jere's lips, feeling how soft and wet they were.

Wren let out a gasp as Jere pulled two fingers into his mouth, biting and sucking and licking them just like he had sucked Wren's cock earlier. The memory was almost overwhelming, and the fact that Jere was doing it was turning Wren on even more. Jere continued to suck and swallow around Wren's fingers, tightening his muscles around Wren's cock at the same time, and pretty soon, Wren felt himself getting ready to come. He kept one hand working Jere's cock, the other being sucked in Jere's mouth, and he carefully raised the heat a little more, knowing that the warmth he was feeling in his hand was only a sliver of what Jere would feel on his cock.

"Come for me," he growled, his words coming out more as an order than he really intended.

Not like he minded, and by the way Jere's body responded, Jere didn't mind it either.

In seconds, Wren could feel Jere tensing and coming around him, and Wren threw back his head in ecstasy and let go as well, coming as hard and fast as Jere did. Wren rocked slowly as they came down, and kept up the motion even as he slid out of Jere, pressing a firm hand to Jere's back to keep him from sliding off of the bed and onto the floor. He rested for a moment against Jere's back, kissing carefully at his neck until Jere turned his head to kiss him back.

Jere smiled up at him when the kiss broke off. "I'm glad we're not at a desk," he managed. "Because all I want to do is cuddle up with you and sleep."

Wren agreed. The bed was far more comfortable than the clinic, especially the front desk. He helped to slide Jere up, noting the wet spot they had made on the blankets. Fortunately, the bed was large enough that the other side would suffice until morning. Jere crawled up to the pillows, leaning back and looking at Wren with a sated expression.

"Have I mentioned how hot it is when you fuck me while still fully clothed?" Jere asked.

Wren smiled. He was undressing now, not eager to sleep in his clothes all night. "You've mentioned it once or twice, I believe."

"So sexy," Jere reiterated, his eyes half-closed.

Wren finished stripping and climbed into bed next to him, pulling him close. "You weren't so bad yourself," he teased, giving Jere another kiss that left them both shuddering.

"You're always sexy," Jere added, shifting until he found the perfect position before falling quickly asleep.

Wren smiled, savoring the memory and the feeling of the day. Jere was sexy, too, and sweet, and wonderful to sleep with. Everything was perfect. He never wanted it to end.

Chapter 4
Threats

Another tropical storm had struck; despite being somewhat distant from the coast, the severity of the weather patterns had propelled the storm inland, bringing rain and high winds. The weather kept people inside, where they were far less likely to hurt themselves.

With everyone avoiding the weather, the clinic was slow. Wren had finished every possible clinic task that he could think of, leaving him with nothing left to do but analyze what happened in the train wreck, and his actions at the veterinarian's office. He knew he should have done better. He should have been more obedient, better at controlling his gift, but he had gotten so spoiled with Jere. He hated to think of what might have happened, and he actually hoped that a patient would come in unannounced, just to pull him out of his thoughts.

When a man arrived, looking healthy, Wren was glad to have something to do. He was curious as to why the man was even there. He was dressed in a suit, looking more like he was there on business than in need of a doctor. Wren assumed he was coming in for a wellness check. Those were often required for passage outside of the state, a response to the potential transfer of the few incurable diseases that had cropped up in the past few years. More states were demanding that travelers be in good health; some even demanded documentation.

"Hello, sir, welcome to our clinic." Wren smiled genuinely for once. Usually, he wasn't so happy to interact with random, unscheduled free people, but today was just dull enough that he was interested. "How may I help you?"

The man gave him a curious look, staring him up and down until Wren had to fight not to squirm away from his gaze. He looked over the clinic waiting room as well, the same evaluating expression on his face.

"Did you want me to get the doctor for you, sir?" Wren asked, starting to feel somewhat alarmed. Some conditions could cause patients to be confused or disoriented, which put them in the category of things for Jere to deal with. Wren dealt with paperwork, not health problems.

The man paused for a moment and then shook his head. "That won't be necessary at the moment," he revealed. "This is the property of Doctor Jeremy Peters, if I am correct?"

"Yes, sir." He considered that perhaps the man was some sort of health official. They came by every few years just to make sure everything was running smoothly.

"And how long has he been in business?"

"About two years, sir," Wren answered, feeling compelled to elaborate. "He started at the end of summer, two years ago. I can get him for you, if you'd like."

The man continued on, ignoring Wren's offer. "You're his property, I take it?"

"Yes, sir."

"Any other slaves?"

Wren drew back a little, feeling more and more nervous as the conversation progressed. Was this the same man that Isis had mentioned? If this was a health inspector, he would be asking to see paperwork, showing identification, and not interesting himself in slaves. He wondered who in the hell this man was, and what he wanted with Jere. A few people had visited the clinic since Jere had started treating slaves last year, demanding to know more about Jere's views and making sure that their facility was still "sanitary." Jere was open and friendly, offering them health pamphlets and tours of the clinic. They had special exam rooms and equipment reserved for slave use. Most people were appeased by the separation in facilities, but something about this visitor seemed off.

"Sir, I think I should get my master."

"I'm just asking questions about the clinic, boy," the man said, his tone calm and his face perfectly blank. He stared at Wren with a penetrating gaze. "You can answer me."

Wren took a step back, looking away. He suddenly wanted to trust the man, to answer his questions, but he didn't know why. He wanted Jere even more. "I know my master would rather speak to you personally, sir."

"Look at me, goddammit!" the man snapped, his composure breaking.

Wren kept his gaze averted. He had no idea what kind of mind gift this man might have, but the insistence that Wren look at him clued him in to a few different possibilities. There were countless varieties of thought reading, emotional manipulation, and control of free will that could be affected with mind gifts, and Wren wasn't willing to find out which of these gifts this stranger might have. If he could have used his own mind gift to fight back, he would have, but revealing his mind gift was far more dangerous than anything this man was going to find out about Jere.

"Jere, I need you out here right now. Someone's giving me a problem." Despite being told countless times that interrupting Jere in the case of an emergency was acceptable, it still made Wren nervous. It was something that a slave shouldn't be allowed to do. He should be able to handle this free man, and if not, he should be able to handle the punishment for failing. But Jere had made it exceedingly clear that forcing Wren to handle uncomfortable situations was the last thing he would ever want, and Wren trusted him. He knew Jere would protect him even from the most irate customers. He had made that very clear in the past, and as unusual as it was, Wren was grateful for it.

Wren pressed himself back against the wall that divided the waiting area from the rest of the clinic and looked in the free man's direction, over his shoulder more than anything. He was afraid of what he might be capable of.

"I'm sorry, sir, my master has given me strict orders. He'll be out shortly."

The man didn't push the issue further. Wren was grateful, but that fact worried him as well. Had he overreacted? An irate patient wouldn't have backed down so quickly, and someone who was angry with Jere wouldn't be so well put-together and calm. Something was off about this man.

They waited, a silent, disjointed stare-down, as Wren refused to meet the man's gaze. He tried to focus on the sound of rain beating against the front door, the wind whistling through the trees, anything but his urge to engage with the stranger. Finally, Wren felt Jere coming out to join them. It had been less than a minute, but to Wren it felt like ages.

Jere had clearly been in the middle of something; he looked disheveled and irritated. Wren could see the faint, powdery residue from the exam gloves that still graced his hands.

"Is there a problem out here?" Jere demanded.

Wren couldn't stop himself from flinching at the tone, even though he knew it wasn't directed at him. Jere was usually so calm and gentle; it was unsettling when he was this forceful and demanding. Jere wasn't even looking at him; he was too busy glaring at the strange man who had invaded their clinic with his cryptic demands.

"Did your slave tell you there was a problem?" the man asked, his smile bright and friendly. It was clearly false.

"Watch his eyes," Wren warned. *"He tried to make me look at him."*

Even as he spoke, he could feel Jere tightening his psychic shields, preventing casual use of a psychic gift on himself and Wren. Wren was thankful for it, but the feeling of that much power wrapping around him made his skin tingle, like it did during a severe thunderstorm. It was easy to underestimate Jere, but he had a frightening amount of psychic power.

"Anyone who's not a complete idiot can feel when their slave is being terrified and intimidated," Jere said coldly. "There's no need for him to feel that way unless there is a problem."

"It seems the only problem here is that your slave has difficulty following orders," the man said, his expression as dark as Jere's.

Wren moved closer to his master, hiding behind him. He trusted Jere to handle this, but he didn't trust the man in front of them. Everything he heard was setting off alarms in his head, and he wanted nothing more than to escape. A crack of thunder made him jump, and he hoped that the weather would excuse some of his bizarre behavior.

"What order did he not follow?" Jere asked.

"I simply told him to look at me and answer a question," the man said, his face looking so innocent that Wren almost believed it. "He refused to do either."

"My orders take precedence over the orders of a complete stranger," Jere said bluntly. "My slave knows better than to answer questions about my personal life. I'm assuming you didn't ask him a question about the clinic hours, or a medical treatment, or anything of the sort. He also has very clear orders to protect himself from anyone who might be trying to use a psychic gift on him, which you've been doing since I walked out to the reception area, and if you don't cease using it immediately, I'll be contacting the Hojer police department and having you removed from my premises."

The man looked surprised, and Wren sensed that he was backing off with his gift. The nervousness and compelling need to disclose information dissipated quickly from Wren's mind.

"You're very prepared," the man admitted. "I didn't expect you to have such strict rules for your slaves, nor did I expect such a distinct separation between your work and personal life; after all, your home and clinic are combined."

"I find that boundaries are remarkably important in a situation like this," Jere pointed out, glaring. "I didn't choose the structure of my property, but then, you wouldn't know that because you're not from around here, are you? Why are you in my clinic taking time away from legitimately ill people?"

The man pulled out a business card, handing it to Jere. "I'm with the State Slave Inspection Agency, a division of the Slave Control, Regulation, and Enforcement. There was a concern submitted about one of your slaves, as well as your abilities as a slaveowner, and the agency is doing a pre-screening to determine whether we will consider a full audit or not."

Their last encounter with the Slave Control, Regulation, and Enforcement Agency had not gone well. During one of Isis's more impulsive moments, she had decided to wander around the town, getting caught by a Hojer police officer and fighting when the officer attempted to take her in to the police station. Despite Jere's best efforts to save her, Nicolette Arnsdale—the head of the agency and main enforcer of slave codes in Hojer — had decided to make an example out of them, sentencing Isis to public whipping. In turn, Jere had publicly insulted Arnsdale, making a spectacle of himself and the agency. Wren knew better than to think that such an offense would go unpunished.

Wren felt his temperature starting to rise, and he forced it to stay stable. The red in his face could be excused as fear or embarrassment, but he could heat a room with his gift. Compared to the damp chill that the storm brought into the clinic, a noticeable increase in temperature would surely give this man something to investigate. He focused on Jere, who seemed remarkably calm. He clung to that calm through the mind connection as tightly as he wanted to cling to Jere for real.

"Did that bitch who runs the agency not have enough fun wasting my time last winter? Was forcing me to publicly beat a teenage girl half to death not enough for her?" Jere snapped. "And just who the hell has been making complaints about me?"

The man shook his head. "Ms. Arnsdale has been specifically excluded from any proceedings regarding this case, given your... adversarial history. This pre-screening is based a complaint lodged by a concerned Arona citizen, based on your recent actions and events that the person claimed to have noticed in everyday life."

Wren went tense. Was this his fault? Had his outburst at the vet clinic been so inappropriate as to call attention to them?

Jere scowled at the investigator. "If you're going to pry into my life, I'd like a better answer."

The man seemed to consider that for a moment. "Your slave recently attacked a veterinarian, sir. And the veterinarian stated that there was something unusual about both of you. We know you're from a free state, but such noncompliance is worthy of investigation."

Wren bit down on his tongue, trying to steady himself. He was terrified of all the things that could be done to them.

Jere, on the other hand, seemed to be growing angrier by the minute. "Actually, as a far more qualified provider of healing to the slave population, I am absolutely certain that any sort of attacks against medical staff by slaves are excused as part of medical treatment. After all, you can't blame a wounded animal from lashing out, can you? So what is this really about?"

The comparison was apt, but hurtful. Wren knew that his lover didn't really mean it, but it still stung to hear it spelled out so clearly.

The investigator shrugged. "While rules for healers are different, our department still felt that the veterinarian's concerns were worth following up on. Your public disapproval of the Agency's policies last winter added to the case, and the fact that you pushed so hard to treat slaves in a human clinic is unusual. Such an action makes you more visible and a target for attention. Our department feels that it is in the state's best interest to investigate the complaint more thoroughly."

Wren felt a cold shock of fear run through his body. Would they investigate today? Ask questions? Take him or Isis somewhere? They had prepared for this, but it seemed inadequate. There was an investigator standing in front of him, and he felt fear he hadn't suffered in years.

"You're interrupting my business. How is this town's only doctor supposed to keep up with new disease threats if he's being hassled over someone else's petty complaints?" Jere pointed out. "There should be a law against these sorts of searches."

"Under current regulations, we are able to search with or without reason. We aren't staging a formal audit yet, but we are evaluating the best use of our resources," the man reminded him.

Jere continued to glare at the man, and Wren was thankful that he was safe, hiding behind his master.

"Like I said, we haven't deemed it necessary to schedule a formal audit yet, but we are considering it. We will make sure to approach your case with the utmost care and sensitivity that we afford all citizens."

When Jere didn't respond, the man continued. "You have two slaves, is that correct?"

"Yes."

"And where is the other one?"

"In the house."

"Can I speak with her?"

"No."

"And you approve of slavery?"

"I own two, don't I?"

"Well, unless there is any indication of an emergency security breach, our policy is to give at least seventy-two hours notice before an official audit," the man stated. "Someone from our office might come by and speak with you or your property in a less formal context, however. On a voluntary basis."

Jere shook his head. "You want to talk, you talk to me. I apologize for any inconvenience, but I've been taught that it's beneficial to be careful. After all, that's why people with physical gifts need to be owned, right? To protect everyone from their gifts, and to protect them from unwanted psychic interference?"

The investigator frowned. "We *will* be speaking with them both if we conduct an audit. It's part of the procedure. It would be far more expedient for you to comply with our voluntary interviews."

"The slaves are mine; unless you're willing to make this a formal audit, I don't want them disclosing anything other than the most basic information that I allow them to discuss with any of my medical patients. I take safety very seriously, and I won't have it wasted because some stupid slave couldn't tell the difference between when to speak and when to stay quiet. As the master, I make the important decisions."

Wren was stunningly proud of his man. Just a few years ago, Jere would have been a stammering, awkward, moral mess, and now here he was, discussing slavery like someone who had lived here all his life. Wren never thought he would be so pleased to hear such denigrating comments made about himself, but they were exactly the right words for Jere to say. The fact that he knew that every other word coming out of Jere's mouth was utter bullshit made it that much sweeter.

"We will be in touch, then. Good day."

They waited silently for him to leave, and only when he was long gone did Wren feel the constricting psychic shields being lifted from him. It was important to protect him and their secrets in general, but with Wren's firesetting gift, everything was that much more dangerous.

Chapter 5
Danger

Relieved, he circled around to face Jere, pressing tight against him. Jere was quick to pull him out of the waiting area and back into the empty halls of the clinic, where he wrapped his arms tightly around Wren and held him close. "Are you all right?" he asked, stroking Wren's hair.

Wren was shaking now, which he thought was exceedingly stupid. He hadn't been shaking when the man had been asking him questions, or even when Jere first came out; why on earth would he be shaking now? But he was, and he knew he didn't have to hide it from Jere. He was safe enough to allow himself to break down, just a little.

"I will be," he said softly, wanting nothing more than to stay in Jere's arms forever.

Jere was kind enough to let him do just that. He stayed there, strong and available, until Wren felt himself calming down.

"What about your patient?" Wren asked, fully aware that he was trying to keep his mind off of anything to do with what had just happened, or what had been threatened. Thinking about work was safe, easy, not a risk for him or Jere.

"I sedated him. He'll be fine when I get back," Jere confessed. It was unlike him to abandon a patient that way. "You sounded scared. I wanted to be out there right away."

Wren smiled up at him. "Thank you. I never doubted you'd be there."

Jere stroked his hand down Wren's back, calming him further. "I was half tempted to stick a scalpel in his face the second I walked out there, just for scaring you. What the hell gives him the right to think that's okay?"

"He's free, and he's a slave agent," Wren shrugged. "He doesn't need any more rights than that."

Jere nodded. "I fucking hate that, but I guess you're right. Still pisses me off, though. You did the right thing. I don't know what kind of gift he had, my guess is some sort of empath or mind-reader gift or something, but he was putting pressure on you. He tried for a second with me, but I could defend. Bastard, picking on someone who couldn't."

Wren just smiled at that. After all this time, Jere was still offended at the way people took advantage of slaves, even if he knew it was not only accepted, but expected. "You took care of it," he reminded him.

"Yeah," Jere said, sounding dissatisfied. "I want to go back to that clinic and lobotomize that vet. How dare she file a complaint?"

Wren tried to smile, but his face wouldn't cooperate. He couldn't pretend that this would be fine. "Jere... I attacked her. I didn't hurt her, not really, but she was trying to heal me, and she was getting too close to my firesetting gift, and I just panicked. I had to get away before she found it for real."

Jere placed a kiss on his head. "It was the right thing to do. You did everything right, just like you always do. I'm sure she couldn't have noticed."

Wren wished he could believe that, but he knew it wasn't true. He had fucked up, both in letting his firesetting gift get out of control, and in fighting back against that vet. He had kept it inside for so many years, hidden it even from the gift-identifiers and his last master, and he had ruined everything by letting his guard down.

"I'm sorry. I shouldn't use it so often. I know it's dangerous—to you, to me, to Isis. We can't afford to draw attention, and we certainly can't afford me slipping up with it. I should go back to not using it. Ever."

Jere looked troubled. "I love your gifts, Wren. Both of them. They're a part of you. Besides, it's not you I'm worried about, not even Isis, really. As strange as that seems, I'm mostly worried about myself. What if I mess up, say the wrong thing, do the wrong thing?"

"You were the perfect master today," Wren reassured him. It was easier than reassuring himself, and it was true. Jere was making great strides in his ability to act the part.

"I still don't like it," Jere mumbled. "I could pretend for a few minutes because I was scared. But what would this audit even entail? Are they going to come in my house and question us for hours? Look through our things? Read our minds? What? I don't know how well I can hold it together if that happens."

"If it happens, which it might not, you'll deal with it." Wren forced himself to smile, false confidence bridging the gap between how he felt and what he wished was true. "I have absolute confidence in you, master."

Jere made a face. "Don't call me that!" he protested.

"Oh, but my darling master," Wren teased. "You're so strong and powerful. How could I ever think of you as anything but that? My master. My lord. My mighty, wonderful man, whom I couldn't imagine life without."

"Well, I'll agree to that last part," Jere told him. "I still want to smack someone every time I remember that I own you. It's not right."

"I'm perfectly content being yours," Wren insisted. "And not just because it means I'm not somebody else's. I love you, and I love knowing that nobody else but you gets to tell me what to do. I trust you with that, more than I've ever trusted anybody else in the world. Don't take that lightly. It's important."

"You're important," Jere reminded him, pulling him close for a kiss.

Wren loved hearing it as much as he loved the strong arms around him and the soft lips pressed against his. He forgot about slaves, masters, and patients, letting Jere's touch lure him into the safety that he loved, and had grown almost dependent upon. Everything was all right when Jere was around. It was what happened when Jere wasn't around that scared him.

"We should get Kieran to visit."

Wren had been anxious after the investigator came by, and he could tell that Jere wasn't feeling much better.

Jere agreed. Kieran was one of Jere's first real friends in Hojer.

She was also an avid anti-slavery activist. They had stayed in close contact over the years, even once Kieran left to attend university in Sonova, the slave-free metropolitan city where Jere grew up. It had been Kieran who had gotten Jere to start advertising his services to heal slaves. A highly skilled empath, she had suffered for years in her home state, unable to block out the agony that the slave population felt. She would be the best resource if they really were facing an audit.

Kieran arrived the next day, looking a little rough.

"Taking my advice about having fun?" Jere teased. He had been gently encouraging Kieran to explore the fun sides of Sonova instead of focusing on coursework and activism.

"You should have given me advice about riding the speed train with a hangover," Kieran mumbled. "Are you getting audited?"

Wren shook his head. "Just a visit. Pre-screening, I guess."

"Harassment," Jere muttered. He explained what had happened with the veterinarian, leaving out the part about Wren's firesetting gift. No matter how much they trusted Kieran, the fewer people who knew about it, the safer they all were.

"The best you can do is comply," Kieran advised. "With the current legal state, that's all you can do. There's a newly proposed law that would help, but I don't even know if it would go into effect soon enough."

"What law is that?" Jere asked.

Kieran brightened, happy to talk about her favorite subject. "They're calling it the Slavery Reformation Act. The medical community on the west coast originally promoted it, after a few cities got infected with one of those weird, mutating diseases. A lot of states are emphasizing healthcare reform in this year's elections, including better treatment for slaves. In Arona, the SRA requires that slaves be treated by human healers, not veterinarians."

"I'm already treating slaves. According to our visitor, that doesn't make me look any better."

Wren agreed. He wished they had never bothered to help anyone outside of their home, no matter how much it pleased Jere or improved life for slaves.

"The SRA in Arona was influenced by both pro-slavery and

anti-slavery lobbyists. It includes some protections for slaveowners — preventing unwanted searches and seizures, making mandatory public punishments illegal. The pro-slavery side is rather pleased by the part where licenses and certifications apply between slave states."

Wren smiled. Kieran had long stopped considering Jere as "owning slaves" so much as "harboring future ex-slaves." Her ambitions were entertaining.

"But there are opponents, especially to the public slave treatment acts. People are so intent on keeping their 'God-given right' to beat and kill their slaves in public, you'd think that we were trying to take away their right to breathe air," Kieran shook her head. "Even the most conservative slaveowners don't do that very often! We've done research, even the pro-slavery side has done research, and it's not something that happens regularly. But so many people are throwing a fit over it. Most don't buy that it presents a disease risk."

"They see it as gradual and intentional encroachment on their rights as slaveowners, and we want no part in that," Wren insisted. If he had owned slaves, he was pretty sure he would feel the same way. It was how he had grown up. "It's too dangerous. We're targets already."

"So why not try to take away the power that the Slave Control, Regulation, and Enforcement Agency has?" Kieran reminded him. "People are panicking about these diseases. This law could get passed before you ever have a chance to get audited."

Jere shook his head. "It's too risky. My life, my clinic... my family doesn't need to be subjected to that."

"Even politics in Sonova are getting heated. Everyone wants to protect their health, and the slave states are a weak link. The candidates backing the SRA are doing well in the pre-election surveys, and the advertising and outreach campaigns are going well."

"Even so... I don't think this is the time," Jere insisted. "There's too much at stake."

Wren glanced at Jere, relieved that he agreed. Between the veterinarian and the firesetting gift, the audit, and their general lack of fit with the community, he was glad that Jere was being cautious.

"Your sister thinks you should do it," Kieran teased. Jere's sister, Jen, had taken it upon herself to connect with Kieran through some of the activist groups they were both members of. "Will you consider it, at least? A doctor supporting a healthcare cause proposed by his own medical school makes perfect sense!"

Wren wanted to reject her again, but Jere was already nodding. "I'll look over it," he promised. "What about the audit?"

"*If* it happens," Kieran reminded them, "just go along with it. It's probably best if I'm less involved. Spend more time with Paltrek; he's the perfect picture of what the slave agencies want."

Throughout the discussion, Kieran kept looking at them nervously. Wren was a little anxious as to what she was going to drop on them next. He and Isis shared a nervous glance. Like Wren, she picked up on the things that the free people in the room missed despite their best intentions.

"Jere, there's this new restaurant I thought we might be able to go check out for dinner tonight," Kieran said, squirming a bit. "The owner might be a good resource."

Wren held back a laugh. She was clearly asking to speak with Jere alone, but desperately trying to be polite about it. It would have been sad if it weren't so endearing.

Jere agreed. He and Kieran left shortly after, leaving Wren and Isis to themselves. Wren missed Jere, even when he was gone for stupidly short periods of time, but he was glad that Jere went out. He trusted that anything important Kieran brought up would be shared with him.

Chapter 6
News

The restaurant was arranged so that each table was almost enclosed with big, tall seat backs and an artificial waterfall that flowed into a large fish tank. Inside were hundreds of fish, edible ones, making Jere wonder if the owners had some sort of gift that allowed them to speed up the breeding process and generate a constant supply of the hard-to-get seafood. Most restaurants were unwilling to reveal their food sources; the genetically modified food that had replaced many natural species was quite revolting to many customers. The fish tank, and the fact that customers were allowed to select their own fish to be cooked, provided a novelty that few people in Hojer had ever seen. In addition, it created background noise that dulled all but the loudest conversations.

As Jere took in the scenery, he recognized familiar faces. Just across the room from him was the veterinarian who had given them trouble, sitting in his town like she deserved to be there. Jere tried not to glare, but he couldn't help remembering the pain she had caused Wren, the threat she represented. She was speaking with none other than Paltrek's father. Paltrek Wysocka, Senior, was probably the wealthiest and most influential man in Hojer. A financial investor and moneylender, he represented the most successful and traditional of Hojer, along with those who hoped to join those ranks one day. Jere could think of no reason why the vet should be here, but he really hoped that she had defaulted on her loan payments.

"I have some news that I wanted to let you decide how to tell Wren and Isis," Kieran confessed. "You know how I'm always on about border crossing and stuff?"

Jere nodded. Crossing the borders into a free state was highly dangerous, but a tried and true method of escaping slavery.

"We've got our rates high, Jere. In the past three months, we have a fifty to eighty percent success rate. That's higher than any other organization of our kind."

Jere was glad that the organization had been improving their rates, but it wasn't enough for him to get excited. He couldn't help but glance over at the vet, her very presence highlighting just how many dangers were out there for him and his slaves. "That's still awfully risky. I wouldn't attempt surgery with a loss rate that high unless the only other option was certain death."

"For some, staying *is* certain death," Kieran reminded him. "We've got it down to an art. In all of those cases, where there was a loss, nothing came back to the master."

"Why are you telling me this now?"

Kieran smiled. "With the elections and the worry about disease, patrol forces are being redistributed for public safety, attention is off the borders. That means a better chance of getting across the borders to freedom. Wren and Isis could go."

Jere's stomach clenched at the thought of either of them taking that risk. When the vet looked over at him, making eye contact for a moment, the feeling intensified. He waited for her to say something, to do something, but she looked away, focusing her attention on Wysocka instead. She had acted so superior in her clinic — in her town — but this was Jere's home. Publicly engaging with him would only bring trouble to her. "They'd have to go separately, I'm assuming."

"You'd want to wait months between them, but we have host houses they could stay in. I think it would be better if Wren came over first, he's more self-sufficient, and you'll still need Isis for the energy thing at the clinic. But then, Isis does seem more likely to run away — "

Jere cut her off. "I appreciate you telling me, but you really need to let me talk to them first. They might not even want to do it." That was his hope, anyway. There was nothing he would love more than to go home to Sonova, to leave Hojer and all the slave states behind and take his loved ones with him, but it was too risky, too uncertain.

If they could all go at the same time, it would still be risky, but the thought of them being separated was more than he could bear. He was certain that Isis and Wren would both see that logic.

"It wouldn't be for a few months, but I'd be out of here the moment I had the chance!"

Jere shrugged. "It's like you said earlier, I don't want to do this without consulting them first."

"Okay," Kieran said, seeming a little crushed. In seconds, she brightened back up again. "Oh, guess what should probably come first, though?"

Kieran was hard to keep down for long. "What's that?"

"Jen and I may have found Isis's parents!"

Jere sat there, stunned. He hadn't believed it was possible. His sister had been rather taken with Isis, adoring the girl's abrasive personality, and had taken her on as a pet project. Jen made it her mission to reunite Isis with her family, bringing in Kieran through mutual acquaintances. Jere would have been irritated if it weren't so perfectly sweet and kind.

"They stuck around town for a year or so before doing anything, probably too scared to search for her. Most families would just try for another child, but there are none on the record for them, slave or free. They both dropped off the face of the earth for a few years, and then this strikingly similar new couple opens up an interstate talent scout business in another slave state. On the surface, they're legitimate; all their travels and inquiries have been work-related. But if you look a little closer and know the pattern, it seems that they've been following Isis for years, but they've always been a few steps behind."

Jere couldn't imagine letting someone take his child in the first place, but mistakes happened. From the looks of it, they had spent the rest of their lives attempting to fix that mistake.

"They were one of the first families to register with the Lighthouse Organization. It connects displaced slave children and their families," Kieran reminded him. "This is one of the first cases we've worked with where the slave is still... well... a slave."

"What does Lighthouse do?"

"It reunites them!" Kieran announced, visibly thrilled at the idea. "Usually through letters at first, maybe telegraphs, and then the family goes to the free state to visit. A lot of them end up moving, starting over. It's so beautiful, Jere, we're actually fixing some of the fucked-up things that slavery does to people."

Jere smiled. "It is impressive. But how would it work, with her not being in a free state?"

"We're still working out the details," Kieran admitted. "We were thinking of sending you to meet them with her. They live in a slave state, so you could take her there, if you're willing. It's a lot safer than having them come to you."

Jere considered it. His last trip outside of Hojer had gone poorly enough that he was starting to agree with Wren and Isis's plans to stay home all the time. Seeing unfriendly faces in public reinforced that idea, and traveling outside of the state meant that they would be subject to further scrutiny. Most states required that slaves be certified for out-of-state travel, assessed like dogs to ensure they would behave properly and not present a risk to the free citizens. "It would mean a lot of planning, and time off work. Won't it take a long time to get them certified?"

"You'd only need to get Isis certified."

Jere waited for the explanation.

"You don't have to take Wren," Kieran suggested, an apprehensive look on her face.

Jere didn't respond, trying his best not to dismiss the idea immediately. He had promised Wren years ago that he would never leave him like that, and the thought of being gone for so long made him uncomfortable. He waited, hoping Kieran would give him another alternative.

"Unless we coordinate it somewhere else, you really can't take him. Redmont, where her parents are, is in the slave state of Brenton, and they have tight restrictions on interstate slave travel due to slave smuggling. They have a limit of one slave per free person."

Jere shook his head, annoyed by the restrictions and the logic of slave states.

"The more people traveling together, the more attention you'll draw to yourselves."

Jere nodded. "I don't want to leave Wren... besides, we don't even know if Isis wants to do this."

Kieran frowned at him. "Jere, haven't you told her we were looking?"

"If I had told her that you and Jen were looking, and nothing ever came of it, she'd be crushed. Trust me, she'd prefer it this way."

"If you say so." Kieran glared at him, a look of annoyance on her face. "You are going to tell her now, right? Because we don't want to invest our people in verifying this couple any further if you're just going to be an asshole about it."

"You know how to do your organizing stuff, I know how to deal with Isis. I'll tell her. And I'll let you know if she wants to go further with it. Or if I do. With this audit—"

"You have all the more reason to get your slaves certified!" Kieran interrupted. "It will make you look more legitimate."

"I'll consider it."

Jere wanted to give Isis as many opportunities as he could, but he needed to make sure that they were all safe. He was much more comfortable when the vet and Wysocka left, and when his conversation with Kieran shifted to lighter topics. Talking about his old college town always made Jere nostalgic, but he never regretted leaving it, just like he never regretted staying in Hojer.

After all, Hojer had brought him Wren.

The house was quiet and dark by the time Jere returned. He left the bedroom light off, trying to be considerate.

He was startled and awed when the room lit up moments later with the soft glow of fire. He turned to look at Wren, who was lying in bed with a grin on his face and a little ball of glowing fire in his hand.

"You always trip when the lights are out."

Jere smiled. He would never tire of seeing the amazing extent of Wren's gifts.

"Did you and Kieran have a good night?" Wren asked.

Jere felt guilty for going out and having a good time without his lover, especially since they had been talking about Wren, but Wren trusted him enough not to worry.

"We did," he agreed, stripping down and climbing into bed next to Wren, watching the ball of fire flicker and burn like a candle. "She gave me some pretty intense news about a new project."

"What's that?" Wren asked, quenching the fire so he could wrap his arms around Jere.

Jere never wanted to risk losing that feeling. He was going to tell Wren about the possibility of escaping to a free state, but even as he tried to imagine the words, he was filled with cold dread at the thought of losing Wren for even six months, or worse, forever.

"It's called the Lighthouse Organization," Jere said instead. "They reunite families with their children who were taken as slaves. Kieran thinks they might have found Isis's parents. My sister is working on it with her."

Jere forced a smile and tried not to even think about the other thing. He would tell Wren... tomorrow, maybe, once it had time to settle in. He could tell Wren and Isis at the same time. When he wasn't as tired.

He worked hard to think up the best excuses, justifying the lie to himself.

"That's good, right?" Wren checked. "I'm getting all sorts of weird mixed feelings through the connection."

That was the damned thing about having such a strong psychic bond, their feelings bled over all the time. When they were being honest with each other, it wasn't a problem.

"There are a lot of potential complications. I haven't even told her we're looking. You don't think she'll be angry about it, do you?"

Wren shook his head, stroking his hands in soothing patterns against Jere's skin. "I think she'll be happy about it. She's always maintained that they'd want her back, I'm sure her judgment is accurate. I would personally kick your ass if you even *consider* looking for my family."

Jere leaned forward, kissing him. "I'd never do that without your permission."

Jere could feel through the connection that Wren believed him. It made it even worse that he wasn't telling him about the possibility of escaping to freedom. But he would wait for it to be safer.

Wren would probably reject the idea anyway. It would be a wasted conversation; Jere could think of far better things they could both be doing with their mouths.

As if to prove it, Jere started kissing Wren more insistently, passionately, clutching at his arms and his hair and every part of him that he could reach.

"You act like you haven't seen me for days, not just hours," Wren teased, touching Jere in return and heating up the space between them.

"I just... I love you so much. I never want to be away from you." That was true, at least.

Wren pulled Jere close, and Jere relaxed into his arms. "I love you too, and I don't think either one of us is going anywhere."

"If I go with Isis, you won't be able to come," Jere admitted. "There are restrictions, you're not even certified — "

"I know. Taking a slave out of state is difficult. It draws attention. I'll be safer here, anyway."

Jere smiled, reaching down to take Wren's cock in his hand and stroking it together with his own, loving the feeling of their skin pressed together like this.

"I miss you even when I'm only gone for a few hours," Jere admitted, working their cocks and holding Wren close. If they could stay like this, the rest of the world would never intrude. Wren would never go away.

"You're sweet." Wren flipped Jere onto his back with ease, pinning him down and grabbing some lube.

Jere loved it when Wren held him down like this; the feeling of Wren's body pressing his into the mattress was so close to perfection that he wanted to come just thinking about it. He didn't, though; he wouldn't do that and risk spoiling the moment. He wanted to draw it out as long as he could, taking in as many of Wren's touches and kisses as possible, letting Wren use his body as he pleased. He could tell that tonight's play wasn't going to last long; it was late, they were both tired, and sometimes, it was the closeness that they both craved more than a long, drawn-out fuck. Still, he wanted to revel in every moment. The feeling of Wren's hands stroking up and down his body possessively, demanding that Jere yield to him, was intoxicating. Jere rocked beneath Wren, hoping to increase the friction between their bodies further still, working both their cocks with his hands so Wren's hands were free to explore. He felt himself growing closer and closer, arching his back to get them both to a perfect angle.

As Wren went from holding him down to kissing him and toying with his nipples, Jere gave in, coming in a series of gasps and moans. He smiled up at Wren's satisfied expression. Wren took his own pleasure in Jere's body, and Jere was happy to let him, not to mention helping him by continuing to stroke him and kiss him. He always loved touching Wren, but tonight they both needed it. Too soon, he felt the telltale signs that Wren was close, confirmed by the way Wren grabbed the back of his head and pulled him up, kissing him forcefully as he came.

Satisfied, they lay back against the pillows, cuddling for a few moments before cleaning up and resting in each other's arms. Jere never wanted to lose this feeling, not for a day, or a week, and certainly not for months, or worse, forever. He couldn't risk Wren getting caught trying to escape the slave state, and he was certain Wren would agree. As they fell asleep, Jere decided to forget all about the first part of the conversation he and Kieran had.

Chapter 7
Planning

While Jere was working the next day, Wren planned with Kieran. Although Wren was pretty sure he knew what "complying" with the slave agency would entail, he wasn't completely sure, and he thought there might be things that Jere would miss. As much as Kieran hated slavery, she had experience with it. Wren trusted her to know what she was doing in this regard; she became remarkably professional when dealing with activist sorts of things. She really did seem pleased to talk with him, and Wren realized he enjoyed it as well. Having friends was such a strange concept, but it was something Wren was starting to feel comfortable about.

And with Jere out of the way, he could drill her on the details of the plans that Jere was so hesitant to enact. Wren had been considering the possibility of Jere taking Isis to meet her parents. Despite the separation and the uncertain footing they had with the threat of an audit, he wanted this for Isis. The girl had grown on him, despite his initial resentment, and he was starting to share Jere's desire to show her a good life.

"I want to plan with you," he told Kieran, giving her a conspiratorial smile. It was fun, playing around and plotting behind Jere's back like this. "I think the opportunity you told Jere about is perfect, but he's a little hesitant, and I want to make it work."

"So, Jere told you what I told him?" Kieran asked, looking uncertain.

"He did," Wren replied, smiling. "And I think it's excellent, but what's really important is getting him and Isis ready to go."

"To meet her parents?" Kieran looked confused, maybe even

guarded.

"Yeah, what else?"

"Uh... nothing, it's not a big deal," Kieran mumbled.

Wren shook his head. Knowing Kieran, she had planned some sort of rally or something that she wanted them to go to, a risk that Wren would never support. "Anyway, Jere's concerned, rightfully so, because he doesn't want to leave me here with anyone. I tried talking about it with him today, suggested staying with Paltrek, but he looked like he was going to cry. Which... I mean, it's sweet and all, and I understand his concerns, but I'm sure I'd be fine. Paltrek is good enough to Jere that I'm sure he'd just lock me away in a room for a few days, and when Jere got home—"

"Wren, no offense, but sometimes I can't tell who is a bigger idiot, you or Jere," Kieran cut him off. "There is no way in hell he'd consider letting you stay in the Wysocka house, and for that matter, neither would I!"

Wren pulled back, frowning. "Excuse me, but I don't recall asking your permission." The old sense of discomfort threatened to creep back in; he had just been quite effectively reminded of his place. Friend? Maybe not. He pulled away, crossing his arms over his chest. The excitement he had felt just moments ago was gone.

Kieran backed down, looking chastened. "Wren, I didn't mean it like that, I just meant that there's another way. You know, I wouldn't let you eat poisoned food, either. I hope if that ever comes up, you don't get all offended at me for looking out for you."

Wren frowned. He did see her point, kind of, but between her protectiveness and Jere's, he felt excessively coddled, and more than a little bit demeaned. He'd let her eat poisoned food right now, if only because he knew Jere could heal her. This was why slaves shouldn't get excited, or trust free people.

"Um, there's a better solution," Kieran said, giving Wren an apologetic look. "Me!"

Wren blinked. "You'd take Isis to see her parents? I don't think she'd go with you."

"No," Kieran laughed. "I'll stay here with you. I stay here often enough anyway. Nobody will question it if I house-sit for Jere."

"Oh," Wren said, shocked by the offer. "I guess... I hadn't really even considered it. I wouldn't want to put you out."

Kieran smiled. "Didn't you at least have friends you could count on when you were a kid? It's not a problem. I'll be happy to help, especially if it makes you stop having hate-feelings toward me. I didn't mean I was going to force you to stop or anything. I just wanted to give you a better option."

Wren smiled. As a slave, depending on things from any person, but especially a free person, was dangerous, but Kieran had always been able to be counted upon. He felt a little guilty for the hateful feelings, and was mortified that she had sensed it. "That's what you get for using your gift on me," he mumbled, blushing.

"I'll consider us even, if you do," she replied.

"Thank you," Wren said, feeling sort of strange. Not quite indebted; Kieran would never ask for anything in return. He was so rarely grateful to anyone other than Jere.

"You're sure you don't want me to look up your family, too?" she prodded.

Wren shook his head. "Not a chance in hell," he warned her. "My family wasn't anywhere near as supportive as Isis's was before I was taken, I could only imagine that it would be worse over time."

Jere approached Isis, admiring the careful work she did for a moment before speaking. For someone who had never hesitated to break everything in the house, she cleaned the medical supplies meticulously, organizing them and putting them back exactly where they belonged.

"When you get a minute, can I talk to you?" Jere asked, feeling oddly nervous.

"Something important?" Isis teased, joining him in an exam room. "Must be, for you to steal away from work with someone other than Wren."

Had it really been a year since he bought her? She had been so difficult at first, but Jere felt like she was exactly what he and Wren needed to balance them out. She excelled at calming clients in the clinic, provided a surprisingly good ear to listen to problems, and never asked for much. It seemed like every day that she got to be happy and safe was good enough for her.

Still, Jere couldn't help going above and beyond at times, and reuniting her with her family fit that description perfectly. He just hoped she would be open to it. "I, uh... I have some news for you."

For the slightest of seconds, he saw fear flicker across her face, the guarded look that she used to wear so often coming back before she crushed it down and set her jaw resolutely. She still tended to assume the worst, although neither Jere nor Wren would ever do a thing to harm her.

"W-what?" she managed, not as successful at hiding the stutter, or the tremble in her voice.

"It's nothing bad, I promise!" He was never sure how she would react to big news. Sometimes she'd shrug and go along with it, sometimes she would shut down completely, sometimes she'd scream and carry on for hours, even if the news was good. She had explained one time that it was the overwhelming emotion that got to her.

Jere hoped he hadn't made a mistake by telling her in the clinic instead of waiting until they got back to the house, where she could have a screaming fit if she so desired. "I just... Kieran thinks she might have found your parents."

Jere stopped, watching as Isis stayed completely still, frozen, not daring to show even the slightest hint of emotion. If Wren had looked like this, Jere wouldn't hesitate to probe a little through the mind connection, but Isis insisted upon maintaining as much privacy as possible. She had never been allowed to have such a thing before, so Jere maintained strict boundaries and respected her wishes. As he waited, he idly contemplated how difficult life must have been before it was possible to peek at the emotions of others.

"I didn't know you were looking," Isis finally mumbled, crossing her arms and drawing back. It wasn't clear whether she was upset that nobody told her, or that it had happened at all.

"I know. I didn't tell you because I didn't want to get your hopes up. I didn't even know at first—my sister and Kieran started it."

"And you agreed to let them spy on my family?"

"I agreed that it was a good idea for them to continue looking,"

Jere said gently. "I was hesitant at first, but I know you always say your parents still care about you. You're right. When Kieran first told me about the reunification program, I knew it would be the chance to find out for sure if they were still out there, looking. I thought it would be a really good opportunity."

"To get rid of me," Isis muttered, looking down at the floor.

"No," Jere said firmly. "After all this time, you still think I'm trying to get rid of you?"

Isis shrugged.

"If I wanted you gone, I've had plenty of better opportunities," Jere teased, ducking down to catch her eye. The joke worked, if only slightly, because she granted him a slight smile. "I've told you I wouldn't ever get rid of you, and I stand by that promise."

"So... so then why?" Isis looked up again, still curled in on herself.

"Because you seem so convinced that they will want to see you. Wren told me he wouldn't speak to me for weeks if I so much as *considered* looking for his family, and I believe him. But I thought you'd be happy to have the chance to see them again. And if the people Kieran found are really your parents, they would give anything for the chance to meet you again."

"Oh." Isis was quiet for a moment. "Are they... I mean, did they look for me?"

Jere could tell that she was trying hard not to seem too eager, but he couldn't imagine being anything but eager at the prospect of seeing long-separated family members. "Isis, they've been looking for you since the day you were taken. They're on all sorts of underground lists, they've moved multiple times in attempts to follow you, they've sold their house and quit their jobs—it's all they've done since you were taken. They never gave up on you."

Isis sank to the floor, sitting and resting her head in her hands. She was silent.

"Are you all right?" Jere asked. She was no longer as likely to scream and break things, but she had a tendency to hide away and hurt herself. The quiet, withdrawn attitude was even more worrisome to Jere than the angry outbursts.

"I don't know. This is just... fuck, it's all I've ever wanted, and I keep waiting to wake up from a dream or have you tell me it's all a joke, but if it's real I don't know what I'll do. It's too much."

Jere let her have a few moments to collect herself. She needed more time to process than most people he knew, but with her memory gift, she had more information in her brain to connect. Worse, she had half a lifetime of terrible, miserable experiences to reconcile. Sometimes she just needed space, and Jere had gotten very successful at waiting. Finally, she seemed to calm down, folding her arms over her knees and resting her head on them as she considered it all.

"It's not guaranteed yet. I mean, Kieran isn't completely sure that they are who she thinks they are; they've changed identities a few times, but from the data on where you grew up and their names—"

"I never told you their names!" Isis interrupted.

"They had someone break into the records," Jere admitted. "I guess it can be pretty easy if you know the right people. Besides, it might be a while before the organization establishes actual contact with them. They're focusing on safety, both for the organization and for the families involved. And it seems your parents, if that is who they are, have gone undercover. We wouldn't want to expose them."

Isis finally lifted her head. "What then? Can I meet them? Talk to them? Could they come here?"

Jere shrugged. "Having them come here would be risky. Usually, a meeting is arranged somewhere else. If they were followed here it could alert people to their, and our, involvement with this organization. You could be at risk of being taken away and I'm not going to risk that. I guess sometimes letters work best."

"They'll be excited that I finally learned how to read," Isis observed.

"I think they'll be proud of you, regardless. They obviously care about you if they're still looking for you after all this time."

"Yeah," Isis nodded. "Does Wren know?"

Jere nodded. "I told him last night. He thinks it's a great idea."

Isis nodded, seemingly unbothered that she was the last to know. Jere shared everything with Wren. At least, almost everything. More often than not, Isis seemed content to sit back and let them make the "adult" decisions, as she described it. She embraced the role of careless teenager more often than not. Jere figured she deserved it; she had missed out on it for so many years.

"I can't wait to tell him about it! Doesn't matter that he already knows, this time I get to tell him!" Isis grinned, suddenly looking happy instead of worried about the possibility.

It was good to see her so excited. While she had a good life with him and Wren, not being hurt or abused, Jere often wondered if it was enough for her. He followed her into the house, smiling as he watched her gush on and on about the news to Wren and thank Kieran for her involvement. As usual, Wren was reserved, smiling gently and nodding at her as she rambled, but Jere could sense through the connection that Wren was happy for her. Kieran didn't even try to hide her excitement.

"Would you have wanted to know I was looking?" Jere asked.

"Like I said last night, I'd kick your ass if you even considered it," Wren replied, playful. *"And not in a way you'd like, either."*

Jere smiled at that. Wren was cute when he made threats. *"Not even your brother?"* he pressed. *"You told me once that you'd like to see how he turned out."*

"Only if he was a slave," Wren answered, after considering it for a moment. *"And only if we could help him. Otherwise, I'd rather pretend that he was free and happy and never have to worry about him again."*

As far as the possibility of freedom, Jere rationalized that nothing was certain yet, so there was really no reason to tell Isis or Wren about it. It would only get their hopes up, and he doubted it was safe enough. Fifty to eighty percent success rate? That meant that twenty to fifty percent failed, and failure meant severe whipping and retraining at best. At worst, it could mean execution or repossession for the slave, and the right to own slaves stripped from the master. Mentioning it would be like teasing, a promise that he could never keep, and he didn't want to put either of the people he cared about through that sort of false hope.

At least, that was the main reason why he didn't want to mention it.

Chapter 8
Influences

Jere didn't have to try to find a reason to keep the chance of freedom to himself. Kieran had only just left for the speed train station when Jere heard a knock at the door. Jere's friend Paltrek was standing there looking hopeful, his slave next to him.

"My father's going to a fundraising campaign," the wealthy socialite announced, raising an eyebrow at Jere hopefully. "He says that Wysocka Enterprises needs to be better integrated into politics, and he's dragging me into it!"

Jere grinned. Paltrek lived with his extremely conservative father and older sister, both of whom treated free people *and* slaves like dirt, for the most part. But Paltrek benefitted from the arrangement, living a pampered life without having to do much work, and being guaranteed a lifetime of success.

"Maybe there will be an open bar," Jere suggested. "Or some suitable people to take home."

Paltrek scoffed. "I'm supposed to bring a guest. My father has reminded me that I'm still 'disappointingly single,' and told me to go make it look like I have respectable connections. He told me to stay away from the bar, too, but that's not happening."

Jere realized that he was the respectable connection that Paltrek Wysocka, Senior, was referring to. The Wysocka family was wealthy and influential; it was a matter of course that they had established a good relationship with Hojer's new doctor when he moved into town. Mr. Wysocka had been friends with the town's previous doctor, but Jere and Paltrek were much closer in age and philosophy. Paltrek scorned his family's image—if not their wealth—and accepted Jere's liberal treatment of his slaves in a way his father never would have. Still, Mr. Wysocka knew that Jere held influence over the citizens of Hojer. Despite Jere's views, Mr. Wysocka respected his business sense and healing abilities.

"I'll get some clothes together for you," Wren's voice sounded in his head. *"You should go out. Have a little fun, show the community how involved and sociable you are."*

Jere wanted to protest, but Paltrek was already going on about how he didn't want to be stuck alone with his family. Jere didn't blame him; Paltrek fit in with his family about as well as Jere fit in Hojer. Paltrek was one of his first and closest friends, one who had stood by him through his struggles adjusting to life in a slave state, through his fight with the Slave Agency last year. His relationship with Paltrek was refreshingly uncomplicated — they went out and had fun, they shared drinks, they shared problems. By the time Wren returned and handed him an outfit, Jere realized that his night was planned for him.

Not long after, Jere was on a speed train, accompanying Paltrek on the short trip to Montrose, the next town over, where the fundraiser was being held. Dane was with them, kneeling at Paltrek's feet. He had been looking at his master gratefully since Paltrek purchased the private car that would allow the slave to stay with them instead of traveling in the baggage section.

"You don't usually bring him out," Jere commented. Paltrek had explained that he didn't feel the need to drag his slave out in public to prove that he had one; he was wealthy enough already.

Paltrek shrugged. "Things are tense at home. He's scared shitless to be left there, even asked me if he could come with me today. Do you know how long it's been since he's made a request like that? I couldn't turn him down."

Jere tried not to show his distaste. He had learned to tolerate Paltrek's use of his slave, much like Paltrek tolerated Jere's permissiveness with Wren and Isis. Dane always seemed willing, if not eager, and Jere knew that he had rubbed off on Paltrek somewhat; Dane was treated far more gently now than he had been when Jere and Paltrek had first met.

Paltrek laughed at Jere's poor attempt to conceal his disgust.

"Delicate outlander sensibilities. One day you'll get over that. You and lover-boy still getting along?"

Jere blushed. "Perfectly, thank you."

"You guys make me sick," Paltrek said, but he was smiling as he said it. He never missed an opportunity to hassle Jere about his relationship with Wren. In a way, it was almost comforting. Jere missed the playful teasing that happened between friends.

"Anyway, thanks for coming with me. My sister's insane, and my father is so into this political business that it's annoying. With the elections coming up, everyone's trying to get Wysocka Enterprises into their pockets, but he won't commit to anyone either way. He's playing them against each other, trying to find one he likes."

Jere nodded politely. "Does he know who or what he's supporting?"

"Whoever allows his business to grow the most effectively. I think tonight's fundraiser will probably secure it. He's been a fan of President Clemente since he was elected a few terms ago — that's the party throwing the fundraiser tonight."

Jere nodded. He had never had a problem with Hojer's president. The only reason he had gone out of his way to target the man's family last year was because the president had ignored Jere's requests to grant an exception to the state slave codes. Otherwise, he knew little about the politics of the state.

The venue was only a short walk from the Montrose speed train station. Jere was pleased to see the lights and hear the music from inside. Hojer was usually dark and quiet at night; few people had the desire or money to pay for event lighting, not to mention hiring people with gifts to amplify the music and speeches loud enough to blare across a dance floor. Hojer had live bands and loudspeakers for special occasions, but the psychic fields interrupted most of the old technology that used to make sound amplification possible.

By comparison, it looked like Montrose was doing well, but with closer to twenty thousand people, there were likely more resources and mind gifts to go around. The venue must have held at least a few hundred people, most dressed in their best clothes, many accompanied by slaves.

Annika found them first, giving Jere the dirty look that she had been giving him since he had rejected her attempts to flirt with her years ago.

"I see you finally made it," she said, glaring at Paltrek. "Daddy's been wondering where you are. I told him you probably had to go pick up some whore to keep you company."

"Nope. Unlike you, I actually have friends to bring to formal events. Looks like you've got Arae, though. She's even conscious and clothed. Did Father tell you that you couldn't take her out of the house looking like she did this morning?"

Annika continued glaring, even as her slave cowered beside her. "If that horrible law passes, I'll never be able to take my slave outside again! Did you know that one of the new laws would ban public beatings that break skin? They say it's unsanitary. Like a little blood would destroy the world or something—it's out-of-control slaves that are going to ruin our society!"

Jere just shook his head. Medically, it *could* end the world, but there was no arguing with this woman. Arae was far from out of control; Jere thought she looked more lifeless and defeated every time he saw her. "It does provide some slaveowner protections."

"This SRA is horrible! It's stealing the rights of law-abiding slaveowners. It's my God-given right to do whatever the hell I want with my slaves, and if that includes beating them bloody, I'll do it!"

"When did you become religious?" Paltrek asked her.

"It's an expression, little brother," Annika snapped. "I'm going to end up arrested if this stupid thing passes, or fined, not like that matters, but I can't be arrested! I'm not some sort of criminal!"

Paltrek rolled his eyes. "All you'd have to do is not torture your slave in public. It shouldn't be that difficult."

Annika scowled enough that Jere felt his skin crawl. The feeling intensified when Annika backhanded Arae and sent her flying a few feet before the girl quietly crawled back to her. He couldn't help but watch Dane, the way he cringed despite his attempts to hide it. Arae was his sister, and as much as Paltrek was laid-back and lenient, Annika was uptight and strict.

"See what I mean?" Paltrek criticized. "You can't even keep your hands off of her when she's doing nothing."

Annika scowled. "I could feel through the mind connection that she doubted me. She knows better."

"Thank you for correcting me, mistress," Arae mumbled, earning another kick.

Jere was certain that Annika had some pretty significant mental problems that she loved to take out on her beaten, starved slave. Jere was sickened by the display, but he didn't know what to say. Fortunately, he didn't have to say anything, because Mr. Wysocka came over, a deep frown on his face.

"If your slave is so ill-mannered that you need to throw her around in public, I can have my assistant take her home and I will deal with her later," he hissed.

Annika turned bright red, and Jere couldn't help feeling pleased by her unhappiness.

"Doctor Peters," Mr. Wysocka said, shaking Jere's hand firmly. "I'm pleased to see you here. You'll be one of the most valuable resources to our city in the future. Your medical care is superb."

"Thank you, sir," Jere said.

"Let's go meet some people," Mr. Wysocka suggested. "There are plenty of people wondering where the rest of my family is, and I'm sure they'd be interested to hear your take on the new laws and the health crisis."

Jere followed along. The fundraiser event benefitted some of the presidential candidates, President Clemente among them. Jere was introduced to a number of politicians and other public figures, all of whom looked at him with a mixture of interest in his healing capabilities and distrust of his upbringing in Sonova.

A local governor of a neighboring town gave Jere a suspicious look. "It's your kind that are pushing for that new SRA. Can't leave well enough alone."

"I'm not formally taking a stance on the SRA," Jere said carefully. "Of course I support the health reform; and as a slaveowner myself, I like that it would make searches and investigations more difficult. I'd rather have my rights at home than in public."

"Our rights should apply everywhere," Annika cut in. "I should be able to do whatever I want with my property."

Mr. Wysocka glared pointedly at his daughter. "Nobody of any breeding should be airing their slaves' issues in public, anyway.

And I will admit that the slaves return in far better condition when they've been treated by a human healer. Doctor Peters here has not only healed my slaves, but has repaired work done by some veterinarians. I'm not sure if I'd say the same for all healers, but I've been much happier having my slaves seen by him."

"Don't tell that to the Human Veterinary Association," the governor cautioned with a laugh. He gestured to the other side of the room. "They're here supporting the new candidate from the Belasso district. The candidate's trying to make it illegal for human healers to treat slaves."

Jere was only slightly bothered by that news. He doubted it would ever become reality, especially with the new diseases and the threat that they posed. Even if such a law did go into effect, he knew that even some of the staunchest supporters of slavery would oppose it — it was a quality control issue. Besides, what he did with his own property was up to him; Wren and Isis would be safe.

What bothered him more was seeing the veterinarian he and Wren had run into. She had hurt his lover and she dared to be in the same room as him? He decided to step outside of his usual comfort zone. "Well, one of them provided some of the most subpar care I've ever seen," he mentioned, pointing her out. "Not only was my slave not healed, he was distressed. She charged twice as much as I would have to do the job right, and she's been harassing me since."

Mr. Wysocka looked over with interest. "She's been seeking a loan to expand her practice. If that's the reputation she has, I don't think I'll be interested in funding it."

Jere was stunned. Was it that easy to buy someone's approval, or to lose it? "Um, you don't have to do that."

Mr. Wysocka shook his head. "I'd rather have an excellent doctor in town than a sub-par veterinarian. I don't even own animals. They're dirty and far too delicate."

"What's she been doing to you?" Paltrek asked.

"I guess she didn't like my attitude or something. I let her know that her clinic was filthy and didn't let her treat my slave further. Now she's claiming that there was something unusual about me, and about Wren, and some investigator came over the other day."

"Bitch," Paltrek dismissed the vet. "The slave agency can get pretty nasty if they want to. The way the laws are right now, some-one just has to make a complaint and you're a target."

"At least now I'm not worried that *I* will be in trouble for what my slave is doing," Annika mumbled, going silent when her father gave her a dirty look.

"You've had the sense to keep a rather low profile since you've been here," Mr. Wysocka reflected. "Where do you think you stand, politically?"

Jere paused. He stood on whichever side allowed his loved ones to be safe, but even voicing those concerns put them in danger. "Well, I certainly won't be supporting the candidate from Belasso, if I want my clinic to keep prospering."

The flippant answer worked well, drawing laughs from the people standing around. Jere continued. "I've seen places torn apart by disease. Hojer is my home, now. I don't want it to end up like that. We need to protect everyone, and we need to protect our business interests as well. My vote will go for whoever can do both of those things. Especially if those things can be accomplished without some regulation agency breathing down my neck."

"I never thought I'd agree with the outlander," Annika muttered.

"It sounds like you're running on the same ideas as our current president is," Mr. Wysocka pointed out. "Clemente hasn't made a stance either way on the SRA. He just says that he'll do what's right for Arona. Of course, that only matters if he can get reelected. He's not making friends by refusing to pick a side. The veterinarians and most in the slave industry are opposed, but the police force, the medical doctors, and the public safety experts are all supporting it."

"It's unnecessary!" Annika complained.

"You just know you won't be able to control yourself," Paltrek said, barely loud enough for Jere to hear from just a few inches away. He felt vindicated that his friend was actually fighting back against his family.

"If we want to make interstate business a reality, we need to appease the sheltered outlanders," Mr. Wysocka said. "Personally, I think the SRA and anyone who supports it are soft, weak, and not fit for a fine state like Arona. Professionally... I think we need to make concessions in order to accomplish our main goals. Survival and success. Wysocka Enterprises was among the first to get involved in the slave industry after The Fall. If we need to adapt to the world again, we will do it with finesse."

Annika looked increasingly less pleased as her father talked. She left without a word, grabbing Arae by her hair and dragging her into a bathroom.

Paltrek frowned at his father. "You know she's dragging the girl in there to vent her frustrations."

Mr. Wysocka shrugged. "She knows I'll disinherit her if she embarrasses me at an event like this. I'm certain she'll gag the girl if she becomes disruptive."

Jere felt his stomach churn. Paltrek had his crass moments, but it was easy to forget just how casually cruel the rest of the Wysocka family was. Image, wealth, and power were all they cared about. Jere had seen it too many times, both when he had visited the Wysockas at home, and when they had paid him social visits.

Some of the other guests moved away, and Mr. Wysocka fixed his gaze on Jere. "I'll make sure that veterinarian doesn't stay in business very long."

Jere didn't want to panic, but he didn't want to anger the veterinarian any more. She had already caused enough problems for him. "Really, I'm sure it will blow over."

"Anyone who so casually burns bridges isn't someone I want involved in my business arrangements," Mr. Wysocka said. "I wouldn't trust her, and I want to make sure my name isn't associated with hers. You, on the other hand, you're a strong connection. With your position, I'm sure you're not in need of funds, but if there's anything I can do for you, please let me know. I'd be happy to introduce you to some of the more established individuals. Help you build a real presence here. I wasn't sure if you'd stick around, but from what my son tells me, you've really started a life here in Hojer. Have you ever considered private employment, instead of state? Wysocka Enterprises would happily hire you as our company doctor. After all, I'm not getting any younger."

"I haven't," Jere replied. He hadn't even realized such a thing was an option. It seemed so elitist, but that was what Wysocka Enterprises was all about. "I appreciate the offer."

"Take some time to think about it. For now, I'll let you boys mingle," Mr. Wysocka said, stepping away from Jere and Paltrek. "I have a few more private transactions to discuss."

As he walked away, Paltrek laughed. "He's going to buy off some candidates," he explained, his voice low. "Tax breaks, regulations, things like that. He'll probably cut his funding to the Slave Control, Regulation, and Enforcement Agency. He wasn't pleased by what they made you do last year, and he gets angry any time they're mentioned. They're getting in the way of a lot of slave business, trying to push all sorts of regulations."

Jere nodded. It would be nice to have the agency not just off his back, but closed entirely. He had no idea how it would work, but the less funding they had, the better off they would be. Jere was thrown by the support that the Wysocka family gave him, but he was glad to be in their good graces.

Annika finally emerged with Arae, who was looking pale and sick. Jere didn't want to know what had happened to her, but he did notice Paltrek reaching down to run his hands through Dane's hair, soothing him.

"Sick of seeing that," he mumbled. "I swear, if there was a suitable place nearby, I'd move out, I really would."

Jere tried not to laugh. He was pretty sure that if the man hadn't left the family home yet, it wasn't just because of a lack of suitable accommodations. Paltrek enjoyed the Wysocka mansion as much as he enjoyed the rest of the benefits that came from having a wealthy and powerful family.

As the speeches and mingling died down, the event became more lighthearted, with an open bar and dancing. The event had already taken a decidedly progressive turn; after some of the candidates gave their speeches, a number of very conservative groups had left, fortunately including the veterinarian who had been giving Jere dirty looks for most of the night. Annika left with them, insisting she wanted to talk to "right-minded" people. Mr. Wysocka stayed, and Jere wondered if he had something to do with getting some of the attendees to leave. The man was only protecting his business, but if those goals aligned with Jere's, Jere was happy to have him as a supporter.

Jere and Paltrek even played around in a friendly manner. Paltrek had ceased his attempts to flirt with Jere when he was sober long ago, but as he got more and more intoxicated, he started again, good-natured teasing and touching and joking coupled with hopeful requests. As the night continued, Jere was actually glad that Dane was there, because it was easier to push Paltrek off on him than to keep turning him down. By the end of the night, Paltrek was happily sandwiched between Dane and another man, a free one, and he seemed as eager to take those two home as Jere was to return to Wren. Jere smiled, pleased to see his friend having so much fun. Dane even looked like he was enjoying himself, the man Paltrek had picked up was mostly sober and was handling Dane carefully.

When they parted ways for the night, Paltrek gave Jere a sloppy, drunken hug, and Jere couldn't stop himself from laughing at it, or the way that Paltrek walked away, one hand down Dane's pants and the other down the pants of the other man he was bringing home. Aside from the knowledge that Dane was a slave, Jere would have thought that Paltrek was just a lucky man taking home two playmates for the night, like his old friends in Sonova used to do. He wondered how different it really was.

Jere was walking home alone, but he wasn't going home alone. He was going home to the most wonderful person in the world.

Chapter 9

Explorations

Wren was only half-asleep when he sensed Jere's return to the area where the mind connection could reach him. He woke up and happily contacted Jere.

"How was it?" Wren asked. A part of him was curious if Jere had made any useful connections, and a part of him just hoped Jere had some fun. He liked seeing his master go out and enjoy himself.

"It went well," Jere replied happily. *"I mingled with Arona's finest and some political people without utterly embarrassing myself, got complimented by Paltrek's father, and finished the night with dancing and drinks!"*

"Did you meet anyone exciting?"

"Not really. I sent Paltrek and Dane home with a new friend to keep them company."

"Was this new friend cute?" Wren teased.

"Not as cute as you are."

Wren smiled at that; even though Jere couldn't see him, he would be able to feel the happiness through the connection. He cuddled back into bed, waiting for Jere to make his way home and join him. At one point, he would have gotten up, maybe even answered the door, but those days were long gone. As a slave, he trusted Jere enough to know that Jere wouldn't hurt him for not doing so; as a partner, he had overcome that anxious new lover stage of his life. Jere would want him to be comfortable, and he was fully in agreement.

He didn't wait long. He heard the door opening, since he had left the door to the bedroom open in anticipation, and he could feel Jere coming closer. A few seconds later, Jere came into the bedroom, smiling as he saw Wren in bed. Jere stripped off his clothes and joined him. Wren reached over and pulled Jere close, tugging him down on top of himself for a long, lazy kiss.

"*I missed you,*" Jere said through the mind connection.

"*You weren't gone that long,*" Wren protested, although he was in no way willing to unlock their lips, either.

"*It was long enough,*" Jere countered, closing his eyes and rubbing his entire body against Wren's.

Wren had been tired earlier, but he had enjoyed his little nap. Even more, he was enjoying feeling Jere touching him. They kissed for a while longer, and then Jere moved lower, taking his time as he licked a slow trail from Wren's neck, down to his chest, where he paused, resting his head and looking up at Wren.

"You up to play tonight?" Jere asked.

Wren smiled greedily. "Absolutely. And I want to feel you inside of me by the time we're done, so keep that in mind."

"Yes, sir," Jere teased.

Wren knew that Jere liked it when he gave him orders, and he enjoyed doing it.

"One day, I want to take you out dancing again. You liked it last time we went, right?"

Wren smiled at the memory. "I liked it a lot. But I like being here with you, too."

"I forgot how fun it could be to go out and do things," Jere admitted. "It felt wrong to be out there without you, but I enjoyed the fundraiser more than I thought I would. I miss things like that."

Wren just nodded. Jere got nostalgic sometimes, but it didn't bother Wren nearly as much as it did Jere. Wren trusted Jere to stay with him even if it meant giving up the life he had once loved.

"Besides, I think it would be fun to watch you flirt with other people, knowing that you'll take me home in the end," Jere suggested. "Maybe pretend we're strangers who just happened to meet up, half-naked, on the dance floor."

"Why would that be fun?" Wren knew he'd be at least a little uncomfortable with a situation like that; at least, if he were in Jere's position. It seemed wrong, dishonest somehow.

"I like the competition. The thrill. Not knowing if I'm going to get picked up, or if I'm wasting my time and might have to start all over again from the start, or go home alone. It's fun to see if you can win. I mean, it would just be pretend, but I still like the game."

"That's fun?" Wren laughed. "Sounds like a lot of uncertainty to me."

Jere grinned up at him for a moment before trailing his tongue down Wren's chest, biting lightly at one of his nipples. "It's a challenge. And besides, all that happens is you go home alone if you're playing for real. There are worse things."

Wren smiled. For a slave, who knew what such actions would bring, but Jere's world was more fun. "And what kinds of rewards come with those challenges?" he asked, running his hands over Jere's body, cupping his ass possessively.

"All sorts of things," Jere said, playfully squirming until he was situated between Wren's legs. "Then you go home, and you get to find out what the other person enjoys. It's like a game, to see who can figure it out faster. You know, what the other person wants, where they like to be touched...."

As Jere spoke, he made his way down Wren's body, using his fingers and tongue to explore. He found the spots that just barely turned Wren on, teasing him and making him ache for more. A glance into Jere's eyes convinced Wren that his lover knew exactly what he was doing, how much the light touches and intentional flicks of his tongue were contributing to Wren's arousal. No matter how many times they had touched each other, Wren was always amazed by how good Jere made him feel.

"You know what I like," Wren said softly, not wanting to interrupt anything. Jere was doing exactly what he liked.

"Yeah, but if you had just met me and taken me home I wouldn't," Jere teased, making his way down to Wren's cock and toying with it lightly, dragging his lips over the head as Wren shuddered in pleasure, but not wrapping his lips around it, yet. "For all you'd know, I might just be a cock tease."

"Is that why you came home and jumped right into bed with me?"

"Maybe I just want to explore," Jere continued. "I mean, I might not have any idea that you like it when I lick and suck your cock like this. I'd have to try it gently at first, to see if you like it. And if I like it too."

As he spoke, Jere made good on his suggestions, taking the very tip of Wren's cock into his mouth, as if he had never done it before. His tongue flicked around it tentatively, and his hands rested on Wren's legs. Wren felt his heart start to race and his temperature rise. He wanted more, but the waiting was only making things better. He lifted his hips to meet Jere's mouth when Jere pulled off, but Jere turned his head aside and smiled.

"See, if I had just met you, I might think that you wanted me to take you a little deeper."

With his eyes still fixed on Wren's, Jere did exactly that, dipping his head low and taking Wren deep into his throat, his tongue driving Wren crazy as he fought to keep himself from grabbing Jere by the hair and just fucking his mouth until he came. When Jere pulled off again, Wren clenched his hands into fists, desperate for more contact.

"Then maybe I'd work my tongue lower, taking it over your hole, dipping in a bit... just to see if you like it, of course."

With each sentence, Jere did as he described, backing off slightly to describe the next action. His words made soft, warm puffs of air blow across Wren's skin. He seemed perfectly aware of how much he was turning Wren on.

"If I just met you and brought you home and you teased me like this, could I just grab you and fuck you already?" Wren asked, curious to see how Jere would reply.

Jere was silent, but he worked Wren's cock more vigorously as he reached and grabbed for Wren's hand. He pulled Wren's hand close and entwined it in his hair. Wren smiled. Jere hadn't exactly read his mind, but he did know his preferences well enough to guess that this was where it had been going.

"Oh, do you like to pull hair?" Jere asked, teasing. "Maybe we should give it a try."

Wren was perfectly aware that Jere knew he loved to do so, but the game was fun. "Yes," he admitted, feeling himself blush. Somehow, doing it was far easier than talking about it.

"I really like having my hair pulled," Jere said, an overly innocent look on his face, like he was just confessing it for the first time. "Maybe we should try it. Maybe you should show me what happens to cock teases when you take them home."

Wren wasted no time taking a fistful of Jere's hair and jerking him down hard on his cock, shivering with pleasure as he felt Jere struggle to accommodate him deep in his throat. He forced himself to wait a few moments before pulling Jere up, glancing into his eyes and seeing the agreement and happiness there before shoving him down again.

"Are you getting all the cock you want, now?" Wren asked, holding Jere's head down as he thrust his hips over and over again.

"*Never enough,*" Jere replied through the mind connection. "*Faster. Until I can't keep up.*"

As always, Wren was careful with Jere, fully aware that his speed gift could give Jere whiplash, not to mention choke him. He knew how much Jere loved to have that control ripped away from him, and he meant to make it happen, working Jere's head up and down until he could no longer detect the careful, artful blowjob skills that Jere had perfected. He smiled as he felt Jere's throat relax, focused only on accommodating his cock. A muffled moan told him how turned on Jere was, and the vibrations seemed to echo around Wren's cock.

Jere's fingers were busy working Wren's ass, gently touching and stretching him with the aid of spit and pre-come. Wren kept his lower body still, letting Jere work his magic, but kept pulling Jere's head up and down on his cock until he was seconds away from coming. He stopped, holding Jere back at the tip until Jere made a little pouty noise of complaint.

Wren smiled, using Jere's hair as a handle to move him over to the other side of the bed and positioning him on his back. Jere happily complied, leaning back against the pillows and shivering when Wren moved on top of him.

"You don't get to do all the exploring," Wren decided, grabbing Jere's arms and pinning them above his head forcefully as he kissed him, feeling Jere's cock hard against his leg.

Wren kissed Jere until he decided they were finished, moving rapidly down to Jere's cock, succeeding in taking Jere enough by surprise that he gasped as Wren took his cock into his mouth in one swift motion.

"Guess you liked that," Wren pointed out a few moments later when he came up for a breath, watching as Jere twisted and grabbed at the sheets in a desperate attempt to stay still and avoid thrusting up to meet Wren. Jere was always considerate of the fact that Wren wasn't comfortable with having his throat fucked so vigorously.

"Let's see what else you like," Wren said, playfully exploring Jere's body. "After all, you're here for my pleasure."

He touched Jere all over, as if he wasn't completely aware of the areas that Jere liked best, and he heated up different spots with his hands, making Jere shudder even more. He worked a finger inside of Jere, warming it until Jere whimpered and opened his eyes, looking a little nervous, but very excited.

"Did you know I had a firesetting gift?" Wren smiled a dangerous smile. Sometimes he did enjoy hurting Jere, just a little. "From the looks of it, you like a little burn."

He kept flitting around Jere's body, kissing here, biting there, almost burning in other places. By the time he was satisfied, Jere was jumping and gasping with every touch, uncertain whether it was going to be sensual or burning hot, a light caress or a stinging scratch. Red patches covered Jere's skin, and Wren felt the heat growing between them as Jere gasped in pleasure.

Wren pulled Jere into the position he wanted him, leaned back against the headboard, his hips angled in the exact right direction, his cock hard and ready. Wren straddled him, spreading his legs around Jere and easing down, brushing his ass against Jere's cock.

"Hmm, would this be something you'd like?" Wren asked, feigning innocence. "Would you like to fuck me? After all, we just met. I don't know if you've earned it, yet."

Jere moaned, reaching up to grab Wren's hips. Wren was a little surprised by the move, but Jere just held him and let his hands trail along Wren's skin.

"I would love to fuck you," Jere said, his voice coming out just barely above a whisper. "My sexy man. Take your pleasure on me. Show me how you want me to move, how you can sway your hips and work my cock for your pleasure. You can do it on a dance floor...

do it on me?"

Wren smiled, easing himself down the slightest bit, feeling the tip of Jere's cock right where it should be. He used his own hand to line it up as he slid down even further, breathing slowly as he felt Jere slipping into him, filling him, and he gasped as he seated himself all the way, feeling the familiar warmth of his lover inside of him. He made a little moaning sound, staying there, feeling his muscles clench and tighten and adjust.

Jere was patient, waiting obediently below him, his hands stroking their way up and down Wren's sides, traversing forward to stroke at Wren's cock every once in a while. "I love you so much," he said, his words somehow coming in time with the gentle pass of his fingers over Wren's skin. It was Wren's turn to shudder, the sweet words going deeper than anything else had.

He started to move, sliding up a few inches, then back down, adjusting and taking it slow. It was hard, sometimes; he did so many things so quickly. For too many years, he had been forced to take this quickly, but Jere was patient, smiling up at him like he was the only man in the world, which maybe he was for Jere. He knew Jere was the only one for him, the only one that he ever wanted to love or fuck or do anything at all with. He started to move a little faster, feeling the slight burn go from uncomfortable to pleasant, and then from pleasant to something even better. He leaned forward a little, pinning Jere to the bed beneath him, and he cried out, pressing himself down hard on Jere's cock.

Jere responded in kind, letting out a sound of pleasure as Wren sped up. He reached up to take Wren's cock in his hand, curling his fingers around it so that every time Wren slid up and down on Jere's cock, Wren's cock was sliding in and out of Jere's fist.

With his other hand, Jere reached up, lightly stroking the side of Wren's face, running his fingers through Wren's hair. Wren loved feeling Jere's fingers in his hair as much as Jere loved having his hair pulled, and he twisted his head, desperate for more contact. As he did, he worked himself up and down, faster and faster, feeling Jere's body rocking underneath of him. He leaned forward, trapping Jere's hand and his own cock between them, and pressed his lips to Jere's, allowing the heat to build. Jere's mouth felt cold at first by comparison, but in seconds, Wren had warmed it with his tongue, plunging it in deep and matching it with the way they thrust together.

He felt himself coming far too soon; no matter how long they had been fucking, Wren never wanted it to end. Jere had worked him up so much with his mouth, and the friction between their bodies combined with the heat Wren was generating. Wren couldn't hold back any longer. He came quickly, making a high moaning noise as he felt himself come across Jere's stomach. He shuddered with the after-effects.

Jere lasted just a few seconds longer. Wren smiled as he realized his own cock had barely started to soften before Jere came as well. Jere clutched lightly at the back of Wren's head and pulled him down for another kiss as he came.

They lay there for a few moments, kissing languidly and shivering with every touch. Wren felt Jere pull out, and he was left with the slight feeling of emptiness. Sometimes, he wanted nothing more than to feel Jere fuck him for countless hours, no matter how uncomfortable it would feel in reality. The fantasy was still worth appreciating.

"I'm glad I get to come home to you every night," Jere declared, giving Wren one last, lingering kiss before gently pushing him off. Jere went and fetched some towels to clean up with, and then they cuddled in next to each other, the warmth still radiating between them, far better than anything Wren could generate on his own. "You're sure it doesn't bother you? I always feel like I'm betraying you when I leave for so long."

"You always come home," Wren reminded him. He never wanted anything to change about that. For so many years, Wren had resented being touched, but now, the thought of spending a night without Jere made him sad and nervous. No matter who Jere mingled with outside, he was home now. Just being with him was enough for Wren. "Someone has to go out and pretend to be a part of this community, right?"

Jere smiled back, a look of relief evident on his face. Wren couldn't hold their respective roles against them.

"Oh, by the way, you got some mail while you were out," Wren remembered, speeding through the house to retrieve the letter that simply had the word "URGENT" stamped on the front. Wren watched as Jere tore into the envelope carelessly, tugging out the single piece of paper. Over his shoulder, Wren saw the words "Slave Control, Regulation, and Enforcement Agency." Receiving mail from them was like receiving mail from an archenemy, and Wren could feel through the connection that Jere was equally displeased by it.

"What's wrong?"

"This." Jere handed him the letter.

Doctor Peters: Due to recent complaints made by community members of Arona, the Agency will be conducting an audit of your property, premises, and slave-owning capabilities. As required by current code, we are providing this notice in writing. Your audit will occur thirty days from the date of this letter. Please make necessary arrangements to attend this event, as your presence is required.

Thank you for your compliance.

The letter was signed by one of the regulation agency workers, but Wren didn't even bother to read the name. As it was, the text blurred in front of his eyes. He was too terrified to focus on anything but what might happen.

"They're going to audit us," Jere said, still in disbelief.

"We can handle it. We'll go through the house, make sure everything is in perfect condition, make sure the clinic is in compliance with everything, and we can do what they ask. We'll get through this, and we'll show them that there's nothing to worry about. At least they gave us a warning about when they'd be coming."

Jere scowled. "Is that a good thing? All I can see it doing is worrying us."

Wren shrugged, trying not to agree with that assessment. "Obviously, they don't think it's any kind of emergency. They're following protocol. We're not top priority or anything. It's like having a business inspected for fire codes, or having the psychic health department check out the clinic. It's routine. They'll come, we'll pass, then we continue on as usual."

"But what if we don't?"

Wren wanted to be brave, but Jere had a knack for speaking his worst fear aloud. "We can't panic. If we panic, it makes it look like we have something to panic about. Consult with Kieran. Paltrek, even, although I'm sure his family has people to handle things like this. They can help you figure out what you need to do. Make sure everything is legal, though I know it is."

For a moment, Jere looked like he was about to disagree. Wren could feel it through the mind connection, the pressing urge to panic and be pessimistic, but then Jere blocked it. "You're right. But I still want to go back to that veterinarian and show her what a human healer's powers can do!"

Jere considered the situation. He knew exactly what Wren meant, and he realized that Wren must have spent years following that same good advice, hiding his firesetting gift, acting normal. It was what had kept him alive for so many years.

Wren smiled. "That would accomplish the exact opposite of what we want. As far as anyone else in this state is concerned, she's just doing her civic duty."

"We've got to call this thing with Lighthouse off," Jere decided. "I know Isis is excited, but—"

"You should still go," Wren interrupted, shaking his head. "Make it look like you don't care, like this is an everyday occurrence."

Jere shook his head. "I can't just up and leave. I have to be here, I have to be ready."

"You have to act normal," Wren cut in. He smiled a little. "Well, you have to act at least a little bit normal. Normal for Hojer. Not normal for you. These are normal slaveowner things—getting certified, traveling for business, all of that. You won't help anything by panicking for the next month, and Isis probably won't be motivated enough to start training for certification if she doesn't have the trip to look forward to at the end. Once you get certified, it will look better. You could both use some practice in how to conduct yourselves, and preparing for the certification will be the perfect opportunity."

Jere frowned, clearly nervous. "That seems... I don't know. I don't like it."

"Well, I never said you should like it," Wren pointed out. He had spent enough years hiding that he knew how uncomfortable it could be, how terrifying it was to think of getting caught. "But it's the normal way to deal with something like this. Trust me."

Jere nodded. He still didn't look convinced, but Wren knew that would take time. They took solace in each other's arms, and Wren tried not to think of the alternative. He couldn't survive without Jere, not after he had grown so comfortable. This had to work.

Chapter 10

International Medicine

Jere wrote up a message to be delivered by telegraph, and gave Wren a desperate, pleading look until he agreed to go deliver it. He wanted Kieran's input, not because he didn't trust Wren, but because he wanted all the help he could get.

While Wren was gone, Jere opened up the clinic. Isis joined him, staying far from patients as usual. Jere had told her about the audit, not to scare her, but because she deserved to know. He had kept enough from both her and Wren, and he needed her prepared for this.

"Can I go stay somewhere else that day?" she asked, giving Jere a hopeful look. "I mean, maybe Kieran could take me somewhere, or maybe I could go hide in the library with Imelda? She likes me, and books are okay."

Jere shook his head. "It's kind of implied that you should be here. It's a test of my ability as a slaveowner — if I just send my slaves away, that's not a very good sign."

"Me screwing everything up won't be a good sign, either," Isis pouted.

Jere could tell that she was scared. He shared that sentiment. "We don't have another option. We'll do it, and hopefully everything will work out. I won't let anything bad happen to you."

"I've been in places that have been audited before. I just don't want to do it here because I don't want to fuck this up. I've usually been bound and gagged while they were there," she said, then got a suspicious look on her face. "Don't get any ideas."

Jere smiled at her. "Trust me, it didn't even cross my mind."

Isis nodded, content with his statement.

When Wren returned, he came with a reply from Kieran. "She said she'll send you a package with a list of things to check and do, and that you should stop 'shitting your pants over every little thing.' She'll talk to you more when she comes to stay with me when you and Isis go to see her parents, but aside from that, just act normal. There's no way out of this. Any attempt to avoid it looks suspect."

"We're still going?" Isis asked. She was clearly surprised, but whether that surprise was pleasant or uncomfortable was hard to determine, even with what Jere could feel through the mind connection.

Jere didn't have an answer for her. He wanted to say no, but the glare Wren gave him kept him quiet.

"We're at least going to follow through and act like we are," Wren said. "It's the right thing to do. We don't need to draw attention to ourselves or make it seem like we're intimidated."

Jere wanted to protest, but the bell at the front desk rang. Before he could say a word, Wren was off to attend it, leaving him staring at Isis cluelessly.

"Wren's probably right," Isis reminded him. "He usually is."

Jere nodded, getting ready for his first patient. He was interrupted when Wren returned, a nervous look on his face. "There's someone here from the International Medical Board. He wants to speak with you."

Even as he walked out to the reception area, Jere could feel his heart racing. Even a layperson could see how tense Jere was. Bullshit in Hojer was bad enough, but what was someone from the International Medical Board doing here?

"Keep Isis out of the way," Jere told Wren.

The man looked official, but not nearly as threatening as the Slave Control, Regulation, and Enforcement Agency investigator had. If anything, he looked as out of place as Jere did.

"Dr. Peters," the man said. "The Board has decided to do a quick check on your clinic. I'll be shadowing you today and reporting my findings."

"Is this because of the fucking vet?" Jere snapped.

"Excuse me?"

"The vet from Pinemont. Barrett, I think her name was. Karmin Barrett. Evil bitch who doesn't know how to do her job."

The man gave Jere a blank stare. "I can only hope that vets here are being used to treat animals, Dr. Peters. We do random reviews; your clinic came up randomly."

From the looks of it, the man probably believed it, but Jere wasn't so foolish. Someone, somewhere had made this happen.

"We're increasing the amounts of checks we're doing across the continent. With the threat of disease and the elections in many of the slave states, we just want to make sure everything is running smoothly. We're based out of Sonova—we commend you for the work you've done here."

Jere didn't buy it. If he was so commended, why were they targeting him?

"There are many people criticizing you," the man admitted. "I'm sorry. I guess it's just a hazard of working in a slave state. It's rare for someone born and trained in a free state to even come out this way."

"Yeah," Jere muttered. He wanted to feel reassured that the inspector was a fellow outlander, but he couldn't. What if the man said something wrong, gave Hojer's officials the wrong impression? Something as simple as mentioning that the slave patients were treated as well as the free patients could draw more attention from Hojer's slave agency, no matter how positive such a comment would look in a more civilized setting.

"If you're interested, the Board maintains a list of vacancies. I'm sure you'd fit better in a more progressive place."

"No, thank you." Jere tried not to be blunt, but the offer worried him. If his problems were so public that officials in Sonova knew about it, he wasn't sure if he had a chance here at all. "Let's just get started."

Isis had been nervous since Wren returned from the telegraph office. The fact that there was another unwanted intruder in their house didn't help matters. Wren had done his best to keep her out of the way of the official from the International Medical Board, but she insisted on hanging around the clinic. They needed her around anyway; she was part of the team that was being reviewed.

"I don't want to be here for the audit," she mumbled. "Or go for certification. Or anything. I just want to be left alone."

Wren agreed, but he knew there was something more to it for Isis. She had been bringing up her parents casually, pondering what they might be like, what the town might be like, where they might be living. She wasn't saying either way if she wanted to go, but Wren could see how hard she was trying to hide her feelings. Jere had a lot of influence on Isis; she would choose to go based on what she thought pleased him. Wren was pretty sure that he didn't have the same sway over her.

"What about the stuff with the Lighthouse Organization?"

"It's probably not even them, anyway," Isis said, dismissive.

Wren raised an eyebrow in her direction.

"It's a lot of work, and they're far away, if it even is them, and Jere can't just pick up and leave you and the clinic and everything else just to go and check something stupid like that out for me, especially with the audit and the medical board and whatever else is going on. There's someone coming into the clinic and interrupting us all the time, obviously Jere won't be able to leave now. It's not even worth talking about."

Wren had been through his own stages of self-pity enough that he could recognize it in Isis. "Jere and I care about you, and Kieran does too. But I know that neither of them has really asked you if you want to go. You say you do, but I have a little more first-hand experience with actually being a slave. I just wanted to make sure you were really okay with this before I make Jere do it."

Isis looked at him suspiciously. "What's your plan?"

"Kieran has offered to stay with me during one of her breaks so that Jere can go with you."

Isis was silent for a moment. "You'd really do that for me? This isn't, like... a joke or something?"

"I wouldn't do something like that to you. I know we've had our disagreements, but I want you to be able to have this."

"What if they forgot about me or something? I mean, it's been nine years. What if they had a bunch of other kids, and they like them better, or they see me and they don't like what they see, or — "

"Just stop it," Wren cut her off. It was easy to see her getting upset, and they couldn't afford that, not with the visitor from the Medical Board lurking around.

Wren motioned to an empty exam room, shutting the door behind them and turning on the sink to cover their conversation. Disinfecting was always the best busy work — a medical clinic could never be too clean. "You know your parents better than any of us do. Were they the type who would abandon you just because you're a slave? Just because of your gift?"

Isis shook her head. "They didn't like slavery. We had family just outside of Sonova, and a lot of them had physical gifts. Sometimes my parents would talk about moving there, away from the 'cruelty.' I didn't know what they were talking about, then."

"See? They're not going to reject you for being a slave, or for having a physical gift. My family made it very clear that I was disowned the moment the gift identifier notified them of my speed gift."

"Assholes," Isis declared. "But what if they just don't like me? Like, what if they want someone nice, or polite, or I mean... I'm fucking damaged, Wren. What if they don't want me like I am? Like, I'm all scarred up, and I do weird things, sometimes, and I'm really jumpy around new people. What if I screw it all up? What if they see me again and they decide that they hate me? Then that's their last memory of me and my last memory of them. I don't want that. I should just stay here."

"Do you really think they would have kept looking for you for all this time just to give up that easily?"

"I'd rather not find that out."

Wren let the silence stretch for a moment.

"You know what, you and Jere have each other!" Isis finally snapped. "I have a vague memory of people who used to care about me like that. I don't want to lose it!"

"It could start being a real, fresh memory," Wren pointed out. "Would you go?"

Wren shook his head. "To see my family? Not for all the fucking money in the world. But I know they don't want to see me. They made it perfectly clear before they let me be taken. That I was a disgrace, a shame to the family... that kind of thing. I'd want to see my younger brother, maybe, depending on how he turned out. If he was a slave and we could find him... but I'd rather he be free and I never meet him again. He'd hate me like he's supposed to; he liked to cause trouble as a kid, but I'm sure he fell in line as he got older. I wouldn't want to see that. But if there was even a chance that my family wanted to see me? I'd throw a fit until I got to go."

Isis smiled at him. "I like it here."

"And nobody will make you go anywhere else," Wren promised. "You're stuck with us. I tried to get rid of you for months. Now that we get along, I'm pretty much as committed to keeping you here as Jere is."

Isis smiled at him, a little. "Thanks. You really think you can convince Jere to take me?"

"Trust me, I can convince Jere to do anything I want him to."

Chapter 11

Convincing

Wren waited for the perfect time to spring his plan on Jere. The official from the International Medical Board made it difficult, but after a few hours of taking notes and getting in the way, he announced that he would be visiting one of Hojer's restaurants for lunch. Wren used the opportunity to corner Jere as he finished up with a patient.

"Jere," Wren said, trying to be tactful. "Come here, I want to tell you something."

Isis looked at both of them and made the face that she usually made when she knew they were going to go spend "alone time" together. He and Jere tried to keep the displays of affection low around her, just to be polite. They tried to keep them low around Kieran, too, but only after she mentioned that she liked to watch. Neither Wren nor Jere was sure if she was serious or teasing, but either way, it effectively halted their explorations in front of her.

Jere followed him into the exam room, smiling wider when he saw Wren pull the door closed behind them. He raised an eyebrow, hopeful.

"Stealing me away for a quickie?" he suggested, seating himself against the countertop and leaning back, a hopeful look on his face. "You know my schedule better than I do. Take me for as long as I'm free. Or at least until the damn Medical Board inspector returns."

Wren came up between his legs and kissed him, teasing for a moment before pulling back. It was hard to resist, especially when Jere moved forward, prolonging the kiss. He put his hands on Jere's shoulders and held him there. "There's something I want to talk to you about first."

"Sex is better?" Jere still held on to the hopeful look.

"Guess where you're going to be a month from now."

Jere looked confused. "Probably right here? Maybe having more sex with you?"

"You're no fun!" Wren sighed. Jere wasn't playing his guessing game. "You're going to be in Redmont, with Isis, seeing her parents."

Jere froze. "What?"

"Look, I know you don't really want to leave Hojer, but Kieran has put so much work into it, and I think Isis deserves this."

"Wren..." Jere started. "I don't disagree, but it would mean leaving you!"

"You won't be gone forever." Wren didn't like the idea of Jere being gone, even for a little while, but he had decided that the benefits far outweighed the risks.

"It would mean leaving you with another person to stand in as your master," Jere clarified, as if Wren had somehow missed this point. "I promised you years ago that I would never do that to you, and I meant it. I still mean it! I'm not just going to dump you off on someone and go running off with Isis. I've explained it to her. She understands."

Wren looked at Jere firmly. He had anticipated a challenge and he hoped to crush it quickly, so they would have time to play when they were done. "Last time Kieran was here, she offered to stay with me. I'm safe and comfortable with her. And I want to do this for Isis. She wants it, and she never really wants anything. Let's do this for her."

Jere was quiet, and Wren could tell that he was wracking his brain to think of any arguments that he could make to keep Wren from being so convinced that this was the right idea.

"What about the audit?"

"You live in a slave state. Audits happen. It doesn't mean you put your life on hold."

Jere frowned as his argument was quickly shot down.

"Babe, if I had the chance to see my family again, I mean, if I thought they didn't hate me... if I was Isis, I would go." Wren wished Jere was a little more acculturated here so his words would make more sense. "When you get taken as a slave, you're told to let family go, to forget them, to pretend they don't even exist. You're told that they've already forgotten you exist. Isis has said a lot of crazy things, but she has always held strong to the idea that her parents are looking for her, that they'll want to see her. I'm not going to crush that."

"Then I will," Jere said, less of a firm statement and more of a suggestion.

Wren smiled gently. "Valiant, but no. Then you'll never hear the end of it from me *or* Isis, or Kieran for that matter, and it won't make anyone happier. Go and do this, because I know you'd do it for me, and I know Isis would do it for me, too, strange as it seems."

Jere nodded, still looking uncomfortable with the idea.

"You might be able to push back against all the harassment you've been getting lately, too." Wren played his final card, the one Kieran had just mentioned in their exchange today. "Isis's parents are talent scouts. I guess it's what they did while they were searching for her, their cover for all the travel they did. They have one of the most successful interstate job placement agencies in the area. It might make people here reconsider the way they treat you if they know you're meeting up with them."

"I don't know who's a worse influence," Jere said. "Between you and Kieran, you're going to get us all killed."

"We'll be fine, Jere. Nobody wants to lose their precious doctor. Kieran has a two-week break from school. That gives you and Isis plenty of time to leave and visit and come back, with a lot of time in between in case anything delays you."

"Nothing will delay me—"

"Speed trains have delays, Jere, we both experienced that," Wren reminded him.

Jere just nodded, agreeing, but not looking happy about it.

"I'll be fine with Kieran."

"Who said anything about you? What am I going to do without you?"

"You'll survive," Wren pointed out. He knew it was a little underhanded, going behind Jere's back and plotting with Kieran, but he figured it was for a good enough cause to justify the actions.

"Kiss me while I think about it? I've missed you all day."

Wren was happy to comply, leaning into Jere's embrace and kissing him, letting his hands roam over and under Jere's clothes. The inspector hadn't just made them all nervous; he had seriously gotten in the way of the casual touches that Wren and Jere usually shared throughout the workday. Wren used the longing to his advantage, knowing Jere would be easier to convince in the short window they had before the inspector returned.

"I can just take her, then?" Jere asked. "Redmont is in another state. One that won't even allow me to bring both of my slaves. How long will it take to get them to allow me to take Isis?"

"Brenton is a reciprocal slave state with Arona. Similar laws, same restrictions. You'll need to get her certified for out-of-state-travel, but that's it."

"Sounds hard," Jere protested, reaching for Wren's cock. "I like this hard thing better."

Wren captured Jere's hand, holding it firmly as he focused on the serious questions first. "The certification takes a few hours. You schedule it, you wait for the appointment. It's like a test, of both her and you. I'll help you get ready. Burghe had me certified a few weeks after he bought me. He liked to drag me around on business trips."

He shuddered at that memory. The things his ex-master had done to him had been terrible, the kind that gave him nightmares for months after the man died. Even now, just thinking about him made Wren's skin crawl.

"Don't talk about him right now," Jere requested, wrapping his legs around Wren's body to pull him closer. "He's pretty much the last thing I want to think about right now."

"Sounds good to me," Wren agreed, pushing the memories away.

"You should fuck me instead. Maybe our friend from the International Medical Board would appreciate seeing me a little more lively when he returns."

Wren laughed. "Are we done talking about Isis and you going to Redmont?"

Jere frowned, clearly disapproving of the idea. "If I say yes, does that mean you'll fuck me?"

Wren placed his hand over Jere's cock, palming it and squeezing down hard until Jere let out a little whimper. "Only if 'yes' means you'll do it like a good boy."

Jere breathed deeply at Wren's words and actions. "Absolutely. Right now, I'll do anything you say."

"Prove it," Wren challenged. "Get your pants off and lean over that exam table."

"Anything you say," Jere repeated, his hands already working his zipper.

Wren wasn't entirely sure whether he believed Jere or not, but he was too turned on by Jere's submission to argue further. Instead, he unzipped his pants and found some sort of medical lotion that would double for lube. He was ready well before Jere was, enough so that he got to help Jere by pinning his body to the exam table and rubbing against him. Jere threw his head back, nuzzling against Wren's neck and sighing happily as Wren kissed him.

Smiling, Wren squeezed some of the lotion out onto his hands, wrinkling his nose at the slight medical scent of it. He wasn't concerned with the scent, he was concerned with the slipperiness of it, and it met that criterion perfectly. He worked some onto his cock, smiling as Jere glanced back at him, eagerly anticipating what was to come. Wren quickly rubbed some of the lotion into and around Jere's ass, fingering his hole roughly.

"Yes," Jere hissed, squirming against Wren's fingers. "More? Please?"

Without waiting or bothering to give warning, Wren plunged into him, satisfying the need that Jere had been begging to have fulfilled since Wren first pulled him aside into the exam room. He worked himself in deep, putting his speed gift to good use. The exam table put Jere at a difficult height for Wren to reach, and he leaned over Jere, pushing his upper body down hard against the cold metal.

Jere's palms landed flat on the table as he braced himself, hissing in a mix of pain and pleasure when Wren pushed harder, pounding Jere's stomach into the edge of the table. Wren heard him cry out, and it wasn't his usual sound of enjoyment. Frowning, Wren pulled out.

"Turn around," he suggested.

"Just keep fucking me?" Jere begged, lying limp over the table. "You feel so good!"

Wren gripped his hips firmly and forced him to turn, putting Jere's back to the exam table. "Up," he ordered, pleased when Jere scooted onto the edge of the table. They didn't have much time, and he wanted to make the best of it. The inspector might not be as critical of the slave-master relationship as someone from the slave agency would, but a doctor wasting patient time fucking an assistant probably wouldn't reflect too well on them. The thrill of how taboo their act made Wren even harder.

"I'll be too high up," Jere protested.

Wren didn't respond; he just pulled Jere into his arms and onto his cock. If Jere's gasp was any indication, he was quite pleasantly surprised, and Wren was enjoying the tightness around his cock just as much.

Jere held tightly to his shoulders, leaving Wren bearing the weight of his body, almost holding Jere up as they continued to fuck. The angle wasn't quite right, so Wren reached out, wrapped his arms around Jere, and pulled him into position, pinning him between the edge of the table and his cock, fucking him hard and fast, banging the exam table against the wall with each thrust. Jere gasped, trying to meet Wren's energetic fucking motions and failing miserably. Wren enjoyed it, though.

"I'm gonna fuck you until you can't keep up," he growled in Jere's ear, pleased when he felt the muscles in Jere's ass tighten around him. "You're no match for my speed gift."

"Fuck yes," Jere replied, his voice barely above a whisper. His hands came up around Wren's neck, holding on tightly and pressing his face into Wren's shoulder, drowning out the satisfied sounds he was making.

It was good that Jere was attempting to be quiet, because Wren was pretty sure that at least the banging of the table against the wall could be heard outside of the exam room. The rooms were built to be sterile, not soundproof, and this sort of activity pushed the limits of what was and wasn't acceptable in the clinic. The thrill of doing something forbidden made Wren even more excited.

As Wren felt Jere about to come, he clamped his hand firmly over Jere's mouth. Jere was left capable of making only a few muffled cries as he came, and Wren gritted his teeth, letting out a only few satisfied grunts as he finished as well, pumping hard into Jere and then leaning him back against the wall, letting him relax.

The inspector came back just moments after Jere walked out of the exam room. Wren had to hold back a laugh at the inspector's confused look — Jere was smiling, a dazed and sated look on his face.

"I had a great lunch," Jere mentioned, trying to be casual. The inspector just nodded.

They finished at the clinic and discussed the plans for Isis and Jere to go to Redmont. Wren filled both Jere and Isis in on some of the real-life details of the certification. He had been through the process only once; Burghe would have needed to re-certify him again soon if he hadn't died when he did. Orders were given to the master, who then passed them on to the slave, and both were rated on their ability to perform as expected.

For Wren, it had been simple; he had been fresh from the training facility and desperate to please, still idealistic and hoping to make a good impression on his new master. He had received a spectacular rating, nearly perfect, but the fact that it was only nearly perfect had earned him a beating that had him coughing up blood for days until his master had finally decided to heal the broken ribs. Wren didn't mention that part, because he didn't want to dwell on it, nor did he want to scare Isis or Jere any more than necessary. They discussed a plan for training — both for Isis, and for Jere. Wren just hoped that it would be enough.

Chapter 12
Training Tools

"Let's do this training thing," Isis suggested, almost immediately after they were finished working. "I want to see what's so bad about it. I mean, I've been a slave forever, I'm sure I can pass."

Wren sighed. He doubted that there was any truth to that statement, and while it was nice to see the girl optimistic about something, he wasn't looking forward to the resulting upset that it would cause.

"All right," he said, figuring he would at least give her a chance. "Here are the rules. From this point on, there will be no questions, comments, outbursts, whining or yelling from you. You will answer Jere only, and you will do it in a respectful way, like you were taught to do at some point. Know what I'm talking about?"

Isis didn't answer, she just narrowed her eyebrows at him suspiciously. It was a trick they were both familiar with, being asked a question that wasn't intended to be answered. He wanted to kick himself for forgetting his own rules so quickly.

"Um, babe, you ask her," Wren mumbled.

Jere looked as awkward as Wren felt, and he turned to Isis with a shrug. "Uh... do you know what Wren's talking about?"

"Yeah, I think," Isis shrugged.

Wren smiled. Maybe more of a hands-on demonstration would work. "The correct answer to that would have been 'yes, master,' or 'no, master,' not 'yeah.' Clear, concise, use the title."

Isis nodded, looking focused on those three things. Wren was just glad that she wasn't upset already.

"Okay, Jere, your rules are a little different. No please, no thank you, and be clear. It's easier for her to follow orders if you give them clearly; don't leave it up to her to guess, because she could guess wrong, which would cause problems."

"I can't even be polite about it?" Jere complained.

"No. We have enough eyes on us already. You have no problem being blunt and offensive to enforcement agents, other professionals, and every other free person you come into contact with. It doesn't add up for you to be polite to your property."

Wren felt a little guilty, but the fact that Isis smiled made it a little better. At least someone could enjoy this, and Jere really did need to practice better habits regarding slave-owning.

"Here's a list of things I want you to do with her," Wren said, handing Jere a piece of paper. He had written it up in a few seconds at the clinic, thinking of the certification he had gone through years ago. "Any mistakes from either of you and we start over. We do it until you both go through the entire thing right, then we'll do something else tomorrow."

Isis pulled back a few inches in her chair, wrapping her arms around herself and eyeing Wren and Jere suspiciously.

"What are you going to do with me?" she asked, her voice on the edge of panic. "Jere, please—"

"I wouldn't tell him to do anything that would hurt you," Wren cut her off before she could panic herself further. "You know me that well, and you know Jere well enough to trust that he wouldn't do it even if I told him to. Some of the things he'll ask you to do will be a little physically challenging, like kneeling for a period of time, and a lot will be unusual or frustrating, but I promise, nothing is going to hurt you."

Isis took a deep breath before nodding.

"Rules back in effect. Show us what you've got."

As predicted, the first few tasks went well. Jere had Isis stand, kneel, stand again, walk across the room, and kneel for a while longer. Easy things that Isis was able to accomplish without hesitation. Wren wasn't yet looking for perfection; poor posture, hesitation, questioning looks, those could all be smoothed out later. For now, it was enough to see her reply to direct orders without showing attitude.

The next order wasn't as direct, though, and even Jere looked at him questioningly.

"*Read what it says. It's on there for a reason.*" He felt bad, making Jere do this, but Jere had to be able to do things like this without looking like he was about to cry. It wasn't Jere who would be hurt the most if he failed.

"Stand," Jere ordered.

The second Isis rose to her feet, waiting for the next order, Jere frowned at her. It was fake, and so was his next statement, but he did his best.

"I didn't tell you to get up!"

"You did so! I just heard—"

"Failed." Wren announced, not surprised at all. He had put the conflicting order in to catch Isis off-guard, because he knew she couldn't resist arguing.

"But I did it right!" Isis snapped, looking furious.

"You're not supposed to argue," Jere cut in, his voice carrying the guilt that Wren could feel bleeding over the mind connection.

"I don't care, I did it right and you know it!" Isis snapped back, growing angrier.

"Isis, if he says he didn't tell you to do something, you don't argue with him, you apologize and get back to position immediately," Wren explained, trying to keep his voice calm. "You did exactly what he said, but the real test was whether you'd fight back or not when he corrected you."

Isis turned red, clenching her fists and glaring. "What the fuck is wrong with you?" she muttered. "Who the hell puts something like that in there—what, did you want me to fail?"

"Isis, I know you know how to stand and walk and all that stupid shit. I know it as well as you do, but I also know that you have a hell of a temper. That *will* fail you. I'm trying to prepare you, and I need you to be aware of things like this so you can learn from them. I never said this would be easy."

"Fine. Whatever you say. Let's start again." Isis wouldn't look at him, wouldn't even look at Jere, she just looked at the floor.

Jere looked helplessly at him, and Wren shrugged.

"From the start, then," Wren cued, and Jere began going through the script a second time.

Isis managed to do as asked, but her movements were wrong. Her attitude was clearly off, and "walk" became "stomp," "kneel" became "flop on the floor," and "yes, master," sounded more like "go to hell." Still, Wren didn't stop, because this was only the first day, and from the way it looked, there were going to be more days like this.

Jere got to "I didn't tell you to get up!" again, looking nervous as he waited for Isis to respond.

She dropped to her knees again, more slowly than she should have, and muttered, "Sorry, master," as sarcastically as possible, glaring down at the floor.

Jere looked to Wren again, shaking his head. "*This is too much!*"

"*Jere, just do it! You both need to be ready. We'll see how she is after today.*"

Jere gritted his teeth and rose to his feet. "Sorry isn't good enough, slave!"

Before Jere or Wren could get a word out, Isis scrambled to her feet and bolted, running to her room and slamming the door before locking it. It was silent for a few minutes before the muffled sobs and pounding started up.

Jere looked at Wren, hurt. "Why?"

"Because she needs to learn not to do that," Wren answered. "I don't like it any more than you do, but if she's going to pass this certification, she's going to need to be able to avoid doing things like that, and you're going to need to play your part more convincingly. She obviously failed, but you didn't do much better."

"Can't I just say I'm lenient?" Jere half-begged. "That I'm a stupid outlander who lets the little things slide and says please and thank you but still is in control?"

"Only if you want to look like an outlander who just had his right to own slaves revoked," Wren reminded him. "This is serious. If you don't want to do it, don't challenge it. Stay here where it's safe. And hope for a miracle during the audit."

Jere sighed. "You're right. I'm sorry."

"Then get this to work. I'll work on a few more lists. Once you guys get through this one successfully, you'll need different things to practice with. They'll get harder, and I'll find more things to pick apart. You both need to be ready."

Jere nodded. As silent as he was, Wren could tell that he was upset, but he was fairly confident that he wasn't what Jere was upset with. Jere wasn't upset with Isis, either, and Wren doubted Isis was too upset with either one of them. Jere was upset at slavery, Isis was upset at herself, and there was nothing that anyone could do about either of those things. They could fix the performance, though, and that was what Wren concentrated on.

Jere waited a few hours before approaching Isis. The pounding on the walls had stopped, but the telltale sounds of movement let him know she was awake.

"Isis?" He knocked at her door. "Can I talk to you, please?"

Jere knew Isis liked time to think before answering. He waited for nearly two minutes before hearing an answer, just long enough to make him consider knocking again.

"Are you mad at me?" she asked, sounding like she was far from the door.

"Not a bit. Wren isn't either. What we were doing earlier, it wasn't real. I wasn't really mad at you."

When she replied again, she sounded closer to the door. "Not even for running away and hiding like I did?"

"No," Jere said. "Not even for that. And I think it was too much to ask for the first day."

The lock clicked, and the door opened. "What about Wren?"

Jere followed Isis back into her room, taking a seat in a chair while Isis sat on her bed, looking nervous. "Wren said that you and I both have a lot to learn. He's not mad at you, but he doesn't think he's asking too much."

"Does he really think I can do it?" Isis asked, looking surprised.

"I suppose so." Jere realized that he was underestimating the girl. "It's not that I don't think you can, I just thought it might have been a little too much all at once. If he had asked me, which he didn't, I would have suggested that he start slowly, let you build up to the harder parts. But Wren wants you completely perfect by the time we go for the certification, and you know how he gets about things being perfect."

"Yeah," Isis managed a weak smile. "I just didn't think you were going to scare me like that. You don't yell at me like that, or talk to me like that. I don't like it."

"I know," Jere agreed. "Believe me, I don't, either. But part of this is getting you prepared for new things that make you scared, or unhappy, or angry, and you have to stay in control when it happens. I will give you my word that I'm not going to lay a hand on you, but that's all I can promise, all right? That, and my word that I won't be upset with you after we finish. Ever. No matter how well or how poorly you do. We're just acting. We have to convince them."

Isis nodded. "Do you think I could stop, like if I wanted a break, or if I needed to calm down?"

Jere shook his head, feeling terrible. "You won't be able to stop at the certification. Besides, some of the things Wren has for us to do are kind of... interlinked, I guess you'd say. Like a puzzle."

"Like a chain," Isis muttered, frowning at the image.

"All right, if you'd rather that," Jere agreed, smiling at her. "I know this is hard for you. But I think you can do it, and so does Wren, and we want to see you succeed."

"I know."

"If it makes you feel better, Wren says I did just as poorly as you," Jere said.

Isis smiled. "He'd be perfect at either role."

"So will we, once we practice," Jere reminded her. "We can do this if we work hard enough."

Isis nodded. "Tomorrow? I don't think I'll do much better again today. Give me until tomorrow to calm down."

Jere nodded. He saw no reason to rush; they had a while before they were planning to leave. He was confident in their abilities, and he liked the idea of learning something new. It kept his mind off of other things, the secrets he knew he should have disclosed already.

After a week of training, the results were abysmal. Wren was displeased to realize that Jere and Isis had only made it through two of the scripts he had given them, and even those were lacking. The harder he pushed, the worse Isis became, and sometimes she just flat refused. Jere made the mistake of trying to cajole her into doing it, which caused a screaming match and a new hole in the wall. It had been months since that had happened, and Jere tried to pressure Wren to call the whole thing off.

Wren reminded him that they couldn't call the audit off as easily as the certification. She needed to figure out a way to behave, and Jere had to figure out a way to help her. If either of them failed, all three of them would suffer. Even more, Isis had a much stronger motivator—the family she had longed to see for so long.

He took Isis aside while Jere was working.

"I know you're capable of this. You and Jere both. You weren't a few months ago, and Jere wasn't a few years ago. But you both are, now. I'm not giving up on either of you."

Isis gave Wren a skeptical look. "I fuck everything up."

"No, just things you're scared of," Wren replied. "Look, everyone's safety depends on this. If I thought you'd fuck it up for sure, I'd be telling him the best ways to incapacitate you for the audit. But I don't. I think you can do it right. Not just to keep us safe, but to see your parents. You want to see them, right? You talk about it all the time. I know it's important to you."

Isis scowled at him for a moment, but she nodded. "I don't want them to see me lose it like this, but I do want to see them."

"Then let me help you and Jere get where you need to be."

Isis looked scared, but relieved. "If you think I can do it, you're probably right."

She and Jere kept trying, but the progress was slow and terrible. Worse was the way that Isis was starting to flinch around the house, cringing when Jere raised his voice, or when someone came too close to her. She was on edge and it showed. It was hard to watch someone who had come so far revert back to such a bad place so quickly. As hard a time as she was having acting like a slave during training, she had just as much difficulty acting like the calm, friendly girl that had become a functioning part of their lives.

Wren decided that an extra training tool was necessary. He took one of the pre-filled passes from the drawer in the kitchen, told Jere he was going out for "supplies," and carefully made his purchase. The owner of the slave supply store gave him a strange look, but all the merchants around town knew him well enough by now not to question his purchases. Jere was good for the money, and he never questioned any expenditures that his slaves made.

He returned home quickly, leaving his new purchase in the bag and sitting it on the empty chair next to where he usually sat and observed the training sessions. He finished the workday as usual and tried to relax before training time started.

Isis was too nervous and so was Jere; they had both come to dread the process so much that it was ruining their evenings. Wren decided to move onto his plan quickly.

"So, things aren't going well," he broke the news. He figured it was his duty to do it, since he was the one orchestrating everything. It wasn't a surprise, but Jere and Isis both looked dejected.

"I'm really trying," Isis protested, her voice becoming shrill immediately. It happened more and more often lately, the shrillness, the protests.

Wren nodded at her. "I know. I know you're trying, and I know Jere's trying, but honestly... I don't think it's quite working out. We have a little over a week before the certification and I wouldn't let either of you go right now. It's too dangerous. There needs to be better progress."

Isis blinked hard, looking away. Jere looked at him with pleading eyes again, and Wren could almost hear him begging Wren to lighten up, to give her another chance.

"I bought something today, something I think will help," Wren said, pulling the bag from the chair where it had sat, conveniently hidden by the table. "Here."

He slid the bag across the table at Isis, who flinched away, but reached out and took it suspiciously.

"What is it?"

"Open it," Wren suggested. "See for yourself."

Isis opened it tentatively, freezing when she saw what was inside. She glared at Wren before reaching her hand into the bag to pull out the collar he had purchased at the slave supply store.

Jere gasped, looking at Wren in shock. Isis just sat there holding it.

Wren started to explain. "I thought—"

The collar flew across the room and crashed into the wall. Isis said nothing, but looked down at the table, shaking in rage and probably terror. Wren understood, he would have been equally appalled, but he had his reasons. He hoped that Isis and Jere would be able to understand them, if not agree with them.

"Will you let me explain?" he asked quietly. "Isis. Will you let me explain why I think that will help?"

"Go fuck yourself," she muttered with no real conviction.

"Wren, love, I'm sorry, but I don't think it's a good idea," Jere protested, frowning. "I wish you would have mentioned this, but I don't think—"

"It's not about what you think, Jere! It's about what Wren thinks, and he thinks I need to be on a collar and leash like some kind of stupid fucking animal!" Isis snapped, her voice finally rising. She glared at Wren, the betrayal far worse than the hatred.

"I don't think that." If anything, Wren had learned from Jere that speaking softly was the best way to calm Isis down. She didn't deserve to be yelled at on top of everything else. He waited, letting her glare, sulk, and finally calm down.

"Then what?" she asked, a few minutes later. "What did you want to prove?"

"I think it's hard for you *and* Jere to differentiate between you acting like a slave and you acting like yourself," Wren said carefully. "I can see it all the time and I'm sure you've both noticed. Isis, when we try to train, you're defensive, rude, and abrasive; the rest of the day you've started getting jumpy and scared again. I know it's hard to do both, so I thought that it would make it easier if you and Jere had a clear sign, a prop that can signify when you start and finish. That's all. I'm not suggesting that you be kept on a collar and leash like an animal, and I'm not suggesting that you deserve to be treated more like a slave. I want both of you to try this out, because I think it could help, and at this point, something has to. If you want to pass this certification, something has to change."

Isis spent a few moments taking it in and visibly calming before nodding. "I guess I cold see how it could work. I'm not happy about it, though."

"I know," Wren agreed. "I'm not either, but we'll just give it a try. Just for the next week. And if it doesn't help, you and Jere get all the rights to tease me about how wrong I was, but for now, I think this is really the best plan. For both of you."

"All right," Isis conceded. "It's not gonna lock or anything, is it? You won't put it on and then not take it off?"

"No," Wren promised, shaking his head. "I wouldn't do that. This is just a reminder. You can feel it there; Jere can see it. It's not going to hurt you, and you're not going to wear it at any other time except when you're training."

Isis nodded, indicating her agreement.

Jere moved to stand. "I'll get it," he said quietly.

"No. Sit back down."

At Wren's order, Jere dropped without question, though he did look confused.

"She gets it," Wren informed him. "Let's start up again. You give the order."

Jere frowned. "Isis, go on, then, grab it."

Isis made a noise of disgust, and Wren shook his head. "No. Try again."

"Isis, please, just get the damn collar," Jere ordered again.

"Jere, come on!" Wren stopped him. "For real, this time."

Jere took a moment to glare at Wren before looking at Isis. "Isis, get the collar."

"Yes, master," she replied, her tone perfect, unlike Jere's.

Wren was surprised; enough so that he didn't want to bother them by making them repeat the interaction again. Isis retrieved the collar, brought it to Jere, and stood in front of him, head down, waiting for orders.

"Get her to kneel and put it on her," Wren said softly.

"Kneel," Jere mumbled, looking relieved when Isis dropped to her knees instantly. He took the collar and put it around her neck, carefully pulling her hair out of the way as he fastened it in place. Isis looked tense, but she didn't fight it.

"I want you both to use this as a reminder," Wren said. "When the collar is on, you're master and slave. Both of you are free to act like stereotypes if you need to. You're not friends, you're not co-workers, and you don't care about each other. Jere, you own this slave. Isis, this man is your master. Both of you need to act like it."

Jere still looked uncomfortable, but Isis seemed motivated. "Can we try again, sir?" she asked, barely loud enough to hear.

"Yeah, I guess," Jere muttered. "A goddamned collar. Let's keep trying."

Chapter 13

How a Slave Should Act

"Wren, I'm not sure what I think about the collar," Jere whispered after getting into bed. "It seems so cruel."

"You and Isis both did better in the past three days than you have in the whole week before that," Wren reminded him. "I'd say it's a success."

Jere frowned, looking unhappy. "She doesn't deserve to be treated like that."

"No, but she needs it." Wren came up to sit behind Jere and placed his hands on Jere's shoulders. "She needs the distinction, and I think you do too. You were both stuck before, and now you're doing well. Clearly, it's helping."

"I don't see why there couldn't be a special training hat or something," Jere continued, sounding just as bitter. "That would be a perfectly good reminder, and a good distraction."

Wren sighed. As hard as Jere tried, he missed things so much, so easily. "Because you both need to remember that she's a slave, love, not just that she and you are both supposed to act a certain way. Keep fighting this and I'll put a whip in your hand and make you hold it the entire time."

Jere turned around, his face showing his shock. "You wouldn't!"

Wren grinned. "It would be a powerful reminder," he countered, knowing that he would never really subject Isis to that much fear. It would be counterproductive; she wouldn't be able to focus on anything. "It's just easier if you keep your real roles in mind. She needs you to be consistent, Jere—you've got to pay more attention to what she needs from you."

"I give her everything she needs! I bend over backward for the girl."

"You do," Wren soothed him, trailing his hands over his lover's skin, barely nibbling at his neck with his lips. "You give her everything she needs in our life, but you have to give her what she needs as a master. You have to pay attention, be more firm when she's doubtful, correct her quickly so things don't escalate, answer her questions before she has a chance to ask them. It's part of being a master."

"It's a lot of work on me. I didn't realize that was such a big part of it."

"It is if you don't want her to suffer the consequences. Lazy masters can just let their slaves suffer for their mistakes; you won't do that to her, I know you better than that. So you have to work harder. You rely too much on words and mindspeak and habits that you've developed with free people—you need to pay attention to other things too, Jere."

"Like what? I feel like I'm missing something."

Wren grinned, a mischievous idea coming into his head. "We'll practice," he suggested. "We can start with some body language sorts of things...."

Jere turned his head, catching Wren's eye over his shoulder. "I think that practicing body language would be a perfect way to spend tonight."

"Oh, do you?" Wren teased. "Well, there's more to it than simple body language. How about you start by getting rid of those clothes for me and then we'll see where we can go from there."

Jere smiled, jumping to his feet immediately and starting to remove his shirt. "I like this plan already. What's the next step?"

Wren stood, grabbing him around the waist and pulling him close, kissing him as roughly as he grabbed him. "Get down on your knees. Try to at least approximate a proper slave kneel."

With a smile, Jere obeyed, moving into something similar to a proper attentive kneeling position. Wren nodded his approval, then went around Jere's body, positioning his knees a little differently, moving his arms where they needed to be, turning his head to face forward instead of looking around. He could tell by the shivers that

Jere was enjoying it, and he felt quite proud of himself when he finished, placing Jere exactly where he wanted him. "Good," he said, smiling. "This is what a proper kneeling position should feel like and look like. Remember it. Maybe I'll quiz you some time. Now stay like that until I come back."

He went to the cabinet where they kept all of their sex toys, plotting out how he wanted the night to go. He had two goals in mind: to have mind-blowing sex with the man he loved, and to give Jere some pointers about slave behavior and the importance of reading body language. He saw no reason why he shouldn't multitask.

"I wish I had bought a collar for you," Wren commented, rooting around their toy box for something suitable.

Jere was naked and kneeling where Wren had left him, at the end of the bed. "We could use the one we bought for Isis?" he suggested, smirking.

Wren laughed at that idea. "She would kill us. She would find out that we used something of hers for one of our — how does she put it? Fucked-up sex games? And then she would kill us. Or whine us to death."

He finally settled on a belt, having had one used as a collar and leash combination on him plenty of times in the past. The prospect of using it on Jere was far more appealing. He checked the buckle to make sure that it wouldn't get stuck or pinch at Jere's neck, and found it satisfactory. He went over and sat on the edge of the bed, looking down at his lover. He reached out, giving Jere's face a familiar caress.

"Are you ready to learn how a slave should act?"

Jere nodded, a shiver going through his body at the thrill of the question. It was a little intimidating, imagining himself as a slave to Wren, but he trusted Wren to be kind with him. Or to be cruel, but in the most sexy cruel way possible.

"Good," Wren said. "But a formal slave should answer out loud. A casual nod might be acceptable, but a formal answer should be given in formal settings."

"Like the certification?" Jere assumed, trying not to wrinkle his nose up.

"Yes. If Isis gets to nodding and shaking her head there, you need to remind her to answer vocally."

Jere squirmed at the idea. "I don't like it."

"I didn't say you had to beat her or anything, I just said remind her," Wren pointed out. "A simple order to answer out loud is adequate."

Jere hadn't even considered hurting her as a reminder; it was the very idea of ordering her to speak when nodding was perfectly adequate that offended him. "Still don't like it."

"Tough." Wren fastened the belt around Jere's neck, slipping the end through the buckle and pulling it snug against Jere's skin. "You both need to do as you're told."

Jere smiled at the feeling of leather against his skin. "I like that," he decided, pulling against the belt a little bit to see how tight he could get it. The soft leather and the light constriction around his neck had his heart racing.

"It feels a lot different when you're not allowed to take it off. For real, not for fun. And it hurts when it's on too tight, or left on for days. Or months."

Jere noticed the slight resentment in Wren's voice. "I know," he said, reaching out to run his hand over Wren's leg. "I've seen it, and I've seen enough of Isis's memories to know how awful it is. This and other things. I appreciate the fact that you even do it with me."

Wren smiled. "It's nice to play with. It's really, really bizarre that this is what people in free states do for fun, but I see the appeal. At least I do with you. I don't think I'd ever want to own a slave for real; I just couldn't imagine it."

"You'd fit in well in Sonova if you went," Jere said, thinking about what Kieran had suggested. The moment the words left his mouth, he realized he risked exposing his secret. "I mean, if you could go one day."

Quickly, he leaned back, pulling against the leash and offering Wren his best seductive glance. "I bet you can use that to pull me right onto your cock," he suggested, changing the subject.

Wren gave his arm a light swat with the loose end. "Don't get distracted just yet," he warned. "There's supposed to be a purpose to this, remember?"

Jere moved in, nuzzling at Wren's legs with his face. "Body language," he recalled. "How slaves act."

"That's right," Wren said, giving him a pat on the head. "Now, here's the challenge: I'm not going to speak. I'm going to move, and touch you, and get you to do things without saying a single word. You're going to watch me, and learn how a proper slaveowner moves and acts, and get at least some idea of how a proper slave moves and behaves, and maybe we can go back to talking later. If you're good."

"Okay," Jere agreed, nuzzling at Wren some more.

A few seconds later, he felt Wren go stiff, pulling back a little. Jere leaned back, looking up at Wren in confusion. "Something wrong?"

Wren looked at him impassively.

"Right, no talking." Jere sat back, trying to figure out what to do next. He gave up trying, and watched Wren instead.

Wren sat silent and unmoving, as if he was waiting for something. Jere wasn't sure what, but since Wren didn't seem upset, Jere committed himself to waiting as well. After a few moments, he relaxed and accepted that there was going to be no way he would ever get Wren to break character. It was odd, just sitting there, but Wren wasn't giving him any clues. Was this it, then? Was this sort of uninformed waiting a big part of being a slave? Jere realized he would go crazy. He'd rather have orders yelled at him than be ignored and left to his own devices like this.

It seemed like an eternity, but Wren finally moved, rising to his feet and looking at Jere. Jere stayed kneeling, feeling uncomfortable and scrutinized. He couldn't resist looking around, seeing what the hell Wren might be looking at.

A sharp tug on the leather around his neck brought him back to attention, making him realize that looking around might not have been the best idea. Jere checked, twisting his head again and earning another tug. He kept looking ahead after that, committing himself to waiting. As he did, Wren poked and prodded at him, not demanding anything, just touching him as if they had all the time in the world. It was unsettling, a turn-off in how methodical it was. It was a game, so it was fun, but Jere didn't think he'd enjoy it very much if it was being done for real. He had felt those same hands touch him in all the same places before, but it felt so different in this context. Like his body was somehow separate from the rest of him.

Finally, Wren came in front of him, taking Jere's chin in his hand and turning his face up so he was looking at Wren, who kept a straight face. Wren let his hand drop, and when Jere stayed looking at him, Wren gave him a little nod. Jere was relieved to know that looking ahead was right, looking around was wrong. Lesson learned. And looking at Wren when he was bidden to do so was also right. He could remember that as well.

A few more seconds passed silently, and then Wren made a motion with his hand, an upward sweep with his palm. Taking a guess, Jere stood, watching Wren for any other clues. When he did, Wren nodded, smiling at him.

Jere felt more proud than he cared to admit. He had no idea how he had allowed his self-worth to get tied up in this, but it was remarkably easy.

Wren dropped the end of the belt, holding his hand up to Jere in a clear sign to stay. Jere tried not to smile, that one was too easy. He stayed in place as Wren made his way onto the bed, waiting for further instruction.

It didn't come. Jere stood there, debating for a while, and then started walking toward Wren, watching him closely for signs or instructions. He thought he saw Wren's head shake, but he couldn't figure out why he would be shaking his head, so he kept getting closer.

This time, there was the slight headshake, but it was accompanied by a very slight frown. Jere stopped, his own face mirroring the displeased expression. Wren stared him down, giving no further signs until Jere took a step back.

Finally, he had pleased Wren. The cessation of frowning displayed his approval, and Jere was relieved to know he was doing well. Still, it left him with the puzzling question of what he was supposed to do.

He knew that slaves were often left for hours without clear instructions from their masters, and patience was a part of that, or at least, that's how Wren had described it. But surely, Wren wasn't doing this as an exercise in patience? That seemed to be a waste of time.

As he considered, he ran his hand through his hair, a nervous gesture that he was only aware of because he had nothing else to focus his attention on. That, and because Wren's stone-like face suddenly shifted to an approving look.

Jere paused, considered it, and then ran his hand through his hair again. There it was, again, just for a moment, approval.

He continued to bring his hand down across his neck, fingering the belt-collar lightly and trailing down across his chest, touching himself tentatively. Wren actually smiled at that, for real, and Jere suddenly caught on to what he was supposed to be doing. He continued, providing something that wasn't quite a striptease, since he was naked already, but rather just a tease, touching himself all over, watching Wren to gauge his reactions. Wren directed him wordlessly, getting Jere to move his hands all over his own body, touching lightly, roughly, whatever pleased Wren. It was intoxicating to be able to communicate like this. It was an effort, but it was fun in context. Jere didn't want to think about what it would be like to be afraid during something like this.

Wren seemed the most pleased when Jere touched his cock, so he did that, again and again, growing hard and eager with every touch. He went from touching to stroking, and Wren sat up, leaning forward to watch as Jere worked himself faster. He wondered if he could come like this, and he figured that he may as well. He closed his eyes halfway, blurring Wren's image for a moment, and he let out a needy sigh as he kept touching himself, getting caught in the sensation for a moment.

A slight cough directed his attention to Wren, who was frowning at him. Jere could tell that Wren was trying to be serious, but the slight upward curve at the corners of his mouth gave him away. Jere stopped touching himself rather reluctantly, and Wren nodded at him. That was a hard lesson, one that Jere wouldn't care to repeat. There was no opportunity to ask to be allowed to come, or even to beg. He just had to accept what Wren offered.

Wren gave him an expectant look, and Jere started touching

himself again, slower this time, watching Wren's face. When he nodded, Jere continued, becoming hard far more quickly than he had last time. When he got right to the edge, he gave Wren a desperate look, but Wren just watched, silent.

Jere kept stroking himself, gritting his teeth to keep himself from coming. He had a hunch that wasn't going to be part of the game.

Just when he thought he couldn't hold out any longer, he saw Wren hold his hand up again, signaling him to stop, and he did so immediately, thankful for the reprieve. Of course, he would have been happier to come, but he knew they would get to that eventually. Wren let him stand there for a moment, gasping and trying his best not to thrust into thin air, and then he motioned with his hand, indicating for Jere to come closer.

Jere took a step toward Wren, watching for the displeasure he saw earlier, but he saw none of that. Emboldened, he moved closer until he was standing right next to the bed. Wren's arm shot out, catching Jere by surprise. Wren used his speed gift to grab the end of the belt that was wrapped around Jere's neck, pulling him closer. Before Jere could catch his balance, he found himself on the bed, close enough that Wren could kiss him.

Jere melted into Wren's mouth, always happy to kiss and be kissed by him. His arms came up to wrap around Wren's body, but they and Jere were pinned to the bed just moments later as Wren flipped him onto his back and lingered on top of him, predatory and dangerous. Jere shuddered at the sight.

When Wren backed off, Jere stayed, drawing a smile from Wren, and indicating that he was on the right track with his actions. Wren moved rapidly, grabbing some lube and stripping off his clothes, returning in just seconds to stretch across Jere's body, pinning him to the bed once more. Wren made his way down to Jere's cock, taking it into his mouth and sucking hard and fast, making Jere struggle to stay still.

He let out a strangled moan instead, and then a cry of protest as he felt Wren's warm mouth leave his cock out in the cold. He sat up, giving Wren a sad look.

Wren just raised an eyebrow at him and then raised a finger to his lips.

Sighing in frustration, Jere committed himself to silence. After a few moments, Wren resumed his task, licking and sucking as Jere pressed his lips tightly together to conceal any of the sounds he wanted to make.

As he worked Jere's cock, Wren also worked his ass, applying lube with his fingers and stretching Jere carefully. Jere was aching to come already, being so worked up, and he forced himself to sit up slightly, catching Wren's eye and giving him what he hoped was a desperate look. Wren needed to stop sucking him so well, or let him come, because Jere wasn't sure if he could hold off any longer.

With a slight smile, Wren backed off, focusing just on his ass.

Jere was relieved not to have to struggle to not come anymore, but the aching desire to do so hurt even more. It was compounded by his desire to get fucked. He had long since been ready enough, there was plenty of lube, and his ass felt ready to pull Wren's cock in, but still, Wren kept teasing him with his fingers.

Finally, Jere started to rock back and forth on the bed, fucking himself on Wren's hand, desperate for any release. He felt a slap on his leg and he stilled, looking up in frustration.

Wren shook his head and slapped him again, and Jere started to move. Another slap, and he moved faster, starting to get the picture. Wren was spurring him on, encouraging him to move faster and more energetically, and Jere was happy to comply. Wren felt so good; the only thing that would make this better was his cock.

This would usually be the point where Jere begged, but he was stripped of that option for tonight. Desperate for contact, but too proud to break the rules of their little game, he curled his legs around Wren's body instead, trying to physically pull him up. He reasoned, in his rather altered state, that if he could just get Wren's cock near his ass, he could probably convince him to put it in. After all, that's the way their bodies were built, they were supposed to fit together that way. They just needed a little help getting there.

Wren seemed a little thrown by the heels digging into his back, but he did move forward, an indulgent smile spreading across his face as he did. Encouraged, Jere tried to pull him up closer, even reaching out with his hands to stroke gently along Wren's back, around to his ass, and then moving around to reach for his cock.

Wren laughed, finally breaking his role. "You are the most un-subtle person I have ever met," he pointed out, grabbing Jere's arms and pinning them above his head again. "I should have tied you before we got started."

"I want you to fuck me," Jere begged. If Wren could break character, so could he. "I'm all hot and ready, and your cock is right there, and I know it wants to be inside of me!"

"Oh really?" Wren asked, rubbing his cock against Jere's ass, tantalizing him further. "You're that good at reading my body that you can tell what my cock is thinking?"

"Yes," Jere insisted, arching his back so he could rub against Wren more effectively. "See, I learned it all. Now you can fuck me."

"Oh, believe me, I will," Wren promised, giving Jere a devious look.

Jere stopped moving, transfixed by Wren's expression for a moment, and once he was still, he was filled with the almost over-whelming sensation of Wren sliding into him, taking him unexpect-edly considering the fact that he had just been begging for this.

"Wren," Jere breathed, his fingers tightening around Wren's hand, which held his arms above his head.

"Shh. I kind of liked the no talking part."

Wren accentuated the order with a kiss, keeping his lips tightly pressed against Jere's to prevent him from making another sound. Jere thrust desperately at Wren, feeling his cock hard inside of him. Clearly, the games had turned Wren on as much as they had Jere.

Lips locked to Wren's, arms pinned above his head, and his ass filled with Wren's cock, Jere felt utterly possessed and he loved it. He could thrust his hips, but he couldn't really move otherwise, and that was perfectly fine by him. He did thrust, and in a few minutes, he felt himself tensing, getting almost ready to come, and his eyes opened, looking to Wren desperately for permission. He felt the slightest nod, and he felt Wren increasing the speed, fucking him even faster until he came, unable to make a sound except a small whine, deep in his throat, which seemed to inspire Wren to kiss him more roughly.

Wren continued to fuck him for a few more minutes, while Jere almost whimpered from the additional sensation. He had been so worked up for so long. Now that he was finished, he just wanted to relax, but Wren was having none of it. He fucked Jere until he was finished, coming hard, and only then did he pull out, leaving Jere shaking.

Jere was left speechless, only able to make a slight whimper as Wren smiled at him and got a towel to clean up.

"See, we don't always need to talk," Wren whispered, climbing back into bed and pulling Jere close.

Jere agreed. There was something especially intimate about communicating without words, and he doubted that he would forget that lesson anytime soon.

Chapter 14
Shutdown

Jere was surprised when Wren handed him a very official-looking letter while they worked in the clinic.

"Can they audit us twice?" he muttered, sarcastic. He wouldn't put it past the regulation agency to try.

"No." Wren smiled a little. He always seemed amused by Jere's suspicion of the state. "It's from the state's medical regulation board. Maybe it's time to recertify the clinic or something."

"Just what we need." Jere finished what he was working on and then opened the letter, expecting a general reminder for some sort of administrative thing that would waste his time and take away from the more important things he was supposed to be doing. What he found instead made him go silent, furiously reading the letter over and over again.

Dr. Peters,

It has come to the attention of the board that your clinic may not be performing to the high standards expected in Arona. A number of community members have complained of long wait times, inadequate healing and lack of attention to detail. These complaints correspond with your recent decision to treat the slave population at your clinic.

We regret to inform you that your practice will need to remediate this issue immediately. Unless you would prefer to schedule a thorough meeting with the Arona Medical Regulation Board, the following actions must be addressed effective immediately:

CEASE TREATING SLAVES IN YOUR CLINIC
INFORM YOUR CLIENTS OF YOUR NEW POLICIES
SUBMIT DOCUMENTATION INDICATING YOUR AGREEMENT

While your medical clinic is privately owned and operated, significant state funds contribute to the upkeep of your clinic and its supplies. In order to continue receiving these funds and operating as a state-certified health clinic, your compliance with these directives must occur immediately. In addition, the International Medical Review Board has been notified of these community complaints. You may wish to check with your Board contact person for additional requests or sanctions.

If you believe this decision has been made in error, you may request a board review in order to address these concerns.

Please direct any questions or concerns to our central office.

Jere threw the letter across the room, ashamed when Isis darted out and even Wren flinched away.

"Bad news?" Wren asked, retrieving the letter and reading it when Jere didn't respond.

"This is bullshit!" Jere snapped. "This is *my* clinic."

Wren nodded, conciliatory. "And it's funded by our benevolent state agency," he reminded Jere. "You don't really have the option not to comply."

"Fuck their funds!" Jere snapped. "I have enough money to run this place on my own for a few years. Maybe I could seek my own damn funding. The Wysockas like me — maybe they could help."

Wren shook his head. "Cutting off the funding is the least of your concerns. If you try to fight this the wrong way, you could be looking at trouble with the International Board. Being shut down in Hojer is bad enough, being shut down everywhere... Jere, that's bordering on practicing without a license. That could mean jail, extradition to Sonova."

That would mean leaving Wren and Isis vulnerable for who knew how long.

Jere stayed quiet for a moment, trying to collect himself. He didn't want to intimidate his lover any more, but he wanted to rage.

He thought it over, thought of all the things that had led up to it. "This has to be the slave agency. This is just another way of messing with us, of trying to investigate, to harass us."

Wren shrugged. "You did sort of torture the president of Arona's daughter a few months ago. You denied her pain relief on the excuse that you were depleted of your energy. Did you really think that wouldn't come with consequences?"

"I did it because of what they did to Isis. I *was* drained of energy, exhausted, too weak—"

"You put the welfare of a slave over the welfare of a free person in a state where that is utterly unacceptable. You rubbed it in their noses and now they're doing the same to you. Consider yourself lucky you're not being shut down altogether."

Jere made a noise of disapproval, but he knew Wren was right. The plan that he and Kieran had concocted last winter had been amazing, hitting the citizens of Hojer and Arona's leader where it hurt the most, but he was not without fault. He should have expected something like this, and he hadn't. He hadn't expected any of the retaliation for doing what he still felt was the right thing.

"Hojer is lucky I'm not shutting it down all together. There have to be other states—other slave states. I could pull out of here, take you both, and move to somewhere that I'm more appreciated."

"Harder than you think," Isis cut in. "Most of the slave states work together really closely. I don't remember much of the spy work they used to have me do, they cut those memories right out of my brain. But the only way this slavery business works is for the slave states to band together. You'd have to go really, really far to get away from it, and even then, the same shit would still happen there. I've lived in dozens of slave states. They're all about the same—except the ones that are worse."

Jere scowled, but he was running out of options. It always came down to this: he had to fit in, or he had to leave and abandon his family. Only one was an option, but he wasn't going to take it lying down.

"I want to talk with Kieran about that SRA," Jere decided.

Wren gave him a skeptical look. "Because you haven't angered the higher-ups enough?"

"I don't remember everything that it does, but I know it mandates that slaves are seen by real medical professionals. It provides some other protections as well. I was perfectly content to leave well enough alone, but if they're going to interfere with both my slaves *and* my clinic, I want a more active role in this. I need it. There's not much I can do, but I can do this."

"I'm sure she'll be happy to hear that," Wren said, but the doubt on his face was obvious.

"I'm not doing this to make her happy. I want to keep treating slaves in the clinic. A lot of owners are already bringing them here because it's inexpensive and convenient, and from the survey we did a few weeks ago, even the biggest assholes seem to like the fact that their slaves are up and ready to work a lot sooner. When I tell people that I'm being forced to stop, they'll be just as angry. Do you really think we should lie down and take this?"

The survey had been another idea passed down by Kieran and her team. Many free people had been outraged when Jere had started offering the service just over year ago, but now that the practice was firmly established and showing positive results, they really did seem to like it.

Wren shook his head. "Fighting it is risking a lot. It's not that I don't agree with you, I'm just saying we need to be prepared."

Jere nodded. "We need to be prepared for the audit, anyway. What's another fight?"

From the look Wren gave him, another fight was more suffering, uncertainty, and risk. He realized just how selfish he must sound, ranting about his clinic when his anger could put Wren and Isis in danger. Challenging the state agencies was a dangerous act, as they had all experienced already.

"Look, I'm not going to go out and campaign or anything like that," he conceded. "I know that would put us at risk, and I'm not going to do that, especially when you don't want me to. I trust you to be smarter about this than I am."

Wren smiled, too tactful to actually say that he agreed.

"But I want to find out more about it, maybe see who I can talk to or how I can help just a little bit. If I have to inform my patients that I can't see their slaves anymore, I should be able to tell them something else. I mean, if the SRA goes through, they'll have to let me see slaves, right? Maybe it will generate more support."

Wren gave in and nodded. "I guess it does make sense that you support it. I mean, I'm sure if you asked anyone from town, they'd all guess that you did. You're a doctor, it's supposed to be for healthcare. And I doubt they'll be pleased that you can't heal their slaves anymore. The local veterinarian will be angry about that; I hear his practice is thriving now that he's able to start focusing just on animals again."

Jere nodded. He wasn't happy about any of this, but at least it made him feel better to know that there would be other people on his side. "We'll lose quite a bit of business."

"We could use some downtime anyway. We need to get any of the anti-slavery literature out of the house, including letters your friends and family back home. And all the things Kieran has sent us to give to 'like-minded' clients need to be gone as well. We want this place to look perfect, and we have to be operating efficiently if we're going to try to challenge this request from the medical board. It will be good to have it all out before the audit, too."

Jere frowned, wondering just where all that information could possibly be stored.

"You sure know how to piss people off," Paltrek observed, laughing. While he visited during lunch, Jere complained about the audit, the clinic shutdown, and his dilemma with finding a safe place to put his personal items. "You'll still be treating slaves personally though, right? Just not officially?"

Jere nodded. "Of course. Anything happens to Dane or any of the other slaves in your household, let me know. I just have to stay sort of underground with it."

"Why don't you just let me hold on to any of your incriminating evidence?" Paltrek suggested. "I mean, my family would destroy anyone who dared to try to go through our things."

"Really?" Jere wasn't exactly surprised; he just hadn't realized he had this many resources in Hojer. It was nice to have that reminder. "I can never tell. I know the rest of your family isn't such a fan of me, or of my views on slavery."

"Yeah, but it won't be a problem. I think there's a dead slave out back I can stuff your things into."

Jere paused for a moment, hoping that Paltrek was joking. He trusted his friend despite their differences, but the casual cruelty that slipped out from the Hojer native sometimes took him by surprise.

Of course, Paltrek's thrilled laugh clued him in.

"You're too easy, Jeremy," Paltrek teased. "Really, though, we have enough money and jewelry and all that sort of shit that we have some pretty heavy security measures. Besides, nobody will think to look in my family's mansion. We're one of the biggest supporters of slavery, financially and politically. Wysocka Enterprises was built on slave labor."

"What do you think about the SRA?" Jere asked. "I mean, I know you're supporting me, and I suppose I'm for it, but... what do you think of it, personally?"

Paltrek smirked. "Dane, have I ever beaten you in public?"

Dane was kneeling at his feet, looking calm and content, like he always was when he was with his master. "No, master."

Paltrek reached down and ruffled his hair. "That's how I feel about it. I think it's fucked up to drag slaves to a veterinarian, to beat them in public. It's even more fucked up to watch. Maybe a smack or something, whatever, but to really beat on a slave? That should be done at home, or in private. It's like taking a shit, you know? Everyone does it, but they do it in the privacy of their own homes, and they don't talk too much about it. And no state agency should come and check up on how you do it."

Jere smiled at that comparison. It was crass, but, then, slavery was crass. "I guess I see your point."

Paltrek rolled his eyes. "Spare me your outlander elitism. You're turning me into enough of a softie as it is with your guilt and your looks and your appeals to my little bitch side, right, Dane?"

Dane smiled at Jere for a minute before beaming up at his master. "You've been very lenient and kind since you started spending more time with Doctor Peters, master. Thank you."

Paltrek laughed. "Yeah. Turning me into some sort of abolitionist before I die, right?"

"There's the medical issue to consider," Jere tried to defend his position. "*Derma cariosus* is a serious threat. Healers can't fix it, and there's no medication. It's modern leprosy!"

"Don't give me lines. I don't believe that some fictional 'rotting disease' is going to get us all—I'll believe it when I see someone who's really sick."

Jere raised an eyebrow. "Just because it's not in Hojer, or even Arona, doesn't mean it can't be. Or that it won't be tomorrow."

"It's a convenient excuse to push the SRA through," Paltrek said, shrugging it off. "But I think it's a good thing. The way people treat their slaves now is nasty. People with any sort of breeding shouldn't be doing things like that. The slaveowner protections are nice, though."

"Yeah," Jere agreed. Those slaveowners protections would shield him from an audit like the one he was about to face, but only if the law went into effect. "Thanks for offering to store my things for me. I really appreciate it."

"Any time," Paltrek replied. "After all, I know you'd do the same for me."

Chapter 15
Pressure Testing

With only a few days left before the certification, Wren was phenomenally pleased with Isis's performance. The collar put her into the right frame of mind, and they moved on to finer details. Wren was tempted to smack the attitude out of her voice, but he limited himself to endless repetition. Isis was familiar with the material; her memory gift and the fact that she had been in and out of training for nine years made her somewhat of an expert.

Still, she didn't know all of it, and she seemed to be confusing some of the most important things. Wren grew frustrated, wondering just how someone with such an infallible memory could have this little knowledge of proper training.

"I remember everything, but I don't see or hear everything in the world. I'm pretty easily distracted, especially when I'm being hurt. That's been most of the time."

Wren softened a bit at that statement, trying to focus on giving Isis the basics of information. The gaps in her knowledge were strange, but they filled quickly.

Jere required considerably more work, and while the standards weren't quite as strict for him as they were for Isis, it was still important for him to maintain his role. It influenced the ways in which the certifiers viewed him and it affected the way that Isis responded.

They had been training for almost two hours, the longest they had done in one stretch. Wren was determined to see perfection tonight, and he knew he could if he pushed hard enough. Again and again, he stopped them, forcing them to restart for such trivial offenses as a lack of firm order, an insincere response, hesitation, a finger out of place. He knew it was harsh, but he knew they could do better.

Finally, after a dozen tries, they did it perfectly, flawlessly. If this was the certification, they would have passed without a question, and from the barely concealed smiles on both Isis and Jere's faces, they could tell that they had done well

"Again," Wren said, carefully masking his pride. He forced himself to look disinterested, methodical, as he had the first dozen times he had put Jere and Isis through this particular script.

"What did we do wrong?" Isis snapped, looking furious.

"Show attitude like that at the certification and they'll probably have you beaten," Wren reminded her, not giving an inch. "Now, do it again, and don't argue back, or we can do all three of the scripts we've done today a few more times."

Tears started to show in Isis's eyes, but she nodded. "Yes, sir," she mumbled. They were trying to work on behavior and verbal responses with people other than Jere, but it was going slowly. Isis absolutely refused to practice with anyone other than Wren, and she only did that reluctantly.

They went through the script again, and while there were no glaring errors, Isis and Jere were both thrown off, nowhere near as perfect as they had been. Isis was scornful and cutting her responses short, Jere was trying to compensate by delivering fewer orders, or by softening his voice. He wouldn't even look at Wren.

"Jere, cut the crap," Wren warned. "You're coddling her. Stop it. It's not working for either of you. And Isis, lose the attitude. You know what you're doing; by this point, I shouldn't need to remind you. You both need to put some actual effort into this, or we'll be doing it all night. Start again."

Isis and Jere shared a glance that almost made Wren smile; they were both so clearly outraged at him. Still, they went through the script again, perfectly this time, almost as perfectly as before. Clearly, they wanted to prove him wrong, and that was the exact attitude he needed them to have. They couldn't just go through the motions when everything was perfect, they had to want it, and they had to hold up under pressure.

"Again," Wren ordered, watching Isis intently.

She surpassed his expectations, dropping to the starting position without question or hesitation. Jere did well also, leading her carefully. It seemed like they were even more determined to perform perfectly to show Wren up, and Wren was glad about it. He was finally seeing what he needed to see. They finished with a triumphant look.

"Again," Wren pushed, forcing his tone to be dismissive. He wasn't about to praise them, not just yet. He wasn't going to let them win this easily; he had another goal that he wanted them to reach. He watched Jere closely, hoping he could make him respond as desired.

Once again, they were perfect, although he could see Isis starting to break down a little. While she was moving and speaking and reacting as expected, there were tears in her eyes, and she looked strained. A harsh word would have her in hysterics. The response was unacceptable, but certainly she was being pushed past her breaking point. He had made them repeat scripts far more times than this, but he had always given feedback. This time, they were doing well, and Wren offered nothing but bored orders to repeat it. Wren doubted the certification would be half as frustrating as this, but he wanted to make sure that they could both tolerate it.

"Again," Wren said, once they finished, fully aware of how defeated Isis looked at the order, at the implication that she hadn't done well enough. He knew how hard it was on her, even more so than Jere, and he actually felt a little guilty for putting her through it. Still, he had another purpose in mind, something that they were lacking. Specifically, something Jere was lacking, but Isis had to go down with him. It was a slave's duty, after all, to suffer for the master.

Silently, Isis took the position on the floor again, ready to start, and when her hands curled into fists, she hid them against her thighs, doing her best to disguise her reaction to what was happening.

"That's right," Wren said, keeping his tone careless and superior. "Keep going. We've got all night ahead of us, and I want it better. You do it enough times, you'll figure out what you're doing wrong."

"No," Jere said, glaring at Wren angrily. "I don't need to do it again, and she especially doesn't need to do it again. We've done it perfectly and you know it, and I will not stand here and see her subjected to this. You either tell her something to change, or you let us move on. She's done enough, and she won't say it, but I will."

Finally, Wren had what he wanted. He smiled, drawing looks of confusion from both Isis and Jere. "That's just it, Jere—she *can't* say it, but you can. You have to. Take the collar off and I'll explain."

They waited for the symbolic piece of leather to be removed before continuing. Isis looked utterly confused, and Jere looked angry. Jere *was* angry; Wren could feel it through the mind connection. It was a righteous, entitled anger, the exact thing that Jere needed if he was really going to succeed. Wren was pleased to have brought it out in him, despite feeling underhanded about his methods. Finally, they sat around the table, Jere and Isis looking at Wren expectantly.

"You both did wonderful tonight," Wren said instantly, smiling at Isis. "You were phenomenal. And Jere, I have to say—your reaction at the end was what I was trying to accomplish all night. I wasn't trying to push Isis that hard, although I'm glad that I did and she was still fine. I'm very impressed with you, Isis. Jere, I was pushing you on purpose. She can't talk back and argue, but you can get away with a lot. You have to be attentive to when she's upset, when she's had too much, and you need to deal with it before it becomes a problem. You can throw a fucking temper tantrum if you want, and it's fine, because you're a free man. You can be every bit as demanding and obstinate as you want, as long as you maintain control of her. Even if all you do is deflect attention away from Isis, it's still worthwhile, and you still need to try to do it whenever you can. It's your job. Think about it; you're a slaveowner, you're educated, you're a doctor—you have every reason to feel superior to these people, and you need to act like it."

"This was about me?" Jere asked, incredulous.

Wren nodded. He had no regrets. It had gone perfectly.

"Bastard," Isis mumbled, looking a little shaky.

"You outperformed him," Wren reminded her, smiling. "Seriously, keep that up and you'll pass without a problem."

Isis grinned at that, able to tolerate compliments a little better as long as someone else was being teased in the process.

"I should really do that, then?" Jere questioned, looking uncertain. "I thought I wasn't supposed to fight back against things? Be a harsh master and all? Act like I'm from here?"

Wren sighed, trying to figure out how to explain it. "It's not that you have to be harsh all the time. You need to come off as firm. Most importantly, you need to come off as being in control at all times. She belongs to you, and it is perfectly acceptable for you to take offense at someone upsetting her. She's yours; you're the only one who gets to upset her. Think about a pet. If you had a dog, and someone else was yelling at it, or treating it badly, it would be acceptable — if not expected — that you would make the person stop. You might even get angry at them. In the same way, you can defend your slave. It doesn't mean that the slave didn't do anything wrong, but *you* are the one who corrects it."

"Her," Jere muttered, absently.

Wren rolled his eyes at Jere's insistence. Plenty of people referred to slaves as objects; Jere's insistence on humanizing everything was sweet, but pointless. "I swear, I'm half-tempted to send you to live with Paltrek for the next week," he threatened. "You could learn some things there."

"You're doing a good enough job of terrifying us," Isis pointed out. "I'm so glad Jere is my master instead of you."

Jere frowned. "I think I can try harder."

"I know you can," Wren agreed. "You're allowed to be an asshole, as long as you come off as a possessive asshole. Don't cry about them referring to her as 'it,' or any of that other stupid bullshit that you get upset about. They can think of her as an object, disregard her, enjoy her misery, whatever. That's normal. Get upset when they are offending you. If they undercut your authority as master, if they take liberties with your property, if they insult you by implying that she's not good enough — that's when you get angry. Stop thinking of her as a person and start thinking of her as a trophy, or a tool."

Isis smiled. "I don't mind being thought of as a trophy," she pointed out. "Better than the other things I've been compared to."

Jere nodded. "I think I can pull it off. It's just weird to think of her like that."

"You're playing a part, Jere," Wren reminded him. "And her safety depends on your ability to play your part well. So does mine.

She's at risk of not seeing her parents, of being retrained—if you perform poorly enough, you could lose your right to have slaves. We don't have long and you both need to be as perfect as you can be. That includes things like this."

"And you'll torture us until we're perfect?" Jere asked, only half-teasing.

Wren gave them both a rather sadistic smile. "I'll keep torturing you after you're perfect, too," he pointed out. "I know you can both handle it."

Chapter 16

A Strong Master

Jere was glad to retire to bed that evening, lying down with Wren in his arms. Jere knew it was illogical, but somehow he felt safer knowing exactly where Wren was, and, more importantly, knowing that nobody else was around them. Despite his best efforts to avoid public attention, he had drawn a lot to himself.

"Aren't you the cuddly one tonight," Wren teased, not protesting at all as he curled into Jere.

Jere smiled, and they both indulged in a long, sensual kiss. "All this bullshit, the train, the audit, the certification... sometimes it's nice to have a little reminder of how much I care about you."

Wren smiled back at him. "Do you really need a reminder?"

Jere kissed him again, and when Wren wasn't expecting it, he tickled him, laughing as Wren squirmed and tried playfully to get away. Finally, he stopped, resting his head against Wren's chest. "No, but it sure makes it obvious."

They lay there for a while longer, content with sharing the closeness, and Jere thought about everything that was going on.

"I'm glad that we're getting ready for the certification and everything, but do you that maybe we should wait on this plan with Isis's parents?" he wondered. "It just seems like too much. Too risky."

Wren drew his hand over Jere's back, making Jere feel calm and safe and secure.

"I think you should still go," Wren said gently. "She's so excited about it, and besides, you have every right to travel. That's why they give you notice for those sorts of things. You can play up your meeting with the talent agency. Show them that you're not trapped here, that you have other options. Hojer doesn't have any claim to you, at least none that you should admit publicly. You can leave whenever you want."

"I'm not leaving you!" Jere protested.

"They don't have to know that," Wren reminded him. "You're a free man, you know. You have to act the part."

Jere grinned at the last comment. Wren was teasing, but the real irony of the situation still burned. "So free that I have to worry about people spying on me. I don't get it. How is it that people don't see how awful this shit is?"

Wren smiled back at him. "They see it, Jere, they just like the benefits more. Who cares if someone might come inspect your ability to be a slaveowner on occasion—you get to own human beings and do whatever you want to them without repercussion. Most people would pass, and if they failed because of something their slave did, they would just put the slave down and get a new one. No harm for the slaveowner."

Jere shuddered. "That's not a benefit in my world."

Wren kissed him. "And that's one of many reasons why I love you. But it's like... you get to play God with other people's lives. It's got to be at least a little exciting, isn't it?"

Jere shot Wren a look of horror. "No! It scares the shit out of me that I have that sort of power over you. Isis, too, but at least I can kind of try and rationalize it that she's a kid, and so, I mean, parents have that sort of power anyway. But if I could just give it all away, I would. I hate it."

"You shouldn't be so quick to be opposed to it," Wren said. "It's a good thing. Look how quickly you got me out of that vet clinic. How safe you've been able to keep us both. That's the kind of power you get from being a master. That's the power that you need. You can accomplish far more as a strong master than you can fighting it."

Jere pouted. "I don't want to be a strong master. Or a master at all. I just want to be your partner. Isis's friend, or guardian, or whatever she thinks of me as. A doctor. That's it. I don't want to be a master, strong or otherwise. I want nothing to do with slavery, nothing to do with being a master."

"Being a master can keep us safe," Wren reminded him. "None

of those other roles can do that here."

Jere smiled up at him. As usual, Wren was able to make the kinds of arguments that really did sway him. "I do want that," he admitted. "Fine. There's exactly one good thing about it. I'd still rather it was someone else. I'm more fit to be a slave than a master."

"Just because you're so good at following my orders?" Wren teased.

"Yes. I like listening to you. And in general, I don't like being the one in charge, not of more than my own life, and medical stuff. I like not having to make the big decisions. You always make them faster and better, and I like knowing that it's you, and I can trust you. I can always trust you."

"I trust you just as much," Wren reminded him. "And you're a hell of a lot better at dealing with Isis than I've ever thought of being. Hell, you're better with most people than I am. You're friendly and kind and you care about people. If the three of us could leave tomorrow, I know you'd still have doubts, because you actually care about your patients. Even though they don't deserve you."

"Yeah, and none of that makes me a good master, at least, not by Arona's standards." Jere was pretty sure that the fact that he was making the very masterly decision to keep the possibility of escaping to freedom from Wren and Isis made him a better master, according to most people here. It still made him feel like a terrible person.

"It makes you easy to work with, which makes people like you," Wren insisted. "You can get away with things because of it. They'd catch on to me too quickly. I'm too demanding, and not at all flexible. Given the choice, I want things my way, all the time."

"You should demand that I be flexible," Jere suggested, glancing up at Wren and giving him a flirty look. "Other people are crazy for not wanting you to be demanding. You're sexy when you're demanding."

"Oh, am I?" Wren took the bait. "Well that's lucky for you, because you're sexy when you're obeying my demands."

"I don't think I really remember what that looks like," Jere said, trying his hardest not to smile. Of course he remembered; every sexy interaction he had experienced with Wren seemed burned into his mind, turning him on for days after. But still, he wanted more. The opportunity to stop talking about serious slave-owning business was welcome, too.

"Well, I guess I'll have to give you a reminder, then, won't I?" Wren replied, clearly fighting back a smile of his own. "Unless you don't really want it. I don't think you were very convincing just a moment ago. I wouldn't want to take advantage of you."

Jere squirmed his way out of Wren's arms, going to his knees on the bed instead. "Please. Take advantage of me. I want you to. Tell me what to do. Be the demanding master that I never want to be."

Wren looked quite happy to oblige Jere in his wishes. He moved quickly, his beautiful, naked body almost a blur, and the only thing Jere regretted was that he couldn't look at him longer. Sometimes he thought he could just look at Wren for hours, memorizing every inch of his skin, as if it wasn't as familiar as his own body by now. But he was happy that Wren was as eager to play as he was, and he smiled when he saw Wren returning with the padded cuffs that Jere had bought so long ago. They were of high quality, withstanding many nights of the pulling and tugging and twisting that they had been subjected to.

"You're feeling flexible tonight," Wren reminded him. "So let's see you get all nice and stretched out for me. On your back, so I can see your face."

Jere moved happily into position, eagerly allowing Wren to take control of his movements and to set the pace, which was rapid and exciting. He felt Wren attach his wrists and ankles to the bedposts one by one, and he pulled at them appreciatively once Wren had finished.

"This is much better." Forget being a strong master; if he could spend every day obeying Wren's orders in bed, he would do it in a heartbeat.

"You like being mine," Wren stated, looking surprised by the fact even after all this time. "Letting me make all the decisions, taking what I want from you."

"Yes." Jere shivered as he felt his excitement start to grow. He felt the light hairs all over his body start to stand up, and he looked eagerly at Wren, waiting to feel where he was going to be touched first.

He was surprised, but not at all turned off when what he felt was Wren speeding away from the bed, returning with a blindfold. Jere obligingly lifted his head, allowing Wren to fasten the fabric around the back, smoothing the knots down so Jere would still be able to lie back comfortably.

"That's better," he heard Wren say. "You were looking a little too curious for my taste. I want you to forget everything else and just focus on what I'm about to do to you."

Jere smiled, feeling the tension drain out of his body immediately. This was perfect, exactly what he needed to relax and re-center himself. He lay there, waiting for the next sensation, smiling as he was rewarded with a light stroke of his cock.

"I'm focused," Jere decided, loving the way that Wren's hand felt on his skin.

"Good." Wren's reply was short. Clearly, he wasn't intending on talking too much, and Jere was fine with that. Actions could be far louder than words, and much more pleasurable, too.

Jere let himself relax, enjoying Wren's light, slow working of his cock. He noticed how good it felt, and he noticed how it coincided with his breathing. As Wren sped up, so did Jere's breath, and he found himself brought quickly to the edge. He had just enough time to wonder if Wren was going to just bring him off immediately, with no further play, and just when he was giving in and about to come, Wren backed off.

Jere whimpered in protest.

"Hush," Wren said firmly.

A second later, Jere felt Wren's body stretching out on top of his, barely making contact. Wren's cock brushed against his leg, Wren's chest brushed against his stomach, and soon, Wren's lips were locking with Jere's.

Kissing him hungrily in return, Jere squirmed and lifted his hips off the bed, eager to grind against his lover, hopeful that maybe he could find release.

No such luck. All his efforts earned him was a smack on the leg, and Wren pulling back from the kiss.

"You stay still unless I tell you to move," Wren ordered. He was clearly trying to be stern, but Jere could picture the barely concealed smile that would be on his face.

"Yes, sir," Jere replied, his tone as playful as the expression he knew Wren would have.

Wren continued to tease him, rubbing his body against Jere's, kissing him, and only rarely touching his cock. Still, Jere grew hard and needy, giving into shameless begging in a matter of minutes.

"Please?" he whimpered. "Please, Wren?"

"What would you like?" Wren replied, his tone deceptively innocent.

"I want you to fuck me. I want to feel you inside of me, right now."

Wren smiled, Jere could feel the expression since Wren had his face pressed to his chest.

"We'll get to that when I'm ready," Wren replied. He spent some time exploring Jere's body with his tongue, working it over his neck and his chest, licking and biting hard at Jere's nipples until he screamed and moaned, the pain and pleasure almost too much to bear.

Wren didn't stop there. He kept going lower, trailing his tongue over Jere's cock. Jere forced himself to stay still, obeying Wren's standing orders not to take him by surprise or shove his cock down his throat.

By the time Wren actually did take Jere in his mouth, Jere was clutching tightly at the sheets, doing his best to keep from thrusting up to meet Wren with every move, desperate and horny. The harder Jere tried to be still, the slower Wren went. The torturous nature of the slowness was made even worse by the knowledge that Wren could go so much faster if he wanted to.

Clearly, Wren didn't want to, and Jere took great pleasure in surrendering to his desires.

Wren brought him back to the edge expertly, taking his time and starting to work Jere's ass with his fingers while he did. Jere loved the feeling of Wren touching him like that, preparing him, and he couldn't help but think of how delicious it was going to be to have Wren's cock buried deep inside of him. He was so busy fantasizing that he barely noticed the temperature increasing, Wren's hands and tongue becoming so much warmer than natural. It only served to increase his arousal, making him gasp and clench tightly around Wren's fingers.

"Please, Wren, I want you now," Jere begged. "I can't wait any longer! Let me take your cock!"

Wren laughed, the act sending excruciatingly pleasant vibrations up the length of Jere's cock and seeming to spread throughout his whole body. Then he was gone, just like that, leaving Jere shamelessly thrusting his hips into the air.

"I thought you said you wanted *me* to make the demands, not you."

Jere could only moan in response. A few moments later, he felt the blindfold being removed, and he blinked at the sudden return of sight. He smiled as he saw Wren next to him, unfastening the restraints.

"I want to feel your legs wrapped around me while I fuck you," Wren mentioned, nonchalant, as if the words didn't make Jere's cock threaten to explode from impatience.

Wren unfastened his arms as well, but seemingly only so that he could grab Jere's hands, pinning them to the bed as he positioned himself between Jere's legs.

Jere trembled. Wren was remarkably intimidating like this, holding him down firmly, his cock ready at Jere's entrance. The look on his face was almost unnaturally calm, focused on what he was doing.

"Don't even think of moving," Wren ordered, a dangerous look in his eyes. "Not so much as an inch. I'll tie you back up and leave you like that all night if you do."

Jere thrilled at the threat. He didn't know if Wren was serious, and he didn't particularly care, because the threat alone was enough to get him even more worked up than he already was. He felt Wren sliding into him, painfully slow, and he fought to keep still, his muscles clenching and releasing almost involuntarily, protesting the slow fucking that just seemed to continue, on and on, until Wren was completely inside.

"Now, wrap your legs around me," Wren ordered, holding them both still until Jere did as he asked. "Good."

With that word, Wren started moving quickly, taking Jere by

surprise as he fought to hold on to Wren's body with his legs. He struggled to take Wren's cock pounding in and out of his ass. Jere cried out in joy, finally getting the fucking he had been begging for, and he clutched tightly to Wren's hand, which was still pinning his arms above his head. With his legs around Wren like this, it was nearly impossible for him to move. He had no other choice but to lie there and let Wren fuck him at his own pace.

Jere had no idea how long it was before he felt Wren's free hand trailing down, grabbing at his cock. Jere yelped, knowing he would be unable to hold off for too long, as worked up as he was. "Wren," he breathed, unable to put any of it into words.

"Don't you think my intention is to make you come for me?" Wren asked, stroking Jere's cock in time with his thrusts.

Jere really wasn't thinking about anything, he was too busy feeling. He squeezed his legs tight around Wren's body, trying to hold him closer, and he came hard, gasping and shaking as he felt Wren come as well.

Jere felt like everything had been drained out of him, all the worry, all the tension... all the bones. He lay there, letting his legs drop back to the bed, waiting for Wren to make the next move. He was enjoying his own bliss far too much to worry about things like cleaning up or speaking.

Wren seemed to have a little more energy, and he got up and brought back a towel, cleaning them off, and cuddling close to Jere.

"Thank you," Jere whispered, pulling Wren's arms around him. "I needed that."

Jere lay there, comfortable and safe in Wren's arms. If he could just stay like this forever, he would be content. But as Wren's breaths evened out into sleep, Jere felt reality weighing down on him again. He knew he was good at playing master, at doing the scripts Wren had made for them. He even managed in the clinic with Hojer's citizens. But would he and Isis really be able to handle a formal certification? It was easy to pretend that Isis was their biggest problem, but Jere's biggest fear had nothing to do with her.

A slave's mistakes could be punished and moved past. A master had no other option but to succeed.

Chapter 17
Certification

Jere and Isis walked into the certification center, the nervousness buzzing between them and creating a terrible feedback loop. Jere could feel the terror from Isis just a little bit through the mind connection, which was the most he ever felt from her. So often, she was a blank slate, a puzzle, giving off almost no psychic presence at all.

Jere checked in and read through the requisite paperwork, Isis on her knees next to him, trembling. He reviewed his information as a slaveowner, Isis's history as a slave, and a bunch of disclaimers for the certification. He was relieved to read that he wouldn't be asked to physically harm her as part of the certification, but less thrilled by the part where he might be instructed to scare or yell at her. The mind-connection would be shut down and monitored by a psychic specialist, preventing him from coaching her at all. He could only hope that they did well.

After returning the paperwork, Jere sat and waited until he was called. A stern-faced team of two men and one woman called him and Isis into a back room, where they were left to stand awkwardly as the papers were reviewed. Jere was pretty sure it was just to make them more nervous.

"Doctor Peters. We've received a special notice about your case."

Jere tried to unstick his tongue from the roof of his mouth, overcome with his own anxiety as well as Isis's. He forced his voice to stay normal. "Oh?"

"It seems that this slave was charged with assaulting an officer last year?" the man asked, pulling another paper from a folder and handing it to his colleagues. "And you want to take her out of the state now?"

Jere did his best to crush the anxiety down and recall Wren's advice on being haughty and dismissive. "She's barely more than a child," he said, trying to look bored instead of scared. "She still had a lot to learn, then, but those bad habits have been most thoroughly corrected. It's not my fault her previous trainers had been lenient and shoddy in their work. Perhaps the state-run training facilities in Arona aren't all they're made out to be."

The man frowned, but seemed to accept Jere's story. The other two colleagues smirked, and Jere hoped that they had been at least somewhat amused by his cutting remarks. Jere was aware that the different agencies, training facilities, and departments that dealt with slaves weren't always on the best terms with one another, each taking turns blaming the others for problems within the system.

"Still, Officer Arnsdale herself has put in a warning about the violent nature of this slave on the behalf of the agency, and we'll be watching closely. We take altercations with law enforcement quite seriously."

"Of course," Jere answered with a smile. "But from what I read, a past charge doesn't disqualify a slave automatically. When she passes the certification, I'll have just as much mobility with her as any slave, correct?"

"Of course, Doctor Peters," the woman said. "Now, why don't you go ahead and sever the mind connection with the girl. Mr. Andrews, to my left, will be monitoring psychic abilities and connections throughout the certification. He'll make sure that there is no connection between you and the girl, and will also make sure that you are not utilizing any abilities to influence our perceptions either way."

"I'm a healer," Jere mumbled, wondering what he could possibly do to alter anything.

"Not all of our slaveowners are healers," the woman reminded him. "It's standard protocol."

"Right," Jere said, blushing. He turned slightly to face Isis. *"This is it for now, kid. Good luck."*

As he severed the connection, he could see it on Isis's face, the nervousness, the sense of abandonment. He couldn't feel it like he could while they were still connected, but he could sense it in the normal way, and he could see her sliding ever so slightly closer to him.

"Doctor Peters, you may take her into the testing room now," the woman said. "Mr. Clark and I will be giving you psychic instructions from that point."

Jere nodded, motioning for Isis to follow him. She did, as expected, but she trembled as she trailed behind Jere.

Jere didn't realize how bothered he would be to not have the connection with Isis. Naturally, he would be uncomfortable if he didn't have it with Wren, but Wren was his partner, his other half. But what was Isis? His ward, perhaps, but that didn't even begin to cover it. She wasn't his child by any means, but she was his family.

And she was his slave, and that thought allowed him to ignore the trembling, to resist the urge to turn to her and ask her if she was okay, to just take her out and go home. Instead, he walked, making sure to look ahead, assuming and trusting that his slave was following exactly two steps behind him, to the left, head down. He wouldn't look, but he trusted her.

Still, he felt relief when he heard the door close behind them, and he felt Isis close, technically too close. Too close was still better than too far away. He waited, wishing that the psychic instructions would come soon, before he got overly anxious.

"All right, Doctor Peters, please place her across the room, and then the rest of the instructions will come." The woman who had spoken with Jere earlier gave directions calmly, like this was something she did every day. It occurred to Jere that she did do this every day with hundreds of slaveowners. A nerve-wracking day in his life was another day on the payroll for her.

Jere started walking again, Isis nearby, leading her across the room to a space where the carpet had clearly been worn down from a number of slaves being forced to stay there in the past.

"Stay," he ordered softly.

The certification process started quickly, and included many of the elements that Wren had trained them for. As the steps started to fall into place, Jere felt himself relaxing, and Isis appeared at least moderately calmer. It was always hard to tell with her, but she was moving more fluidly, her face taking on a calm, focused look.

The man and the woman alternated orders. Jere could hear both their voices in his head; sometimes one would pick up where the other left off. The initial steps were simple, one-directional tasks that had Isis walking, standing, sitting, spinning, and kneeling. As they became more complicated, she and Jere both rose to the occasion, Isis obeying more quickly and Jere giving orders more firmly. Jere started to feel hopeful that he and Isis could accomplish this.

Instead of the voices in his head from the psychic connection, the next order Jere heard came from a speaker in the ceiling.

"Slave, remove your shirt."

The man's voice was calm and crisp, and Jere couldn't help feeling betrayed by the order from the voice that had been gently giving him his instructions through the psychic connection.

Isis touched the hem of her shirt, looking at Jere with a questioning look. As training demanded, she didn't protest or speak, but she did pause, waiting, looking like she was asking permission. It was acceptable for a slave to confirm an order from her master; Wren had told him that.

"Obey," Jere ordered, nodding at her to confirm. He held his breath, waiting, wondering if she would do it or not. They hadn't prepared for this at all; nor had Jere heard of such a thing being part of the certification. Isis refused to wear short-sleeved shirts; Jere had no idea how she would respond to an order like this.

Setting her jaw, Isis did as ordered, standing there silent and small. Jere could feel the shock of the credentialing team when they saw the scars that covered her, and he was somewhat curious as to whether this was the reason why they had ordered her to undress. Had this been in the warning from Arnsdale? Was this a display of power, or a sick exercise in curiosity? He waited, as did Isis.

"Slave, remove the pants."

Isis didn't need to be told again, she simply did as ordered, keeping eye contact with Jere as she did. He could see the tears starting in her eyes, and he was amazed when she folded the articles before setting them aside, as if this were nothing out of the ordinary. They had never trained for this, never, because neither Jere nor Wren had considered these sort of orders part of the certification.

"Sir, walk across the room and touch your slave."

Jere was shocked at the order, and he felt his eyes widen. Isis glanced down, her body still and tense as she waited, wearing only underclothes.

"Excuse me?" Jere asked, startled. He wondered if he had misheard the request.

"Walk across the room and touch your slave," the voice repeated. "We need to see how she responds to touch."

Jere hesitated for a moment, then walked over to Isis, placing his hand lightly on her shoulder. She didn't move, which he was grateful for. Not only was this strange, it seemed highly unnecessary. After a moment, he dropped his hand and waited, casting his eyes toward the wall that he knew the certifiers sat behind. He couldn't see them, but he stared them down anyway.

"Continue, sir," the voice intoned. "Touch her in a more familiar way. Slaves are meant to be used, after all."

Jere felt the rage, and he could see Isis tensing up again. There was no way he would do this to her, there was no way that he would *let* this be done to her or to himself! He was furious at the very thought.

"That is absolutely unacceptable," he stated, his voice firm and clear and loud. Isis winced at the volume, but he continued. "I am not going to do something like that in public, and I am appalled that you would dare to suggest it."

"Sir, it's part of the process," the voice explained through the speaker again. Jere assumed that the man was reluctant to engage very closely through the mind connection at this point. "A slave is expected to tolerate sexual touch, and that needs to be verified. Surely you're not appalled that we imply your slave can be used sexually?"

Jere turned his body to glare, recalling Wren's words to be more confident, stronger, to be all the things that Isis was but couldn't be right now. "I am taking offense at the idea that you would *dare* to order a free man to engage in an unwanted sexual encounter!" he declared, his tone rising further. "While my sexual preference is my personal business, be aware that I am not in any way interested in females — the very presence of a half-naked woman in front of me is offensive, and I've tolerated it this long because I thought you had a valid reason for suggesting it. At this point, I am feeling very much harassed, and I would like a clear explanation of what is going on."

He heard whispers and rustling of papers for a moment before the speaker disconnected, and after a few moments of silence, the man's voice returned again, a bit chagrined.

"Of course, Doctor Peters, we would never suggest such a thing or attempt to force you to partake in any activity that you did not feel comfortable with. We had assumed that this was a sex slave, but it is clear from your description that the girl is used primarily as a research and medical assistant, commensurate with her gift in memory ability. We certainly meant no offense, and we certainly didn't intend to harass or bother you in any way. We'll move on."

Jere nodded, feeling relieved, but still enraged. The thought that someone would even *try* to force his hand on an issue like this was horrifying. This was why Wren had insisted on getting him to stand up for Isis, to prevent things like this. Had he not spoken up, Jere had no idea what he might have been ordered to do.

A few more commands were given, both through the speaker and through the mind connection. Jere was quite pleased that the first was an order for Isis to dress herself. A few times, conflicting messages were given over the speaker, described to Jere as a way to see where Isis's loyalties were, but each time, she passed easily, obeying Jere in spite of anything else she had heard. She kept her eyes on him, as if he was the only person in the world who mattered at all. Jere was beaming with pride, and he knew that they were very, very close to succeeding.

"*Doctor Peters, for the next part, we need to make sure that the slave remains cooperative even when faced with punishment,*" the woman explained. "*With her watching, you are going to walk to the wall directly behind you, where you will find a small panel with a whip. You are to remove it, walk back to your spot while keeping it in clear view, and then call her over to you. Have her kneel, facing away from you, and once she does, that exercise will be completed and you will be given your next orders.*"

Jere couldn't help feeling nervous, because, again, this had never been practiced. "*Is this a standard part of the certification?*" he asked, although he was already walking to fetch the whip. "*I've never heard of this!*"

"We do different things for different slaves," she explained, evasive. *"Given the history, we feel it is important to verify that the slave can perform according to very stringent standards."*

Jere seethed, but said nothing. This was revenge for insulting Arnsdale last year. He picked up the whip and held it in front of him as he walked, ensuring that Isis would see it, guaranteeing the stricken, panicked look that crossed her face.

Once he reached his spot, he stopped, looking at her with what he hoped was compassion.

"Come here," he ordered, his own anxiety increasing as she walked over slowly, her face begging to ask why.

Finally, she reached him.

"Turn that way and get on your knees," he ordered, his voice feeling too thick, like it was coated in syrup.

Isis was still for a moment, looking at him in confusion. Slowly, she started to back away. "I didn't do anything!" she muttered, increasing the distance.

On instinct, Jere reached out toward her, hoping to pull her close, hoping her words hadn't been heard, but as his hand went out, she flinched and moved a few more feet away, eyes wide in panic.

Jere felt his heart start to race. Failure. That's what this was. Failure.

"That was unsuccessful," he muttered, before the certifiers could have a chance to do so. "What do I do now? Is this a complete fail?"

"Of course not, Doctor Peters," the woman told him, a touch of amusement in her voice. *"You can correct it. Correct the behavior as you would normally; we will give the next order once we feel that appropriate measures have been taken."*

Jere tossed the whip aside, resenting the fact that he had ever picked it up.

"You're welcome to use that, sir," the man pointed out.

"I prefer to use a mind-bind as punishment on this one," Jere said, his voice low and threatening. It wasn't his intent, but Isis went pale at the mention. He waited a moment, increasing the dramatic effect.

"Isis, come here."

Isis obeyed immediately, but she was sobbing as she took the first step. By the time she reached Jere, she looked ready to be sick, and she dropped to her knees next to him.

"Please, master. Please, no, I'll be good, I promise! I'm sorry. Please, don't."

Jere felt bad enough that the girl was acting this upset, but what was worse was the fact that she wasn't acting, and neither was he. She *was* this upset, and he was going to use a mind-bind on her.

"You had your chance to be good," he told her, his voice harsh and empty. He placed his hands on her shoulders. "You know what happens when you aren't."

Feeling nauseous, he initiated the mind-bind, the ugly, cruel procedure that he had successfully avoided through all the times she tried to kill herself, through the public whipping, through everything else. He initiated it, and she stilled under his hands, unable to do anything more than blink and breathe, and only because he allowed her that.

"That seems rather unusual," a voice commented.

Jere sighed, realizing he would have to explain himself. He didn't want to make up an explanation, he wanted to go home, but that wasn't an option. "Look at her skin. To hit hard enough to hurt would mean doing significant damage, and she's become quite accustomed to it. The thing that scares her more than anything is a full mind-bind, the lack of control. You saw how upset she became, and your person should have been able to sense it from her psychic reading. This... this is torture for her."

A rustling noise was heard through the speaker, and Jere could feel through each of the three free people in the next room that there was a consensus.

"She came obediently when I called her to me because she knows these are the consequences," Jere lied easily. "I should have mentioned it beforehand; she knows I wouldn't choose to whip her. It's a waste of my abilities."

"Then why did she become so upset when you had the whip?"

Jere barely had to consider his response. "Illogical situations are frightening. I should never have agreed to something I would never really do. A whip in another's hand wouldn't have been so upsetting. A good slave attends to its master's moods; she knew there was something wrong with the situation. This is expected."

"How long can you hold her like that?"

"Hours," Jere answered honestly. "She doesn't fight it, and I have level one superior healing capabilities. It enhances the mind-bind. I could hurt her like this; if I wanted to, I could even stop her heart from beating without expending too much additional energy. I have very fine control, as is necessary for my profession."

"You can control involuntary movements and bodily functions?" the woman asked, surprised. "Seeing that would be quite impressive."

"It's highly dangerous," Jere answered, horrified that they were even suggesting such a thing. "I will demonstrate other movements, however, if you'd like."

They quickly went through a series of demonstrations; giving Jere instructions through the mind connection, and watching in awe as he controlled Isis's body, making her raise an arm, turn her head, and kneel. Jere couldn't help noticing that the girl became increasingly upset by the invasive procedure, but there was nothing else he could do, no other way in which he could demonstrate his control. He refused the more dangerous and invasive procedures, on the grounds that it presented a health risk, but the rest, he complied with.

After a while, they allowed him to release her, and he withdrew the mind connection quickly. After only a brief moment of disorientation, which Jere rushed to explain was normal, Isis dropped to her knees, cowering and waiting for her next command. She seemed the perfect picture of a subdued slave.

They gave a few more orders, and Jere and Isis were both able to follow them. Jere could tell that Isis was nearing her limit, and in truth, so was he. This hadn't gone as well as planned, and he just couldn't wait to have it all over.

Chapter 18
Results

Jere was relieved when he was instructed to take Isis to a private room to wait for results. He went quickly, with Isis following closely behind. He took a seat, watching uncomfortably as she went to her knees beside him.

He was quick to re-establish the mind connection. The fear and nerves were so much more intense than usual. Jere had to force himself to stay calm in the face of all the emotion. He wished badly that Wren was there; his calm presence would help to anchor both Jere and Isis. He resented the state for forcing him to do this all on his own.

"*Are you okay?*" Jere asked immediately. He was supposed to be the one protecting her, but he was as helpless as she was in the context of this certification.

"*I'm sorry,*" Isis replied, obviously struggling to hold herself together. "*Jere, I'm so sorry! I fucked up, I know. I didn't do it right, I screwed up, I screwed everything up, and I never should have tried this! I failed, didn't I? They're going to tell you that they're going to fucking take me away, aren't they? They're going to fucking take me and put in some sort of training facility, or sell me, or –* "

"*Stop!*" Jere ordered, hoping to curb her terror. "*I'm not letting anything happen to you. And they said that we didn't fail because of that, anyway. Please, calm down. You didn't do that bad. Just a little mistake. It's okay. Everything else was perfect. That has to mean something.*"

"*You should have just beaten me! That's what they wanted to see.*"

"*It's done,*" he said, idly. "*They'll tell us what they want us to do, and we'll do it. You're not going anywhere; I'll throw the biggest fit this*

145

shithole state has ever seen if they so much as try. For now, we wait."

They were summoned into the room where they were greeted at first, facing the three people who were to decide their fate.

The woman spoke first, smiling slightly. "Doctor Peters, you'll be pleased to know that you and your slave have not failed certification."

Jere started to breathe again. Isis didn't fail, and neither did he.

"The majority of the certification went well, although there were clear indications of hesitation and reluctance on your slave's part on numerous occasions," the woman continued. "On a ten-point scale, the slave's responses were typically rated as a three or four, with a few incidents rising to five. In general, we consider anything higher than three to be in a concern range. Her movements were judged as awkward, which usually indicates a lack of practice, but given the significant past injuries we noted, that did not impact your scores. Still, it did not make a very good impression. Verbal responses were stilted and sparse, but appropriate. Perhaps you are wise to disallow her from speaking most of the time."

Jere listened carefully, resisting his urge to argue back, to say that Isis had done well enough, resisting the desire to just get up and walk out. Jere knew that they were far from finished. This was a part of the certification process as well, and he could no more walk out of this than he could walk out of the certification itself. He envied Wren's firesetting gift; a small wastebasket fire would be appreciated at the moment.

"Of course, the major point of contention, one which our team debated for a while, was the outburst," the certifier said, frowning as if the memory offended her. "The refusal to cooperate, verbal defiance, and especially the attempt to flee were problematic. Following the incident, we found it unusual that you would not immediately correct the behavior, but wait for instruction."

She paused, and Jere felt intensely scrutinized. "I would have, elsewhere," he mumbled, unable to just sit there while she glared at him. "I was unsure what the protocol would be in a place like this. I didn't want to mess it up."

"You didn't grow up in a slave state," the woman continued. "In fact, your record indicates that you've only been a citizen for two years. You have clearly learned a lot, but the reactions you showed are not typical. Someone from a slave state would have instantly corrected the girl with the whip in his hands; instead, you chose to wait for instruction and use a mind-bind."

Jere didn't want to defend himself, because that would make it look like he had something *to* defend.

"It seems that your excellent grasp of mind-bind capabilities and ability to think creatively are strong assets. Because of this, and because of the slave's compliance despite the aversive nature of the correction, we as a committee feel that you have proven that you are capable of exerting adequate control over her. It is clear that she struggles with unfamiliar situations, but then, you do as well. You seem able to provide a consistent, calm environment and firm correction."

"Thank you." Jere had used the mind-bind mostly because he didn't trust himself not to look clumsy with a whip, nor was he willing to subject Isis to it again. It seemed that the choice had unexpected benefits.

"The committee has decided to grant a conditional pass, based primarily on the slave's history of violence and the small yet significant flight attempt," the woman informed them. "From this date on, you will need to keep your slave within three feet of you at all times. Any attempts at violence, disobedience, or flight should be immediately contained. It's a safety concern, you understand."

"Of course," Jere answered. "I'll make sure she stays close."

The woman smiled, a pitying look that one would give to someone who missed the punch line of a joke. "The slave must be restrained at all times while she is in public with a regulation grade collar or harness that is securely locked to a regulation grade leash that is no more than three feet in length."

Jere sat for a moment, processing the information. "Oh," he said, startled. "I... I guess I can get those."

The man sitting to the side had been preparing paperwork, and handed a stack to Jere, along with a pen, to sign agreement to the terms. "It starts today. We can place her in a holding cell until you return with them."

Isis whimpered and dove closer to Jere, nearly hiding under the chair. He turned, prepared to defend her with his own body, if needed. He wasn't sure it was the best decision, but letting her be placed in a holding cell was absolutely out of the question. Her behavior would revoke any conditional pass that she might have earned. He wasn't sure if that would be worse, or if his being put in jail for assault would be worse

"Can't I purchase them here?" Jere tried, stalling. "Or... I could keep her in a mind-bind while I go to purchase them?"

"That will not be acceptable." The team clearly wanted to get on with their day, not argue with an overprotective slaveowner.

Jere could feel Isis panicking next to him, and he struggled to come up with anything that would allow him to stay with Isis. He had gotten as far as considering paying a random person in the waiting room an exorbitant sum to leave and purchase the item when one of the certifiers spoke up, looking confused.

"Sir, I believe the bag you checked when you arrived today has the requisite items," the woman said, a little hesitant. "I saw it when I was walking by the bag inspection area — that *was* your bag, wasn't it?"

Jere was startled. It was his bag, but he hadn't packed it. In fact, Wren had been kind enough to pack up all of the paperwork and everything else that he and Isis would need.

"I... I must have forgotten," Jere stammered. He felt stupid, but he certainly didn't want to admit that his other slave had packed the bag, and purchased the items inside of it. "You know how things can build up in there. Purchases you forget."

The woman gave him an odd look, then glanced at a slave who was waiting nearby. "Go get Doctor Peters the bag, please."

The bag was brought quickly, and Jere was allowed to take out the collar that he and Isis had become familiar with, as well as a sturdy leash that neither of them had ever seen before.

He was glad Wren had thought ahead, and he nodded to Isis, who quickly moved to kneel in front of him, bowing her head slightly as he fastened the collar around her neck and attached the leash. Remembering the caution about having it securely locked, he rummaged through the bag further, pleased when he felt cold, heavy metal against his fingers. As though it was normal, he pulled it out, twisted the key inside, and attached it, complying with the requirements.

Silently, he reviewed the documents, signing where necessary. In addition to the leash requirement, she was on some sort of probationary period. Any sort of violation could result in removal or re-training, and the certification would only be good for one year, instead of the typical five years that was usually granted to a master after certification.

Still, Jere was pleased. They had passed and they were able to go home. Further, they would be able to go and visit Isis's parents, and they would look better during the audit.

He waited until they had cleared the certification center before asking her anything, wanting to be out of the watching and judging eyes. Finally, a few blocks away, he glanced at her and smiled.

"Congratulations," he told her, utterly sincere.

She burst into tears. A few more blocks passed before she was calm enough to speak.

"I almost failed, Jere," she mumbled, horrified. "They could have taken me away, taken Wren away, and for what? Because I got scared and panicked? They could have kept me there. They could have kept me there or taken me away!"

"They didn't," Jere said firmly. "You passed. We passed."

"It was too close," she muttered, her breath coming short and stilted, as did her words. "I could have ruined everything."

"You didn't. You did okay. And if you want to try next year, I'll be more than happy to take you again."

Isis glared at him, but she looked more relieved than anything else. Glaring was normal from Isis, reassuring, almost. When she was angry and glaring, it meant that she was capable of rational thought.

"How did he know?" Isis asked. "Wren. How did he know, and why didn't he tell me? Why didn't *you* tell me?"

"About the leash thing?" Jere checked, watching as the girl nodded. She looked at him like he had been expecting it. "I didn't know, that's why. Do you think I really would have sat there and tried to figure out where I could come up with a leash and collar if I knew that there was one in my bag?"

"I guess not."

"Wren... my guess is that he just thought it might be necessary, but he wouldn't tell you because it would worry you, and he wouldn't tell me because I would have tried to object. But we know he's always right. I just trust him at this point."

"He's good at details like that," Isis admitted. Her hand came up, tentatively fingering the collar. "Is it weird that this isn't really that uncomfortable? I mean, don't think I like it or anything, and the second we get home, this thing is coming off and I'm never leaving the house again, but he picked a nice one. I've had a lot worse things around my neck."

Jere smiled. "Like you said, he's good at details. And next time we try this, maybe it won't be a problem."

Isis cast a skeptical look in his direction. "Did you think I was joking when I said I'm never leaving the house again?" she retorted.

Wren felt Jere's presence in his head far before he and Isis reached the house, and just the presence calmed him.

"We passed!" Jere informed him, the second the connection was strong enough to make out actual words. *"We'll be home soon."*

Wren let out the breath he had been holding for hours. *"Give Isis my congratulations!"*

He waited, too impatient to sit, too fidgety to stand. He cleaned things that were already clean, rearranged some supplies, and tried to wear his nervous energy down. It was difficult for someone with a speed gift. Finally, he settled on playing with his fire gift, boiling some water, charring some scraps of paper, things like that. He was getting so much better at it; using it for well over a year had made him much more able to use it with ease. He doubted he would ever feel as fluent with it as he did with his speed gift, but then, he had been using that for so much longer, and he got to use that in public as well. The firesetting gift was so restricted as to be a novelty, even to him, and more often than not, he forgot that it was even an option.

It was his little secret, his and Jere's. So dangerous, so powerful, and a secret just for the two of them. Jere was supportive and encouraging, and Wren's skills with his firesetting gift flourished in that support. He just hoped that his fluency with the gift wouldn't prove to be a liability; the difficulty he had holding it back at the veterinarian's office terrified him. He was more worried about the upcoming audit than he even wanted to think about.

When Jere and Isis arrived, Wren was surprised that a sturdy strip of leather connected them.

"Hi — oh." Wren took in the sight, realizing what it meant.

Jere ushered Isis inside quickly, digging around in his pocket. He rushed to unlock it, but Isis seemed relatively unbothered.

"We passed!" she exclaimed. "I can go and see my parents, and I'm not going to get taken away or anything and neither are you!"

"Thanks." Jere turned to face Wren once he finally had the collar off. "I never would have thought of this... even if I had, I never would have agreed to it."

"You could have told *me*," Isis added, but she was smiling.

"Yes, so you *and* Jere could have suffered through you being even more anxious than you already were," Wren said dryly. "Besides, I didn't even know if you'd need it."

"They told Jere to whip me! That wasn't fair."

Wren raised an eyebrow. He didn't remember any part of that from his own certification.

"There was some sort of special note on my file, not to mention on Isis's, so they were more than thorough," Jere told him. "I liked it better when all people knew about me was that I was a doctor."

Wren shuddered. A more than thorough certification process most certainly couldn't have been enjoyable for either of them.

"Now I know what a mind-bind feels like from you," Isis mused, looking far less upset than Wren had imagined she would.

"A mind-bind?" Wren was shocked that Jere had been allowed to do that.

"They insisted I punish her 'as usual.'" Jere explained. "What the hell was I supposed to do? Show off how uncoordinated my efforts are and give her the chance to panic? The mind-bind worked better. Apparently I impressed them with my mind-bind abilities."

"And you scared the fuck out of me," Isis added. She glanced at

Wren. "Has he ever told you that he can *stop somebody's heart* with a mind-bind? And they were worried about *me* being dangerous!"

Wren laughed. He knew that Jere was perfectly capable of ending someone's life with his healing gift, but he didn't realize how. Wren glanced at his lover, who was looking bashful and ridiculously harmless, given what he was capable of.

"I wouldn't have really done it," Jere muttered. "But I can. I've made people's hearts beat, so I assume I could do the reverse. It scares me to do mind-binds, especially outside of the context of medicine. I've used it mostly to stop seizures, or to sedate someone for a procedure when other methods don't work, but never as a punishment. That's malpractice!"

"It's fine," Isis insisted. "I passed, and now I pretty much know never to do anything that would make you put me in a mind-bind again. Definitely worse than being whipped, except I guess it was done and over sooner."

"It puts on a good show," Wren pointed out. "Hojer wouldn't want to lose a healer as powerful as you are, not with the threat of disease. I think it's good that you showed that skill off."

Jere frowned. "I won't do it again."

Isis shrugged. "You'll do what you need to," she said, matter-of factly. "My job is to not panic and fuck things up, yours is to deal with me if I do. And it if makes you look powerful, good! Maybe they'll leave us alone in the future."

Wren grinned. Sometimes he felt like Isis was the most reasonable of all of them.

Isis glanced at Wren. "Oh, and I'm on some sort of probation thing, so if I fuck up again in the next year, they take me away for retraining or something. So... I'm not leaving the house. Maybe I'll be okay with going outside, maybe. At night. When nobody else is around. But definitely not leaving the property."

Wren smiled at her. He sort of agreed with her plan. "How do you think this is going to impact the audit? They didn't say anything about it, did they?"

Jere shook his head. "Not a word. I don't even think they know about it. Maybe it's too new, or maybe the communication isn't too open, or maybe they had enough things to lecture me about."

Wren nodded, relieved. That would be the last thing they needed on top of everything else.

"I didn't mess that up, too, did I?" Isis asked, clearly concerned.

Jere just shrugged, giving Wren a clueless glance.

"Probably not," Wren told her. "They are technically separate things. The certification was for your behavior and safety if you're taken out of state, the audit is going to be for how Jere conducts his house according to Hojer laws. Getting certified, even provisionally, proves that Jere is a responsible slaveowner who does things like take his slaves for certification."

"Should you go for certification?" Jere asked, clearly inspired.

Wren shook his head. "I wouldn't push for it, now. Scheduling one for me will just make it look like you're trying too hard. Or like you're seriously about to leave Hojer for another slave state. One day, we should probably get it done, and maybe I can go somewhere out of state with you."

"Like a vacation?" Jere suggested smiling at the very thought.

Wren nodded. "Something like that."

"And I'll be...?" Isis prompted, sounding not at all thrilled at the idea of being left behind.

"Locked in your room for a week or so," Wren replied, not missing a beat. He smiled at her outraged look. "Well, you aren't planning on leaving the house ever again, what's the difference if you're just safely locked away in your room?"

"Very funny," she replied.

"We'll all go somewhere together," Jere told her. "Or get someone to stay with you. You know I'd never do anything like that to you."

Isis actually managed a smile at that. "*Again*, Jere," she teased. "You'd never do anything like that to me *again*. You locked me in my room for weeks, remember? I didn't forget, you know. Memory gift and all? I always remember."

Chapter 19

Something to Remember

Kieran arrived a few days after the certification to stay with Wren while Jere and Isis were in Redmont. They spent some time reviewing safety measures, making sure that everything in the house and the clinic was in perfect shape.

"You're sure it won't look unusual that I'm leaving?" Jere checked.

"Taking a vacation is normal, Jere," Kieran reminded him. "Besides, this is supposed to be a business trip. It's good for doctors to stay current with new treatments, even if it means that you're gone for a while. Hell, it might even send a message to the town."

"In what way?" From what he could see, he was leaving, as planned. It showed that he wasn't scared, but that wasn't much of a message to send.

Kieran gave him a conspiratorial smile. "Have you announced your reasons for taking time off at the clinic?"

"I put my notice in when we made the plans months ago."

"Public announcement, Jere," Kieran prompted. "What do you think of making a very public announcement that your 'business trip' is also going to entail interviewing in a few other cities? After all, your practice is being limited, here. It makes sense that you would seek better employment."

Wren smiled. "And you can show Hojer exactly how unfortunate it will be if they're out a doctor for a few days. It would be quite a pity to have to deal with sickness, mild injuries, or hope the speed trains are working to get to the emergency clinic."

"Exactly," Kieran agreed. "Last time, before you came? When

Doctor Burghe died, Hojer was left without a doctor for a few weeks. Nobody wants to come here and be a doctor, at least, nobody good. It's a way to fight back against that ridiculous shutdown notice."

"That's wildly unethical," Jere mused. "I think I'm okay with that."

"I can help you draft a letter to send as a press release," Kieran suggested. "Get it sent to the newspapers. Word will spread fast—people are paying more attention with the upcoming elections."

Jere gave Wren a questioning look. "Is this a good idea?"

Wren nodded. "People here like punishment. They'll be expecting something like this. It shows that you'll fight back."

Jere nodded. It was unethical, but he could justify it. He wasn't really doing anything different than what he had already planned, and as he watched Wren and Kieran draft the press release, he started to feel a little vindicated. He had been threatened; he was backing off from Hojer for a few days.

He hand-delivered the press release, feeling better once it was gone. He could enjoy his last night in Hojer, spending time with Wren before they left.

"I'll miss you," Jere said the night before he left, leaning closer to brush his lips against Wren's. "I miss you every time I'm not with you."

"Afraid you'll forget about me?" Wren teased, tightening the grip he had around Jere's body, letting his fingers move around of their own accord, feeling Jere's back, the strong muscles there.

"Don't think it's possible to forget you," Jere admitted, giving him a smile. "But, if you want to give me something to remember you by...."

Wren grinned. He could think of lots of good things for Jere to remember him by. He gave Jere's ass a playful squeeze. "And what might you be thinking of?"

"Maybe a few things I can look at while I'm gone," Jere said, blushing a little.

"Should I get a pen and write my name in a little heart on your ass?"

"Not like that! I was thinking... maybe some bite marks. Maybe some handprints. Maybe some things I can't see, but I can feel."

"Like a tender ass from getting fucked so hard it hurts?" Wren suggested, squeezing hard at Jere's ass with his hands.

Jere nodded. "And I was thinking...I mean, if it's not too weird...."

"Jere, just say it before I get tired of waiting and shove my cock down your throat," Wren whispered in his ear, pleased when the threat made Jere shiver. Some of the lines that people had said to him in the past were actually quite sexy when repurposed with Jere.

"I used to play with fire sometimes, back in Sonova," Jere admitted. "Nothing crazy, that would last forever or anything, but a little bit. Enough to leave a little bit of a mark for a day or two."

"You're asking me to burn you?" Wren considered it. He wasn't nearly as opposed to it as he once would have been; he had scratched and hit and poked at Jere with knives, and he enjoyed slapping him hard enough to leave handprints on his face. Jere liked pain and Wren liked giving him that pleasure. Sometimes he took his own pleasure in it, more often than not.

"Just a little?" Jere asked, looking hopeful. "I'm not talking third-degree burns or anything. More like a sunburn. A little red spot."

"I'll think about it," Wren decided. He wasn't sure he could actually summon up the ambition to do so, and more importantly, he wasn't sure whether he'd be able to do so safely or not.

"Okay," Jere replied, a satisfied smile on his face. "Oh, and I also want the bite marks. And handprints. And the sore ass. And a lot of fucking. And I want you to kiss me. Now that you know what I want, will you do it to me? Fuck me? I want to feel you."

Wren smiled, nodding his agreement. Just talking about all the things he was going to do with Jere was turning him on; he couldn't wait to actually enact the fantasies. "Take your clothes off," he ordered, smiling as Jere rushed to obey. He stripped while Jere got naked. Jere came back, crawling up to kiss him, and after a moment, Wren broke it off, pushing Jere down. "Get me started."

Jere went to work happily, sucking at Wren's cock with expert skill. As he did, Wren played with his firesetting gift, warming up his hands, getting them to the temperature that he knew would burn another person. He tested it on his own forearm, working hard to suppress his own abilities that would prevent him from being burned. He had years of practice with that; all the years in the training facility and when Burghe owned him, his safety depended on suppressing that part of his ability, so that when they tortured him with fire or lit cigarettes or cauterizing tools he wouldn't prevent himself from being burned and give away his secret. It was a useful skill despite how sad the circumstances of its development were.

After a moment of holding his heated hand up to his forearm, he saw a slight red mark that faded almost instantly. He knew Jere wanted more than that, but he would have to see what happened. As it was, when he touched the sheets he was afraid that he would set them on fire. He decided he would start slow and warm, working his way up to hotter temperatures when he could focus properly on it. It didn't help that Jere was distracting him with a wonderful, expert blowjob.

When Wren had had too much, he pulled back, flipping Jere onto his stomach, and lubing his ass up quickly. Jere squirmed a little at first, but settled into the rhythm that Wren created. Wren slid his fingers in and out of Jere's ass a few times before driving his cock deep inside.

Jere gasped, and Wren was pleased to have taken him by surprise. Certainly, Jere wasn't expecting this so soon, but Wren had many plans. He fucked Jere hard and fast, wrapping an arm around his body to hold him where he wanted to, and leaning forward to kiss and bite at his neck and back. As Jere struggled to keep up with the pace Wren was setting, Wren bit harder, leaving a nice set of teeth marks all over his back and making Jere cry out.

Giving in to the wonderful tightness and the sounds Jere was making, Wren came, forcing Jere to hold still as he finished, quite pleased that Jere hadn't come yet.

Jere made a sad little whimpering sound.

"Quiet," Wren cautioned, giving him another bite. "I'm not done with you yet."

Jere shuddered, allowing Wren to move him as he wanted. He eased Jere off of his cock and moved him to the center of the bed, placing him on all fours and tilting his head up.

"Stay," he ordered, giving Jere's ass a slap that was hard enough to make Jere jump.

He went to the toy cabinet and returned with a few items, laying them out for Jere to see. A riding crop, a silk scarf, and a big dildo.

"Damn," Jere mumbled. "I guess we really aren't done yet."

Wren lifted his head higher by his hair, forcing Jere to look up at him. "You aren't done until I say you're done, and I'll be fucking you again, so don't think that I'm done yet, either."

Jere smiled back at him, blissful and aroused.

Wren started with the dildo, working it into Jere's ass easily and making Jere moan. It was thick and unyielding, and he could tell that Jere struggled to take it.

"I like your cock better," Jere decided.

Wren responded by pushing the dildo deeper inside of him, until Jere whimpered.

"Now, you just hold that in there, or I'll put it in deeper," Wren threatened, pleased as he could see Jere's cock getting harder at the very mention of the threat.

He picked up the riding crop next, tapping it all over Jere's skin in a random pattern, making him jump from surprise instead of pain. Once he got Jere all worked up, he started hitting harder, leaving little red marks behind, interspersing them with harder slaps with his hand. For some reason, he felt far more comfortable leaving handprints than marks from a riding crop. He also found it far sexier to mark his lover with his own handprints.

But, in the span of a few minutes, he realized he was pretty damned comfortable with leaving marks with both, because Jere was covered in little red welts. His ass and thighs had taken the brunt of it, turning a bright, cherry red, with little bruises starting to show through in spots. Wren paused, proud of his actions.

"Think you'll remember this?" he taunted.

Jere could only whimper his approval. Wren reached around him, grabbing his cock and finding it hard. It was always nice to have the confirmation that Jere was still enjoying the games they played.

Wren shifted gears, taking up the scarf and climbing into bed behind Jere, watching as his lover struggled to shift his weight on the bed, and watching the big dildo slip a few inches. Wren reached out, grabbing it and twisting it, making Jere howl. He twisted slowly, agonizing Jere as he worked it out, and then he added more lube and shoved it back in hard, leaving it there for the time being.

He went over Jere's body with the scarf, the light fabric teasing his skin, making Jere wriggle and squirm and cry out, especially when he went over the most intensely abused parts of his skin. Wren loved making Jere squirm like this, and if Jere's rock hard cock in his hand was any indication, Jere loved it as well.

He made a few more passes with the scarf, and then a few more with his hand, until Jere was almost melting into the mattress. He smiled at the sight, then he wrapped a hand around Jere's waist, holding him in place as he grabbed the dildo and fucked him hard with it, until Jere was begging.

"Please, Wren, please fuck me!" He cried, "I want you inside of me. I want you now."

Jere continued begging, growing more and more desperate until Wren finally eased the toy out one last time, smiling at the way the muscles in Jere's ass continued to contract, trying to hold something in. He eased Jere onto his back, propping him up against the pillows with care. Positioning himself between Jere's legs, he lined up his cock, thrilled when Jere continued to thrust up at him. "Please," he reiterated. "It hurts so bad."

Wren wasn't completely sure what Jere was referring to, but he didn't really care, either. Jere was smiling, and he hadn't asked to stop. Wren trusted Jere to take care of himself. He liked that Jere was hurting for him, and he liked knowing that Jere would have his marks and a sore ass to remember him by.

After waiting just long enough to ensure that the muscles in Jere's ass would have tightened up somewhat, he plunged into him, smiling as Jere's legs came up around him, holding him tight.

"Is that what you were waiting for?" Wren teased, sliding in and out of him slowly.

"Yes," Jere answered, gasping as Wren kept the pace steady. He winced a little with the deeper strokes.

"Sore already?" Wren asked.

"I want to be even more sore," Jere reminded him, reaching up to put his arms around Wren's neck. "I want you to fuck me all night. I can sleep on the speed train tomorrow."

Wren kept fucking him slowly, then took his hands and wrapped them around each of Jere's forearms. He slowly sped up, and as he did, he increased the heat in his hands, slowly and gently, almost unnoticeably.

It was a while before Jere caught on, his eyes growing wide, and his gaze redirecting to Wren's hands around his arms. "You're going to..." he started, stopping with nothing else but amazement in his voice.

"You still want it?" Wren checked, struggling to maintain the speed and the heat and the conversation at the same time.

"Absolutely," Jere replied, fearless. His eyes widened with excitement.

Wren went quiet, doing his best to concentrate. It was easier to increase both of his gifts at the same time. As he fucked Jere faster and faster, he felt his hands growing hot, radiating against Jere's skin. Finally, he felt the temperature go far higher than he had ever taken it before, especially while playing with Jere, and he heard Jere yelp in pain.

"Should I stop?" Wren asked, keeping the temperature stable.

"No," Jere replied, keeping his eyes on his lover as Wren burned him and fucked him hard.

Wren kept it up, increasing the speed until Jere cried out and came around him, unable to hold anything back after that. Wren stopped the heat immediately, stroking his hands up and down Jere's arms to spread the residual warmth, and admiring the red marks he had left behind. Wren fucked Jere even harder until he came as well, finally realizing that Jere was completely limp beneath him, gasping and smiling with his eyes closed. Wren took a few minutes to revel in the wonder of fucking Jere and coming inside of him once again, then eased himself out carefully, satisfied when Jere made a little sound as he slid out.

"Was that good?" Wren asked, lying next to Jere.

"*That was beyond good,*" Jere replied, not even moving his mouth.

"Did I hurt you too much?" Wren asked, a little nervous. He knew he hadn't done any permanent damage, not even enough to raise welts or blisters, but he still wasn't sure that they both hadn't gotten carried away in their moment of passion. He had enjoyed the activity far more than he expected to.

"No. I could maybe use some ice, though."

Wren smiled, leaning over to kiss him first. "I'll be right back with some."

A few seconds later, he returned with ice and a washcloth, and he lovingly cleaned up Jere's entire body, paying special attention to the handprints, crop marks, and bite marks on his back, and the burns that were barely visible on his forearms. There was one large spot on the inside of each of Jere's wrists where Wren's palms had been in contact, five smaller ones wrapping around the outside from Wren's finger tips. They did look like little sunburns, and seeing his handprints encircling Jere's skin was almost enough to turn Wren on again.

They were both exhausted. The second Wren put the towels and ice away in the bathroom and came to lie next to him, Jere scooted over and pulled Wren's arms around him.

"Thank you," Jere said quietly, sounding half-asleep. "That was amazing. You're everything I ever wanted."

It was probably just a tired statement, Jere had certainly meant to say that the experience was everything he had ever wanted, but Wren liked the version that had come out of Jere's mouth far better. He smiled, pleased and proud of himself. He never thought he would be doing something like this with his gift, but now that he had tried it, he realized that he enjoyed it very much. He hoped that the memory of tonight would sustain them during the days Jere was gone.

Chapter 20
Separation

After a short walk, Jere and Isis stood at the ticket counter at the Hojer speed train station.

"Two for the train to Redmont?" Jere asked, nervous. He hated any public interactions where he was forced to appear as a master with a slave, and the fact that it was Isis made it even more uncomfortable. Isis tried so hard, but she still made mistakes, and mistakes at this point could be detrimental. The threat of probation and retraining tempted Jere to just put her in a mind-bind for the entire trip, but he reminded himself that he had to trust her more than that.

"One regular, one slave class?" the ticket man asked, bored.

Isis gripped his arm tightly.

"Uh, no, uh..." Jere fumbled. "I want her with me. She's not leaving my side."

Would she even be allowed to travel slave class like this? Of course, the fact that the leash was trailed down the back of her coat to hide it didn't make the collar and leash very obvious. Jere wanted it that way, for Isis's dignity, which she didn't care about at all, and for their protection. A slave on a leash drew attention, and attention was undesirable.

The man at the ticket counter nodded. "So you want a private car, then?" He smirked. "Well, can't say I'd blame you there. Train rides can get awful lonely."

Jere tried to hide the look of disgust as he passed over the exorbitant amount of money that was being demanded. Since it was an interstate train ride, an officer checked their boarding passes, identification cards, and the certification documents for Isis before letting them on the train. Jere didn't relax until they had been shown their car, and the door closed tightly behind them, a sign hung outside indicating that they were not to be disturbed. He reached into his pocket to pull out the key that locked the collar around Isis's neck and tossed it to her.

"For when we're in private," he muttered, still horrified that it was necessary.

Isis smiled at him, unfastening the lock quickly. "Look, it's my own damn fault. It doesn't bother me, really. You know Wren picked the most comfortable collar he could find. Like a little pillow around my neck. Don't get all weird about it."

Jere made some sort of sound between a grunt and a whine, expressing his disapproval more clearly than words ever could.

"I think it bothers you more than it does me," Isis offered. "I've been collared plenty of times before. Or the straitjacket, you remember that. The guy you bought me from. He used to keep me in that all the time. That fucking thing hurt, and I hated it. I've had sweaters that are less comfortable than this collar, so relax."

Jere nodded, agreeing with her if only because it seemed fair that she get to make her own decisions about what to be upset about and what not to.

"I haven't been in this part of a speed train since I was little," Isis recalled. "Since I was living with my parents. When we went to visit my cousins, we'd take one. I used to love looking out the window and seeing everything."

Jere shifted over to the seat closest to the door. "Enjoy the view," he offered, smiling when she accepted happily.

Jere had taken his share of speed train rides, although he had taken few this long since moving to Hojer. The vast expanses of land that stretched between cities were rather impressive. The storms that had covered the area had left many things soaking wet, adding to the nearly swampy areas that already existed. In the spring, it would have made the vegetation grow, but this late in the season, it just piled against the leaves that had fallen from the trees, creating a sparkling, multicolor blanket across the ground. They even sped past the few ghost towns that hadn't survived The Fall; this many decades later, the buildings were crumbled and the old automobiles had mostly turned to rust. It was like looking into a museum, and Isis stared at it all in silent fascination.

Before they knew it, they were off, standing on the ground of another state.

"Wish it was a free state," Jere muttered, looking around.

They arrived at their host's house later in the day; in addition to the time they had spent preparing and traveling, there was a small time difference between the two states, and it was already growing dark. The organization stayed away from hotels, as they presented too much of an identification risk, preferring instead to arrange for visitors to stay with one of the planted members of the organization that lived nearby. They had arranged to meet with Isis's parents the following day in case there were any sorts of delays from the speed train. They made introductions with their host quickly, with Isis hiding almost behind Jere. The woman gave Isis plenty of space, but shook her head at the collar.

"Dreadful things," she remarked, scowling. "How any government can make that a requirement for a human being...."

Jere agreed, but he didn't say anything. She showed them the small spare bedroom that she had made up for them, and gave them permission to help themselves to any of the food in the house. With that, she made her departure, keeping to herself for the rest of the night.

They settled into bed somewhat early, tired from the time change and stress of the speed train ride. Jere had gotten little rest the night before, but as he settled in to sleep, he remembered why. The memory brought a smile to his face. In the dark, he traced his fingers over the handprints that were burned onto his arms. They were fading quickly, but he could still feel them; when he pressed his own hands over the marks, they warmed up enough to sting. The reminder of Wren was wonderful, and Jere fell asleep thinking of the way Wren's eyes had looked when he had been holding him down.

"Is it stupid that I miss him already?" Wren asked, just minutes after Jere and Isis left for Redmont. "I can still feel him. He's probably not even through the first speed train station, and I already miss him."

"There's nothing wrong with that," Kieran informed him. "He's your partner. That's normal."

"Slaves don't have partners," Wren mumbled, intent on holding onto his self-pity as long as he could. "They have masters.

"You gonna pout all weekend?" Kieran asked.

"Maybe," Wren replied. He saw no point in lying; Kieran could sense his emotions with her gift, and he was feeling pretty miserable.

"Well, is there anything we could do?" Kieran pressed. "I mean, I could study, but that's boring. If you want me to help out around the house or anything, just tell me. I'm going to let you lead here, I mean, it is your house."

Wren smiled. She was trying so hard, and he guessed that she was just as uncomfortable owning him as he was being let behind. "Well, there is a project that I've wanted to tackle for a while," he revealed. "Isis's bedroom is still rather destroyed from when she first came here, and we haven't really gotten a chance to clean it up. She hates people being in her space. She's covered it up with rugs and artwork, but it should be fixed properly, especially before the audit. I figure, now would be the perfect time to get in there and patch up the holes in the walls, get rid of the broken furniture, clean the carpet, things like that."

"That... sounds fun," Kieran said, clearly trying to summon up some enthusiasm and failing miserably.

Wren laughed at her. "Thanks for trying, but I get it. Maybe not what you were planning for your vacation?"

Kieran blushed. "I'm not really good at that sort of stuff. But I mean, I'll totally help, if you want me to! I can try, at least."

"Okay. You can start by writing me out a pass to go to the hardware store and get some supplies."

Kieran stared at him in open-mouthed horror at the suggestion, making Wren laugh even more. He took off, finding some paper and a pen, and wrote out his own pass, pushing it to her to sign. She took it reluctantly and signed her name where indicated.

"I can't believe I just did that. It's like I'm a part of it, now! I'm...
I'm a slaveowner!"

Wren laughed, taking the pass and putting the pen away. "I'll
be sure to have them put it on your headstone if you die by the time
I get back. It will read: 'Kieran Stellan, proud slaveowner and abolitionist.' Really confuse everyone."

That made her laugh. "I guess it's not that bad. But I still don't
like it."

Wren shook his head. She and Jere really were both so reluctant
to accept the privilege of slaveowning. A master like Jere was every
slave's fantasy. He had argued the point with Jere on numerous occasions, and all Jere could come up with to explain his feelings on
the subject was that owning slaves was just "wrong," and "terrible,"
and all sorts of things like that. Wren supposed that having been
a slave for years made him look at the issue from a more practical
standpoint, accepting the benefits it offered in exchange for the few
drawbacks. After all, if you were going to be in a slave state, it only
made sense to want to be a slaveowner. It was just a fact of life.

He made his way to the hardware store, quickly picking out the
supplies he needed. He waited as the cashier took his time charging
and recording the purchase, making plans for when he got home.

Plans that were disrupted the moment he stepped outside of the
store.

"Well, if it isn't the missing doctor's little play toy," a rough
voice said.

Before Wren could so much think of using his speed gift to escape, he found himself surrounded on all four sides. Someone with
a mind gift levitated him off the ground, leaving him squirming and
flailing in the air. As he struggled, he was moved behind the store-
fronts, into a back alley.

"Please," Wren said quietly, trying his best not to panic. "Let
me go."

"We hear your master got mad that someone's trying to keep
the dirty *lacklers* out of his little clinic," one of the attackers taunted.
"Decided to just leave us all here to die. Do you remember last time
Hojer didn't have a doctor?"

Wren remembered it quite well; he had been the one to kill his former master, starting a chain of events that brought Jere to him. He didn't answer, though. He knew it would only make the situation worse.

"What's the matter, having a hard time now that your master's not here? We thought we'd send him a little welcome home message."

Wren felt his temperature starting to rise, but forced it down, smashing it deep inside of himself like he had for so many years before Jere. They couldn't find out; no matter what they did to him, he couldn't let his secret out. He longed for Jere, for his mind connection, but there was none.

Kieran would never demand something so invasive, not like a proper slaveowner would.

Wren scanned the faces of his attackers. He knew a few of them; he had filed their paperwork at the clinic. "Please, just let me go home," he repeated, trying to stay calm. "We can forget this ever happened. I can pay you. Nobody needs to know."

"We don't want your fucking money. But we do want someone to know," one of them replied. "Tell your fucking *lackler*-loving master just what can happen if he doesn't stay in line. To you, to the little girl he keeps hidden in his house. He acts like you're both some prized possessions, but everyone knows you're just his whores. We want to remind him what you're supposed to be used for."

"Don't do this," Wren begged. "My master will be furious."

"What are you going to do, report me to the police? Think they'll believe your story, or do you think that they'll believe that you were so lonely and sex-crazed after your master left town that you begged us all to take our turns with you?"

Wren said nothing. He closed his eyes, focused on suppressing his fire gift, and waited for it to be over. He couldn't fight them; to lay hands on a free man was asking for whipping or worse, and he couldn't escape them. He could contact someone with his mind gift, but it was even more dangerous. He'd rather take whatever they would do to him than risk exposing his other gift. He steeled himself as he felt his body twisted and turned in the air, and he tried not to make a sound as he felt hands tugging at his clothes. He reminded himself that they weren't planning on killing him; they were going to rape him, probably beat him up, and then send him back to his master. He had lived through far worse. He just hoped he would be in a condition to wait for his master.

He wanted to be sick as he felt his shirt being peeled away, as hands made their way across his skin. The same spots that Jere could make feel so good made him feel dirty, violated.

"Tell us you want it," one of the attackers ordered. "Beg us to fuck you and we might stop when we're finished."

Wren clenched his jaw tightly, refusing to participate. Jere would be home soon, and he would heal the injuries. His pride earned him a slap in the face.

"Guess he wants it rough."

Wren felt hands at the button of his pants, ripping them open instead of bothering to unfasten them. He didn't fight. He couldn't. All he could do was focus on suppressing his gift.

"Get him hard," one of the attackers suggested, a cruel smile on his face. He jerked Wren's pants down, just past his hips, trapping his legs. "The little whore's come-stained clothes should let the doctor know just how much he enjoyed this. I say we hold on to them and mail them later, just to make sure he gets them."

Wren was surprised when his cock seemed to take on a life of its own. He felt his heart racing, his cock growing hard, his breathing becoming rapid and shallow. He looked from one assailant to the other, trying to figure it out, and then he realized that someone was using another mind gift on him. They were controlling his hormones, making his body respond even as every other part of him yearned to escape. The humiliation of losing control brought tears to his eyes.

The conversation surrounding him was just as awful. "I'll take his mouth, you'll take his ass?"

"Maybe we can all join in! Two in front, two in back. All slaves are good for, anyway."

Chapter 21

Parents

The morning after they arrived in Redmont, Jere and Isis made their way over to her parents' house. Standing at the door, Jere felt every bit as nervous as Isis looked. In the same way they did when they took the speed train, they had fastened the collar around Isis's neck and threaded the leash down her back, where it couldn't be seen. Walking closely, it was impossible to tell whether Jere was holding it or not. In case of danger, it was easy for him to reach out and grab it the handle from her pocket, as though he had been holding it all along. If all went well, it would stay there, out of sight, covered by the thick turtleneck sweater that Isis wore, covering the collar as well.

Jere raised his hand to knock, hesitating for a moment. "You ready?"

She nodded, looking scared but still eager. "I'm fucking terrified. They'll like me, right?"

"They're your parents. And they've been looking for you for years. I'm sure they'll love you."

Jere knocked. The exact dates of the visit were kept from the prospective families to keep them safe in case of interference.

A small woman came to the door, an open expression on her face. "Hello, how may I help you?"

Jere knew that only part of the nervousness he felt was runoff from Isis's emotions. "My name is Jere. I believe the Lighthouse Organization has been in touch with you?"

The woman's eyes widened. She hurried them in. "I heard that there had been a match...."

"They said that it would be best not to let you know too many details in advance," Jere apologized. "We were just supposed to show up and—"

Jere let his words trail off as he realized that the woman wasn't so much as looking at him. She had fixated on Isis, and tears had started to form in her eyes.

"Mariah?" she said, finally.

"Mommy?" Isis replied, her voice slipping higher into a child-like tone. "Holy shit, I didn't believe I'd ever see you again."

Jere stood back, silent. Isis had never mentioned her birth name to him, the name she had before it was reassigned when she was taken as a slave. Isis stiffened in her mother's grip, but didn't pull away like she did from everyone else. Jere could tell that she grew uncomfortable the longer the embrace lasted, but before too long, the woman had stepped back to look at her daughter.

"Mariah, I didn't think we'd ever find you! We've looked for so many years...."

The woman was sobbing now, clutching Isis's hands, and Isis looked like she was doing all she could to hold back tears as well.

"It's all right, Mom. Everything's fine. I'm okay."

"I just..." the woman smiled through her tears, then turned her head. "Nathan, Nathan, come here!"

A man appeared in the hallway, as unassuming as his wife had been. "Aurellia, what—"

He stopped speaking as he took in the sight in front of him.

Isis was struggling to tolerate the hugs that her mother was forcing on her again, and doing a rather admirable job, but Jere could tell that she was at her limit. The man in front of them wasn't small by any means, and he had a rather imposing presence. He strode over to his family with determination. He placed a hand on his wife's shoulder, pulling her back a few inches, and unwittingly allowed Isis to retreat closer to Jere.

"It's her, Nathan!" the woman exclaimed, elated. "She's come back to us after all this time!"

"Is that really you, baby girl?" Nathan asked, stepping directly in front of Isis.

"It's me, Daddy," Isis mumbled. "I made it."

He reached out and took her hands, pulling her closer to him. Jere could sense her anxiety.

"I'm so sorry, honey," he said. "I never should have let them take you. Never. Your mother and I should have left the moment we heard they were coming, should have fought—should have done anything."

He tried to pull her closer and Isis squirmed away.

"I never thought I'd get a chance to see my little girl again." Nathan confessed, stepping closer.

Isis glanced over, panic and confusion evident on her face and through the connection. "Jere," she pleaded. She was scared, helpless to stand up against the people who loved her but didn't know her well enough to avoid making her uncomfortable.

Jere stepped between Isis and her father, putting a firm hand on Nathan's chest and pushing him back. "She doesn't like to be touched."

Nathan shoved him back, challenging. "She's my goddamned daughter!"

Jere didn't fight back, but he stayed in front of Isis. "She is your daughter. She also doesn't like to be touched. I would hope that you would respect this if you care about her as much as she's told me you do."

Nathan glared at him, the expression eerily similar to the one Isis had given him so many times in the past. "That true, Mariah?" he asked, never taking his eyes off Jere.

Isis started sobbing. "I'm sorry, Daddy," she mumbled, drawing close to Jere and pressing into his side.

Jere pulled her close, letting her hide.

Nathan was still glaring. "So you get to hug my daughter and I don't?"

"Isis and I have been through a lot," Jere said quietly. "She trusts me."

"I'm her father! You buy her and trick her into trusting you and I'm supposed to believe that? What? Are you the only person who's allowed to touch her? You sick fucking bastard!"

"Nathan, stop!" Isis's mother was grabbing his arm. "Stop, he brought her here! He's her master, don't upset him! He could hurt her—we might never see her again!"

Nathan's face went white at the implications. "Please, sir, I apologize—"

"It's okay," Jere cut him off, horrified by the man's desperate apologies. "Nobody is going to hurt your daughter. I don't want that any more than you do. She's just overwhelmed and scared. Please, calm down."

Nathan nodded, embarrassed. "Mariah, honey, I didn't mean to make you uncomfortable."

Isis pulled away from Jere a little bit, wiping at her eyes with the sleeve of her shirt. "It's okay. You didn't know."

There was silence for a moment, and Isis broke it. "So, I guess I should introduce you. Mom, Dad, this is Jere. He's my master, and he's like the best fucking person in the world, and I don't know what would have happened if he hadn't found me. Jere... these are my parents."

Jere stepped forward, shaking hands awkwardly and exchanging greetings.

"And, um... I go by Isis now," Isis continued, looking more confident. "I have since I was taken."

"Mariah," her mother pleaded.

"Isis." The look on her face was determined. "It's who I am now. Who I've become. I'm not... I'm different than I was back then. It's been a long time, and I'm different. That's what I want to be called."

"It's a pretty name," Nathan tried. "Hard to see how they got it out of Mariah, but who knows how they pick those slave names anyway."

"I kind of picked it," Isis explained. "It's... a long story, but it's my name. I like it. I'm so happy to see you."

Isis's mother beamed at her for a moment. "Well, why don't you sit down, maybe we could have tea, get to know each other? Mar— Isis, would you like a hot cocoa, honey? We have money for the real kind, these days, but you always liked the imitation kind when you were younger. You said it was sweeter. I know it's silly, but I've always kept some around."

Isis smiled excitedly. Jere tried not to laugh. It was clear that

Aurellia still thought of the teenager as a little girl. Isis was perfectly thrilled to soak up the affection.

"Are you hungry?" she asked, clearly trying to squeeze in as much mothering as possible. "I could make something. I don't even know what you like, it's been so long. Do you like the same things? You were so picky as a child."

Isis laughed. "I eat everything now. You learn not to be picky when you're starving – uh, from a lot of travel. Yeah, the speed train food is pretty bad – how about if I help you make something?"

Jere could feel the tension in the room. Her parents had to know the conditions slaves were subjected to. Isis had come to accept the facts of her enslavement, but her parents looked horrified at the possibility.

"Don't you dare tell them, Jere!" Isis warned through mindspeak. *"They don't need to know everything I've been through. Not yet. Or ever."*

He nodded as she followed her mother out of the room, leaving him alone with her father.

"It's, ah, it's nice to meet you, sir," Jere managed, feeling out of place. "You have an amazing daughter."

"What the fuck did they do to her that she doesn't like to be touched?" Nathan asked, unable to look Jere in the eye.

Jere could see where Isis got her temper – not to mention her language. He tried to keep his own voice quiet. "Everything you could imagine and then some. Please keep your voice down; she doesn't want this discussed, and I'll respect her wishes enough to keep the details private. She doesn't like to talk about it. But I'm sure you know the kinds of things that happen to slaves. I guarantee she wasn't immune to any of it."

Nathan nodded, looking bitter. "And you?"

"It stopped when she got to me. I wouldn't hurt her."

"How long have you had her?" Nathan asked. "How long have you owned my daughter?"

"Just over a year," Jere answered. "She's come a long way. She had it rough before I bought her, but she's happier now."

"As a slave?"

"I treat her as well as I can." Not only had he agreed with Isis that he wouldn't discuss the details, he didn't feel right discussing it without her there. It was her business, not his, and not her father's.

Isis and her mother returned quickly, some hastily prepared snacks between them. They sat, and Isis's mother eyed up Jere critically.

"So, Jere, Isis tells me you're a doctor?"

"I was recruited to work in Hojer a little over two years ago when my former mentor passed away."

"Jere hates it in Hojer," Isis supplied. "Because it's in a slave state."

"But you stay... because of the money? Slave states do have more funds, although interstate business is really where it's at. It helps to just get out of this place every once and a while."

Jere shrugged. "I've adjusted somewhat to living in a slave state. But mostly I stay because my partner is there, and now because Isis is there. I've built a life in Hojer. I wouldn't leave it—I wouldn't leave *them*."

"You have a business partner?" Aurellia asked.

"Jere's in love with his other slave," Isis grinned. "Wren's the actual reason he stays in Hojer. I'm just extra baggage."

Nathan made a disapproving sound. "You bought a slave to fall in love with?"

"I inherited him," Jere explained. "The falling in love part was secondary."

"Do you all get along well?" Aurellia tried to keep the conversation light.

"Wren and Jere are like older brothers," Isis explained. "Older brothers who do gross sex things with each other, but I guess that's okay. They love each other more than anything else ever, and they leave me alone, and I get to do pretty much whatever I want. I help at the clinic, and I've got things for drawing, oh, and I learned how to read, and Jere's taught me how to do all sorts of medical things!"

Jere relaxed as Isis took over the conversation. Her parents both seemed taken aback at her enthusiasm, but they were most shocked by her lack of comfort with them. She was less uncomfortable around her parents than most people, but they were still new. She clearly wasn't about to get too far from Jere, and he didn't mind. She might be their child, but he considered her as much a part of his family as his blood relatives. There was no way he would risk her getting hurt, even from such well-intentioned people.

The day disappeared rapidly, and Jere allowed himself to fade into the background. It was dark before he gently suggested that they should be leaving; their cover story of making a business arrangement would only allow them to stay for so long.

"Where are you going?" Aurellia looked offended at the idea of her daughter leaving again.

"We're staying with a contact across town," Jere said vaguely. "It's safer that way."

"Well, surely she could stay here?" Aurellia pressed, glancing hopefully at Jere. "I mean, *you* could always leave."

Jere felt Isis beginning to panic, and he firmly ended the conversation. "Isis stays with me. I have a permit to bring her here on the condition that she is within eyesight at all times. I'm not breaking interstate slave laws, and I'm not drawing attention to the Lighthouse Organization or myself."

"I just thought..." Aurellia let her question die. "We're holding a networking event tomorrow for international job seekers. Would you be able to attend? I know you're not really looking, but it matches your cover story and it would give us a little more time to spend together. We can always use another guest speaker."

Jere wanted to agree, but he could already feel Isis panicking. She stood up stiffly, casting a pleading look at Jere. "You're right. We should go before it gets too late."

"We'll think about it," Jere said.

The goodbyes were hurried and tense. Isis suddenly seemed ready to bolt out the door, despite her parents' attempt to keep her around as long as possible.

As happy as Isis had seemed all day, she escalated into full-blown panic as they walked back to the host's house. Jere could see it in the way she held herself, the way she dug her fingernails into her palms.

"Are you okay?" he asked.

"I don't want to talk about it." Isis's tone was short, and her words were clipped. "Please. Don't make me talk about it outside."

Jere respected her wishes, grateful that she could ask him for this instead of throwing a fit like she used to. They walked back to the host's house in silence, and he gave her some time once they arrived to calm herself.

After a while, she came and looked at Jere desperately. "Let's just go. Please, Jere, let's leave town tonight. We can go to the speed train station, get an overnight train, or wait until morning. I don't fucking care, let's just leave. I want to go home, Jere."

As many times as Isis had caught him off-guard, this was unexpected. "Isis, we've got tickets booked already. I'd really like to attend this event your parents mentioned – it would do a lot to show how serious I am about this healthcare issue. Besides, don't you want to see your parents again?"

She started sobbing at the mention of her parents. Jere began to guess at what was wrong. He was still surprised when he heard her next request, almost inaudible through the panic.

"Please don't leave me here."

"I've put up with you this long, do you really think I'd leave you here now?"

"You will. You're gonna go spend more time with them at this stupid thing, and then you're going to tell me I should stay with them, but I can't!"

"What are you talking about?" Jere asked, confused. "The 'stupid thing' is so you can spend more time with them and so I can send a message to people in Hojer. I'm doing this for you and to prove a point."

"You brought me here so you could get rid of me! You wouldn't sell me to anyone else, but you'll sell me to my parents, or you'll fucking give me to them, and I don't want to stay with them!" Isis finally looked up at him. "All I've ever wanted was to see them again, to go back home, but this isn't home anymore! And I'm not going to that event. I'm sorry I made you come all the way here just to take me back, but please, Jere, please don't leave me here! I can't do it!"

Jere was struck by the panic in the girl's voice. "Isis, when I leave, I'm taking you with me, and nobody is going to convince me otherwise. Me and Kieran and Wren – we set this up because we care about you. We thought this was something you wanted. Nobody is trying to get rid of you. I need you around the clinic, and I need you to go to this event with me."

"I'll fuck up if we go out in public. Go without me. Tell my parents you sent me home already."

"They know as well as you do that it doesn't work that way. And I'm confident that you will do just fine. You've been perfect during this whole visit."

"No."

Jere didn't bother to ask, he just waited for her explanation. She glared at him for a few minutes before speaking again.

"I can't see my parents again and tell them that I don't love them enough to stay with them."

"It's not that you don't love them —"

"I shouldn't want to keep being your slave when I could just be my parents' daughter again. What's wrong with me? I'm a slave, not a real person anymore. I can't love anybody, and I can't ever be normal!"

"Just because you don't want to stay with them doesn't mean that you don't love them." Jere thought it was quite logical of her to want to return to Hojer; as far as he was concerned, she wouldn't be very safe with them. While they were pretending to be legitimate business owners, a close examination of their history would reveal the family connection, placing them and Isis at risk. "You're capable of love, but you're also capable of making decisions that are right for you. You don't have to live with them to prove that you love them, or that they matter to you."

Isis was silent for a few moments, calming slightly. Finally, she looked at Jere. "Before I met you, it wasn't just that I was miserable, I really didn't have a purpose. If I go back with my parents, that will be true again! I'm sixteen fucking years old, Jere, what am I supposed to do? Go to school? Listen to spoiled kids talk about their first kiss and going out on their own when I've already had *everything* done to me, and been on my own for longer than I haven't? I can't do it. I'd be miserable."

"I'm not asking you to do that," Jere reminded her. "I'm asking you to attend an event with me and see your parents again."

"I have a purpose with you; I have work, and you and Wren don't pity me or think there's something wrong with me. You know the most terrible parts, and it's still okay. How could I even start to tell them about it? What am I supposed to say the first time my mom sees the fucking scars all over me? I can't. I've spent so long wishing for them to find me, like that would make it better, but it's worse. I just want to pretend none of this ever happened."

Jere let the words sink in, the happiness with their home in Ho-jer, the fears and hopes and dreams that had been crushed. "It did happen. It's still happening. There are so many things I can never get back for you, but this was something that I could. And I need a favor from you in return. You can say goodbye tomorrow and never talk to them again if that's what you really want, although I doubt that's the case. You can keep in contact with them on your terms."

"After I go to your stupid event, right?" Isis snapped. A moment later, her anger was replaced by obvious terror again. "I can't see the look on my mom's face when I tell her I don't want to stay with her. Tell them I died or that you locked me up or something. Go to the event by yourself. Just take me home and I won't complain about anything ever again. I'll do anything. I'll find a way to pay for the tickets, I'll—"

"Isis, you know that's not what it's about. Your parents deserve to see you, and I want to take them up on their offer. This is a perfect opportunity."

Isis glared at him. "Then you'll have to beat me unconscious and drag me there, because I won't go willingly!"

Jere sighed, letting his head drop down. This was supposed to be something good for her, and he couldn't tell if he was making it better or worse. But he knew she was capable of thinking of people other than herself when she wasn't overwhelmed with fear. "Isis, do you really think I'd do that?"

"Don't care!"

Jere chose his words carefully. "I'm not dragging you anywhere. And I will completely support your decision to stay with me in Ho-jer. I'll help you explain it to your parents if you want me to. But we're not leaving. And I need you to go to this event with me."

"What's gonna happen there?" Isis asked, giving him a suspicious look, but not refusing.

"I'm going to put the word out to other states that Arona has done a terrible job treating its slave population and make it clear just how bad it will be if unqualified healers try to address the new diseases. I'm going to try and get our damn clinic open again and make it clear that I can move to another state and leave Hojer unattended if things get bad. I'll keep you right next to me, the whole time, and if anyone so much as looks at you wrong, I'll make one of their eyeballs explode."

Isis smiled a little at the last part. "I really don't want to go, Jere."

"I know."

"I guess since you never ask me to do things I don't want to, I kind of have to when you do ask?"

Jere just smiled. He wasn't above playing on her guilt.

"Am I being selfish? For not wanting to stay with them?"

"You're doing what's best for you. And if your parents are half the people you've made them out to be, they'll agree."

Isis nodded, not looking completely convinced. "Thank you. For all the nice stuff you do for me. I won't do anything bad at the event tomorrow."

"I know," Jere said. "I trust you. Now, do you think we can get some sleep?"

Isis nodded and they went their separate ways. Jere lay there for a while, wishing he was home. This was the part where he was supposed to talk to Wren, so Wren could explain it and kiss away his doubts. Instead, Jere rolled up a spare blanket and wrapped his arms around it, wondering what he was going to talk about tomorrow.

Chapter 22

Repairs

Wren felt his heart pounding, half from fear, and half from the arousal that was being forced upon him. The gift to manipulate someone's sexual arousal was dangerous, horrifying, and one of the many mind gifts that qualified someone to be a free person.

One of his assailants had moved in close enough to touch, dragging his hand along the stiff length of Wren's cock. Wren wanted so badly to burn them all, but his humiliation and suffering seemed a fair enough price to pay for his long-term safety. He gasped and tried to twist out of their grip, but the psychic hold that suspended him in air was far too strong. He felt one of them moving behind him, and he knew that he would feel the pain of one more.

As Wren waited, tense, he heard another voice adding to the mix.

"Avery Waters and Preston Lorelle," the voice called from a distance, sounding almost friendly. "If you'd like to keep your jobs at Wysocka Enterprises, I'd suggest you get your asses back to work."

Wren dared to open an eye, shocked to see Paltrek standing in front of him, looking regal despite the fact that he had obviously slept in the outfit he had worn the night before. Dane stood silently next to him. Wren's jaw dropped, just a little, and a moment later he crashed to the ground. To his relief, the arousal dropped just as quickly, and Wren felt his body coming back under his control.

"We don't even work today," one of the attackers mumbled. Either Avery or Preston, Wren assumed.

"Unless you'd like that to be a permanent arrangement, I'd be heading home," Paltrek announced, arrogant as ever. "My family doesn't like to employ criminals, and you're about to damage someone else's property, someone who I happen to be friends with."

"Fuck this, I'm out of here," one muttered, quickly followed by the other.

Wren watched in amazement as Paltrek stared down the other two. "I don't know who you are, but I promise you, I will find out. My family owns half this town — chances are, you work for me, or maybe we hold the loan on your house, or maybe we make investments if you're well-off, which I doubt by your poor choice of clothing and midday activity. Why don't you move along before I make some arrangements?"

The last two attackers scowled, but took off quickly. Wren was left curled on the ground, uncertain of how to proceed.

Paltrek waited a moment before taking a few steps over to Wren and offering him a hand. Wren flinched away at first, but took it cautiously, rising to his feet and doing his best to replace and straighten his clothes.

"Did they hurt you?" Paltrek asked, his tone gruff.

"No, sir," Wren said, trembling. "Because you were here. Thank you so much."

Paltrek shrugged. "You're lucky. If I hadn't been passed out in that house over there last night, I wouldn't have come across you."

"Yes, sir," Wren replied, still shaken. He still couldn't believe Paltrek had shown up.

"Lucky it's a small town. Only a few routes to take when you want to avoid being seen."

"Yes, sir," Wren agreed.

"Thought Jeremy would have taken you with him," Paltrek mused.

"He couldn't, sir. He had to take Isis."

Paltrek just nodded. As far as Wren knew, Jere hadn't shared the plan to reunite Isis and her parents with anyone else. While it made little sense that Jere would bring Isis along instead of Wren, Paltrek wasn't one to question Jere.

"Who the hell did he leave you with, and why they hell wasn't that person here instead of me?"

"Kieran, sir," Wren mumbled. "She didn't know. We didn't even think... I just came out to get a few things."

Dane was already picking up the spilled purchases without a word.

"Fucking idiot," Paltrek snapped, leaving Wren uncertain who he was referring to: Wren, Jere, or Kieran. "Let me guess, no mind connection?"

Wren just shook his head, feeling stupid. He should have known better. It was never truly safe for slaves to be out alone, and with the press release that Jere had dropped on the town just before he left, things were even more tense than usual. He shouldn't have left the house, especially not after Jere left town.

"Want one?" Paltrek offered. "A mind connection. I won't do anything weird with it; I'm not that good with the damn things anyway."

Wren looked up at him suspiciously. It would keep him safer, but he couldn't bear the thought of having Paltrek inside his head. More importantly, he didn't know how he could keep tamping down his firesetting gift for so long. Already, it felt like it was trying to tear his way through his skin, burning him up from the inside. "No, thank you, sir."

Paltrek shook his head. "Don't leave the house without one again," he ordered. "You'll end up dead. Or worse."

"Yes, sir," Wren agreed, taking his things from Dane.

"Come on, I'll walk you home."

Wren just wanted to speed home and pretend nothing ever happened. "It's fine, sir. I don't need —"

"That was an order, not a fucking invitation," Paltrek snapped. "Come on. Jeremy's helped me out plenty; the least I can do is get your ass home safe."

From anyone else, the sharp orders would have been intimidating. From Paltrek, they seemed overdone, like he was trying not to seem worried. After all, the intimidating heir to a wealthy slaveowning family wouldn't rightfully be so concerned about a slave.

True to his word, Paltrek walked Wren home, not just to the house, but right to the door and inside. Kieran came to greet them, looking surprised to see Paltrek.

"Are you a fucking idiot?" Paltrek demanded, not bothering to say hello.

"Why are you here?" Kieran asked, glancing from him to Wren. Her eyes widened, and Wren felt the probe of her empath gift. "What happened to you?"

"He got jumped because Jeremy pissed some people off, and he had no way to defend himself because someone didn't bother to establish a mind connection with him before sending him out alone," Paltrek cut in before Wren could speak a word. "You have a responsibility, to him and to Jeremy. Don't accept temporary ownership if you're not gonna do it right!"

"I, I won't," Kieran stammered.

"Good!" Paltrek snapped. He nodded at Dane, who turned to leave. "I see him out alone again and I'll have a mind connection with him. The two of you can figure out how to explain to Jeremy why I'm in his boyfriend's head."

"Thanks again," Wren said, the words falling silent as the door slammed.

Kieran stared at Wren in horror. "I am so, so sorry," she said. "Wren, I never thought—"

"I'm fine," Wren lied. "They didn't hurt me."

"They terrified you," Kieran stated the obvious. "And if Paltrek hadn't been there—"

"I'd rather not think of that."

Kieran went silent for a moment. "I should have gone with you. I know you do it all the time, but this clinic shutdown, and that press release—I'm the one who encouraged him to put that out! I incited this. I just didn't think... it was just a short trip!"

Wren nodded. "I need to go shower and change clothes. I'm fine, though, really."

He was lying, and he knew Kieran was letting him lie about it. He went the bedroom that he and Jere shared, ripping his clothes off and flinging them away, the angry tears that he had been holding back spilling out. It had been so long since he had been so afraid, so helpless. He had grown used to Jere protecting him that he had forgotten how to protect himself. Not with his gifts, but as a slave— avoiding empty sidewalks, moving quickly, begging effectively... things he never should have had to do in the first place. The rage built as he thought about his enslavement, pushing against the firesetting gift he had held back so hard, and he felt it erupting. He picked up the clothes, intending to throw them away, and a second later they ignited. He stood there, watching them burn, even as they were clenched in his fists. They played with fire often enough that they had dispensed with the smoke detectors, which was good, because thick smoke filled the room. A few seconds later, he heard Kieran knocking.

He took a deep breath, burned the remaining fibers to embers in a hot, white blaze, and then called out, "I'm all right. Just burning my clothes. In the bathtub. I'll be out in a few minutes."

Kieran was silent for a moment, and Wren wondered if she was going to barge in on him. Wren had no plans for moving. Let her see the fire.

"Okay. Do what you need to."

Wren glanced down at the pile of ashes and laughed.

He took a long, hot shower, keeping it warm long after the hot water ran out. He scrubbed at his skin until it didn't feel violated anymore, until all the dirt and gravel that had dug into his hip when he was dropped to the ground had washed out. He heated the freezing cold water until it should have burned him, and smiled when it didn't. Releasing the pent-up energy felt great, and he returned to the dining room clean and freshly dressed.

"Better?" Kieran asked.

"Yep," Wren replied.

He made his way into the clinic, relieved to be in the familiar environment where he felt safe, comfortable, in control. While Jere was gone, Wren was keeping an eye on it. A few people still wandered in, and a few even pestered Wren for some traditional remedies, which he dispensed obligingly. In between, he and Kieran quickly became engaged in the tedious but strangely rewarding process of fixing up the room. Drywall plaster smoothed out the walls evenly, fresh paint hid any mistakes, and a thorough scrubbing of the rest of the walls and the carpet made the room look brand new.

"Do you think you'd ever want to go ahead and try to get to freedom?" Kieran asked as they worked.

Wren was startled by the question. It was so strange, so idealistic... "Maybe one day," he said dismissively. "It's just not realistic.

I'd rather focus on things I know I can do, help get the clinic cleared for seeing slaves again, pass this audit, things like that. I think that's the best I can do right now."

Kieran looked disappointed. Wren was surprised that she had taken his statement so hard, but then, she did tend to get overly involved in the feelings of others, due to her gift. Wren just figured she could sense how bitter he was at knowing he was never going to have an opportunity like that.

Wren just didn't realize how much he would miss Jere until he was gone.

Maybe for free people, things like this were okay, because there were no potentially terrible consequences if their partner didn't come home after a vacation. They could move on, find someone new, maybe get some cats or one of the new hybrid animals that were being bred with the skills of mind-gifted individuals who could easily combine genes from multiple species. For a slave, none of that was true. For a slave whose partner also happened to be his master, it was even less true. If anything happened to Jere, Wren was certain that his entire life would collapse. If his trip to the damned hardware store was any indication, it would be a rapid, painful collapse. He would rather die than see that happen. Instead, he busied himself with cleaning, almost resenting how quickly he could do it with a speed gift.

"Wren, you're going to worry yourself to death," Kieran pointed out. "Not to mention kill me with chemical smells. Let's play a drinking game."

"Why are you trying to get me drunk?"

Kieran laughed. "Who said anything about getting *you* drunk? I want to get myself drunk. It's a Hojer tradition for me. Before I left for school, or met you or Jere, pretty much every day when I woke up, I would get pass-out drunk so I would forget that I was still here."

Wren liked the game, and the drinks helped. He had to admit that he felt better once he was occupied instead of just worrying himself into a frenzy.

"Do you think Isis will be able to see her parents again? I mean, after this trip."

"Probably," Kieran said enthusiastically. "And who knows, maybe one day, she'll make it to a free state, and then she could see them or anyone else whenever she wanted."

"Yeah, wouldn't that be nice?" Wren was on his third drink, and such possibilities seemed not only possible, but wonderful. Reality was still intruding, though, so he knew it was just fantasy-talk.

"Hell, if she wasn't so young, I'd push harder for her to do it now," Kieran mentioned. "With our new program and the awesome success rates we've been having? You and Isis and Jere could be out of here in six, maybe, eight months? It's a pity you guys weren't interested in it, although you guys are always dreadfully safe. We're working on getting our rates higher."

"What?" It was so typical of Kieran to get all excited about some successful program that was being run in another state. "Where is this happening, and when's it coming to Hojer?"

Kieran stopped, staring at him. "Oh," she said, looking guilty. "Oh, shit."

Wren stared back at her. "What do you mean, 'oh shit'?"

Kieran winced before she continued speaking. "The eighty percent success rates we've had *were* out of Hojer. Our new project manager, the new steps we've taken, the new people we've hired on both ends to make sure things go smoothly..."

Wren considered it, not just what Kieran was saying in general, but what it could mean for him. "Eighty percent success rate?"

"Well, fifty to eighty. I... I thought Jere told you."

Wren shook his head. "He didn't mention a word of it to me or Isis."

Kieran looked nervous. "Shit, Wren, I... I thought he had told you! That's why I didn't tell you sooner. I thought it would be better coming from him, you know, I can get overly pushy sometimes, about things I really care about. I thought if he had the opportunity to tell you, he could do it better, more objective and stuff, so —"

"That fucking asshole!" Wren snapped, throwing his cards to the floor. He didn't want to play anymore. He didn't want to do anything, except maybe find out every detail about this opportunity, and maybe take it, right now. "He knew, and he didn't tell me? How long has he known?"

"I'm not sure—"

"How long has he known!" Wren snapped, feeling the temperature of the room start to rise. He couldn't let that secret out, and he dug his nails into his palm to remind himself of that fact. When that didn't help, he finished the rest of his drink. At least the flush on his face could be explained by the alcohol.

"A while," Kieran admitted. "A couple months. I told him when I told him about finding Isis's parents."

Wren sat silent and fuming. "I'm going to kill him. I'm going to wait until he comes through that door, and I'm just..." he held his hands up, making a choking motion. "That son of a bitch!"

Kieran sat there nervously, letting Wren rant and rave, growing angrier and less coherent with every sentence, and with every intermingled drink of alcohol. Finally, when he had gone quiet, she tried to be helpful. "I think he was maybe trying to protect you?"

Wren shook his head. "I don't care why he did it. We've had this argument before. Him and his fucking decision-making. And lying to me. It's ridiculous. Like I'm some sort of stupid slave who can't be trusted to make my own decisions."

"I'm sure that wasn't his reason," Kieran said. "You know Jere doesn't think that."

Wren poured himself another drink from the pitcher, adding some extra liquor to it.

Kieran recoiled from Wren's outpour of emotion. "I take it you're not up to playing the game anymore?"

"I'm playing the other game. The traditional one you told me about earlier." The one where he drank until he passed out. It sounded silly earlier, self-destructive and childish. Now, it sounded like an excellent idea. If he wasn't conscious, he couldn't reveal his fire-setting gift. More importantly, he couldn't hurt so bad. More than when he was outside of the hardware store, he felt alone now.

"Oh." Kieran silently finished her drink and poured another one in camaraderie.

"Don't try to keep up. Speed gift. Faster metabolism," Wren

explained. Full sentences seemed like too much of a challenge. He wanted to be angry and intoxicated. Speaking took far too much effort away from both of those things.

"Maybe he just hasn't found the right time to tell you yet?" Kieran suggested. "He said he was going to. There's been a lot going on."

"If he was going to tell me, he would have done it all the other times he's had a chance to," Wren reminded her, furiously pounding his way through another drink. "He's given me this weird look a few times and when I ask him why, and he says 'nothing' or gives me some excuse. Or starts kissing me or fucking me. I can't believe I fell for that! I've used that excuse enough times to know how it works! I can't believe I had to find it out from *you*!"

Kieran flinched.

"It's not you. I'm sorry. It just sucks to have to hear it from someone you're not in love with."

Kieran nodded. "It's a huge betrayal."

"Fuck you, stop reading my emotions," Wren mumbled, pouring yet another drink. "Maybe if you're lucky you'll get to see me break down and have a fucking panic attack."

"He won't leave you," Kieran said. "I think he's scared he might lose you, so scared that he'd risk upsetting you this badly. If you get caught...."

"That twenty percent?" Wren asked, flippant. Twenty percent wasn't a bad chance at all. "I'd go right now if I had the chance. Just tell me when and where, I'd be there. Speed gift, that makes it easier, right?"

"Yes, but it takes a lot of planning," Kieran cautioned. "You should talk it over with Jere first."

Wren finished his drink. "New game. Every time either one of us mentions his name, I drink until I don't want to choke him anymore." It was supposed to be an attempt to make light of the situation, but Wren only ended up feeling more hurt. He couldn't even think of the man he loved without feeling betrayed and angry. The alcohol burned his throat, but it dulled the angry fire inside of him, at least for the night.

Chapter 23

Networking

"I am not wearing that thing!"

Jere ducked as a collar and leash flew through the air, nearly missing his head. "Isis, there is no way we can hide it for an entire networking event. It works when we're walking somewhere because I can be close enough to you that it's not noticeable, but I'll need to be moving around, shaking hands, giving a speech—"

"How the hell are we supposed to explain it to my parents?"

Jere sighed. He wasn't looking forward to that part either. "We'll just tell them the truth. You're a little volatile, and Arona's certification agency is evil and biased."

Isis continued to glare at him. "I never should have agreed to this."

"I'm glad you did."

Isis said nothing; she just dug through her bag of clothes, finding something with a lower neckline than what she had been using to hide the collar during the rest of the visit. "If I'm going to wear it, I'm going to show it off. And it can't pull as much if there's not clothes over it."

Jere just nodded, grateful that she was cooperating. He had spent part of the morning planning out what he wanted to say, consulting their host to find out what similarities and differences there were between Redmont and Hojer. He had never been much for public speeches... actually, he had never been much for public anything, but the chance to put Arona's leaders under as much pressure as he had been under during the past few weeks was too good to pass up.

They arrived at Isis's parents' house first; once she had given up her urge to flee back to Hojer, she had requested some time to talk with them. She was the picture of the perfect slave on the walk over, just a few inches away from Jere, the onerous leash loose between them.

Aurellia answered the door first, a smile on her face that quickly disappeared when she saw the leash and collar.

"What have you put on my daughter?"

Jere stepped inside, Isis following him quickly. "A little accessory required by Arona's certification agency."

Jere knew that the situation was unsettling, but he wasn't prepared for the slap that followed. Isis's mother seemed to share her daughter's explosive temper, and only her husband's quick move of grabbing her arms and pulling her back saved Jere from being pummeled further.

"You bastard!" Aurellia screamed at him. "How could you let someone do that to her? You see her as nothing but an animal!"

"Aurellia, stop!" Nathan begged, struggling to hold her back. "Please don't upset him. Remember what he could do to her!"

Jere watched in shock, the slap stinging more than really hurting. He could understand why she would take it out on him. If the roles were reversed, Jere knew he would doubt someone in his position.

"Mom, it's not Jere's fault!" Isis protested. "It was because of me. I screwed up. I lost it at the certification and couldn't behave."

"They were biased," Jere added.

"Because of the trouble I caused last fall," Isis reminded him. She looked at her parents with determination. "Jere has done nothing but keep me safe, no matter what stupid shit I do. If he could, he'd burn the damn collar, but it's the only thing allowing me to be in Redmont right now. It's worth it."

Aurellia and Nathan were silent for a moment. Jere could feel their eyes on him, on Isis, watching the way that she clung to him and defended him.

"I'm sorry," Aurellia said quietly. "I never meant to offend, or to hurt you. I just got so angry seeing her like that. Don't take it out on her."

"I'm not going to hurt your daughter because you slapped me," Jere muttered. "It wouldn't be the first time I've gotten hurt for the girl. This is why we wanted to come over before the event—we didn't want to surprise you."

"We're glad you did," Nathan agreed. "We actually have something to discuss with you."

They moved into the living room, where Isis practically glued herself to Jere.

"We want our daughter to be safe with us. We'd like to make an offer to buy her."

Jere felt Isis tense next to him, ready to bolt out the door. She looked at him desperately, shaking her head.

"I'm sorry. That won't be possible."

"We're her parents," Nathan argued. "She's better off with us. We have more resources now. We can take care of her. She'll never need to worry about anything, or work, or put herself in danger."

"Baby, we want you home with us," Aurellia tried. "It will be good here. We'll have fun, I promise!"

"I want to stay with Jere," Isis mumbled, her eyes fixed on the floor. "I'm sorry." Silently, Isis added for Jere's sake, "*You tell them. I can't.*"

Jere sighed. Isis hated to use mindspeak; if she was using it, things had to be pretty serious. "She could probably explain it better, but from what I could understand, she isn't willing to try to fake a normal life. Being back with you reminds her of everything that she's lost. She has a purpose back home, she gets to do pretty much whatever she wants without worrying about hurting anyone or letting anyone down. She is invaluable to my clinic, and she has a small group of people who know her and care about her."

"She's a child, she doesn't know what she wants!" Aurellia protested.

"Yes I do," Isis cut in. "I want to go home. With Jere."

"But we care about her!" Aurellia changed tactics. "We love her! We'd do anything for her!"

Jere suddenly realized that Isis was more free as his slave than as a free child. "Then let her go back home without a fight. This is what she wants, and this is the best decision. She'd never be able to have a life with you. What's she supposed to do, sit around the house all day? What about when you're gone? Your business and travel needs take you from state to state, to free states, all over. Even if you start traveling alone, leaving one of you here with her, it puts a lot of stress on her. And she wouldn't have anything of her own to be proud of."

"We can shut our business down," Nathan insisted. "We can keep her safe!"

"I'm sorry, but no, you can't," Jere countered. "You couldn't keep her safe nine years ago, and you wouldn't be able to keep her safe now."

Isis started crying, and her parents both glared at him, but Jere stood his ground.

"And you would?" Nathan challenged.

"He has," Isis added. "So many times. No matter what I fuck up, he fixes it."

"I don't plan to stop now, even if it means taking her away from you. You're both registered on terrorist lists. I have decent standing in Hojer and I have enough social history that I'm not really questioned. And I care about her more than anyone else in this world, except the two of you. She's safe with me."

"Why are you helping her? What is she to you?" Aurellia asked, suspicious.

Jere was quiet for a moment, trying to come up with the right answer. He felt Isis watching him, scared and curious, and he could see the doubt on her parents' faces. "She's the little sister I never had. I love her—not like I love Wren, but she's part of my family. I just want the best for her. Right now, that's staying with me."

Nathan glared at him. "I guess we'll see if that's the right choice."

Jere nodded, certain that Nathan hated him for being right. "I've always done the best I could for her." He hadn't always succeeded in protecting his family; Wren and Isis had both experienced that firsthand.

"We can write letters," Isis suggested, her voice still shaky. "And maybe we can visit again. I get to try the certification again next year, and if I do better, they won't make me wear a collar. I can probably do it right, next time."

"Honey, is this really what you want?" Aurellia asked, tears in her eyes.

Isis was quiet, thinking about it for a moment. "Yeah. I'm sorry... I love you guys, but I can't stay. I like my job. I get to help people, and I like Wren and Jere and what we have there. It's my life, now. Maybe you can just pretend I'm off at school or something. Rich kid boarding school. I get to train with a doctor. Plenty of kids would love this chance."

"All these years, we thought we'd find you and save you," Nathan admitted. "I guess you're already there."

Isis smiled. "I didn't do anything. I just got lucky and Jere found me. But I'm not just going to let it go. Please be okay with this?"

Jere watched as her parents struggled with the decision. He assumed they were speaking telepathically. He had no idea how he would respond in the same situation, but for Isis's sake, he hoped they could understand, or at least pretend to.

"Maybe we'll do more to promote slave rights and decent treatment," Nathan decided. "Isis, we want you to be happy, and we'll support your decision, but you have to understand that we can't really be okay with anything as long as you're property."

Isis shrugged. "That's fine. I think I'm the only one who's okay with that. Jere's always bitching about it, Hojer's all crazy, I guess these people at this networking thing are upset about it. I don't need you to be okay with slavery. I just need you to let me stay with Jere and not try to make me feel guilty about it."

Isis's parents obviously weren't thrilled about the idea, but Jere hadn't expected them to be. He was proud of Isis for being able to stand up for herself, and thankful that her parents had relented. They accepted it enough not to fight it or make Isis miserable, and that was enough for him.

The event was larger than Jere expected, with plenty of people from different states and professions. He was thankful for the nametags that everyone wore, because they told him where the attendees were from and what their position was. Some had even added phrases like "hiring" or "seeking a job" to the tags, readily identifying themselves to anyone who was interested. Keeping with his announcement in Hojer, he wrote in "exploring options" on his own tag. Isis helped herself to a tag and scrawled "clinic assistant, Hojer" on it. None of the other slaves wore nametags, but none of them wore collars, either. She smiled at Jere as she attached it, staying close as he began to mingle with the rest of the crowd.

A healer from Denville, a small town on the edge of the Arona border, caught Jere's attention almost immediately. "You're from Hojer? What do you think of the new slave reform? I'm really hoping it will pass. The last few months, people have been bringing their slaves across the border to my clinic, insisting they want someone who knows how to treat humans. We can't keep up with the patient flow."

Jere smiled. "I'm in favor of it. I had been treating slaves in my clinic, but the state shut me down. It's killing my business, and I hate seeing the mess that animal healers leave when they try to heal humans."

"It's so ridiculous," the other healer said, shaking her head. "I've lived in slave states all my life—I used to think there was such a big difference, but once I got my gift... you can't tell one from the other. Humans, you know? We all have the same bodies. We're all at the same risk."

"Absolutely," Jere agreed. "I just hope the reform passes."

"Well, if it doesn't, we'll probably be looking for another healer. Do you have a pen? I could write down my contact information."

"You can tell me, ma'am," Isis suggested. "Memory gift. I remember everything for my master."

The healer nodded, giving Isis the details before walking off.

"Thank you," Jere said, surprised to see her taking the initiative.

"Don't thank slaves, it makes you look like an outlander," Isis teased, barely loud enough for Jere to hear. She followed him closely, taking more contact information, and Jere was surprised to feel like he fit in.

After a while, Nathan let him know that he was due to give his speech. He sat toward the front of the audience, listening to the previous speaker discussing the need to recruit more medical professionals, and it was suddenly his turn. With Isis by his side, he made his way up to the podium.

"Hello. I'm Dr. Peters, from Hojer, Arona. I'd like warn you about some things that are going on in my hometown, things that might have a major impact on your patients and clinics."

He had their attention.

"The 'rotting disease,' as it was once called, or *derma cariosus*, as most of us refer to it, may have mutated to a contagious and deadly form. It's spreading across the west coast, and a few days travel by an infected person could bring it to this part of the world. As medical professionals, we are all aware that it won't be the last of such mutations. Some of you might remember your grandparents telling stories about the time after The Fall, when disease wiped out a substantial portion of the population. Any means of preventing contagion is necessary. Right now, Arona, like many states, is proposing a reform to their existing slave codes, requiring that slaves be treated in human clinics, providing the best treatment."

Someone near the front called out, "Humans need human clinics more!"

"They are human. Homo sapiens, if you prefer. Regardless of whether a human has a mental gift, marking them as free, or a physical gift, marking them as a slave, every human shares the same DNA. More importantly, they share the same virus transmission patterns as free people do. With the influx of new and treatment-resistant diseases that are occurring across the globe, it is vitally important that we take into account the health of every human being."

Jere listened carefully, noticing the people who commented that they agreed, the people who argued that they couldn't handle the traffic, and the people from more progressive states who seemed surprised that Arona didn't already have such laws in place.

"I obviously have no major problems with slavery," Jere reminded them, playfully gesturing toward Isis. "What I have a problem with is the risk that my state is exposing the general population to. We are reducing herd immunity. I'm sure none of you think this will affect your practice, but if this thing grows out of control, Arona will become a magnet for disease. If you're on a border state? Sorry, you get it too. The same is true for other states—we need to do this together, and as leaders in healthcare, we need to make it clear to our friends, our patients, and our politicians—the best treatment is for *everyone*."

It was frightening and exhilarating to have so many eyes focused on him. They were listening, just like he would have. Their profession united them more than anything else.

"The Arona Medical Regulation Board has forced me to stop treating slaves in my clinic. Those of you who own your own practices should find out if your state's medical board is capable of doing the same. And all of you should investigate more about your patients and their travel histories. I'm sure nobody has made you aware of Arona's new restrictions, but I'm letting you know personally: slaves from Arona, and by association their owners, may not be in the best of health. Like many of you, I'm exploring my employment options—if I leave Arona, I'd like to go out knowing that new potential candidates know exactly what they're getting into."

Jere ended his speech with a question and answer session, explaining how the clinic shutdown had occurred, what the potential reform in Arona would entail, and what his position was like there. He answered honestly, but he made sure not to shy away from any of the unpleasant details. He wanted them to know. The event went late, and Jere followed up with many of the attendees personally. Whether they were truly interested or just seeking gossip, he didn't care. He was tired of staying quiet while bigoted government agencies dictated his life. He thought the networking event had been a remarkable success, and he was amazed that Isis had held herself together flawlessly.

The next morning, they visited Isis's parents one last time. Isis tolerated a tearful hug from her mother and an awkward handshake from her father. Neither of Isis's parents could look Jere in the eye, but they both muttered a bitter "thank you" as he and Isis walked out the door. He didn't hold it against them; he knew that their anger was directed around him, at slavery and masters in general, and not at him personally.

They walked to the speed train station in silence. Isis seemed content enough after saying goodbye to her parents, but since then,

Jere could sense the overwhelming misery and loss.

"Isis, I'm so sorry," he started. "I know this had to be hard—"

"I can't handle talking about it until we get home," she mumbled, moving to sit next to him and taking him by surprise.

As if Jere wasn't surprised enough that she was sitting next to him, she went nearly limp, flopping against his side and crying quietly. After a moment's debate, he put his arm around her, providing the human contact he knew she craved in spite of hating it so much. She nestled in and sobbed until she fell asleep, leaving Jere to contemplate the entire situation. Isis had spent her entire life as a slave wishing to be reunited with her parents, only to realize that it didn't solve anything.

Chapter 24

Reconnecting

Jere's train was delayed, and Wren was pacing anxiously. Finally, he heard footsteps and the doorknob turning. He rushed to open it, surprised when he got an armful of Isis.

"God, Wren, I missed you so much," she said, glued to him. "Everything was hard and nobody knows what it's like to be a slave and I couldn't stay with my parents because they wouldn't understand and even though Jere tried I know he doesn't really get it but you do, right? You get why I wouldn't want to be free, to be with them?"

Wren tried not to be too shocked by the fact that Jere seemed to have informed Isis about the possibility of freedom before informing him. For a moment, he was glad that Jere didn't have the mind connection with him yet. He felt the need to guard himself.

"I do get it," he admitted.

Jere gave him a helpless look and shrugged. Finally, Isis pulled back, composing herself.

"Do I get to say 'hello' to my man, now?" Jere broke in, teasing. "I think I want to put my hands all the places you just did!"

"Gross," Isis rolled her eyes, but she was still smiling.

Wren felt his heart start to race and his temperature soar as Jere approached him, looking tired and happy. Between the betrayal and the eagerness to see Jere again, he was burning up. He pulled Jere into his arms and kissed him, putting everything aside in favor of being with him again.

"The connection," Wren mumbled, once their lips separated. "It was so weird without you."

"I know," Jere agreed. "I'll put it back."

Wren would have protested, except he really didn't want to have that conversation in front of Kieran and Isis. He did his best to shield his emotions before Jere made the connection, but his success was limited.

"Wren, what — "

"Later, Jere. We can talk later about why you didn't feel the need to tell me about the possibility of being free."

The look on Jere's face almost made up for it, and Wren had to admit that he felt rather triumphant knowing that he could inspire that much horror and shame. Good. Jere deserved to feel horrified and ashamed.

They spent the better part of the night talking about the trip, giving Isis the opportunity to gush about everything that had happened. Would he go back with his family if everything was different, if they wanted him back, if Jere wasn't his partner? He would find himself in the same crisis as Isis did. What would he study, office management? An awful lot of time spent learning how to do something he excelled at already.

If the people of Hojer were willing to attack him just because Jere announced that he was considering other options, what would they do if they thought he was serious about leaving?

That night, Wren was glad to feel Jere next to him. He was surprised to realize that he didn't even feel like yelling at him, at least, not right now. The relief he felt at knowing Jere was home safe was almost canceling out the anger. He sat next to Jere and put a hand on his leg.

"I, uh... I guess you found out."

Jere didn't even try to hide the fact that he had been keeping secrets. Wren wasn't sure whether to be more irritated about that or less. A part of him had hoped that Jere had suffered a minor head injury or something, anything that would explain the lack of disclosure besides intentional betrayal.

"Found out? How could there be something for me to find out? I thought we *weren't* keeping secrets from one another anymore?"

"I didn't—"

"Jere!" Wren cut him off. "You didn't what? Didn't think I'd find out? Didn't think I'd be upset? Didn't think I'd want to know that there was a realistic option to be free some day? Or, oh, how about this — you didn't think I deserved to have that kind of input into my own life? I'm just a slave, no matter how many times you tell me otherwise. When it counts, that's how it works, right?"

"You're my partner!" Jere protested.

Wren tried to hold his anger back, to cool the fire that threatened to burn him alive. "You can choose to be my partner or my master. I can't. It's always in the back of my mind that I am a slave and you own me. The fact that you can even *try* to forget it reminds me just how much more important reality is for a slave."

The slave would feel obligated to tell the master about a big, life-changing opportunity. The master could hide it as he saw fit.

Jere was quiet for a moment. "I didn't know if you'd choose to stay with me and I was scared you'd leave."

"And so you'd rather just trap me here, make sure it wasn't a possibility" Wren asked, no less offended by that excuse. "Shit, Jere, why don't you just chain me to the fucking door so I can't get too far away from here?"

Jere was silent.

"Oh, I'm sorry, is that one of those unthinkable things that I shouldn't say?" Wren challenged, hoping to goad Jere into a real fight. When he had been jumped, it had been so easy to just comply. The only times he had ever felt like fighting for anything were when he was with Jere.

"No. You're absolutely right," Jere replied, looking down.

Wren wanted to stay angry. There should be some sort of consequences for something like this, right? The thought gave Wren an uncomfortable feeling, thinking of all the consequences he had experienced in his life, none of which were from Jere.

"I'm sorry. I fucked up. I did something that I knew would hurt you. It was shitty."

"That's a better start, at least. Jere, you've had the opportunity to leave since day one, you never did. Did you really think that the only thing keeping me here was the fact that I can't actually leave the state?"

Jere shrugged. "A part of me always wonders. Would you stay, or would you leave me? This is a convenient relationship for you, but is it more?"

"Of course it's more," Wren said. "If it was just about convenience, I'd just let you keep being nice to me and fucking you sometimes without doing all the hard relationship shit that we do. I wouldn't care about you like I do, or trust you with everything. I love you, and I love the relationship that we have. Even when it's bad, it's still good. Why do you think that I would leave you?"

Jere seemed to calm down a little, looking at Wren with no less guilt in his eyes. "I thought you'd want to be free."

Wren sighed. "Of course I want to be free. It's not like the opportunity comes with no strings attached. There are a lot of other factors to consider about that, and none of them are small. First off, there's the safety risk! You're the one who convinced me I didn't want to die. I'm pretty serious about surviving. I don't like risking myself like that, not to mention you or Isis. I'm not completely self-serving, you know. And more importantly, there's what you and I have."

Jere shrugged. "I know. I just... I didn't know what would be more important."

"Surviving is important. You are important. Right now, as far as I see it, that means I stay."

"You deserve to be free," Jere muttered. "You shouldn't let me hold you back, or Isis, or anyone."

"Nobody would be holding me back," Wren insisted. "Holding me back would be something like not telling me about an opportunity to leave, or not allowing me to leave. I am *allowed* to leave, right?"

Jere winced. Wren felt guilty, but only slightly. He was still furious that Jere had kept it from him.

"Yes. I'd allow it, and I'd support you in whatever way you needed."

The idea of freedom was enticing, but the idea of leaving everything he had ever known or loved behind was terrifying. "I keep going back and forth with myself, and it doesn't help that I'm pissed off at you, either. I wanted to just fucking leave when Kieran told me, just to spite you, but I know that's stupid. And then I wanted to stay, because I don't want to leave you, even when I'm really pissed off at you. And now... I just don't know."

If Wren was caught, getting found again would be unlikely, and having the opportunity to try for freedom again was even less so. There was a chance that they would never see each other again. That was if Wren wasn't put down immediately.

"I still need some time to think about it. This is all just reaction—I'm mad at you, I want to go. I love you, I want to stay. I want freedom, I want to go. I think of the danger, I want to stay—I want to give this some proper thought. If I stay, I'll always regret not going, and if I go, I'll probably always regret not staying. Either way, I'll regret not considering it for longer, not taking more time with it and thinking about what I really want. I need this."

"I thought I could protect you from that problem. You'd never have to wonder 'what if?' You'd just be here, safe, never knowing the difference."

Wren raised an eyebrow at the man he loved. "You wanted to protect yourself from losing me, don't pretend it was something that it wasn't."

Jere was quiet for a moment. "It was mostly that. But a little part of me wanted to protect you from it. I want to protect you from everything that could ever possibly hurt you."

Wren smiled. "Okay, I believe that was true. But I'm a big boy, Jere. I can handle this."

"I want everything to be easy for you."

"It never will be. I'm a slave. You can't make it easy, but you can share things with me. If I can get beaten and almost raped for you, you can treat me like an equal who's capable of making decisions."

Jere looked up at him, hurt. "I never thought you weren't! I just—"

"You just wanted what you wanted, and you didn't want to risk me doing something else," Wren cut him off. "Stop it. You tried to protect me in the most demeaning way. Don't sit there and act like I should be grateful to you for lying to me. Jere, we were supposed to be in this together. You spent months lying to me, to Isis, to Kieran... what the hell?"

"I was just scared," Jere muttered. "I wasn't thinking clearly."

"No. You weren't."

"It was stupid of me."

Wren kissed him again, rediscovering the lips that he had missed so much while Jere was gone. Jere was scared and insecure, both feelings that Wren had far more experience with than he ever wanted to. Wren wanted to be angry, but there were so many emotions competing for prominence, he didn't know which ones to attend to and which ones to push aside.

"Please don't do that again," Wren asked. "I love you, but I can't take that kind of deception. It makes me feel like you don't value my opinion, like you don't even value *my* input into *my* life."

Jere nodded. "I just don't know what to say."

Wren could think of a lot of things to say, but he was pretty sure that he shouldn't say any of them right now. "This was a huge decision. We should have been able to make it together, like we agreed to. You had so many opportunities to tell me, and you didn't. You chose every fucking day to lie to me. I was so angry. I'm still angry. But the whole time you were gone, even after I found out, I just kept thinking about how much I missed you and how I didn't want anything to happen to you and Isis."

"So, you're staying?" Jere asked, hopeful.

"Still need time to think about it, Jere," Wren reminded him. "You've had months to process this, you know. It's new to me."

Jere nodded, looking away in guilt. "Well, if you want to talk, I'm here. I can't guarantee that I can be unbiased. You know I want you here with me."

"I don't expect you to be. Hell, you could have spent the last few months adamantly trying to convince me to stay. I just need a chance to think. I'm not packing my bags yet, especially not because of this. I'd like to say otherwise, but I might try the same thing if I was in your position."

"Yeah, and you wouldn't get caught," Jere pointed out. "You've always been better at planning than I have."

Despite the joke, it was clear from the look on Jere's face that he knew he had done wrong. Still, Wren appreciated the playful tone. It was their first night back together. Wren didn't want to ruin it by being angry.

Wren flipped Jere onto his back, pinning him down so he could kiss him more thoroughly. "You know I love you," he pointed out, accentuating his words with bites to Jere's neck.

"I love you too," Jere agreed, squirming underneath of him. "And I won't do it again. I promise. Thank you for being so understanding."

"Remember a long time ago, you told me that what you wanted to do when you were angry with me was to talk about it and work it out?"

"Yeah." Jere smiled at the memory.

"Well, I guess that's how I feel," Wren admitted. "I may or may not have wanted to hurt you in a variety of creative ways the other night, but what I really want is for us to figure out what went wrong. This keeps being a problem, and that's not okay. It worries me and it hurts me, and yes, it pisses me off."

Jere gave him a guilty look.

"It's just... you're home, now, and nothing bad happened to you or Isis, and I don't really want to spend tonight fighting about it," Wren admitted. "I have all these things I want to do with you, and arguing isn't really on the list. I don't want to waste tonight being upset. I want to put this on hold, just for a little while, just until we can get connected to each other again. I want you back. Maybe I'll be angry at you some other time, but right now, I just want you."

"You have me," Jere replied, smiling.

"I have something else I need to tell you, too." Wren tried to think of how to say it, but it just came spilling out. "I got jumped, tossed around a little bit, almost raped... and then, weirdly, saved by Paltrek."

Jere stared at him wide-eyed, and Wren could feel through the connection how much it terrified him.

"I'm fine," he insisted, recalling the events as quickly as possible. Jere deserved to know. "I got a few scrapes and bruises, just because the person who was levitating me dropped me a few feet onto the ground. They scared me; that was all."

"They would have done worse!" Jere reminded him.

"They didn't," Wren countered. "I'm all right. We know to be more careful now."

"Wren, I'm so sorry," Jere said, still horrified. "I never should have left! I shouldn't have made a bullshit announcement that I was leaving, and I definitely shouldn't have been out acting like I was going to get another job somewhere."

Wren shook his head. "No. It's not your fault. This didn't happen just because you left. It happened because you left, and because we pissed off the town by threatening to take away their doctor, and because of the way slaves are treated, and because Kieran and I were careless, and because people are terrible. It happened because I can't defend myself here. I don't have that right, or that ability. And it's fine, because you have friends here, and I guess I do, too. You can heal the bruises I have from where they dropped me and we can work through this."

"Where are you hurt?" Jere asked. As always, he seemed so eager to do what he did best.

"You can heal me before I fuck you tonight. And then we won't talk about it anymore, at least not tonight, because it is still upsetting, and I don't want that sort of thing in bed with us tonight. Just you and me. We can get back to unpleasant things tomorrow, after I thoroughly have my way with you."

"Okay," Jere nodded, instantly agreeing. "Whatever you say, my love. I'm yours to command. I'll do whatever I can to make it up to you."

Wren grinned, looking up with an evil glint in his eye. "Oh, don't worry. I'm not done with you, yet. I want to be there when you tell Isis, and when you tell her that you've been keeping it from her. That's how you can start by making it up to me. Well, after the sex. God only knows what she'll request of you. Probably ice cream; she's a hell of a lot easier to please than I am. Even if she requests the special-order kind that comes from actual cow milk, it will be easier than making this up to me."

Jere made a face, the idea of telling the most volatile member of the household that he'd been keeping secrets clearly not appealing to him. "That's just cruel. But I guess I deserve it."

Wren smiled. Isis needed to know anyway, there was no reason why he shouldn't get to enjoy the telling. There was a small, sadistic part of him that enjoyed the idea of Jere suffering through the discomfort of confessing this to Isis, and essentially being indebted to both of them. The very thought of enjoying that was a little unsettling, but Wren had learned to accept the darker part of himself.

"Now, let me give you something else you deserve," Wren whispered into Jere's ear. "Not to mention something I've been missing out on for a long time."

Chapter 25
Hot Passion

Jere was thrilled at Wren's words. He had honestly expected Wren to be angrier at him, but perhaps Wren really was just happy that he was home. Maybe there would be hell to pay later, but right now that didn't seem important.

What seemed important was the way that Wren's lips were nibbling and biting at his earlobe, working their way down across the sensitive skin of Jere's neck. Jere turned his head, trying to catch Wren's lips with his own, but Wren was quick to respond, grabbing him roughly by the hair and turning his head away again, exposing his neck even more.

Jere complied instantly, going nearly limp and breathing deeply when he felt a sharp bite on his skin. He loved it when Wren was controlling like this, and clearly, that was the plan for the night.

"Feels good." Jere's voice came out much shakier than he imagined. He would never get used to how quickly Wren could make him unravel with just his mouth and his hands.

"We haven't even started yet."

Wren's voice was harsh and threatening, the words growled into Jere's ear quietly.

The mood set, Jere lay back and waited.

"I said you were going to heal me first," Wren reminded him, his voice still low and growly in Jere's ear. "Or were you going to try to skip that until later?"

"No!" Jere protested, only to be shoved away as Wren stood next to the bed and started undressing. For a moment, Jere worried that he had really offended his partner, but Wren gave him a slight smile. Jere watched in silence as Wren revealed the red skin, bruised and torn from gravel, along his hip and ribs and arm.

"It's clean," Wren commented. "Just needs healing. Itches like hell."

Jere waited for his cue. "May I?" he asked, finally.

"Crawl."

Jere's breath caught at the casual command; Wren had been picking a speck of dirt off of his skin, but when he spoke, he flicked his eyes up to meet Jere's. They were cold, quiet, and hard. It took Jere a minute to realize what he was even supposed to do, but when he did, he obeyed, crawling across the bed on his hands and knees.

Wren smiled as Jere reached him, and Jere was encouraged enough to place his hands lightly over the injured skin and heal it, making it flawlessly smooth in just seconds.

"Good boy," Wren said, reaching out and giving Jere a pat on the head. It could have been demeaning, but Jere craned his head, closing his eyes slightly as he tried to stay in contact.

Before he could process it, Jere felt his hair gripped tightly again, pulling him away, then pushing him down on his back. He gasped and let Wren get him started at his own pace, knowing that any attempt to take control on his own would be rebutted. Jere enjoyed the way that Wren took charge, and he happily relinquished his control over the situation.

Poised above him like a predator, Wren worked his teeth and tongue across Jere's skin, tasting his lips, biting his earlobes, licking and biting at his neck. Even the slightest attempt by Jere to change the course of their explorations was met with sharp, swift punishment—a roaming hand pinned down, a twitchy leg smacked, an adventurous tongue shoved away by a rough hand. Jere just relaxed, content to respond to Wren's touches.

It seemed like forever before Wren even bothered to move below his shoulders, and when he did, his actions became goal-driven and almost methodical. He stripped Jere's shirt off in one quick motion, unfastened his pants roughly, and jerked them off, along with his underwear, leaving Jere naked. Once he finished, he sat back, giving Jere an appraising look. Stripping wasn't the fun for tonight; being naked was.

Jere smiled, reaching for him. "Now that you've unwrapped me, are you going to play with me?" He felt like a toy, given to an eager child.

Wren just gave him a dark smile. He didn't bother reaching for Jere's hand. "I think I want you wrapped up in something else."

Silently, he got up off the bed, still staring Jere down. Jere lay back, waiting.

"Get off the bed."

Jere obeyed, getting out of bed and standing next to it, waiting for further instructions. He smiled; he liked playing games like this with Wren, taking orders from him.

"Now get on your knees and close your eyes."

Again, Jere obeyed, dropping to his knees, closing his eyes, and feeling his arms dangling at his sides, seeming out of place. It was only seconds before he felt Wren grabbing them roughly, pulling them above his head, tying them tightly together with some of the soft rope they had purchased. Wren let them go and brought them in front of him of Jere, who was unable to get too comfortable because of how tightly and thoroughly they were tied. The knots went from Jere's wrists, almost all the way to his elbows, not just restraining his arms, but immobilizing them. Jere resisted the urge to open his eyes and admire Wren's handiwork.

He didn't have to resist for long, because he quickly felt a blindfold placed over his eyes, tied tightly behind his head. He waited, feeling his muscles tense as he waited for the next contact, the next command, anything from Wren. It seemed like he waited forever.

A hand in his hair pulled him to his feet, and he stumbled, unprepared. Wren caught him around the waist before he could fall, turning his body and all but throwing him onto the bed. Jere couldn't help but wonder whether that little accident had been planned, and he grew hard at the thought. It was rare that Wren manhandled him this way, and he was enjoying every minute of it.

Wren positioned him on the bed like an art display. Jere had landed on his stomach, and Wren was quick to hold him there, pinning him with a hand in the middle of his back until Jere stopped trying to turn over. Once Jere went still, he felt Wren move, taking Jere's bound hands and attaching them to the headboard, pulling the rope taut so Jere's arms were stretched. Once he finished with that, Wren went to Jere's legs, tying each one separately to the foot of the bed, leaving Jere wide open and exposed. Jere waited, eagerly anticipating the touches or kisses that he hoped would come next.

He jumped as he felt a scratch instead. It wasn't that hard, it was surprising more than anything, as Wren dragged his short, perfectly maintained nails down Jere's back, heating up little lines as he did. Jere couldn't tell whether the heat was from the scratching or Wren's gift, and he didn't care. It felt good, despite the pain.

Wren was strangely silent. Jere hadn't noticed it too much at first, but as they continued, it became increasingly apparent. There were no little whispers of affection, not even teasing comments, there was just touch. Not that Jere minded; he was quite enjoying what Wren was doing to him. Even the silence had its own appeal, forcing him to focus more on everything else that was happening. Combined with the blindfold, Jere felt like all he could do was wait for Wren to touch him. The feeling was mostly sexy, but given the conflict between them, it left Jere a little uneasy as well. A part of him wondered if it wouldn't serve him right if Wren just left him there, alone, all night.

He probed slightly at the mind connection, wanting to make sure that everything was okay. He was allowed access for a moment, and he found pretty much what he had been expecting. Quite a bit of lingering, residual anger and confusion, hurt, gratefulness, and underneath it all, the deep, lasting love that he had come to associate with Wren. Jere started to smile, then he yelped, feeling a hand connect smartly with his ass.

"Ouch!" Jere protested, trying to turn his head to give Wren a dirty look. The position he was tied in made it difficult, not to mention the blindfold.

A matching slap landed on the other side, gentle this time, and it was followed up by a light, soothing caress.

"If you have a question, you could ask me," Wren pointed out, his hands squeezing Jere's ass cheeks, abusing the already stinging skin.

"Just wanted to make sure you were okay," Jere mumbled, embarrassed at being called out like that.

Wren continued kneading his skin, then gave his ass a few more slaps, all lighter than the first one. "You like that?" he checked, pausing.

"You know I do."

"Yes, and when I want to check, I ask you," Wren replied, landing a few more smacks, harder now, but still arousing. "It seems like you're having difficulty with the asking part."

Jere made the connection quickly, he wasn't that stupid. Checking the connection first instead of simply asking was right up there with keeping secrets from Wren in terms of underhanded things he had done. "Wren, I'm sorry, I—"

"Hush," Wren ordered. "I don't want apologies. I want to play with you. Not another word until I'm finished with you. And if you even *think* of using the mind connection, you'll regret it."

Jere went silent, a little fear starting to enter his mind. He didn't dare probe the mind connection at all; while Wren hadn't made any sort of real threat, and while he trusted that Wren wouldn't actually do anything bad to him, he knew he would regret it. Wren was trusting him to play along, and more than anything, he would regret breaking that trust again.

Wren was still and silent for a few minutes, leaving Jere to grow increasingly anxious. He could still feel Wren's weight between his legs, his warm hands resting on his ass, the lingering burn of the scratches down his back. Jere shivered, more out of excitement than anything, and a few moments later, he felt Wren resuming, slapping lightly at his ass and legs once again, warming the skin there. After a few passes, the slaps stung more, and Wren drew it out, moving so slowly for someone who could move so quickly when he wanted to. Jere whimpered and squirmed, torn between the light pain and the almost overwhelmingly arousal.

It seemed to continue forever. The slapping and scratching, the warmth—Jere was positive that Wren was using his gift now, adding heat to his already scorched skin. He struggled to stay still, and when it was too hard, he struggled against the ropes that restrained him. They were tight, very tight, and Jere was thankful for it. He started to whimper as Wren continued relentlessly, slapping him over and over again, stopping only to scratch red hot lines of fire across his ass.

Just when Jere thought he couldn't take it anymore, couldn't bear another little bit of pain on his already inflamed skin, he felt it stop, and he felt Wren's hands spreading his ass cheeks apart, dripping some lube that rolled down his skin, stinging as it came in contact with the fresh scratches Wren had left him with. Wren had to have known; he was dripping it all over, from all angles, and Jere tried not to squirm too much in response. Wren was quick to work it inside of him, opening Jere up with his fingers in a greedy, possessive way.

Jere was in utter bliss. The slight edge of fear that he felt, knowing that Wren was still a little bit angry with him, made everything even better. The fact that he couldn't see or speak, and could only hear the wet sounds of slippery fingers and flesh rubbing against flesh enhanced the sensation even more.

He felt Wren shift, above him, and felt the telltale signs of the mattress depressing slightly where Wren's body waited, ready over his. Jere forced himself to relax, preparing his body for the moment when Wren would push his way inside of it. He could have used a little more warm-up, but that wasn't his decision. Like everything else, Wren was calling the shots tonight, and as he felt Wren's cock sliding into him slowly and deliberately, he whimpered, unable to do anything else. It burned, stretching him almost to the point of pain, but Wren was kind enough to distract him from it by digging his fingers into the flesh of Jere's ass, spreading him further apart, grabbing Jere's hips, lifting him for better access. After what seemed like forever, Wren was fully inside of Jere, and Jere pulled at the ropes that kept him attached to the headboard, desperate for something to hold on to.

Wren didn't move, didn't thrust, he just filled Jere, who could feel his muscles pulsating. When Jere tried to move, he found himself pinned tightly to the bed, a sharp elbow at the back of his neck. He gasped in surprise and excitement, and he struggled to decide whether to relax or try to work the muscles in his ass to please Wren.

He soon realized he didn't even get to make that decision.

The shift from slow and deliberate to fast and punishing happened too quickly for Jere to keep up. One moment, he was trying to adjust to Wren's length inside of him, the next, he was thankful for the ropes that bound him to the bed, because Wren was fucking him mercilessly, driving deep into him and then pulling almost all the way out, sliding back inside before Jere had the time to even notice what had happened. Jere gasped and cried out as Wren used his body hard, fucking him without taking Jere's pleasure into account at all. That simple realization had Jere squirming, pressing his own cock into the mattress, desperate to find release.

Once Wren had him in the perfect position, he resumed the rough slaps to Jere's ass, striking him in time with his thrusts, making him cry out. It felt good, and it hurt. Where Wren's hands landed, they were hot; not warm, but burning hot, hot enough to leave marks if Wren didn't move them away so quickly. The harder he hit, the harder he pounded into Jere, and Jere didn't know whether he could take much more.

"Wren—"

Before Jere could utter any of the desperate pleas he was planning on, Wren's hand clamped firmly around his mouth.

"I am far from finished with you," Wren growled, his hand pressing purposefully against Jere's teeth, forcing him to crane his neck backwards. "I told you; I am giving you what you deserve tonight, and I'm not stopping until I think you deserve it."

Each time Wren thrust into him, Jere felt the pressure on his jaw, on his neck, and all through his body. It scared him; Wren was usually so much more careful than this, but he enjoyed it as well. As rough as it was, Wren was still being cautious, guarding against real injury while making Jere pleasantly uncomfortable. The fact that Wren was controlling everything about this experience was perfect.

"You're lucky I don't burn a handprint across your face," Wren hissed, warming the hand over Jere's mouth just a tiny bit. "Maybe then you'll remember to open your mouth when you have something to say."

Jere could only shudder at that threat. The pain would be awful, and the humiliation would last for days.

After a few minutes, Wren relaxed his grip on Jere's mouth, at least enough that Jere stopped worrying about pressing his teeth through his lips. He parted them slightly, feeling Wren's fingers still resting there, and he licked lightly at them with his tongue, enjoying the warmth he found there. Wren responded by bending his middle and ring fingers inward, working them into Jere's mouth while holding his head still with the rest of his hand. Obediently, Jere began to suck, working Wren's fingers in time with the rapid thrusting in his ass. He felt completely and utterly at Wren's mercy, and while it was a little intimidating, he absolutely loved it.

Wren came first, thrusting deep into Jere's ass and squeezing his hand tightly around Jere's jaw, nearly gagging him with how deeply his fingers were in Jere's throat.

Jere took it, sucking harder at Wren's fingers, clenching his muscles around Wren's cock. He whimpered at the feeling, and he ground into the mattress, seeking his own release. Wren's hand pressed down hard on his back, pinning him, and Jere moaned. Reluctantly, he stopped moving. Wren's fingers withdrew from his mouth as his cock withdrew from Jere's ass, and Jere was left feeling empty and unfulfilled. He whimpered, not sure if he should risk speaking again so soon. If Wren had more planned for the night, Jere had no desire to spoil it.

"Oh, did you want to come?" Wren taunted.

Jere nodded eagerly.

With a laugh, Wren reached underneath of Jere, wrapping his hand into a tight fist around Jere's cock. He didn't bother to untie him or touch him further, he just lent his hand. "Go ahead."

Jere drew a breath. His pleasure was an afterthought tonight. A purposeful afterthought. Wren had taken what he wanted from Jere, and now he was throwing him the scraps. Jere accepted, rocking his hips and thrusting into Wren's hand. It was strangely erotic in its humiliation; he was so desperate to come that he would take this over nothing. Wren didn't help; didn't move his hand, or squeeze his fingers at all. Despite the blindfold, Jere could feel Wren's eyes burning into him.

"Better hurry up," Wren said, so calm compared to the heat his body was generating. "I might just get bored and leave you here before you finish. See if you'll hump the mattress like an animal or beg me to come back."

Jere trembled, working harder, wishing he had a hand free, or the ability to change angles at least. He was trapped here, helpless, blindfolded, bound. The fact that he knew Wren well enough to realize it was intentional made it that much more alluring. Despite the angle, he came quickly, pressing his face into the mattress to avoid crying out.

When he finished, Wren unwound his fingers from Jere's cock, wiping his hand clean on Jere's back, a final touch that left Jere gasping in shock and arousal once again. Wren got up off the bed without a word, leaving Jere alone. He lay there, wondering if Wren might just leave him tied there all night, covered in both their fluids. The fantasy held its appeal, but Jere really wanted to spend the night cuddled with his lover. He had missed him so much.

Wren returned quickly, and Jere actually flinched as a warm washcloth came in contact with his skin, wiping away the sweat and the come and the lube and soothing the scratches Wren had left on him. Jere relaxed, letting Wren take care of him. He was as gentle and meticulous as always.

Once he was cleaned to Wren's satisfaction, his arm and legs were untied, and Wren pulled him over to the clean side of the bed and into his arms. Only then did he take off the blindfold.

Jere glanced up at him, a little surprised to see Wren smiling. He started to open his mouth to speak, but then thought better of it.

"You can talk now," Wren told him indulgently, stroking a hand down Jere's back.

"That wasn't all play, was it?" Jere asked, cuddling into Wren's arms.

"You liked it anyway," Wren pointed out, not denying it.

Jere sighed happily. He had more than liked it, regardless of the motivation behind it. If Wren wanted to sort out his anger that way, Jere was more than happy to play along.

"I liked it a lot. And it doesn't mean I didn't get your point. I need to communicate better, and trust you more."

"Yeah," Wren agreed, cuddling him close. It went quiet for a few moments.

"I love you," Jere reminded Wren. "No matter what happens, that will never change. I fuck up because of what I'm lacking, not you. I knew I should have told you from the start, I just didn't because I was weak and scared."

"I know," Wren replied, kissing him softly. "And I love you, too. It doesn't fix everything, but it makes it better. I wouldn't trade having you here with me right now for anything in the world. Even if we do fuck up sometimes."

Jere lay in Wren's arms, feeling safe and happy in spite of everything. He didn't have to be perfect; there was room for both of them to make mistakes. He would rather that he not keep making the same one over and over again, but if he did, perhaps he just hadn't learned it well enough the first time. He tried so hard to protect Wren, but it was just too easy to get caught up in the same old patterns. As much as he wanted to pretend that Wren was just another lover, an equal that anyone would recognize as such, Wren's welfare depended very much on him. Stupid shit like lying to him about the chance to be free, provoking people who offended his delicate outlander sensibilities... all he was doing was putting Wren and Isis in danger. He had to adapt, and he needed Wren's help with every step of that process.

He vowed to continue to try, for Wren and for himself. He owed it to both of them to do that much.

Chapter 26
Audit

The next morning, Wren watched, amused, as Jere let Isis in on the secret he had been keeping.

Isis shrugged. "So? I don't mind you making decisions like that. I don't want to go anyway. I like it here."

Wren laughed. It was so simple for her. No debating, no beating herself up over what could be. She didn't want to go, so it didn't even matter that Jere lied about it. He wished he could forgive so easily—he wasn't as angry as he had been before, but he needed time to heal, to trust again.

"What?" Isis asked. "I can't fucking live on my own. I like living with you guys. If you decide to go, I'll go, too. I'd rather not risk it, but if I have to I will."

"I should let you know too that I kind of got jumped," Wren mentioned, explaining the story quickly. "I think your plan to never leave the house again was pretty solid. We have to be careful, especially with the things Jere was saying when you were in Redmont."

Jere got up to make breakfast, which Wren knew was an attempt to appease him. He appreciated it, and he appreciated the chance to see what Isis thought of the news.

"Are you really thinking of leaving?" she asked.

"I'm considering the option. I don't even know if I've made up my mind yet."

"If you go, Jere goes, and I'm going too. That's not even a fucking question. It will just happen."

Wren shrugged. "Who knows, maybe Jere won't go." He wondered how much of Jere's secret-keeping was because he wanted to keep Wren out of danger, and how much of it was because he wanted to keep Wren in Hojer. After all, it wasn't like he'd have a lucrative job in a free state.

"Why the hell would he stay? He hates it here."

"He's starting to fit in better here. There are benefits to staying in Hojer. He's playing the political card pretty well now. He's got friends, a job, lots of money... he could find another slave, or another boyfriend. Or both."

Isis gave him a critical look. "You're being stupid. Jere would cut himself up into pieces and ship them one by one in little boxes if that's what it took to get back to you. You're his favorite person ever. He loves you. Like... really loves you. You're not a slave to him. He likes me, in a different way. I don't know if I'm a slave to him; maybe I'm just a kid to him. There's not that much difference, especially if you're treating them well. My parents are like you guys."

Wren smiled. He and Jere had happily settled into the routine of a married couple. "I want the chance to think about it. I might never get the opportunity again."

Isis rolled her eyes. "There will be other chances. It will probably get safer and better planned in a few years. Or maybe if we just wait long enough, slavery won't be so bad."

Wren didn't know if he was capable of waiting that long. There was a time in his life when he would have been elated that he was being treated well and getting his basic needs met. The more he had, the more he wanted. The only way that he could have it all was to find a way to be free.

But as Jere returned, bringing some slightly overcooked food along with him, Wren couldn't help but smile at his strange family. They would miss him. That was something he had never had before. As alluring as freedom was, could it ever be worth more than this?

While they finished their meal, the calm of the house and clinic was interrupted by a loud knock. Wren answered, as usual, speeding to the door casually and opening it before Jere had a chance to wonder who it was.

"Early audit," Wren's voice in his head was the only warning Jere had. A moment later, he heard the footsteps of a stranger moving through his house.

"Auditor's here early," Jere informed Isis. *"Sorry, but I need you ready."*

He waited, seated as was proper, and let Wren bring the intruder into his house. The few seconds in which Wren was out of sight and Jere was still sitting stupidly in his dining room seemed like hours, but Jere knew it was the proper thing to do. Wren had made that clear on many occasions.

Wren flashed a tiny smile as he entered the room. "There's an auditor here to see you, master."

Jere tried not to cringe at the title. It was easier now, there had been enough practice while they were getting Isis ready that the term itself wasn't utterly repellant. It was just the fact that it was coming out of Wren's mouth. He stood, nodding stiffly at Wren, and looked at the auditor. It was a different one from before.

"You're not scheduled to be here for almost another week," Jere pointed out.

"There was a change in schedule," the auditor informed him.

"I have patients waiting!"

"As long as there are no problems, this won't take long. Besides, your patients will appreciate that their doctor is cooperating with the Slave Control, Regulation, and Enforcement Agency."

As if Jere had agreed to anything, the auditor introduced himself and informed Jere of his rights and responsibilities. Jere thought the whole thing was bullshit. He didn't care who this man was, or why anyone might believe that this was a good idea, and he certainly didn't feel that he had any rights. He put on a smile and agreed with everything.

"I'll start by doing a brief visual inspection of the area," the auditor explained. "Do I have your consent to look into files, closets, and that sort of thing?"

"Of course," Jere agreed, nodding at him. He didn't really have a choice, but he was glad that they had cleaned the place up a little. They could never be too careful.

"Thank you. After that, I'll be asking you and your slaves a series of questions. I prefer to be alone while interviewing."

Jere nodded. They had expected this. Everyone had prepared him, and Wren and Isis were ready for the experience. The preparation didn't make it any more desirable, nor did the early visit. "That is perfectly acceptable, but the mind connection stays activated." This was perhaps an uncommon request, but it was perfectly allowable. According to some people he had talked to, it was advisable. "I have many private issues that I would rather not have discussed. Health privacy, patient information, that sort of thing. I am obligated as a part of my profession to protect this information."

"That will be fine," the auditor nodded. "The agency has no interest in exposing professional secrets."

Jere was glad that this was going somewhat peacefully. "If you don't mind, sir, can I ask what your gift is? I was told that sometimes this could be used as part of the process."

The auditor nodded. "I can easily ascertain whether someone is telling the truth or not," he said. "In response to a direct question. Do I have your consent to use this today?"

Jere nodded. "Yes." He didn't want to agree, but he had no choice. To deny the auditor that request would be to prove his guilt.

Jere gulped as the auditor made his way around the house, giving each space a cursory inspection. He had no idea what the man was looking for; perhaps a torture dungeon, perhaps a group of runaway slaves. Regardless, he found none of those things, just the usual. Coats in the closet. Shoes. Silverware in the drawers, brooms in another closet. If the man had anything to say about the massive amount of clothes he found in Wren's old room, he said nothing. It only made sense that a doctor would provide adequate clothing for his slaves. Jere just hoped it wasn't too obvious that Wren only used the room to store off-season clothes. The guest rooms were hotel-plain and empty, making for very fast inspections. The master bedroom was a little slower, and Jere felt himself blushing fiercely when the man opened the cabinet where their rather massive collection of sex toys lived.

The auditor noted something on the clipboard he carried with him, making Jere's heart race. Jere couldn't help moving a little closer, trying to peek at what he was writing before he died of nerves.

"Doctor Peters, I've seen my share of bedroom games," the auditor said, clearly irritated with Jere's hovering. "If this is what you're the most nervous about, you'll be fine. Nothing wrong with tying a slave up and having your way with him."

Jere backed off, a little amused that the man had automatically assumed that it was Wren who was being tied up. That was probably for the best. Still, Jere was relieved when he left their bedroom.

That relief was short-lived, as he approached Isis's room, where she had managed not to destroy anything else since it had been repaired. She sat in there, as she had insisted it was the most comfortable and contained place in the house.

The auditor seemed a little surprised by her presence, startling when he saw someone in the room, but collecting himself quickly.

Isis rose to her feet, almost bowing at the man. "Hello, sir," she said, absolutely perfect.

The auditor just nodded at her. He looked through her room, and her things, and Jere went to stand next to her, feeling her anxiety bleeding through.

"You've had some problems with the girl," the auditor reminded Jere. "She's supposed to be leashed in public, am I correct?"

"We're not in public," Jere protested, earning him a glare from Isis. "I mean, yes, but I don't bother inside the house. She's perfectly under my control, and I don't need the hassle."

The auditor just nodded.

"What is it that you do around here, girl?" he asked, looking at the art supplies that she had actually put away in her closet for once.

"I... I help at the clinic, sir," she mumbled, taking a few steps closer to Jere. "I help my master."

Jere moved closer to her. "She's got a memory gift. She takes all my notes for me, assists with whatever I need."

"Sounds useful," the auditor said, dismissive. "Let's go see the clinic."

Jere left Isis there, smiling at her, proud of how well she had done. He led the auditor into the clinic, followed closely by Wren, who was eager to play the part of the good slave.

The auditor noticed the signs indicating that slaves could no longer be treated in that location, directing former patients to the nearest veterinary office. "Having some problems here, I see?"

Jere tried not to seethe too obviously. "The state medical regulation board is concerned that I am overexerting myself treating the slave population. The case is under review."

The auditor nodded, perhaps unwilling to step on the toes of the other agencies. He checked the clinic thoroughly, and Jere even mentioned the cellar, which was checked as well, barren except for some spare furniture and extra supplies.

The auditor seemed just as happy to leave that place as Jere and Wren always were.

"The visual inspection is unremarkable," the auditor said. At Jere's confused expression he clarified, "You passed this portion."

"Thank you," Jere said, pleased. He knew there was more to come. It wasn't the house or clinic he was really worried about, it was the interview portion.

The auditor looked from Wren to Jere. "I'll take you first," he told Jere. "Send your slave away, please."

Jere tried not to bristle, but he knew this was part of the audit. "Wren, go wait in another room."

"Yes, master."

Jere still hated those vile words.

The auditor asked him a series of boring, pointless questions; how long he had been in Hojer, how many slaves he owned, past, present, and future, how they assisted in his work and personal life, what kinds of discipline Jere had used and planned to use in the future. Overall, the auditor seemed pleased with the results.

Then the man moved on to more difficult questions.

"Are you opposed to slavery, Doctor Peters?"

Jere considered it for a moment. No lying. "Yes," he nodded. "Personally, I mean. I think it's an inefficient and cruel way of arranging a society."

"And yet, you own slaves?"

Jere shrugged. "I try not to let my personal beliefs get in the way of business or productivity. The practice here is not to hire assistants, but to purchase slaves. I would never compromise my medical treatment due to a lack of appropriate help."

"You treat your slaves very kindly," the auditor said, his face a blank. "Do you make and enforce rules for them?"

"I enforce all the public rules of Hojer and Arona, and do my best to ensure that those rules are not allowed to be broken."

"What was the purpose of your recent trip out of state?"

"Business." When the auditor didn't ask another question, Jere continued. "I went to network with other medical providers. Other healers. I'm considering other employment opportunities."

"Did you attend an event and criticize Arona's current slave codes?"

Jere frowned, suspicious. Gossip traveled quickly, at least when you were being scrutinized. "Yes. I wanted to draw interstate attention to what I see, as a healer, as major deficits in policy."

The auditor was silent, writing notes. Jere wanted to see what he was writing, but he held himself back from looking. He wondered if he had been too brash, too provocative. They just had to get through this audit, and he would leave all of this alone.

The auditor switched to another topic. "Are you a member of any abolitionist or anti-slavery organization?"

"No." He wasn't. Kieran was, but he wasn't.

"Are you now planning, or have you ever planned to help a slave escape to a free state?"

"No." He was suddenly overwhelmingly glad that nobody had decided to go through with that plan.

"You're an associate of a Miss Kieran Stellan?" the man switched topics again.

"Yes. She's a friend of mine, and she goes to school at my alma mater. We speak frequently and discuss life in the city. I lived there my entire life, before accepting the position here."

"Are you aware that she is associated with anti-slavery activism groups on campus?"

"Of course," Jere answered, perfectly calm. He had discussed these sorts of questions with Kieran, and she had emphasized the importance of being truthful. "Last I checked, Hojer allowed for dissenting political beliefs. I have friends who are vegetarian, but it doesn't stop me from eating bacon when a shipment comes in."

The auditor actually smiled at that, just a little. He asked more and more questions, of different specificity, but in the end, he found nothing of worth from Jere.

"I'll take the male slave next," the auditor said. "If you have patients waiting, I'm sure you can check in with them now."

"I'll wait," Jere muttered, even as he was summoning Wren.

Jere was terrified and angry, but he could feel that Wren was calm, going through the motions in the accepting, compliant way that he had. Wren was good at this sort of thing. Still, knowing that Wren was trapped away from him in another room made him far more nervous than he liked.

Wren came out with a smile. *"Relax, Jere. He asked what my gift was, and how Burghe died, and he asked what I do around here and he asked about activism stuff. I'm sure I passed."*

Jere just smiled at him. Of all of them, Wren was the one he had never doubted.

"You can get the girl," the auditor told him, looking calm and bored.

Jere figured that the man must do hundreds audits every year. He went to find Isis in her room. "Your turn. He's waiting for you in the other room."

She wasn't amused. "I'm scared. Don't make me?"

"You'll be fine," Jere promised. "Come on, just talk to him. It'll be quick, only ten minutes or so, that's all he spent with Wren."

Isis paled, looking like Jere had just told her she was to be tortured for an hour. To her credit, she went willingly enough, making her way to the room and walking in, casting a nervous look at Jere as he closed the door.

He poked at the mind connection a tiny bit, not wanting to be too pushy, but still wanting her to know he was there. She went from nervous to panicked in just a few seconds, and Jere was on his feet and walking in that direction as the door opened back up.

"Care to tell me why the girl is lying in response to every question I ask her?" the auditor asked, suspicious.

"Please, I'm not lying!" Isis begged, huddled on the floor.

Jere didn't even have time to think. He just went to her, putting himself between her and the auditor.

"She's not lying," Jere insisted. "I don't even need to know what you asked; if she said she's not, she isn't!"

The auditor looked stunned by Jere's defense. "Well, you certainly believe her. What is her gift? I can't get her to answer me truthfully."

"She has a memory gift," Jere explained. "The physical kind. She remembers everything that she sees and hears."

The auditor considered it for a moment. He pulled out a wallet and handed his identification card over to Jere. "Give that to her and have her memorize it, please."

Jere did as he was asked, and after a second or two, Isis nodded, indicating she was finished.

"How old are you, girl?" he asked.

"Sixteen, sir."

"Are you forty-eight years old?"

"No, sir."

The auditor sighed, glancing at Jere. "My apologies, Doctor Peters. I'm misreading the girl. The way her gift works, anything she's been exposed to comes up as true. According to her results, since she has imprinted my identification card on her memory, it appears that she's lying when she says she's not a forty-eight year old man."

"That's interesting," Jere admitted. He wasn't familiar with this particular interference between gifts, but there were plenty of similar phenomena documented in the literature.

"You can still ask me questions, sir," Isis suggested. "I'm not going to lie about them. I know I'll be in a lot of trouble."

Jere was familiar enough with Isis's performance that he could tell she was acting, but she was putting on a good show. She was the perfect slave, just for a few minutes.

"That will have to suffice."

Jere left again, feeling slightly reassured, and he could hear Isis and the auditor talking. After only four or five minutes, the auditor opened the door.

"I'd like to see the other slave again, please."

Jere felt ready to attack. "Why?" he snarled, despite the fact that Wren was already moving forward.

To his credit, the auditor didn't so much as blink at Jere's outburst. Wren went with him, and this time, Jere could feel him panicking, struggling to stay calm. If he thought he had any chance of killing the auditor and getting away with it, he probably would have.

It seemed like they were gone forever, but it could only have been a few minutes before the auditor came back out, Wren following him silently. Wren gave Jere a disappointed look, shaking his head slightly.

"What's wrong?" Jere demanded. "Why did you talk to him again, what did you ask him?"

"Dr. Peters, I'm sorry to inform you, but I've consulted with the Slave Control, Regulation, and Enforcement agency regarding the details of your case. Our team has decided that we will need to take one of your slaves for additional evaluation at our facility."

Jere stared at him in shock. It couldn't be true. He wouldn't let them take either Wren or Isis.

"I'll give you a few minutes to make your decision and finalize anything you need," the auditor informed him. "We'd prefer the male, since you've had him a while longer, but the female would work as well. I'll be waiting outside, and one of the members of the Hojer police department will assist. Thank you for your cooperation."

With that, the auditor left, and Jere stared at his slaves. Isis burst into tears.

"It was my fault!" she cried. "I'll go. I fucked up at the certification, and my gift is broken or whatever..."

"No." Wren's voice was quiet. He was obviously terrified, but he was still holding himself together. "It wasn't you; it was me. I brought the attention anyway, at the vet clinic."

"Bullshit, Wren, you're perfect!" Isis protested. "I fucked this up. I'll go."

Wren shook his head. "You can't. If you go, you'll fuck it up for both of us. I know you don't mean to, but you will. If you go and fuck it up, they'll take me anyway. It has to be me."

Isis didn't protest, and Jere didn't know how. He knew Wren was right, but he also knew that Wren had so much more to lose.

Wren continued addressing Isis. "You need to stay here and help Jere. Help him get me back. I'm counting on both of you."

Isis nodded silently, accepting the truth in a way that only those from a slave state seemed able to do. Jere just stood there dumbfounded and speechless.

Wren came over to him, pulling him close and holding him tight. "This isn't goodbye," he promised.

"I'll burn this entire fucking state to the ground if it means getting back to you," he added, his hands warming over Jere's back.

"I love you," Jere managed, but it didn't seem to mean anything. He had failed, somehow, he was incapable of protecting those he loved the most. He watched as Wren turned and walked out the door, where the auditor and police officer took him by an arm on either side and marched him away.

The audit was over. Wren was gone. Jere felt more lost than he had since arriving in Hojer.

Chapter 27
Evaluation

At first, Wren had found the audit more interesting than anything else. It was a strange thing to find interesting, and he acknowledged that, but being asked questions like he mattered was something that he wasn't very used to, especially as a slave.

The questions hadn't even been that uncomfortable; a lot of "yes" or "no" answers, basic facts about what he did, questions about the rules of Hojer and how they should be followed. The man asked him about the small altercation he and Jere had had years ago, when Wren was caught out without a pass, but the auditor seemed content with Wren's answer that his master was busy with a patient and couldn't be bothered to write a pass for a slave. It demonstrated disregard for Wren's safety more than anything else, and the safety of a slave wasn't even worthy of considering in an audit.

The auditor asked all sorts of inane questions about smuggling slaves, and being part of anti-slavery organizations, and things like that. Clearly, whoever had been making complaints about Jere and his mastering abilities had no idea of what was really going on, and just wanted to set him up to get him into trouble. It was nothing more than a ploy to cause problems. The auditor looked bored by the fact that he was even conducting the audit; Wren figured he had somewhere else he wanted to be. The most uncomfortable question he had asked was whether Wren was primarily used for sexual purposes, and Wren could feel himself blushing. The man just shook his head as Wren explained that he also helped in the clinic and kept up around the house. The auditor muttered something about him being as shy as his master, which Wren didn't really understand, but he was glad the man let it go. He had no interest in discussing their sex life.

Right up until the end of the interview, Wren thought that they would pass with flying colors.

And then the auditor had given him a strange look.

"What's your gift, boy?"

"Speed, sir," Wren had answered, calm and content. But the auditor didn't seem to buy it.

"Has that always been your gift?"

Occasionally, when someone was young, they showed signs of multiple gifts. Some people's gifts fluctuated wildly, changing on a daily or even hour basis, but by the time they hit puberty, the gift had usually settled into one solid gift. The chances of having two were so rare as to be almost impossible.

"I had a little variation when I young, sir." Wren had sat and hoped that the line of questioning would stop. He had no desire to discuss his early gifts, and even less desire to discuss the one that had persisted throughout his life.

"Tell me again what gift you have."

"A speed gift, sir."

When they brought Wren to the evaluation facility, the first person he faced was a gift identifier.

"Look this one over," the auditor announced, releasing the hold he'd had on Wren since they left Hojer. "There's something off about his gift. It was in the original notice from the veterinarian, and I can't get a good read about him. See if we can find something to justify our hold on him."

The speed train ride had been miserable; for a few minutes, he still had his mind connection with Jere. He thought he would be able to maintain it, but it was ripped away from him. He knew it wasn't Jere's doing, and he knew he wasn't far enough from his master that the connection had failed, but he wasn't going to risk himself by probing with his own psychic abilities. He could only assume that some other member of the slave agency had interfered, severed the connection, pulled him away from Jere.

"On your knees, slave."

The order was chilling enough to jar Wren back to reality. Looking down at the floor meekly, he knelt in front of the gift identifier, dreading the moment when the man would probe his gift. Would it be different now that he used it more often?

He felt the uncomfortable presence of someone intruding on his energy, exploring, violating. He squirmed, but focused on repressing the firesetting. He had to do it; he had done it for so long.

Jere's mum had detected the firesetting gift almost instantly, and she had described it as "latent" back then. Wren had worked so hard on developing it over the past few years.

"You do have an odd presentation," the gift identifier muttered, taking a few steps closer to Wren. He reached out his hand.

When Wren flinched away, the gift identifier cuffed him in the head. "You should know better than that," he chastised. He didn't seem overly angry, and Wren's slight resistance didn't slow him down at all.

Wren sat silently, tolerating the feeling of the man's hand on his head, strengthening the ability of the identification gift. He tried to remind himself that only the weakest gift identifiers typically worked in these sorts of facilities; rural outlands had few natural resources of that sort, and people from free states who could identify gifts were rarely interested in relocating unless their gift was weak and rather useless. His suspicions were confirmed; while he felt the probe of his gifts, he could tell that the man was confused.

"Is there anything we should know about your gift?" the man asked.

"No, sir," Wren lied. "I have a speed gift. Not even a particularly fast one."

The gift identifier pulled back, and Wren felt an overwhelming sense of relief. Maybe this would be it; maybe they just wanted to evaluate him a little more. The gift identifier stepped into the hallway, not even bothering to close the door behind him.

"Send him for a full medical evaluation in addition to the standard questioning."

Wren's hopes were dashed to nothing when he heard those

words, and he remained kneeling, afraid of what was coming next. In just a few minutes, he was collected by a free person in uniform, one who carried a short stock whip on his belt. Wren waited for a command, but felt himself being pulled up roughly by his arm instead. He fought to keep himself from pulling back.

He was taken into an examination room. A part of him wanted to feel comfortable in the familiar medical setting, but the only comfort he could imagine was being back with Jere, in their own clinic. In any other setting, an examination room promised nothing but pain.

The doctor entered from another room. "Strip," he ordered, not bothering with any of the formalities that Jere would have with any patient.

Wren shuddered. Either the doctor had such an inadequate healing gift that he couldn't even assess Wren's health without visually inspecting him, or the order was meant to be intimidating. Even those with the most limited healing gifts could assess a person's medical condition with just a touch and their psychic gift.

Wren removed his clothes quickly, reminding himself that compliance would get him the best results, as well as trying to show off his healing gift as much as possible. He wanted to make an impression — an impression that clearly conveyed his one and only gift.

The moment he complied, the doctor reached out, grabbing him by the neck. Many healers worked best when they were in contact with their patient's head, but Wren only felt the threat of strangulation. He fought the urge to resist and reminded himself to keep his firesetting gift well within his control. He felt the uncomfortable sensation of someone pushing into his head and he gritted his teeth.

"Don't fight me, boy," the doctor warned, triggering an instant memory of Wren's former owner. "I can make this tolerable, or I can make it hurt like hell."

"I'm sorry, sir," Wren mumbled. Healing had always hurt, from the moment he was taken as a slave until he met Jere. Jere had showed him how to let someone in willingly, how to welcome someone's psychic gift into his own, but how much of that depended on his firesetting gift? It was all mixed up and confused in Wren's mind, and he decided that resisting the psychic intrusion like he always used to was far less dangerous than doing anything that might alert the evaluators about his second gift.

As expected, the searing pain coursed through his body, making his head pound and his stomach churn. He felt dizzy, and he could sense someone else's presence inside of his head. The doctor had made his way in, with no effort made to shield Wren from the discomfort.

He felt the doctor assessing his health, checking his organs, his blood levels, everything inside of him through the healing connection. With Jere, even before they meant anything to one another, the process felt limited, respectful. Now it felt too rough, too deep, like he was being violated. To add to it, the doctor's free hand started moving all over him, feeling inside of his mouth, around his neck, over his stomach and between his legs. Wren squirmed, feeling his temperature start to rise, and he earned himself a rough slap as a result. That only made the firesetting gift more active, and Wren jerked his way out of the healer's grip.

"Stupid whore," the doctor snapped, stepping out into the hallway.

Wren curled into a ball, knowing that the repercussions for resisting would be severe. The healer would probably be too weak for any sort of long-term mind-bind, which meant restraints, and once he was restrained, Wren knew he would have no chance of fighting back.

His predictions were true, and even as he sat there, struggling to hold himself together, two guards came in with heavy chains between them. For once, Wren wished they had just come with medical restraints. He didn't fight them, but he whimpered as the cold metal was pulled tight around his ankles and wrists, then attached to a set of shackles on the wall. He was pinned there, helpless. Even if he could burn his way out, the chains would still hold him. He wondered if they knew.

The doctor began the examination again, rougher this time, and he paid more attention to Wren's responses. Wren closed his eyes, trying to think of Jere, trying to focus enough to hold his firesetting gift at bay. He didn't listen to the doctor's questions, and he didn't respond, even when the man slapped and kicked him. He was silent until he heard a familiar voice in the hallway.

"The male?" Nicolette Arnsdale, the head of the Slave Control, Regulation, and Enforcement Agency, was engaged in a very heated conversation with one of the evaluators. "What did he do? I thought it was the girl we were interested in?"

"Actually, it's both of them, and the doctor. They're starting all sorts of trouble—some sort of altercation with a veterinarian."

"Karmin Barrett?" Arnsdale asked. "She's the head of the Human Veterinary Association. Lately, it seems that they're the only professional organization supporting our agency. We should take her concerns very seriously."

Wren listened, grateful to have something other than his stupid gifts to contend with. He could listen to this information, take it home to Jere, use it for... he didn't know what he would use it for, but he liked the thought of doing something useful. He hoped it could destroy everyone in this building.

"A few community members have submitted anonymous reports of other violations," the doctor continued. "Co-mingling of slave and human medical treatment, poor clinic quality due to the amount of time treating slaves. Dr. Peters is associating with a number of known abolitionists and terrorists, but we don't have anything solid on him, yet. I've been trying to find any sort of marks or identification that would indicate involvement in something like that, but this one seems clean. Of course, those sorts of criminals would never leave evidence that easy. There has to be something, though."

"We'll find it," Arnsdale said. From the sounds of it, she hadn't taken kindly to her last interaction with Jere. Being called out for abusing a child, even a slave child, wasn't something that would be forgotten easily, especially when it happened in public.

The telltale click of high heels announced her entry into the examination room, and Wren prayed that he would pass out quickly. While the healer was still prying around in his mind, Arnsdale walked over to Wren and grabbed his hair, prompting him to open his eyes.

"I always knew there was something off about your master," she hissed. "Nobody fights that hard because he had to take a day off of work. What is his real purpose? Is he a spy? Is he trying to sabotage our agency?"

Wren was stunned. This was about Jere? "No, ma'am. He's a doctor. He's just from Sonova."

Arnsdale was quiet. She glanced at the doctor, who seemed to be monitoring Wren's responses both physically and psychically. "Watch for any irregularities."

The doctor nodded, and Wren felt the psychic energy increasing, jabbing into his mind uncomfortably.

Arnsdale questioned him about everything she knew about; Jere's arrival in Hojer, his relationship with Kieran, quite a bit about Isis, the SRA. Wren was able to answer her questions easily, and after a few had passed, he felt more in control. He could handle this. The woman was grasping at straws, and Wren had years of experience holding back his gift. As the interrogation progressed, he felt himself growing more confident as Arnsdale became more frustrated. She was trying desperately to link Jere with some sort of crime or corruption, but she had nothing to go on.

"What about before Dr. Peters owned you? Were you this much of a problem, then?"

Wren frowned at the change of course. He liked it far better when they were talking about Jere.

"I was owned by Hojer's previous doctor, ma'am. Matthias Burghe."

"I remember Dr. Burghe," the doctor said. "A good man. Never gave us any problems, never tried to bring in garbage ideas like this Dr. Peters is doing. I'm sure he healed his own slave, but he wouldn't have lowered our professional standing by advertising that he would treat slaves in his clinic. Good healers are few and far between; we need to save those resources for the people who truly deserve them."

Wren shuddered at the thought of his last master. The man had tortured him for years. The only kind thing he had ever done was to choose Jere as his successor.

"And how did your new master come to inherit Dr. Burghe's property?"

"I was left in his will, ma'am. Along with the clinic. They knew each other from Sonova University."

"Didn't he die of a heart attack or something?" Arnsdale asked. "Maybe he was poisoned. Did Dr. Peters have anything to do with his death?"

"No, ma'am. It was a fire. My master had no idea until he was summoned by Dr. Burghe's lawyer," Wren supplied, trying to act disinterested. Still, he felt his gift spark at the memory. Jere didn't have anything to do with Burghe's death, but Wren had killed the monster with the same gift that he was trying so hard to hide.

The doctor glanced up at Arnsdale. "That seemed to upset him," he reported.

Arnsdale let a smile cross her face. "A fire? Was it accidental?"

Wren tried to remind himself that the woman had no idea what she was looking for. "I believe so, ma'am. I don't remember much of it. I was burned badly. I nearly died."

"How convenient."

Arnsdale stepped out, and Wren wondered for a moment if she was going to research the case, maybe leave him alone for a while. She returned just a few minutes later with a small cauterizing gun.

"Let's see if we can revive your memories."

Chapter 28

Press Conference

For a few minutes, Jere could do nothing but stare at the door in shock. It was Isis who finally broke him out of his reverie, her sobs catching his attention.

"I'm sorry," she repeated, over and over again. "I should have done better, I should have done better at the audit, or something, my gift—"

"This isn't your fault," he said quietly. He had to be strong, not because it would do him any good, but because Isis didn't need him breaking down and becoming useless, and neither did Wren. If he wanted to fix any of this, he had to take action.

"I need to send a telegraph to Kieran, and I need you to start working on some things for me," he told Isis, hoping she would calm down if she had something to focus on. "There's a book of slave codes and rules in my office. I'd like you to look through it for me, see if there is anything that can help us out. Keep an eye out too for anything related to slaves being seized, or evaluations, or—"

"I'll just memorize it," Isis muttered, her voice still shaky. "That way, you can ask me anything you need."

Jere nodded. "We're gonna get him back," he promised. "And I don't care what happens to Hojer while I do."

Jere went to the clinic and treated the patients who were waiting there as quickly as possible. He didn't blame them, but they were keeping him from Wren. When he had cleared the waiting room, he put out the "emergencies only" sign. It was his job to keep them alive, but he wasn't about to be wasting time on wellness checks and colds.

As soon as the clinic was under control, he sent his telegraph and began reviewing as much information as possible about Arona's healthcare laws and The Slavery Reform Act. He had been hesitant to get involved, but if they dared to take Wren from him, he wasn't afraid to fight back. He had no greater goal than to see something about this state's legal system collapse.

Kieran arrived the next morning looking almost as distraught as Jere felt.

"I'm in," he announced, before even saying hello. "I want in on the SRA. Make me your speaker, make me your example."

Kieran was clearly surprised, but she nodded. "As a whole, it's still receiving sort of shaky acceptance. There's a lot of unhappiness that the healthcare part is tied up with other slave acts. It's a little too conservative for the passionate anti-slavery activists, but still too radical for the really pro-slavery ones, so that's kind of a problem. We're catching the middle, but the edges are kind of unhappy on either side. Which is stupid, because the anti-slavery types should see that this is progress!"

"I remember when you first started getting interested in this, you were ready to just burn down the house of any and every slave-owner. That's where I'm at, now. I want Hojer to realize that passing the SRA is in their very best interest."

"It will mean a lot to people to see you supporting this. Now you're not just the outlander doctor, you're one of them. You're having your slaves, your life, your livelihood messed with. This makes you the perfect example — I just wish that it was different, for Wren's sake."

"I plan to do more than support it," Jere muttered, unwilling and unable to even think about Wren at the moment. He would collapse if he did. "Should I be worried about my safety? Or Isis's? I assume Wren is safe wherever he's being kept."

Kieran gave him a nervous look.

"What?" Jere demanded.

"I got in touch with an inside contact we have in the slave agency," Kieran said, apologetic. "They're not just keeping him there... they're questioning him, Jere. Probably more. I'm not sure about the details —"

Jere blinked back the tears that he could feel in his eyes. "All the more reason to move quickly."

"They won't kill him. He's a bargaining tool."

Jere shuddered. They would probably do everything *but* kill him. He couldn't think about it. "What about townspeople? Me and Isis?"

"Jere, if they hurt you, they're losing their doctor. After what those guys did to Wren while you were gone? I'd be worried, but I'd still do it. They're not just angry, they're afraid. I really think that Hojer's need for a doctor is going to outweigh the threats of having a potential abolitionist in the town."

"Have there been any sorts of attacks?" Jere asked. "I mean, aside from Wren. Any documented ones on people who are actually involved."

Kieran shook her head. "Right now, it's protests against big businesses, industries, politicians. They have the most influence in things like this. They influence the elections, they influence the way that the population thinks. Small players like yourself are being left out of it. This sort of legislation is happening in bigger states than Arona. Remember, something happens to you and all these people in Hojer lose a doctor—not what anyone wants in case there really is a disease risk in the future. Nobody from here is going to push that issue; at least, they haven't anywhere else. I'd keep a close eye on Isis, but I doubt she's going anywhere, anyway."

Isis just nodded. She had made it very clear that she wasn't going out that door or away from Jere in any circumstances.

"Do you know how to make this public?" Jere asked.

Kieran nodded. She began doing what she did best, organizing the best way to create chaos and promote her "cause." This time, it was Jere's cause as well. And he had a surprise planned for his loyal patients.

The next day, Jere made his first public appearance to promote The Slavery Reform Act.

Isis knelt on the floor next to the podium, assuming her rightful place behind and below her master. A few feet of leather connected them, and for once, it didn't bother Jere. Isis was even tolerating it surprisingly well—from the moment Kieran suggested that having a slave present would not only increase his sympathy, but make sure Isis was safe while Jere was out of the house, Isis had been accepting of the choice. The fact that Jere was sending off enough psychic energy to make strangers on the street flinch helped as well.

Jere looked out at the crowd that had gathered for the speech Kieran had arranged in just a matter of hours. He recognized most of the faces. He had treated most of these people. Those from out of town were easy to identify, they banded together, often with signs or nametags indicating where they were from or what organization they were associated with. The Human Veterinary Association was strongly represented, but Barrett was nowhere in sight.

"My name is Jeremy Peters. As most of you know, I'm a healer—I've met most of you, healed you, treated your wounds, kept you healthy. I'm standing here to make sure you continue to be healthy."

He had the attention of the crowd, at least for now. He wondered how many thought he was going to tell them that there was a new infectious disease in their town. He considered doing so, even though it would be a lie.

"For now, you are safe. But the 'rotting disease' is spreading. As Hojer's sole doctor, my job is to keep you safe. All of you. And that includes the slave population."

There was a quiet rumble from the crowd as participants aired their many grievances on the subject. One especially loud voice called out "*Lacklers* aren't people!" The slur against slaves was impolite, but all of the discussions on the controversial topic devolved to this level rather quickly.

"Whether slaves are 'people' or not is a matter of philosophy, not a matter of medicine," Jere answered, his tone of voice as carefully guarded as his emotions were.

"Nobody here has that disease!" another audience member protested. "If a slave gets it, we can just shoot it, anyway."

"And risk putting contaminated blood into the air?" Jere reminded the audience, looking appalled. "We don't know how this disease spreads, and we won't know how future diseases will spread, either. By mandating proper medical care, we can fight this if — or when — it comes to our town. It's only a speed train ride away."

"So do your job!" someone called out.

Jere smiled at the invitation. "That is exactly what I am doing. I'm here to let you know that the passage of the SRA is vital to Hojer's continuing health. But you should know that already. Just in case you don't, I'd like to make it very clear — providing subpar treatment to any part of the community places you all at risk. I'm making it my mission to reduce that risk by implementing some new safety measures."

The crowd listened, attentive. The fact that his clinic had been running on "emergencies only" for the past two days already had their attention. "As many of you know, the state agency has revoked my ability to treat slaves at my clinic — but it has not revoked my ability to treat free people. However, this places everyone at increased risk. To ensure safety, there will be additional screening procedures for all patients. The current partial closure is a safety precaution as I review the best treatment methods for a epidemic. When I reopen on a full-time basis, I will have established a quarantine area and a new set of safety precautions. I, or my assistant, will be taking information about your travel history, the slaves you own, and any symptoms. Everyone will be subject to additional health screenings. Those of you who have untreated slaves, or who have traveled recently may be quarantined away from the other patients. Unfortunately, this will take considerably more time and resources."

"Any healer can provide good enough treatment for a slave!" one of the members of the Human Veterinary Association called out. "We can stop disease just perfectly."

Jere set his jaw. "Medical research has proven otherwise. I'd be happy to provide you with some of that research. But I am not just standing here as a medical professional. I am standing united with you as a slaveowner and a business owner."

Jere looked down at his note cards for a moment, trying to hold back the tears that threatened to fall at the thought of Wren. "Half of my business has been shut down. My slave was seized yesterday, through no fault of my own. Nobody has told me any specific crime, or timeframe in which I can expect him back or any details other than that he's being 'evaluated.' I know many of you spend significant amounts of money on your slaves, and for good reason – they are valuable assets. The current regulatory agency, however, feels it is their right to seize these assets, at any time, without documentation or warning. Even if you don't care about healthcare, do you care about your property and privacy?"

Even the dissenters went quiet at this, looking outraged.

"They can't just take our slaves!" someone protested.

"That's private property!" another agreed.

"They absolutely can," Jere said quietly. "The Slavery Reform Act includes significant protections for slaveowners as well. The restructuring of the current Slave Control, Regulation, and Enforcement agency into the Slave Regulation Board will include a number of new protections for slaveowners, one of which includes an immediate halt on unreasonable or warrantless investigations. Each citizen is responsible for taking the appropriate care of their slaves, and The Slavery Reform Act is designed to increase participation and assistance in complying with new regulations. It isn't trying to stop slavery, it's trying to save our system."

"What do you get out of this?" someone challenged.

Jere laughed, a cruel sound that was so unusual coming from him. He wanted to say that he got the satisfaction of bringing this backwards-ass shithole into the modern world, but he knew that wouldn't be an acceptable answer.

"Well, I get half my business back in the clinic, for one," he said, pretending to playful. "Someone else is making decisions about how you can treat your property – and, how slave-related business can be run. With one assistant seized and another's physical mobility limited by yet another restriction, I doubt the medical clinic will be running very efficiently at all for a while. Add in the additional health screenings... I'm going to be very busy."

"I've already waited two days to get a damn appointment!" someone yelled.

"And I am sincerely sorry about that," Jere said. "But medical safety is paramount. If the SRA passes, you might see your clinic functioning properly again. I want nothing more than that. But I'm not willing to sacrifice safety for efficiency. When I moved here from Sonova, I grew to understand that owning slaves was a right, a way of life, and I wanted to embrace that mentality. Now, I wonder if it's just another way for your lawmakers to exercise their control over your lives. I met with a talent agency not long ago. I don't want to leave Hojer; it's become more of a home to me than anywhere else in the world. But if I can't trust that my possessions and my business will be safe under the current laws, I can't remain here. I am certain that many of you would feel the same if it were your slaves being seized, your businesses being shut down. I believe in Hojer, but not like this."

The speech continued for a while, with a question and answer session that Jere hit hard on. He had some supporters because of his position, but the fact that he had actually lost one of his slaves to the agency that many already saw as overreaching won him considerable support. Of course, there were plenty who still opposed him, who still opposed the SRA based on all of the slavery related things that it encompassed, but Jere had made quite an impression. Someone even offered to start a petition to free Wren, and no matter how futile Jere thought it was, he was pleased with the support.

Once he finished with the press conference, he returned to the clinic and started implementing the safety plans he had discussed. He set up separate exam rooms, quarantine areas, and dragged some of the chairs from his house into the waiting area to seat the additional overflow patients. His average exam times jumped from twenty minutes to almost an hour, and the questions he asked irritated and enraged his patients. At the end of the day, he chose the most severe patients to treat and sent the rest home, encouraging them to try again in the morning or to take a speed train to one of the emergency clinics. He was frustrated and out of options, but so were the citizens of Hojer.

Chapter 29
Summoned

After the press conference, Jere was appalled with himself. As much as his words had been inspired and passionate, he was going against every medical ethic he had ever believed in. He had played every card he thought possible in his desperate attempt to push the regulation agency, to get Wren back. Fighting corruption with corruption. He was mortified when he saw the newspapers over the next few days, prominently displaying his decisions and the comments criticizing the delays at the clinic.

To add to the shame, Paltrek came over the following day, laughing and congratulating him.

"Looks like you finally came to your senses, doc," he teased. "Slavery—the future of Hojer!"

Jere just shook his head. "I said that people shouldn't be shot because it would spread a disease that might not even spread that way. I called Wren an asset! I'm turning patients away and subjecting them to overpriced procedures to prove a point!"

"They're getting your message," Paltrek reminded him. "That's all you could hope for."

"I hope for Wren to come back unharmed," Jere muttered. He still could barely bring himself to think of his lover, much less say his name. Only four days had passed since he had been taken, but for Jere, they felt like months. He had pestered Kieran incessantly for information, but all he could get out of her was that Wren was alive and hadn't revealed anything incriminating. She wouldn't answer his question of whether he was being tortured, but Jere knew that meant he was. If he thought he had a chance, he'd storm every

243

state facility until he found him.

"Right now, they'd be complete idiots to do anything else," Paltrek tried to reassure him. "You're basically going around calling the current agency slave-snatching idiots — they do anything permanent to Wren, they're confirming it. That's riot level bullshit, right there. People are already angry about their favorite doctor suffering under the evil state's restrictions. All they need is a little push."

"I guess. I don't care what happens as long as I get Wren back. If this passes, he won't ever have to worry about being caged in a veterinary clinic like an animal again. Or beaten in public. After all, contaminated blood or sweat or tears could infect free people."

"I like the part about the inter-state agreement," Paltrek decided. "Right now, it's a goddamned process. Stupid licensing and testing to take slaves out of state. It's ridiculous. Pay a fee, sure, but to have to go someplace and have things tested? Screw that. We're supposed to be a united country, not a bunch of... separate ones."

Jere nodded. Paltrek wasn't exactly the most eloquent political speaker, but he made a point pretty well.

"You're sure you wouldn't want to help us speak or promote things?" Jere asked, hopeful as ever. He knew that people would receive Paltrek's frank, slaveowner-centric views far more easily than the views of an outlander, and he would take any help he could get in his crusade against the people who had stolen his partner. "You have more sway than I do, being from here and all."

"Have you lost your mind? I wouldn't be caught dead doing anti-slavery bullshit like that. Besides, my father has a professional team on the issue already."

Jere was surprised. "He's supporting it, then?"

Paltrek laughed. "His business is supporting it. His personal views are that the SRA is a waste of time and an exercise in soft-hearted idiocy, as he put it. But professionally, he's started paying a lot more attention to international investments. He doesn't want to be left behind, and he has some partners pressuring him to get with the times. He's rich enough that he'll continue to do whatever the hell he wants, but Wysocka Enterprises is formally in support of the election candidates who support the SRA. He's specifically told me to stay away from anything that might 'muck it up,' including saying anything in public. Thinks I'll be too much of a pushover and say something about the actual slaves."

"Thanks for letting me know," Jere said. The support of a major financial figure was fantastic. Wysocka Enterprises had quite a bit of influence on the public and politics. "But, if you ever change your mind, the pushover side would be happy to have you."

"Yeah, and get kicked out of my father's house and be disinherited?" Paltrek reminded him. "No thanks. Besides, I don't really have the urge to hang around Kieran. She's weird. Always has been. I figure the other anti-slavery people are like that, too."

"She has some choice things to say about you, too," Jere pointed out. He found it rather strange that his two closest friends outside of the house more or less hated each other, but he was getting good at juggling the relationships.

"I'm sure," Paltrek said. "I hang out with you already, and I'm already getting enough shit for that. Now that you're not new and interesting anymore, the only thing you've got going for you socially is that you're a doctor, and a damn good one, and so you kind of get a pass on being all weird and radical and promoting stupid shit like this. I like you, personally, but most other people are suspicious. They can't tell if you're really invested in Hojer's safety, or if you're really just supporting the SRA. My father said that he respects your business sense and healing abilities, but nothing else."

Jere dismissed it. He wasn't exactly concerned with what Paltrek's father thought of him personally; his public and financial endorsement of a similar cause was enough. The man's wealth didn't impress him at all; he might be a big deal here in Hojer, but Jere had seen the truly rich and extravagant while living in Sonova, and they made the Wysocka family look like commoners.

"Then again, he values his business sense more than anything else, including me, and maybe including Annika, so I guess that's not all that bad," Paltrek mused. "You can be in Daddy's good graces, even if I can't."

Jere didn't want to be in the good graces of a man like that. He had heard enough stories of how Paltrek, senior, treated his family and slaves to know that he wanted to be nothing like the man, ever.

"I'd watch my back if I were you," Paltrek mentioned. "A lot of people agree with you, at least on the slaveowner protection bits, but plenty just see it as an abolitionist move, which we all know it is."

It was a risk; this sort of action put them prominently in the spotlight; worse, against the popular view of how to treat slaves. It was potentially dangerous.

"I don't think anyone will do anything," Jere decided. "As of now, I'm still maintaining my image as the town's doctor. After all, I should be interested in health, and this is being billed, largely, as a healthcare reform. So, if I just stick to that idea, I think I'll be fine. The current regulation agency isn't pleased with me, but they weren't before. Let them be angry."

As they spoke, they were interrupted by a knock on the door. As Jere had forbidden Isis to go anywhere near the door in case of any sort of danger, he got up to answer it himself, his heart racing when he saw a speed messenger.

It could be a notice to come and retrieve Wren, or it could be something terrible.

When the messenger waited, Jere opened the letter and read it over quickly. When he finished, his heart was still racing, but more from uncertainty than anything else.

The president of Arona had summoned him for a meeting.

"Sir, do you have a reply for President Clemente?" the slave prompted. "He's eager to set up a meeting as quickly as possible."

Jere nodded, still staring at the letter. There was no indication of why Jere was being summoned, or what the outcome might be, or why the man who had ignored his request to spare Isis from the ordeal she faced last year was suddenly so interested in his life. "When should I come?"

The slave gave him an apologetic look. "President Clemente would like to see you as soon as possible, sir."

"He means right fucking now," Paltrek interpreted. "It seems you've made an impression. Why don't you go ahead and go, I'll make sure everything here is taken care of."

Jere gave him a curious look. The only thing to really "take care of" was Isis, and he didn't think Paltrek would care.

"Jeremy, you're a target," Paltrek reminded him. "I'll make sure your house and your little girl are safe. I know you'd do the same."

Jere nodded, relieved that he could trust his friend. Isis wasn't pleased with the situation, but Jere convinced her to just stay quietly in her room, a solution she and Paltrek both supported. He changed out of his work clothes and into something nicer, something that seemed more appropriate for a meeting with the leader of Arona. For as many times as he had come into contact with the man, they had never spoken or been formally introduced.

His speed train ticket was already purchased, which made him wonder just how certain the president was that he was going to respond. If he hadn't, would there have been some sort of threat? Or was the man just that sure of Jere's desperation. In any case, he arrived at the Capitol building quickly, and the same slave who had delivered the letter escorted Jere to an office. He walked in hesitantly, but determined to get some sort of results.

"Doctor Peters," the president introduced himself. "I'm Eldred Clemente. The president of Arona. I'm very pleased to meet you."

Jere shook his hand and sat down, but didn't speak. He had done enough speaking yesterday; he had nothing to say unless it was for a damn good reason.

"You created quite a stir with your speech last night. My office hasn't received this many inquiries since I took this position. I don't quite know what to do with it."

"Well, you've ignored them in the past," Jere reminded him, bitter.

President Clemente nodded. "The girl," he recalled.

They were silent for a moment, staring at one another. Jere wondered if the president knew where Wren was, knew what was being done to him. He wondered if he knew that Jere had denied pain relief to his daughter last winter. He wondered if any of it mattered.

"Is there a real threat of disease?"

"Yes. It can come, and if it's not this one, it will be another. If it's not halted, it could wipe out the entire town. It's happened before. I could provide research—"

"Don't bother." The president gave Jere a warning look. "We've received hundreds of complaints about the functioning of your clinic over the past few days. Do you really think that inconveniencing your patients is an appropriate way to retaliate? You have a job here, Dr. Peters."

"Yes. I do. My job is to take appropriate measures to ensure the safety of Hojer's residents. That includes mandating additional screenings and health checks. It's in the state's codes, and it's in my contract with the town of Hojer."

"This has nothing to do with safety!"

Jere smiled. He had done his research. "Other cities have implemented similar restrictions. I am well within my rights to run my clinic as I please. You're always welcome to hire additional doctors — maybe that's what's necessary."

The president shook his head and looked at Jere, defeated. "What are the chances of another healer coming to Hojer? You've gone to other states and called it a 'magnet for disease.' You've openly announced that business is so bad here that you are looking for other jobs. If that disease comes to Hojer, would any other healer even take your position?"

Jere scoffed. He could be honest with this answer. "The chances of another healer taking my position in Hojer are slim on its best days. The best training clinics are in free states. People are progressive there. Nobody of quality wants to come to a rural town like this and take on this much responsibility and isolation. If an outbreak occurred, that number would reduce drastically."

The president scowled. "Is this all a show? A scare tactic? Would you even be able to heal them?"

"I'd do a hell of a lot better than anyone else around here," Jere snapped. He wondered if he should hold his tongue, but he didn't care anymore. If Wren wasn't returned, he would leave, and he'd take Isis with him. Even if Wren did return, a part of him wanted to leave, move to another slave state. He'd let Hojer flail until they found a doctor, and he'd hope that they never would.

"I'm facing significant pressure from both sides, Dr. Peters," the president revealed. "Traditionalists hate the SRA and won't re-elect someone who supports it. Progressives love it and won't re-elect someone who doesn't. It's the people in the middle I need to appeal to, and most of them don't care about politics or values or anything. They want to know that they'll be safe, that they are doing the right thing. You're an attractive public figure. You're quiet about almost everything, so people think that anything you say is important. You're more educated than most people here, and they realize that. You've upset my state, called out the slave agency, and now you're not even healing people in a timely manner."

"I'm drawing attention to many major problems."

"I agree that the current Slave Control, Regulation, and Enforcement Agency has grown far beyond their intended power, and should be replaced with the Slave Regulation Board, as indicated in the SRA. You made a strong argument for why this SRA should matter to Arona, and I can't disagree with it."

"Why?" Jere spat out. "You've never challenged any of their decisions before."

"No, I haven't. In the past, the majority of the population supported the agency; if I wanted to stay on the right side of my people, I needed to go along. But things are changing. Just in the past few hours, I've received a stack of telegraphs from individuals and organizations demanding that I take action against the Slave Control, Regulation, and Enforcement Agency. I've received another stack panicking about disease and clinic availability. And I received a very lucrative offer of campaign support for my elections, contingent upon my support of The Slavery Reform Act."

Jere had to force himself not to smile. Mr. Wysocka must have offered the president a significant sum to sway him this quickly. For the first time in his life, Jere appreciated the level of political corruption that could go unchecked in places like this.

"As president, I am being held accountable for all of the problems that are occurring. I need to change that, or my term will certainly end. Taking a very public stand on this issue puts me in a good position in the future. I'm hoping that my active involvement will push the issue in my favor."

"As a supporter of the SRA myself, I would appreciate that involvement," Jere said, resisting the urge to ask why he was hearing this. He assumed that Arona's leader would tell him soon enough.

"I plan to publicly announce my support for The Slavery Reform Act today," President Clemente said. "I would like to tell the people of Hojer that consultation with our experienced doctor helped to push me in the scientifically sound direction, and that you will be helping to advise my team on matters in the future."

"Why me?" Jere asked. Surely, there were other activists the president could have supported, other households he could have helped. He could have hired anyone with a pattern analysis gift to do research, even someone as horrible as Annika could handle basic reporting of facts.

"You're convenient," the president said. "You're highly visible. You're one of my biggest problems, but I can't just get rid of you. And you have significant motivation to go along with my requests."

Jere wasn't sure whether that was a threat or just an observation. He figured it was a little of both.

"You understand the value of working from a conservative, scientific perspective. You can promote evidence over emotion. I suspect that will be the best route to take as we proceed."

"We?"

The president sighed. "You will accompany me to deliver the news to the public. You have considerable sway over this community and I want to take advantage of that. It benefits you quite a bit, so I can't see any reason why you would refuse."

Aside from the fact that he had basically just threatened Wren and Isis, Jere didn't either. "I'll be happy to provide whatever you need."

Clemente smiled. He didn't look happy; he looked accomplished. "I also wanted to inform you that I will be arranging for the release of your male slave. By the time you leave this office, he should be ready to return home with you."

Jere stared at him in shock, not certain whether he believed it or not. After a moment, the president slid a piece of paper over toward him. It was a presidential pardon, the likes of which Jere had sought last year, but had been denied. It freed him and Wren from any accusations, and stated that the seizure and subsequent evaluation had been made in error.

"I don't understand."

President Clemente gave Jere a tired look. "I know what you did to my daughter last winter," he said. He should have been angry, but he just sounded tired.

Jere waited, nervous. If the man knew what he had done, how and why was he helping him?

The president slid over a photograph of Wren, tightly restrained to a table, covered in cuts, bruises, and burns. His eyes were only half-open, but Jere could see the pain, the distant look in his eyes. He hadn't seen Wren look that way since he had first arrived in Hojer. He grabbed the photograph, crumpled it, and threw it across the room.

"If you mention a word of this to anyone, or if you try to leave before this election is over, I'll revoke that order and put your little pet back into the hell he's been in for the past few days. Normally, I would have a problem exploiting you like that, but given your history with my family, I see it as putting us on equal footing."

Jere nodded, silent. He had never planned for his act of rebellion to have such far-reaching consequences when he did it last year, and he certainly never thought it would end well for him or Wren if he was found out. He still wasn't sure that it was working out well.

"As far as anyone is concerned, I believe that the SRA is right for Arona," President Clemente explained. "I think that the healthcare reform is in Arona's best interest, and I am siding with the progressive political parties that are most likely to keep me in office into the future. The Slave Control, Regulation, and Enforcement Agency is going far past their reach; as the president of Arona, I am taking the control back from them to prove a point and show Arona's citizens just how committed I am to helping them maintain their property rights. I am overruling their decision to engage in harassment, which is why I'm releasing your slave and granting you and your household amnesty for the remainder of the election period."

Jere nodded, uncertain of what to say in response. Thanking the man seemed insincere, since he had no idea how many strings this favor would come attached with.

"Your speed train ticket to the evaluation facility has already been purchased; it leaves in twenty minutes. You should leave now so you're not delayed. My press team will stop by your clinic later today; I think that would be a perfect place to announce the latest news. You will also announce that you have found a way to speed up these exams—keep your additional procedures if you must, but stop the slowdown. Stop turning patients away."

Jere was on his feet immediately, eager to put things in motion. He wanted Wren back in his arms more than he wanted almost anything else in the world. As he turned to leave, he was stopped by a final statement from the president.

"I've put in a recommendation regarding the state of your clinic. It should be cleared for the treatment of slaves in just a few days. After all, Hojer will need a place to treat slaves if the SRA passes."

"Thank you," Jere said, pausing for a moment to contemplate the situation before dashing out the door.

He was finally going to retrieve Wren.

Chapter 30
Reinstated

Wren had no idea how long he was interrogated for. There were no windows to judge night or day, and the people just kept hurting him, asking him questions.

At first he thought the cauterizing gun would only be a threat, but he soon found out that the threat was real. So were the beatings he got for fighting against the restraints, for screaming, for banging his head against the wall that he was restrained to.

He managed to knock himself unconscious once, but after that, they made sure there was something padding the back of his head.

They mostly asked about Jere, about the anti-slavery activists. At some point, Wren realized that drawing his torturers down the wrong path would be the best way to keep them away from his real problem, his cursed gift, the damned firesetting that had done nothing but plague him with problems since he was taken. He distracted himself from the pain by creating elaborate stories, tales of deception and plots against the state, making sure that all of them were so unbelievably false that even the slightest investigation would disprove them. His efforts only served to infuriate Arnsdale more, as she continued to seek the answers to her question.

What was Jere doing in Hojer?

Who was behind his actions?

Why were they trying to destroy the fabric of society?

Wren felt some satisfaction at knowing that the woman was so far off in her assessment; she was paranoid about her position, her agency, when what she should have been focusing on was Wren's gift. In between torture, when Wren was left alone to suffer, he fantasized about just how fun it would be to burn the place to the ground, to inflict wounds on them like they had on him. They knew his gift was doing *something* when they burned him, but as far as the healer could tell, his speed gift was simply speeding up his heart rate and increasing his temperature. Wren let them believe it, even as he held the firesetting gift hostage inside of his own body, knowing it would betray him if he dared to let it escape.

A part of him simply thought Jere would rescue him. He would get help from Kieran, or pay someone off, or maybe make good on all those healer threats he had made and murder his way through the evaluation facility, but Jere never came. It was those moments when he started to doubt his partner that it became hardest to control his gift, even harder than when they burned the most sensitive parts on his body in an attempt to get him to confess to something that didn't even exist. Arnsdale told him that Jere was promoting the SRA, that he had met with talent scouts who would set him up with a more lucrative job in another state.

Wren didn't want to believe it, but she shoved the new reports in his face, forcing him to read the quotes that Jere had made, the ones that showed how little he cared about the petty needs of a community that violated his rights, the ones that reminded everyone how overqualified he was for the position, how he found slavery "repellant," and "an invitation for disease." Arnsdale showed him the list of places where Jere was supposedly looking for work, including a number of states without slavery.

Slowly she convinced him that Jere had given up on Wren already and moved on to his real passion—ending slavery, even at the cost of ridding the world of slaves by euthanizing them all. It didn't make sense at first, but as his mind twisted, he started to believe it. After days of no sleep, food, or rest, he trusted nothing other than his desperate instinct to hide his firesetting gift.

When the torture stopped, he assumed they were just figuring out what to do with him next.

"You're a mess," a new doctor stated, shaking her head. "I can't believe this is what I come in to."

Wren had long since stopped replying. He waited for the pain, the psychic jolt, whatever the new doctor was going to do to him.

They had gone through three already, wasting valuable psychic energy hurting and healing him while monitoring his response.

This one didn't seem interested in hurting, though. In just a few minutes, Wren was amazed to feel the burns healing, the welts that covered his body closing up, the nausea and dehydration subsiding. Once the ringing in his ears stopped, he could hear Arnsdale ranting about something in the hallway, but he couldn't hear what it was.

"What are you going to do to me?" he asked the new doctor. He was so tired, but he knew that if he gave up completely his gift would betray him somehow.

"Executive order," the doctor informed him. "I've only got a few more minutes to make you presentable."

The words didn't make sense, and Wren didn't try to make them. Perhaps they were going to put him on display somewhere, take him to a research facility, publicly execute him. He had heard of worse.

The new doctor not only gave him his clothes back, she helped to dress him as well. Wren just stood there staring at her, confused, as she guided his limbs roughly through the holes. When she finished, she tried to balance him on his feet, but he sagged. He was simply too weak; she hadn't healed him well enough in such a short time, and his body was drained.

The next raised voice he heard was Jere's, and Wren wasn't sure whether to be excited or terrified. Had any of the things that Arnsdale said been true? Was Jere really just interested in promoting some cause? It didn't make sense, but then, why hadn't Jere wanted him to have the chance to be free? Why had he let Wren go without a fight, and why had he spent all of his time on some stupid fucking SRA instead of attending the real problem—the fact that Wren was being tortured.

Those doubts faded the second that Jere came into the room, pushing past the guards and reaching out psychically, probing for Wren's energy. Wren felt Jere in the room and wanted to welcome him, but the lingering doubts gave him pause. He just wasn't sure what was real and what wasn't.

"Wren," Jere said the moment he saw him, the relief evident on his face. "Shit, what did they do to you?"

Wren didn't answer. He couldn't. He had been so quiet that he almost forgot how to speak.

Jere rushed over to him, shoving away the doctor who was still trying unsuccessfully to get Wren on his feet. In a moment, Jere's arms were around him, and before Wren even had the chance to try and protest, he felt the familiar presence of Jere's healing gift filling him, renewing his energy, giving him the strength to stand up on his own. When he was strong enough, he pulled away, earning him a very confused look from Jere.

"I want to go home," Wren said, breaking into tears as he fought to speak. He didn't know whether Jere had abandoned him or betrayed him; all he knew was that Jere was with him and he was fixing everything properly. It only made Wren feel weaker.

The trip out of the evaluation facility was a blur, as was the short walk to the speed train station. It wasn't until they were safely hidden inside of a private train car with the door closed that anything started to make sense. Jere told him about the SRA, the threats he had made to leave Hojer, the unexpected support from the business community in both Hojer and the surrounding towns in Arona. He told him about the meeting with President Clemente, the one that resulted in Wren's release and the reopening of the clinic. Wren was glad that it resulted in his release, but a part of him resented Jere for how busy he had been—doing everything but saving Wren. But then, wasn't that what Jere had accomplished anyway? Wren went along with it, accepting his master's decisions.

"I'm so sorry, love," Jere said over and over again. "I never should have let them take you. I never should have let them come anywhere near you. Are you sure you're okay? When I started healing you, there were so many things wrong, things they only healed on the surface. What did they do to you? Why did they hurt you?"

It didn't matter, but Wren answered anyway, his voice raspy and dull. "They tried to make me confess to things you never did in the first place. They thought you were some sort of spy, some sort of planted weapon. They have no idea that it's me who's wrong. They had no idea about the gift. They still don't. Even when they burned me, I hid it. I kept waiting, but you never came."

"I couldn't," Jere admitted. "I didn't know where you were, I didn't know what they were doing to you."

"So you just decided to get involved with the SRA? Maybe if you had stayed out of it like we agreed to, they wouldn't have hurt me so much!"

Jere was silent for a moment. Even though they had yet to connect through the mind connection, Wren could tell that Jere was suffering from guilt. It didn't make things any less fuzzy or confusing.

"I had nothing else that I could do," Jere said. "I tried... there were no other avenues. I arranged that press conference because I was furious, because if they were going to ruin my life and yours, I was going to make damn sure that everyone in Hojer knew that they were doing it. I wasn't going to go down without a fight, but I don't know *how* to fight. That was the best I could do."

Wren shook his head. He didn't know what he expected Jere to do, either, but that certainly hadn't been it.

"That's what caught President Clemente's attention," Jere reminded him. "I'm not some sort of vigilante, I don't have that much going for me... I save lives, I'm good at it, and that was the only thing I had to use against them. I had to make it bigger than you or even the clinic. I had to pretend to be cold, uninvolved, act like this was a business decision, not a personal one. That's what they understand. All they understand is pain, death, money. They have no idea how much I love you."

"I just need to sleep," Wren mumbled, cuddling up to the back of the speed train seat. When he felt Jere's fingers running across his leg, he jumped and jerked away. Jere looked at him with a mix of horror and what Wren hoped wasn't anger.

"I'm sorry," Wren whimpered. He just couldn't stand the touch, not yet.

Jere looked crushed, but he nodded. "Take your time," he said. "I'm here whenever you want me. To talk, to heal you, to put the mind connection back. Or not. You do what you need to do."

Wren needed to sleep, and the short speed train ride just left him craving more. The walk back to the house was silent, and it was all Wren could do to tolerate Isis's joy when he returned. Paltrek was there, babysitting, from what Wren could tell, and Wren had no idea whose life he was returning to. He made his way down the hall, but the thought of climbing into a bed that he shared with Jere in the same room where he once burned his master to death turned his stomach. He made his way into what was once his bedroom, the one that was now used for storage of off-season clothes, and climbed under the covers like he could hide there.

Chapter 31
Shaken Up

Wren wished that the change of setting made him more comfortable, but it seemed unnatural. Maybe this was officially his room, but the only time he had ever really spent in here was when he and Jere were fighting. He hadn't even fallen asleep before Jere came in, and a part of him wondered if Jere was really going to force something on him, touch, healing, anything.

"I've mixed up some Crucial Care and brought tea," Jere said, avoiding eye contact even once Wren looked up at him. "And there's some water here. I'm so sorry, Wren... there was nothing else I could do."

Wren just nodded, looking at the beverages with disgust. He would drink them later, he knew it, but he'd rather not do it while Jere was staring at him. It was so typical of Jere to try to doctor him; it was how Jere always dealt with conflict. In a way, it was comforting.

He slept through that night and the better part of the next day, vaguely aware that there were people gathering outside, that Jere was away from him. He woke only to drink the vile healing beverages and use the bathroom before collapsing again. He wished the tea was still warm, but when he thought about using his firesetting gift to warm it, the burns that were still healing inside of his body seemed to ache again and he thought better of it.

When he finally woke, it was growing dark outside. He made his way to the kitchen, found some food, and glanced at the pile of mail that was building up in the spot where they always set it. He scoured through it until he found the newspapers from the past few

259

days, reading in fascination about Jere's endeavor into the political field. To anyone else, Jere's speech might have looked planned, but Wren could tell that much of it was anger, fury even. He had thrown a full-blow fit when Wren was seized, and he had let it become public on purpose. From the looks of it, plenty of people had been swayed.

As he started to feel better, he realized just how quickly and effectively his reasoning had been tampered with. He had been trying so hard to protect his firesetting gift that he had let himself bleed dry. He knew how much Jere hated causing problems or even being noticed in public. He had done both to get Wren back.

Isis and Jere came in from the clinic, chatting about the massive surge of clients they had gotten since they were allowed to treat slaves again. From the sounds of it, everyone in Hojer had simply been waiting, hoping that Jere's ability to treat slaves would be restored. Wren couldn't help smiling; Jere was really at his best when he was healing.

"You're awake," Jere noticed, a smile spreading across his face.

"I'll give you guys some time alone," Isis suggested. "Let you guys get all the sappy shit out of the way without me."

For a moment, everything seemed normal. Wren laughed, nodding his thanks to Isis as she made her exit. But that left him alone with Jere, and he still couldn't forgive him for everything.

"Are you all right?"

Wren didn't know how to answer. "No," he said, honest, but then he shook his head. "Yes... I mean... I'm not dying or anything, Jere. I'm not about to have some sort of breakdown. But I'm not all right, and I need you to heal me, but it makes my skin crawl when you touch me. It hurts."

Jere nodded. "Part of that is the injuries that aren't healed under your skin. The rest... I don't know everything they did to you, but I have an idea."

"So it's in my head."

"Doesn't make it any less real."

Wren was willing to try to rid himself of the real part though. "Heal me. And do it right—I don't even care if it hurts. I know it can hurt to heal over a bad healing job. Just make me feel normal again."

"Okay. Do you want me to put the mind connection back?"

If he was being honest, that was the last thing that Wren wanted, but a part of him insisted it would make him feel more normal. "Yeah."

Jere didn't look like he believed him, but he agreed anyway. They went into the living room, sitting next to each other, and Jere placed his hand on Wren's head. In just moments, Wren felt everything tingle, not quite hurting, but not feeling good, either.

"Sorry, love," Jere whispered, running a hand through Wren's hair. "Your nerves aren't very happy about being rearranged. I'm not hurting you, am I?"

Wren shook his head. So many other things hurt far worse in ways that nobody could heal. Jere was talented, though, and before Wren knew it, nothing hurt. He felt the burns disappear completely, the effects of the days of dehydration and starvation vanish, and when he looked at Jere, he could see just how sapped his lover was.

"I think I can manage the remainder if I just rest a little," Wren reminded Jere. "No need to bleed you dry for me."

"I would." Jere had stopped the perfectionist healing, but he looked at Wren desperately. "If you wanted it, I would."

Wren shook his head. "Just put the mind connection back."

Jere nodded, and with a brush of his hand, the old connection that had been so active for years buzzed back into life, linking their energy and letting Wren into Jere's emotions. He was amazed by how relieved Jere was, how excited, how hopeful. He was surprised how scared he was.

"I'm okay," Wren promised. "I'm just shaken up."

"I was so terrified that I'd lose you," Jere admitted. "I've always thought I was doing enough... I thought you'd be safe."

"We both did," Wren reminded him. On impulse, he leaned into Jere, pleased to feel his lover's arms around him again. He still wasn't sure how close he wanted to get, but this was a good start. Now that Jere was back with him, everything seemed safe again. His firesetting gift was tucked inside of him where it belonged, and all he had to do was work on forgetting everything that had happened to him. He wanted to go back to normal.

"Do you want to talk about it?"

"No," Wren decided. A part of him almost flinched at answering so bluntly. He had been slapped for giving answers like that so many times in the past few days, but Jere just nodded. Wren figured his emotions were giving him away; he had been hiding them quite well during the evaluation, but now that he was home, even he could tell that he was projecting emotions strong enough for everyone else to feel.

"Did you tell Kieran that you got me back?" he asked, thinking about how difficult the empath would find it to even be around him right now.

"Not yet," Jere realized. "I was so happy to have you back, and then the clinic opened again... I really should let her know."

"I'll go," Wren suggested. The opportunity to get out of the house seemed spectacular.

"Are you sure you want to go alone?" Jere asked, a nervous look on his face.

"Yes," Wren decided. He wanted the opportunity more than he wanted almost anything else at the moment.

Jere didn't fight it, but Wren could tell how uncomfortable it made him. He gave Jere a kiss, wrapping himself in the feeling of Jere's skin for a few more minutes. It was becoming familiar again so quickly.

"I can make time to come with you," Jere offered.

Wren shook his head. "Nothing will happen to me; if it does, you'll come for me. Besides, I need to do this. I can't just hide. It's not healthy."

Jere nodded, and Wren was glad he understood. Wren had spent so long learning not to be afraid of things; he couldn't stand the thought of unlearning it. He was nervous as he left, checking twice to make sure he had a pass, and more than a few times during the quick trip to make sure Jere was there in the mind connection. There he was, dependable as always.

Wren was comfortable in the telegraph office; nothing here reminded him of anything. There was a wait, because of the approaching voting day, and he stood patiently in line, surprised when one of the slave employees eyed him up.

"Excuse me, are you Doctor Peters' slave?" the girl asked. She had three envelopes in her hand.

"Yes," Wren said, nodding.

"Would he mind if I gave these to you instead of delivering them?" she asked, her voice barely a whisper. "We're so busy. I won't get through everything today, and I'll be in trouble."

"Of course," Wren said. "Not a problem. I'm his authorized receiver for official mail. I can sign for you, if you'd like."

The girl's face lit up with relief. "Thank you so much!"

She subtly shoved all three envelopes into Wren's hand, as well as the receipt proving she had delivered it. She gave Wren as smile as she hurried off, likely to get more messages to deliver.

As he waited in the long slave line to send his telegraph out to Kieran, he glanced at the telegraphs Jere had received, wondering if they were from his mum, or maybe his sister, or even Kieran. He was surprised to see two major hospitals and a town mayor as the senders. Looking casual, as though he had any right to read the private correspondence, he opened them and examined the content.

Three job offers; all unsolicited, in response to the press release that they had sent out. The move had been a taunt to Hojer and a reminder to clinic patients, but it seemed that some hospitals had taken note of Jere. One could be easily discarded; it paid less than half of what Jere was making in Hojer, and was in a slave state. The other two were more unsettling—one was from a distant slave state, not one that was reciprocal with Arona, but it paid nearly double, and came with a full-time staff and free assistant. The other was a hospital in Sonova. It didn't pay as well, and it didn't come with as many benefits... but it wasn't in a slave state. It was in Jere's home city, the city he loved.

Wren had always wondered what would happen if Jere got some sort of invitation to take an amazing job back in Sonova. Would he really turn it down just to stay with Wren? Would he regret missing it? Suddenly, Wren understood exactly why Jere hadn't said a word to him about the possibility of freedom. Wren was frozen, terrified, and he hadn't the slightest idea of what to make of it.

"Are you okay?" Jere checked in through the mind connection. *"You feel off, scared. It just hit me."*

Wren wanted to shield it, but he didn't. *"There's a big line here. Something just reminded me of something unpleasant."* He wasn't completely lying. The thought of Jere leaving was unpleasant.

"All right," Jere agreed. Wren could feel the warmth through the connection. *"See you soon. Love you."*

Wren smiled slightly. He loved Jere, too. And he loved that he was in Hojer. He folded up the telegraphs, sticking them into the inside pocket of his jacket. He would tell Jere about them, but maybe after the SRA had been voted on. It was only a few days away, and they needed the time to relax. They had all been so stressed lately.

When he got home, he forgot all about the mail. He was tired, as was Jere, and they fell into Wren's bed, into each other's arms. All he wanted was to be with Jere, and to hope that the SRA passed successfully. He was starting to feel like that might be enough.

Chapter 32
Flames

It was days before Wren could stand the thought of fire again, much less the thought of being in the room where he had burned his master to death.

No matter how well Jere had healed him, he couldn't erase the memories, and Wren just kept feeling the burns on his skin, the way that the "evaluators" had touched him, all over, while he waited helplessly to be saved. A part of him wished he had just burned them all alive.

Jere had been kind enough to try and excuse him from the clinic, but he needed the work, needed something to feel normal. A part of him screamed to give up, to go back to how he had been before, but the deal that Jere had arranged with President Clemente and the new protections that The Slavery Reform Act could grant him gave him the tiniest bit of hope. He was going to get things back to normal, him and Jere, or maybe they'd even make them better. He just kept reminding himself of that fact every time one of the terrifying memories forced its way into his consciousness. He was determined to regain a sense of normalcy, and one of the things he wanted most was to feel comfortable fucking Jere again.

Business at the clinic was still slow, and he and Jere had hours to play and touch and explore each other.

"Get in the shower," he told Jere, just a few minutes after they closed up in the clinic. "I think I'm ready to go back into our bedroom again."

Jere didn't say anything, but the wide smile that spread across his face conveyed his feelings pretty quickly. Wren spent some time gathering the supplies he wanted to use that night, shuddering as the memories kept creeping back in. He had been through worse than this, he reminded himself, preferring to think about Jere.

Once everything was set up, Wren stripped off his clothes and joined Jere in the shower, startling him for a moment as he grabbed him from behind, wrapping his arms around Jere's waist and pressing against his back. It felt good not to be the one being startled.

"Welcome back," Jere said, turning in Wren's arms so that they were facing each other. He leaned in, pressing his lips lightly to Wren's.

Wren trembled at the touch, but for the first time in days, it was a good tremble. "I didn't want to miss the opportunity to join you."

He loved kissing Jere, and touching him, and there was something strangely erotic about the simple act of showering together, reaching around his wet, slippery body to grab some soap, or to adjust the angle of the showerhead. Even when they weren't fucking, or even touching, there was a sparking current of eroticism between them. More than anything else, the feeling anchored Wren in the moment.

He made up for the extra time Jere had on him in the shower with his speed gift. Hindered only by the constraints of the water pressure, he was able to soap up and shampoo his hair in mere seconds, standing there and smiling as the water did its work, washing the suds down the drain, swirling with the ones coming off of Jere. On impulse, he reached over and entwined his fingers with Jere's, watching the pattern.

"I missed you so much," Jere admitted.

"Me too." Wren wasn't too proud or shy to admit it anymore. "I knew I'd make it back to you. I belong here. With you."

Jere leaned into him. "I love you. I always want to be with you."

Wren held him close, thrilled with the calm, contented love that he could feel from Jere. His words, his body, his emotions — they all told the same story, and it mirrored Wren's feelings. "I love you, too."

They stood there until they were rinsed clean in the stream of water, then they took turns toweling each other off. It was nowhere near as efficient as taking care of the action by themselves, but it was more fun, and more intimate, just like showering had been. Not only that, but it provided them with an opportunity to touch and tease and work each other up—an opportunity which they both needed.

By the time they moved to the bed, Wren's hair was nearly dry, his short style lending itself more to quick drying than Jere's did. They maneuvered into bed, legs and arms and lips all mixed up together, and they stayed that way for a good long while until Wren pulled back, separating a little.

Jere smiled up at him. "What are you planning?"

Wren tried to hide his own smile. "Whatever makes you think I'm planning something?"

"Because you're always planning something devious to do to me in bed," Jere replied, smiling even wider.

"I may have something in mind." Wren had quite a lot in mind; he had been planning it for days. "It's been a long time, remember?"

"And so you sit around and think up sexy things to do to me?" Jere was clearly looking forward to it, despite having no idea what Wren was planning.

Wren pulled himself back, then stepped out of bed. "But of course. Can I restrain you?"

"I thought you'd never ask. Want to blindfold me, too?"

Wren shook his head. He needed to see Jere's face, to make sure they were both safe. But he wouldn't say that out loud. "I want you to see what I'm doing to you." He watched, pleased with himself, as the words made Jere shudder, his eyes growing wide with excitement.

Wren retrieved the cuffs that they were both so fond of, quickly attaching Jere's arms and legs to the frame of the bed, keeping his legs spread wide for easier access. He felt his own pulse race at the sight of the cuffs, and not entirely for good reasons. He forced the bad memories away.

"I thought we'd start with a nice massage," Wren said, pulling out some oil and pouring a generous amount onto his hands.

"I can think of some other uses for that oil," Jere teased, earning him a smack on the inside of his leg, enough to make him yelp and squirm. "That hurts! The oil makes it more stingy."

Wren could tell his lover was playing. He appreciated the playfulness. He dipped his head down to kiss and bite at the spot where a faint red imprint of his hand decorated Jere's leg. "Don't be such a smart-ass, then."

"Maybe I'll just save it for when I'm lying on my stomach. I like it better when you're slapping my ass."

"I'll keep that in mind," Wren taunted. "But for now, you're all locked up. Can't go anywhere. I could just keep smacking you like that for hours if I wanted to."

Jere's smile indicated that he wouldn't actually be opposed to that at all. Still, Wren had other plans for the night besides hitting Jere until his skin glowed, and his plans started with lots of oil and lots of touching. He worked his way up and down Jere's body, getting his muscles to relax and making his skin glisten, each touch making them both grow harder and harder. Once he was satisfied that his actions had achieved their desired goal, he gave Jere a long, lingering kiss, and then eased himself out of the bed.

"Wait just one minute," he teased, speeding out of the room to grab a cup of ice and returning with it just as quickly. Jere remained where he was cuffed, looking completely comfortable in a way Wren could never understand, but had certainly grown to appreciate. For Wren, restraint was one of the most terrible tortures, a fact that had recently been reaffirmed. But Jere loved it, and Wren had come to love restraining him. He shut off the lights when he returned, leaving them both in the near-darkness, as the sun was just about to set.

"I thought you wanted me to be able to see," Jere teased. "Going to be dark soon."

Wren smiled, walking to the nightstand and pulling out a few candles. He hadn't so much as warmed a cup of tea since his return; a part of him wondered if he had killed the fire inside of him forever. He risked glancing at Jere for a moment, relieved to see a patient, intrigued smile. Whether Jere knew it or not, that patience was more attractive than anything else Wren could have imagined at the moment. He cleared his mind of everything but Jere and fire, focusing his attention on the candlewick. In just seconds, it ignited, a clear yellow flame glowing at the tip.

"That will never stop being amazing to watch," Jere admitted.

Wren felt a part of him shift back into place. The candlelight flickered in the room, making shadows dance and creating an eerie, sensual look. He lit a few more, placing them strategically around the room to make light. Then he took a few more and placed them on the bed, unlit.

"Guess what's even more amazing," Wren challenged, stripping his clothes off and coming to straddle Jere's hips, smiling down at him.

"You?" Jere tried.

If it had been anyone but Jere, Wren would have accused the person of being insincere. Jere meant it, though, and it was as apparent from the look on his face and tone of his voice as it was through the mind connection. Wren blushed, adding more heat to their already steamy situation.

"I was thinking more along the lines of this," he said, holding up an unlit candle.

He held it directly above Jere's chest, where Jere could see it from the position Wren had left him in. Wren could easily hold it there, not having to strain or stretch at all, and he had a good view of it, as well as a good view of Jere's face. As they watched, Wren slowly focused his energy again, holding the candle and thinking not of a flame, as he did when he was lighting the candles with his gift, but of the wax, and how it would melt in a flame; not catching fire, but just warming up enough to turn it to liquid. He concentrated for a few moments, and finally, he was rewarded with the sensation of warm wax dripping down his fingers and onto Jere's chest.

Jere was silent, his mouth partway open, the edges curling into a smile.

Wren took that as encouragement, and he used the opportunity to focus his energy even more, heating the wax to a higher temperature before letting it drip down.

Jere gasped as the hot wax hit him this time. Wren drew the dripping line from side to side, making little zigzag patterns. He heated it a little more and dripped some onto Jere's nipples, making him squirm and moan.

"You're enjoying yourself?" Wren checked. He knew Jere well enough that he trusted Jere to tell him to stop if he needed a break, but it still made him feel better to check.

"Yes, so much! Don't stop!"

Wren felt quite proud. He had taken control of his gift once more, and he had reduced Jere to near-speechlessness in just minutes. He continued to heat and drip the wax, paying special attention to the sensitive areas around Jere's neck, his nipples, and then working his way down. Jere squirmed, moaned, and cried out as Wren played with the temperature, seeing just how much his lover could tolerate. There was certainly pain with some of the drops of wax, but more than anything, Jere seemed to be enjoying himself. Then again, Jere enjoyed pain in ways Wren would never understand, but loved to exploit.

Wren moved lower, covering Jere's stomach and upper thighs, laughing as Jere first squirmed, then held completely still as Wren brought the stream of hot wax closer and closer to his cock.

"Be careful?" Jere whispered, and Wren smiled, imagining that it was the embodied voice of Jere's cock saying the words.

Wren gave him a wicked smile. His eyes caught Jere's, and as they did, he brought the wax closer and closer. Jere didn't know it, but Wren was subtly lowering the temperature, waiting for it to be just perfect, and letting a large pool of it collect. He centered it over Jere's cock and let it pour, smiling at the nervous and excited squeal that came from Jere in response.

"Shit, Wren, fuck, that feels so good!"

Wren smiled. He was pleased to realize that he had gotten the temperature right, after all. He was more concerned with it being too cool than too warm, but judging from Jere's reaction, it was plenty warm enough to excite him. Wren would never do anything to risk putting Jere in actual danger.

As Jere continued to moan in enjoyment, Wren went ahead and covered his body in multiple colors and patterns of candle wax. He was pleased to see Jere's cock harden, twitching the tiniest bit along with the rest of his body each time a fresh part of his body was touched by the wax. Here and there, Wren dragged his thumb over the wax, peeling it off of Jere's leg, off of his stomach, off of his cock. The oil Jere was covered in made it much easier, and where it hadn't hardened yet, Wren took an ice cube and froze it before peeling it off, sometimes only to replace it immediately with newer, hotter wax.

Eventually, Jere's whimpers and pleas devolved into desperate begging to be fucked, and Wren was absolutely thrilled with that idea. He played with Jere a little more as he used his other hand to alternate between stroking Jere's cock and playing with his ass, slipping in and out, using the oil for lube. Jere was quickly rocking against him, trying to take him deeper, making Wren slip up a few times and get candle wax in places he wasn't intending, like Jere's cheek.

Jere stuck his tongue out, licking at it. "Still feels good," he announced, giving Wren a salacious wink. He licked along his lips as well, staring into Wren's eyes in a needy, sexy way.

Wren couldn't wait any longer. He slammed the hand that was holding the candle against Jere's shoulder, squishing the warm wax against his skin, and he slammed his cock into Jere's ass, thrilled as Jere let out a whimper when he tried to accommodate Wren so quickly.

"Wren," Jere breathed, pulling tight at the restraints. He let out a strained gasp that was somewhere between pain and pleasure. "It burns."

Wren had buried himself deep, but he forced himself to still instead of pounding in and out like he wanted to. "Too fast?" he asked, trying not to sound too disappointed.

"Harder," Jere demanded. "Fuck me harder. I like the burn."

Wren needed no further encouragement. He clutched at Jere's shoulders with both hands and pounded in and out of him repeatedly, making Jere gasp and cry out with each energetic thrust. Jere did his best to match Wren at first, bucking and twisting and thrusting up to meet Wren, but Wren would have none of it. He pinned Jere more forcefully by his shoulders and increased the pace, fucking him at a speed no natural human should ever be able to obtain, until Jere finally stopped struggling and just lay there, a blissful expression on his face as Wren took his pleasure.

It wasn't long after that Jere came, sending warm spurts of come between them. Wren smiled at the feeling, pleased to know just how much he had made Jere come undone. Jere trembled for a few seconds before going rather limp, breathing heavily and moving in time with Wren's thrusts. Wren kept at it for a few more minutes, enjoying the lack of resistance he had from Jere, as well as the very sated expression on his face. He flicked a few bits of wax from Jere's shoulders, making him twitch involuntarily, and that tiny movement set Wren off, making him come at the very reminder of the effect that he had on Jere.

Wren kept slowly thrusting, working himself in and out of Jere as he came, soon settling inside of his lover. He loved how close this made him feel to Jere, the way their bodies seemed to become one big mass of pleasure. He lay on top of him for a while, tracing his hand along the patterns he had made in the wax, working his lips over Jere's skin.

After a few moments, he pulled out and slid off of Jere, who was still lying there peacefully and quietly, a contented look on his face.

"Want to get the cuffs and the wax off?" Wren suggested gently.

"If you want," Jere mumbled, turning his head into the pillow. He seemed perfectly content to sleep cuffed to the bed, covered in wax, but Wren doubted it would be comfortable after a few hours.

Wren uncuffed Jere's hands and legs, wiped the come away with a towel, and began to carefully peel and chip away at the wax. He had done this to prove something to himself, and he had succeeded. His gift wasn't crushed inside of him, his mind wasn't destroyed — he had come back to exactly the life he had left. All it took was a few candles and the deep, enduring love of the most amazing man in the world. He noticed how Jere's breathing slowed and steadied with each touch, and realized that Jere had fallen fast asleep. Wren decided that the rest could wait until morning. He crawled up into bed next to Jere and turned him so that Jere's back was to him, placing all the wax on the other side. He put his arms around Jere and held him tight, pleased when he felt one of Jere's hands come around his and squeeze.

"Thank you," Jere whispered.

It was all he managed before falling asleep again, but it was plenty for Wren. A part of him thought that he should be the one thanking Jere, not just for bringing him home, but for being a part of feeling comfortable with himself again.

Chapter 33
Attack

With Wren back and the clinic opened for full business, things were getting back to normal. After they had finished up work at the clinic for the day and gotten dinner out of the way, they sat together in the dining room, playing a card game and conversing and teasing one another when the conversation got in the way of paying attention to the card game. They stuck to games of chance and luck instead of skill; Isis's memory gift and Wren's speed gift prevented most games of skill from being fair in any way, so simple games were much more fun for everyone involved.

Jere was in the middle of playing a card when he heard the startling, unmistakable sound of glass breaking, followed by yelling and jeering from outside. Isis screamed, and Wren was on his feet in seconds to investigate. Jere trailed behind, wishing he could move as quickly. When he reached the living room, he wished he hadn't.

Situated at the front of the house, the living room had a big window that faced the front of the property, toward the main road where people approached the house and the clinic. When Jere first looked, he was confused as to how the curtains were blowing outside. It took him a minute to process the fact that there was a gaping hole in the window, the night wind pulling the curtains out through the hole. The sight sent a chill through Jere's body. Unrecognizable yells and curses came through the open window, and the outlines of four or five people running and throwing more things were enough to fill him with terror. He could make out the phrase "slave-lover" and "outlander," but not much else. He glanced at Wren in horror.

"You guys, what's—" Isis followed close behind, pale and terrified, but her words cut off with a scream as something else made its way through the hole in the window, catching the curtains, couch, and carpet on fire.

Jere felt the panic rising. "Go! Get down in the cellar," he ordered, striding toward the front door.

"Jere!" Wren called after him, held back by Isis, who was clutching onto his arm and still screaming. She tried to pull him away, toward the cellar, and Wren tried just as hard to shake her off.

Jere ignored them both, intent on opening the door and destroying whoever dared to threaten his family. He had no clear plan, but suddenly, the possibility of a heart-stopping mind-bind seemed quite appealing. He had no concern for himself, only for protecting Wren and Isis.

By the time he opened the door, all he saw were the backs of the people as they fled away from his house and away from the town. Five figures, running away as quickly as possible. Jere didn't yell or threaten; he didn't need to. They had taken off at the first sign of resistance, like cowards, only willing to intimidate and threaten.

The fire inside of the house lit up the yard, and Jere cursed as he noticed that large chunks of the ground had been ripped up by some sort of mind gift, crudely spelling out the words "gift traitor" in the remaining dirt. The removed soil and grass was piled in front of the door; clearly, the attackers hadn't realized that it swung inward. Not only had they tried to light the house on fire, they tried to make sure nobody could follow them.

With every bit of fury and panic he had, Jere threw out a psychic warning and request for help. He wasn't a physically intimidating man, but his gift was strong, and the intensity of his psychic message was enough that he could feel unknown people recoiling, as if he had shouted too loudly in the middle of a quiet room.

Trained attendants at the police station picked up the message.

"*Sir, is there a problem?*" a voice asked.

"*I've been... vandalized, attacked.*" Jere tried to clear his thoughts enough to send them clearly. But there was smoke and fire, and what if there were more? Outside wasn't safe. There was no good way of dealing with fires, so inside wasn't safe, either. "*Send help to 141 North Meadow Lane, and catch the five people running north from here!*"

"*Someone will be on the way soon, sir,*" the voice promised him. "*Stay in a safe place. Is anyone hurt?*"

"*I'm the fucking doctor!*" Jere snapped. "*Just catch the bastards!*" He broke off the connection, needing his energy and attention to deal with what was happening to his home. Even as he looked at his living room, he could see the fire spreading quickly, consuming more and more. The smoke was worse, as the furniture was mostly smoldering, not quite caught on fire, yet.

Jere turned, looking at Wren and Isis. "I thought I told you guys to go to the cellar!" he snapped, panicked. "They won't kill me, but you're fair game! You need to be out of here, where it's safe!"

Isis just clung to Wren, sobbing, and Wren shook his head. "Not without you."

"Dammit, Wren—" Jere started, then stopped, looking at his lover's face. Wren was as terrified as he was, and just as unlikely to leave. He had been jumpy around fire ever since he had returned from the evaluation, and Jere wasn't sure just how well he had gotten over the torture they had subjected him to.

"Fine, we'll all go." Jere moved toward Wren and Isis, planning to push them into the cellar and lock them down there until they were safe. He wouldn't risk the attackers coming back.

Wren glanced at him, clearly sensing that something was amiss. He looked over at the fire. "We have to deal with this."

"Just get somewhere safe!" Jere wished that Wren would just do as he asked. He started to cough from the smoke. "Forget the house, just go!"

Wren gave him a determined look, detached Isis from his arm, and pushed her onto Jere. Dodging Jere's attempt to grab his arm, he walked further into the living room, which was burning quickly now that the fire had taken hold.

"Wren, what are you doing?" Jere asked, his voice rising as he watched his lover step into the middle of the flames. He watched in horror as Wren calmly picked up a blanket and placed it over the fire, singeing it all over, then tossed it aside.

"Wren, stop, there's too fucking much!" Isis pleaded. "Let's just go!"

Jere realized exactly what Wren was doing. He watched as Wren made his way to the center of the fire, where it would burn the hottest, the flames parting for him as he did. He spread his hands out over the flames, not getting burned by them, but absorbing them, stopping them as quickly as they spread. He didn't look out the window, or at Jere, he just stared straight ahead, taking the flames into himself as if it were nothing. Jere was terrified that someone from the police station would come, but it all happened so quickly, it was started and finished before he could even summon up a proper sentence in his head to try to convince Wren to stop. He had no sooner realized what Wren was doing and the fire was gone, smoldering here and there.

Wren followed up by speeding from place to place, crushing out the still-smoldering embers with the charred blanket he had used earlier. In seconds, he was finished, and he returned to where Jere and Isis were standing, shocked.

"Now, we hide," he said quietly, grabbing Jere's hand and pulling him along.

The cellar had been cleaned up considerably since the first time Jere saw it, but he still didn't like it. It was dark and creepy and full of bad memories, and despite the fact that Isis had taken to hiding down there when life became too much for her, it still had more crawly things than Jere was comfortable with. Regardless, it was a safe place without windows or doors, just the one entrance through the stairs. They would be safe there until the police arrived. Unlike the rest of the house, it was also free from smoke. They went down and sat at the old table and chair set that had been found while the cellar had been cleaned out. Jere still had yet to let go of Wren's hand, and Isis was all but glued to his other arm, still shaking.

Jere realized that she wasn't the only one shaking, and he took a few deep breaths to steady himself.

"They ran away," he recounted, still terrified by the experience. "They took one look at me, and they ran away. I didn't get a good look at any of their faces. The police are coming. I'll get them to keep someone stationed here until this is over."

Wren nodded. "That's probably the best decision," he admitted. "You think it's because of your involvement in the SRA?"

Jere shrugged. "I can only imagine," he admitted. "I had no idea this would happen. I never wanted any of this to happen. I should have stayed out of it!"

"But what you're doing is right, Jere!" Isis protested, composing herself barely enough to make the words come out. "They're wrong, not you."

She sniffled a bit and then drew back, as if she had suddenly realized that she was touching another person. She settled herself just inches from Jere and Wren, the physical proximity indicating exactly how scared she was.

Jere shook his head. "They just fucking tried to burn us out!"

"It's fine," Wren said softly. "It's out. They're gone."

It was silent for a moment while everyone caught their breath and processed the horror of what had really just happened. It was almost too much. If he had another choice, he'd back out of the SRA and everything else he'd threatened. If it wasn't for Wren's hand clutching his, he would probably be as panicked as Isis was. Wren was oddly calm, guarding his side of the connection. Jere let him take his space, just squeezing his hand and offering him a small smile.

It was Isis who broke the silence.

"So... you put that fire out," she stated.

Wren nodded.

"You have a speed gift... and like, a fire extinguishing gift?" she asked, looking at him curiously.

Wren sighed. Using the free hand that wasn't still clenched tightly around Jere's, he made a small ball of fire appear, balancing it on his hand like a juggling ball.

"Firesetting." He swirled his hand a little, for a dramatic gesture, then closed it, extinguishing that one as easily as he had extinguished the one in the living room. "I can start it and stop it. Never stopped one that big before, though."

Jere was glad that his heart was already racing, because that little display would have made it pound even more. He waited for Isis's response.

She was quiet for far longer than Jere would have guessed that she would be, and he even felt the tiniest poke at him from her side of the mind connection. He was startled and undefended against it since she so rarely initiated anything of the sort.

"You knew!" she said, scowling at Jere.

Jere nodded. She had caught him.

"I can't believe neither one of you told me," she said, frowning. "Jerks."

It was so out of place, and so typically Isis, that Jere couldn't help but laugh. The revelation that Wren had a second gift, the fact that their lives had been threatened and the house almost burned down, the fact that police were on their way to the house—none of that really seemed to matter to Isis; at least, not nearly as much as the fact that both Wren and Jere had been misleading her. It was so ridiculous, and the fact that he was laughing at it made it even worse.

"What?" Isis asked, shrugging. "It's really rude. You guys like... went out of your way to keep this a secret from me? For a year? That's shitty. I get that you're all older and saner and stuff, but only one of us is a trained spy, and it's not either one of you. Trust me, I can keep secrets."

"It's really dangerous if this gets out," Wren tried to explain. His face was as red as Jere assumed his own was, and Jere guessed that it was because he was equally ashamed of hiding things from the girl they both considered to be a part of their family.

"Well, yeah," Isis said, shaking her head. "You'd be some sort of freak, like I was as a kid. They'd want you for special slave things, and being a special slave is never good."

"Yeah. Pretty much," Wren agreed. "That's why we didn't tell you at first. It was dangerous information; if it got out, it could really destroy me. We didn't tell you, and then... we just kept not telling you."

Jere looked at them both nervously. They definitely didn't need any more conflict here, and they certainly didn't need any more threats.

Isis raised an eyebrow at him. "What?" she asked. "Am I supposed to get all weirded out or something? You two are the best people ever, and I'm used to keeping secrets. I'm not going to tell anyone or anything."

Jere breathed a sigh of relief. It was strange to be so indebted to the girl. It had always been the other way around. But somehow, this seemed acceptable.

"Thank you," Wren said quietly.

Isis shrugged. "It makes sense, now, how you could sometimes heat things up so quickly. Like, if I was watching you boil water for tea, it would take like ten minutes, but if I was gone for a minute, it would be done when I came back. Makes a lot more sense than thinking I had just spaced out for a while, although, I do that a lot, too, so that's not completely impossible. Makes sense why the stove wasn't always hot, either."

Wren nodded. "I thought I was being subtle about it, but I've been trying to use it more. I've grown careless. I didn't realize it until they took me for the evaluation."

"You could have told me about it and used it all the time," Isis pointed out. "You guys didn't trust me, though. Now you'll see that you were just being dumb."

"We appreciate it," Jere admitted. "It could really destroy things."

Isis shrugged. "I have no reason to want to destroy this. I like it here."

Jere wondered why he had ever doubted Isis.

They waited nervously in the cellar until Jere felt the mental presence of someone upstairs, someone who identified himself as part of the police force. He instructed Isis and Wren to wait downstairs while he went up and gave his statement to the officer. He explained how his very loyal slave had risked his own safety putting the fire out. He showed the officer the singed blanket, explaining that Wren had used his speed gift and his own hands to beat the flames out.

"Can I see his injuries for documentation purposes?" the officer asked as he filled out some forms.

Jere paused. There weren't injuries, because Wren had never really been in danger. The fire had moved aside for him as easily as pulling a curtain.

"I'm sorry. I healed him as soon as the fire was out. I'm a healer, and I mean, he deserved the reward..."

"Not a problem," the officer assured him, documenting his statement. "In the future, you might want to have a complete record of it and get someone else to witness it for insurance reimbursement."

Of course, that's what people here would be worried about. Getting payment for the healing services of the slave that had saved their lives. "I... it's not a big deal. It's easier to heal fresh injuries."

The officer nodded. "I guess you'd be the one who would know. Do you want surveillance on the property?"

Jere didn't really *want* surveillance on the property so much as he knew it was necessary. "Yes, please," he agreed, trying not to look too uncomfortable with the idea.

The officer laughed. "Don't worry, we just send a slave out. Can't waste important people, but the slave can sit out in the cold and watch, and let us know if anything happens. He can patch up your lawn, too. Looking like it is, you're asking for more trouble. Keeps the peace if we clean up the vandalism."

Having a police slave would be the perfect solution; the slave wouldn't have the psychic abilities to eavesdrop on their mindspeak conversations, and would be too well-trained to eavesdrop physically. "Thank you."

"Nobody will mess with the slave," the officer assured him. "They wear our uniforms, like our dogs do, and penalties for harming police property are pretty severe. Chances are, someone is just trying to scare you, and they did a damn good job of it. It's not a surprise, not with that slave law you're promoting, and your threats to leave us hanging here."

Jere squirmed. The officer was speaking conversationally, probably entirely unaware of how uncomfortable he was making Jere. "I suppose so. I just... I value healthcare, and I value my privacy as a slaveowner. Seems strange that people are so opposed to those things."

The officer laughed. "People hate change, and they aren't too fond of outlanders' ideas. I don't really care either way, but I'd rather have a good healer. And I can't wait for this election to be over. People are getting way too excited about things, rioting and protesting in some cities. We don't need that here."

"I completely agree. I'm so sorry to bother you with this."

"Just doing my job," the officer replied. "We need to keep our doctor and clinic safe, right? Don't know what it is about this place that attracts fire."

The officer finished the details of his report, provided a copy of the report number for Jere to use when contacting his insurance company, and left with a smile.

Jere shuddered, waiting until the officer left and was replaced by a uniformed slave before calling Isis and Wren up.

"Are you sure you're okay?" Jere asked. "I'm so glad nobody was hurt."

"I'm glad *you* weren't hurt," Wren pointed out, a serious expression on his face. "We can't do this without you. You can heal us if we get hurt. If you're hurt... you can't abandon us like that."

Jere nodded, realizing just how important it was for him to be there as their master. They needed him in ways that nobody else could stand in for.

"I think it's good you were here," Isis pointed out, giving Wren an admiring look. "That was pretty much the coolest thing I've ever seen."

Wren blushed. "I've never gotten *that* reaction to my gift. Ever. Even when I first found out about it, I was horrified. I was so different from everyone else I had ever met. Another slave at the training facility I was placed at found out and wanted me to burn the place down—even Jere was a little intimidated when he first found out."

"I think it's awesome," Isis repeated, drawing a smile from both Wren and Jere. Jere was pleased to see someone appreciated Wren's gift for the good it could do, not being afraid of it.

Having the police slave linger around their home was uncomfortable, but at least the slave would keep to his business. The slave was more symbolic than functional, but the attack had been symbolic. It made sense to respond similarly. It was worth it to maintain their safety. He just hoped that it would be enough until the SRA was voted on. He didn't care if it passed or not, he just wanted to fade from the public eye.

Chapter 34
Voting Day

Just over a week after the house was attacked, the SRA went to a vote before the lawmakers. It was only one of a number of similar laws that were being proposed in addition to the elections, but the SRA was what everyone was talking about. From the looks of the crowd that had gathered outside of the city building, supporters of either side were evenly distributed; plenty were eager to see it pass for healthcare, human rights, or slaveowner privacy issues. The other half was still furious that such an atrocious bill had even been proposed, much less having the potential for passing the vote. Events and protests had been staged all day, and Jere and Wren found themselves wandering through the crowds, amazed and awed by the outcry. Jere had never seen this many people gathered in one place in Hojer, much less been in the middle of it.

"There are even people here from other towns," Jere said, barely audible over the crowd.

"Other states," Wren corrected, pointing to a few groups on the sidelines. Many held signs and banners indicating who they were, where they were from, and why they were attending.

It didn't matter that this was an issue primarily for Arona; it was part of a nationwide sweep of similar attempts. People were both thrilled and offended by that idea.

Slaveowners and slaves alike were milling about; some were even demonstrating their gifts in an attempt to justify whichever side of the argument they were on. A free person with a gift of manipulating matter had staged a small demonstration, easily ripping up the ground below him and forming it into different shapes. He made holes in the ground spell out the phrase "LOGICAL HEALTH-CARE," rearranging the holes into the medical staff symbol just moments later. He gave Jere a nod when he walked by.

Jere was shocked by the outpouring of support. He knew that there were plenty of people who didn't support slavery, or at least, didn't support the brutal conditions of slavery that were acceptable in this state, but seeing it right in the center of Hojer was something else entirely.

"I almost feel like I'm back home," he told Wren, too amazed and cautious to speak the words out loud.

Off to one side, Wysocka Enterprises had erected a massive display. Like the man who owned the company, it was professional and reserved. Free gifts and snacks were being handed out, each emblazoned with the simple marketing words: "Support Progress. Support President Clemente. Yes on SRA." Mr. Wysocka had made his decision, putting his desire for prosperity above everything else. Jere smiled at him; as little as he cared for the man, his support would be important.

A surprising number of slaveowners were in attendance, bringing their slaves along with them as a matter of course. Plenty seemed to be in support of the SRA, and had their slaves holding signs with phrases like, "HUMAN DOCTORS FOR HUMAN BEINGS," and "HERD IMMUNITY." A few had even brought animals, cleverly decorated with signs reminding people that they were the ones who should see veterinarians, not slaves. One had even taken it to a comedy level, pinning a sign to her dog that said "NO on The Slavery Reform Act! Keep my vet too busy to neuter me!" Plenty of people walking by stopped to pet the dog, and the dog's owner was quick to inform them of the benefits of the new SRA to their slaves, their pets, and to the general population.

A table with a sign identifying the group as the "New Veterinary Association" was nearby, offering free health scans for dogs. Jere recognized Hojer's vet among the group, and realized that there must have been a split in the larger Veterinary Association. He read over some of their signs, pleased to realize that there were a number of vets voluntarily refusing to treat humans except in cases of emergency. They emphasized pride in their gifts and profession, and had a number of vets visiting from free states as well. The partnerships must have been quite lucrative.

Jere had always dismissed protests and lobbying as someone else's problem, and he still wasn't completely sure about how he felt about being involved so prominently. The gathering made him feel a little better about his role. These weren't people complaining about idealistic notions or searching for some sort of utopia, they were all vested in rational goals with real reasoning behind them. The fact that Wren and Isis would be safer after the SRA was passed made it even better.

"*I wish Kieran and Isis could see this!*" Just for a moment, Jere could pretend that they really weren't in Hojer at all.

Wren shook his head. "*Isis would be having a thousand panic attacks, and Kieran would be overwhelmed with the emotion.*"

It was true. Isis had actually laughed in Jere's face when he asked if she wanted to go, reminding him that wearing a leash and collar and being around a whole big crowd of people were pretty much two of her least favorite things. Kieran was still in Sonova, dealing with things on that end and generally avoiding being associated with the SRA or Hojer. She was pleased with her involvement, but it didn't make her hate Hojer any less, nor did it make the people of Hojer like her any more.

"*Besides, it's not all good.*" Wren pointed to the other side, where some of the more ambitious opponents of the bill had gathered.

"What the fuck are they doing?" Jere asked, appalled.

From the looks of it, they were publicly brutalizing their slaves for no reason; a slap here, a kick there. One was pinned down by some sort of gift, naked and spread-eagle on the ground. A sign next to her read, "use me," and Jere could only imagine what sorts of horrors the sign referred to.

"*They're exercising their rights,*" Wren answered, seeming only slightly less disturbed than Jere by the scene.

In contrast to the well-worded and clearly prepared signs that the supporters of the bill and their slaves wore, the other side had quickly scrawled messages onto pieces of scrap paper, or, more often, onto the bare skin of their slaves. "Slaveowners need control," was a popular one, as well as descriptions of offenses that the slaves had committed, everything from breaking property to disobeying orders. One had the word "runaway" scrawled across his chest, old scars from past whippings prominently displayed on his back. The scars were made more noticeable by the fact that they were lit up by some sort of gift. When the mistress clapped her hands, the soft blue light illuminating the scars grew brighter, causing the slave to writhe in agony. Jere had no idea what was causing it, and he had no desire to find out.

Suddenly, the fact that he was in Hojer, not in any place that he would ever willingly call home, was painfully obvious. There were law enforcement agents everywhere, but they did nothing more than observe. After all, those actions were perfectly legal.

Some of the more creative, or perhaps, less prepared people had gone a step further, carving the messages into their slaves' skin, the shallow, bloodied gouges spelling out crude messages like "no on 3," and "*lacklers* need control." Jere was startled to see the derogatory term so prominently displayed, especially in a context where so many people were out, including families with children.

The Human Veterinary Association, with Barrett at the head of it, was offering "free samples" of healing—clearing the canvas for new messages to be cut into the slaves' skin.

"Why are they doing this?" Jere wondered aloud, still shocked by the sheer display of callousness and brutality. "They're not making their case any better. They're making it worse! They're worse than animals, torturing slaves for fun. For fuck's sakes, there's kids here! They shouldn't have to see this. I shouldn't have to see this!"

Wren moved closer to him. They were still in public, so it wasn't like they could really comfort one another, but the sheer physical closeness made him feel a little better.

"*They're acting out,*" Wren replied. "*Like naughty children, about to have their favorite toy taken away. They know it's going to end, so they're going to make damn sure that it needs to go. I don't agree with it, either, but there's nothing we can do.*"

"Even after it passes, they'll just get a fine or a sentence to go to a training class." That was the agreement that had been written into the SRA. Offenders wouldn't be penalized with jail time or severe fines; the focus was on re-education and rehabilitation. Jere thought it unfair that the same people who would beat their slave to a pulp for dropping a glass of water would get sent to a two-hour public safety course, but everyone who was more experienced with this sort of thing had assured him that this was the best course of action. It was the most likely to be enforced, and the least likely to go unapproved.

He and Wren continued to walk around, making an active effort to stay away from the more gruesome protests, chatting with supporters of the bill. Jere was their expert, the scientific professional who provided the emotion-free decision making and information based on research. They liked him, and they liked the way that he subtly protected Wren from everything, making sure to place himself between Wren and the angry protesters, shielding him from questions or comments that had the potential to go badly. He wasn't clearly coming across as being in love with his slave, but he was demonstrating the ways in which slaveowners could protect their assets.

The officials were debating inside, casting their vote for state and local issues and collaborating with other cities to report the results of the state issues. It seemed to take an eternity before any word was heard from inside. Jere thought idly of the olden days when people could watch the proceedings on television screens or through the Internet, getting instant updates. It seemed so strange that so much information could pass so quickly back then, especially without the use of mind gifts.

Someone with a mind gift received the first news — the spouse of one of the political members inside of the building. He had a loudspeaker, and he started announcing the results of the vote. The Slavery Reform Act wasn't the only issue being debated in this year's election, although it was arguably the most controversial. The results on zoning for a new city park came first, followed by a proposed tax change for small businesses. As each issue was approved or denied, the large crowd became more and more incited.

Finally, the results of the vote on The Slavery Reform Act were revealed.

"Approved, with a final vote of six to five in favor!" the person called out over the loudspeaker, excited. His side was clearly that of the supporters.

The crowd exploded. There were cheers, cries of protest, and cries of pain from the slaves who were unfortunately positioned on the receiving end of many of the dissenters' anger. Jere watched in amazement as someone sent up little beams of colored light with a mind gift, filling the sky with a scene that reminded Jere of the fireworks that Sonova held every year in celebration of the survival of the human race after The Fall.

The beautiful festivities only lasted so long before the ugliness of the state destroyed it.

The party opposing the bill took out their anger on their slaves, slapping and screaming at them, yelling loudly about their "rights" to do so. Clearly, their rights were extending to other people's slaves as well, and even to some free people, as tensions quickly came to a head and fights started to break out. The few moments of happiness and peace came crashing to a halt, and the Hojer police department struggled to contain the scene.

In addition to the free officers from Hojer and the neighboring boroughs, police slaves had been dispatched. Jere watched with wide eyes as one was ordered to place himself between two free people who had started brawling. The slave obeyed, but within seconds, he was snatched up by an angry mob, thrown to the ground and kicked repeatedly. Vandalizing police property was a crime, but with all the commotion, the crime was overlooked. The free police officers had bigger things to worry about, protecting the very free people who were causing the damage.

Against the background of screamed curse words and insults, the police slave was set ablaze by one of the spectators. Some arrogant free person was flaunting the same mind gift that Wren had to hide every day, and Jere couldn't reconcile the brutality as he watched the slave writhe and scream as his skin blackened and turned to ash. Jere was a healer, but he couldn't heal this; Wren had a firesetting gift that could stop it, but he couldn't risk revealing it. Jere covered his nose with his hand, blocking the smell of burning flesh, and he felt relief once the slave finally stopped struggling.

The tormenters moved on, leaving the body and seeking out another victim.

Jere was startled as he was bumped from behind, nearly falling but for Wren's quick intervention, catching him around the waist.

"Look at it, putting its dirty *lackler* hands all over its master," the person who bumped them snarled, glaring at Wren. "Maybe we should take this one and teach it some manners."

Chapter 35
Costs

Jere wasn't much of one for physical confrontation, or confrontation at all, for that matter, but he pulled Wren behind him and shoved the aggressor away from both of them, sending a spark of psychic pain along with his shove.

"Touch him and I will make your stomach digest you from the inside out," he growled, dropping any sort of reasonable hold on his psychic abilities.

Jere sometimes forgot what a threat he posed, especially when he was enraged. The psychic energy nearly crackled off of him, and the fact that he had been able to assess the man's entire health from the single second of contact he had with him indicated exactly how focused Jere was. The man backed down, muttering something about Jere being crazy, and a stupid, sentimental slave-lover, but he retreated. Other people gave him wide berth as well.

He turned to Wren, who actually pulled back a little, whether from the excess psychic energy, or the rage on Jere's face.

For once, Jere was pleased to be intimidating. "We need to leave."

Jere shielded Wren's body with his own. The crowd had devolved into a riot; psychic energy and weapons of all sorts flew in every direction. While the crowd mostly contained their violence against free people to fistfights, slaves of all sorts were subject to any combination of aggression. While some seemed caught up in the chaos by accident, many others were being volunteered by their masters, pushed toward the angry crowds like sacrifices. One of the slaves was being drowned with psychic water, another was being thrown into the air and dropped to the ground repeatedly, another's head was slowly being squeezed by an unknown force until her eyeballs threatened to pop from her skull. Jere couldn't understand how places like Hojer ever decided that those with physical gifts were more dangerous than those with mind gifts.

They made their way home quickly; nobody considered bothering them as they made their way through the crowd. If they hadn't seen or heard Jere's outburst, they could feel the psychic energy from him, and it was something no rational person would choose to contend with. They moved quickly away from the crowd and toward the outskirts of town, where the house was. Jere didn't drop his guard or his psychic presence until they were well out of range of everyone else. Once he did, he was shaking.

"Are you okay?" he asked Wren, forcing himself to calm down a little.

"Yeah." Wren offered him a grim smile. "You scared me for a minute, but I'm good now. Thank you."

"Sorry I scared you," Jere said. "He was threatening you. I needed to make sure he realized that wasn't acceptable."

"Could you really do that? The stomach digestion thing?"

Jere considered it, then nodded. It was technically possible; not like it was something they taught in medical school, but they were taught how to repair tears in the stomach lining and how to control the flow of stomach acid, so changing the fine details of that process would certainly result in something like that. "Yeah. I'm not sure if I would, but I think just giving someone heartburn after a threat like that would be enough to scare them away from you."

Wren smiled. "You're creative. Even Burghe never thought of that one."

Jere laughed. He wasn't sure if the statement was a compliment or just a general statement of horror, but either way, he appreciated that Wren seemed grateful for his intervention. "I'll be damned if I let anyone hurt you. And things seemed out of control enough back there that I might have even been able to get away with it."

"It was pretty bad."

"I didn't expect that. I thought there would be some excitement, some people who were disappointed, but I never expected there to be such a fucking riot!" Jere exclaimed. "People lose their minds over this shit. I don't even know how they're going to break that mess up."

Wren shrugged. "Doesn't matter much to me. We're out, safe, and on our way home. And it passed!"

Jere forced a smile. He was glad it had passed, but any happiness he felt was overshadowed by what he had just witnessed. The few riots he had seen in Sonova had never ended in murder or torture. He put his arm around Wren's waist, needing the closeness. Everyone who would oppose the gesture of affection was surely back in the riot, and besides, it was perfectly acceptable to "use" a slave like this. Jere was relieved to feel Wren's warmth against his skin.

They returned to the house quickly, nodding at the now-familiar police-issued slave stationed outside the door, and coming inside where Isis was eagerly waiting for them.

"Did we win?" she asked, ignoring any sort of social niceties.

"Barely, but yes," Wren informed her, smiling.

"It was six to five, meaning that one person could have voted differently and it would have gone the other way. But it worked, and it's law now, so no more public beatings, or killings, and we're going to see an increase at the clinic, hopefully."

"Hopefully?" Isis asked.

"Well, some people might just opt not to take their slaves anywhere for medical treatment," Wren observed. "It's a risk, but then, there's also the 'no intentional killing' clause."

"If the master is just going to let their slave die of illness because they're too fucking mean to take them to a doctor, they'd probably be better off dying anyway," Isis decided. "I wished so many times for someone to just let me expire. Assholes never did."

Wren nodded his agreement, and Jere looked at both of them with barely concealed horror in his eyes. Jere wasn't about to argue, because Wren and Isis had both expressed those very same wishes to him when he first acquired each of them, but it was still rather unsettling to hear it discussed in such casual terms.

"Well, let's just hope most of them make it here," he mumbled, trying to hide his discomfort. He could still smell burning flesh, whether it was real or not. It seemed etched into his senses, the same way as the horrors he had witnessed were etched into his memory.

"Silly outlander," Isis teased. "Slave state riots are always bloody. Lots of property damage makes a statement. But free people in slave states are good at following laws; they've been doing it their whole lives. The new laws will change things, I mean, once they pass. And until then, we can stay at home."

Isis was blunt, but Jere had no doubt that she had seen a riot or two in her life, or at least heard about one. She and Wren both seemed pleased by the results, if not the process, and Jere tried to see it like they did. It was just hard to think of a pile of dead, tortured humans as property damage. For once, he approved of Isis's chosen method of handling problems. Hiding seemed like an excellent idea.

The three of them busied themselves preparing the clinic for the injured that were sure to be on their way. As they did, they pondered what the passage of the SRA could mean for the clinic, and for Hojer, and for them.

"Maybe one day we won't have to even think about running across the border," Isis mused. "Maybe it'll be like... okay here, or maybe it will be easier to leave."

"Like being allowed to free slaves?" Jere asked, considering it. It would make everything so much easier. He could consider tolerating living here if he could have Wren and Isis freed, allowing them at least some sort of legal protection.

"Or being able to move out of state with them," Wren suggested. "Slaves are property in this state; fine. But you can move out of state with a couch, or a set of silverware, you should be able to move out of state with a slave as well."

"And then once you get to another state, then they'd be free," Jere nodded. "Damn, I want to see that happen before I die."

"We're taking the first steps," Wren reminded him. "I don't know whether it will ever happen, but as Kieran loves to point out, this is progress toward the cause."

Jere nodded. "It really is. I never even thought we'd get this far."

As they talked, reveling in their small victory and hoping for the future, Jere felt an intense presence in his mind, only moments before hearing a harsh, rapid knocking at the door.

It was Paltrek, and unlike his usual careless self, he sounded miserable and angry and sad. *"Help her, Jere. Do whatever you can."*

Confused by the message and the knocking at the door, Jere got up and answered. It was proper for Wren to answer, but given the threats and the strained political situation, they had decided that he would stay away from the door as often as possible. Jere wondered what Paltrek was so upset about, but he assumed it was family issues. He opened the door without concern, eager to tell his friend about the success of the SRA. While Paltrek hadn't been active in any of the campaigning, he had supported Jere. As much as the riot had been awful, Jere was starting to accept the upside, to feel like he had done the right thing.

The sight in front of him crushed any of the happiness he had just been feeling.

Dane stood there, the tattered remains of Arae's body cradled in his arms.

"Help her. Please."

Jere stood in the doorway in shock for just a few more seconds. He knew this was a possibility; the atrocities he had watched during the riot had made that very clear. But it wasn't supposed to harm someone he knew. He had taken inventory of the people he cared about; he thought everyone was okay. He didn't want to believe it, but there was no denying the effects that the SRA had caused. The few minutes of cautious success he had felt crumbled when faced with the reality on his doorstep.

"Please, Doctor Peters, please!" Dane begged, sobbing as he shoved his way into the house, pushing Arae's charred and dismembered body toward him.

"What happened?" Jere forced the words out through his throat, even though it felt like it was about to close up on him.

"Mistress Annika," Dane sobbed. "She cut her and burned her and beat her and did everything... please help her!"

Wren responded before Jere had a chance to do more than stand there in shock. Wren was on his feet, helping Dane and Arae to the clinic, where he instructed Dane to lay the girl on an exam table. Jere followed blindly. He had distanced himself, barely, from the slaves he saw being tortured on the street. Seeing someone he knew reminded him just how real this was, and how wrong. He had seen things like this in emergency rooms before; he had done a rotation that had coincided with a massive building collapse and subsequent fire, resulting in hundreds of people losing limbs and lives and being burned over massive percentages of their bodies. But that had been a disaster, a terrible mistake of engineering. Jere knew that this was no mistake. This had been done intentionally; each of the wounds had been inflicted by hand or with a weapon. By the looks of it, Arae had been alive and conscious for most of it.

With a shudder, he placed his hand on her burned flesh, seeking any sign of life or hope. When he didn't detect it, he moved his hands to her head, cringing as he came in contact with the patches where hair had clearly been ripped out in chunks. He closed his eyes against the tears that were forming, and tried to find any sign of life to make a connection with.

"I don't think she's—"

"No! You have to help her!" Dane screamed, dropping to the floor and begging him to save his sister's life. "You have to, please! You can't just let her die! You're a healer! You can fix her! Please, fix her."

Jere doubted it, but he was willing to try. His medical ethics demanded it, and his affection for Dane demanded it even more. With great reluctance, he pushed his way into what was left of her psychic energy, which was fading with every second.

The dream-states of the recently dead were one of the most terrifying things Jere had ever experienced, and he had fortunately only experienced it twice before in his life. Usually, it was during a risky surgery, and he could feel the patient slipping away with him there, the dream-state being ripped away from him, as if the walls around him were suddenly disappearing and leaving him hopeless and bare. This was different. From the moment he entered, he was thrust into nothingness. While entering a person's mind for mind-healing often had a detached feeling associated with it, entering the mind of someone in this state was like falling, faster and faster, with nothing to hold on to, nothing to guide or ground himself with. Jere's stomach churned and he tried in vain to find something to latch on to, a residual heartbeat, a flicker of a brainwave, anything.

He found nothing.

He struggled to even locate her organs, the faint traces of psychic energy guiding his healing gift to where they should be, but leaving him cold and empty, like everything else. He fought, he struggled, but all he could ascertain was that she had been dead for many, many minutes. As quickly as Dane must have carried her here, her body still warm before cooling down to match outside temperatures, she was likely dead before he even picked her up. Jere kept trying, pushing his healing gift to the maximum strength that he had possibly ever used it at once, but there was nothing left to heal. A healer's gift depended on life and energy, and when there were neither of these things, his gift was utterly useless. Bringing Arae back to life would be as futile as bringing the exam table to life.

Utterly crushed, Jere fought his way back to reality, emerging and gagging as he did. He was happy to leave the horrors that he had experienced, but it left a stain on his own psychic energy, the same way that touching a dead thing might leave bacteria on one's skin.

He pulled back, horrified by it all, and what was worse, he had to look at Dane and break the news to him.

The look on his face must have done it, because Dane crumpled into a broken mess. "No," he kept repeating. "No, I didn't let her die, I didn't let her die!"

Wren looked at Jere, a desperate, hopeful look on his face. Jere just shook his head, sadly. "I'm so sorry," he managed, and he wasn't even sure who he was apologizing to. Dane? Arae? Himself? It didn't matter, because no amount of healing and no amount of apology was going to fix any of this. "She's too far gone."

Dane launched himself across the room, grabbing at the medical equipment and throwing it left and right, digging through for something.

Jere just watched, letting him have his moment of grief. Wren glanced at him for guidance, but Jere shook his head.

"Can you go handle the clinic?" he asked Wren. He wasn't sure how much time had passed or how many patients had shown up, but he could hear people. Hurt, angry, scared people were filling his clinic, and someone had to be out there. *"Lock the door from the outside when you go."*

Wren nodded, dodging Dane as he slipped out the door. Jere didn't really want to be trapped in a room with a grieving man, but he saw no other alternative. He watched, helpless, as his best friend's slave found scalpels and sliced them into his skin haphazardly, as he found medications and took them without regard.

Jere wondered just what victory they had really achieved. This was slavery. It was miserable and brutal, and he couldn't demand that Dane contain himself. He was always so tightly controlled; he deserved a chance to lose control instead.

Dane proceeded to try and destroy everything he could in the exam room, including himself. He didn't come near Jere, didn't even look at him, but Jere could feel his pain. There was nothing else to offer him. Slaves weren't given funerals; Annika would probably view the death of her slave as nothing but an inconvenience. The rest of the Wysocka family would probably be too busy keeping up appearances. Jere watched silently, giving him the only things he had to offer — a slave exam room full of replaceable items and the privilege of breaking down completely.

He waited until Dane exhausted himself, falling on the floor and sobbing. Jere went to him and placed him in an unconscious state, a hand on his head interrupting the flow of blood and oxygen to the conscious parts of his brain. Once that was completed, he healed the cuts and bruises Dane had inflicted on himself, cleared his body of the toxins he had poured into it, and did his best to avoid noticing how destroyed Dane was, even in the dream state. While it wasn't as horrifying as Arae's, it was still unpleasant, shut down, half-created, and the projection of Dane was as unresponsive as the real one.

He withdrew quickly, the healing only taking a matter of minutes due to how recent the injuries and poisoning had been. When he did, Wren was back and waiting for him with a sedative. He didn't even have to think about it before slipping the needle into Dane's arm, injecting him with enough to keep him out for the rest of the night.

Wren was helpful, as always, cleaning Dane up as well as possible, wiping the blood and tears off of his skin as neatly and proficiently as ever. He and Jere carried Dane out of the clinic and placed him in one of the spare rooms, tucking him tightly into bed and leaving him there, dreading the moment when he woke up.

Chapter 36
Waste

Jere went to find Isis, who was hiding in her room, sitting in the far corner looking terrified.

"She's dead, isn't she?" she asked, shaking.

Jere nodded. "I couldn't help her," he admitted, feeling useless.

"I can't get it out of my head. Seeing her like that. Burned. Jere, she didn't have an arm. She was missing her fucking left arm!"

Jere shuddered. It had been too much for him to process. He had just taken in her general state, and then her dream state, but it was true.

"Why?" Isis asked. "Is this because of the SRA?"

Jere nodded, still feeling sick. "Yes. It wasn't supposed to happen this way, but it did. This was never supposed to happen."

"I'm gonna stay in here for a while," Isis said, not even moving from the spot she was curled into. "I'm sorry, I just can't."

"It's all right," Jere said softly. "Have you hurt yourself?"

Isis shook her head. "Can't," she admitted. "Too scared. I think of blood, and it makes me think of her."

"Okay," Jere nodded. "Tell me if you need anything later."

Isis nodded, putting her head on her arms and sitting there. Despite her limited psychic presence, Jere could feel how viscerally upset she was, how terribly this had bothered her. Confusion and regret and guilt swirled around, and Jere could feel his own emotions bleeding back and forth between them, increasing it on both sides. He pulled back on his own connection, letting her have her space, focusing on Wren. Unsurprisingly, Wren was handling this well. He wasn't pleased about it, but of course, Jere wouldn't have expected him to be pleased about it. Wren might be a little callous sometimes, but he didn't actually enjoy it when other people suffered. He was apathetic, and Jere envied him that.

He walked out of Isis's room, leaving the door slightly ajar in case she needed anything, and came to stand in the living room, lost. Wren came up and held him tight, providing Jere with the strength and security that he needed to even be able to think.

"We knew it was going to happen one day," Wren said quietly. "Annika is a fucking monster."

"I didn't think it would be this bad," Jere replied. "And Dane...."

"He'll be all right," Wren reminded him. "It's amazing what people can live through. And the rest of the patients need their doctor if they're going to continue to live."

Jere wanted to just stay in Wren's arms, but he couldn't. How had they been celebrating less than an hour ago?

"Aw, fuck." Paltrek's voice cut through Jere's reverie, and he turned to find his friend standing just inside the doorway; in the chaos, the door had been left wide open, and Paltrek had clearly taken that as an invitation to let himself in.

He looked at Wren and Jere without a thought or judgment of the position they were in, and shook his head. "She fucking killed the girl, didn't she?"

Jere nodded. Normally, he would have made at least some effort to move himself out of Wren's arms, but not tonight. Everything had been too stressful, too terrible, and Paltrek already knew enough about Jere's private life anyway. What did it matter if he saw Jere cuddling with his slave, or his partner? Paltrek knew that they were one and the same, and Jere had just tried to revive his sister's dead slave. The time for secrets was over.

"I tried, Jeremy. I heard what they were doing, and I got there as fast as I could. I had to fucking drag her out of there. They were on her like... like vultures, you know? Everyone ripping and cutting and burning and —"

"Please don't describe it," Jere interrupted him, forcing himself to sit up. "I saw what she looked like. I'd rather not hear the details."

"I tried to stop her, I told her that our father would be furious at her for making a scene, I told her it was illegal, I told her she was being a horrible, awful bitch, but she just kept going!" Paltrek shook his head. "And so did the rest of them. Arae... she wasn't the only one, Jere. There were five, at least, as far as I could tell."

Jere shook his head. "What the fuck is wrong with them? Why now?"

Paltrek shrugged. "I need a drink," he muttered. "Where's Dane?"

"Sedated in the guest room," Jere told him.

"Jesus Christ."

Jere could feel the fury emanating from him. "Paltrek, don't be angry at him, he needed—"

"Don't fucking accuse me of being angry at him, Jeremy!" Paltrek snapped, standing up and walking toward the liquor cabinet on his own for the first time that Jere had ever seen. "I'm not a fucking monster like they are. I'm angry, but not at him, and not at you. I'm angry at my sister, and at the people she associates with, and I'm angry at myself and my father for not trying to stop this sooner. Jesus, Arae was a good girl, and Dane is going to be fucking crushed over this, and none of it should have happened!"

He stormed out, returning a few seconds later with a half-full bottle of vodka and draining a good portion of what was in it.

"You were there when they released the vote and said the SRA passed," Paltrek continued, barely blinking as the alcohol burned his throat. "I saw you, and I saw you and Wren take off just a few minutes later, which was the smart thing to do. The fucking police should have made everyone disperse, but they didn't, they thought they had it under control. I don't know if you were there when the fights were breaking out, but everything got worse, people kept picking at each other, and then the people who were against the SRA decided to hold a grand demonstration to show how damaging the new SRA really was."

"By breaking all the laws of it?" Jere asked, shaking his head. It was possibly the stupidest demonstration he had ever heard of, but then, riot mentality never was that logical to begin with.

"The SRA doesn't pass into law until tomorrow," Paltrek told him. "Because of the health risks, they're rushing it into effect, but they want to give everyone until tomorrow to find out about the results and make changes accordingly. So these fucking assholes, they decide that the best way to exercise their rights 'while they still have them' is to do... that. To beat up their slaves. To kill them. While it's still legal."

"To prove what!" Jere demanded.

"How the fuck should I know?" Paltrek asked, taking another long pull from the vodka bottle. "Goddamn animals that they are. I think they just did it to ruin everything. Nobody was fucking celebrating once that started. People were screaming, running... the sounds from the slaves as they burned, as —"

Jere held up his hand. "No details," he reminded Paltrek.

Paltrek nodded. "Anyway, it escalated into a riot. I did what I could, but it just wasn't enough. I couldn't get to her fast enough, and when I did, they fucking pushed me back, telling me to keep my hands off of someone else's property. The only reason I even grabbed Arae when I did was because they had already thrown her on the pile of bodies."

Jere shuddered at that image, and felt Wren responding similarly next to him.

"I gave her to Dane, hoping there would be something you could do," Paltrek admitted. "And then I got into it with my sister, and our father was there as well, and he came by, and we fucking dragged her home. She's screaming bloody fucking murder the whole time about how we're assaulting her, how we're hurting her, after what she just did to that girl. First time in a long time that Daddy and I have agreed on something, but she was making us look like shit, and she needed to be off the street. Things are bad out there, Jere, I'm surprised the clinic hasn't gotten hit with emergencies yet."

Jere shook his head. "It has. It's not as bad as it could be. There are a few other healers out there, from other states, other counties. They came to support the passage of the SRA. You know, solidarity from the medical field. They must be handling most of it, at least for now."

"The patients in the clinic are the ones who got away quickly," Wren supplied. "But they're getting more severe."

Jere knew he was needed, and Paltrek seemed to get the hint. He got up and left, muttering something about making sure his slave was alive and unharmed. Jere knew fully well that Dane was fine, and he suspected that Paltrek knew the same. He was relieved to see his friend care so much.

Jere didn't have much time to reflect on Paltrek and Dane's relationship; he had injured patients to heal. He and Wren made their way to the clinic, where Jere gagged at the lingering odor of burnt flesh and death. There was still a corpse to be disposed of.

"I'll deal with it," Wren said quietly, giving Jere's hand a quick squeeze before taking off.

Jere wanted to cry. He couldn't imagine handling any of this without Wren; he couldn't even imagine spending a day in this house without him.

He was glad that the ban on treating slaves in his clinic had been lifted, because there were a number of slaves and free people with injuries ranging from cuts and burns to more gory disfigurements. Between him and Wren, they were able to keep up with the flow, clearing all the patients from the waiting room long enough for a break. He came back inside, finding Paltrek sitting next to Dane, his expression as empty as the liquor bottle next to him.

Finally, Paltrek picked his head up. "How'd Dane take it?" he asked, his expression hardened and waiting for the news.

Jere shook his head. "Not so well. That's why he's sedated."

Paltrek shook his head. "Jesus, did he do anything I should be concerned about? I'd hate to have to come down on him after he's been through something like this."

Jere felt irritated at Paltrek for even suggesting such a thing. He couldn't even formulate a response.

"He's just trying to keep things normal, babe," Wren cautioned him. *"He feels horrible, look at him! He doesn't know any other way to respond. This is something he can deal with."*

Jere relaxed a little, realizing that what Wren said was true. He forced himself to look at Paltrek, and he did look terrible. He looked closely, and saw a bruise on the side of his friend's face.

"Are you hurt?" Jere asked surprised. "I can heal it if you want."

Paltrek shook his head. "Annika got a few good punches in on me," he admitted. "And I started a fistfight with someone when the results came out. Don't bother healing it."

Jere nodded. If Paltrek wanted to suffer with the pain, he would let him. "Dane got a little self-destructive. He's devastated. His sister just died. He needs support."

Paltrek nodded. "Figured," he answered. He finished the bottle. "That fucking bitch sister of mine," he muttered.

"Yeah," Jere echoed.

"Is it okay if I stay here tonight?" Paltrek asked. "I'm not about to carry Dane home, and you're probably right. I should be here with him."

Jere nodded. "Yeah, of course. Do you want us to get another room ready, or —"

Paltrek shook his head. "Dane sleeps in my bed all the time," he admitted. "I don't mind sharing with him. Fuck, right now, I just want to make sure he doesn't just fucking off himself."

Jere went quiet, nodding his agreement.

Paltrek's eyes widened. "Jesus, he tried, didn't he? You think he's going to? I'll beat his ass if he tries to kill himself on my watch!"

Jere actually mustered a smile at that threat. It sounded cruel, but it was so well-intentioned and heartfelt that he couldn't help appreciating it.

"It wasn't a very coherent attempt," Jere informed him. "I think he just wanted to destroy something. He's hurting. Take care of him."

"Yeah," Paltrek agreed. "God, I drank too much. And I can still remember it. The screams... this was sick, Jeremy."

"You want a sedative, too?" Jere suggested, only half-joking.

"Don't tempt me," Paltrek muttered. "No, I'll just go to bed. Thank you for trying with Arae. I knew it was probably going to be futile, but I just had to try. For her, and for Dane."

Jere nodded. He had felt exactly the same way. He wondered if everything they had been trying for during the past few months was for nothing. It might feel different in the morning, but right now, it felt like such a terrible waste.

Chapter 37

Benefits

Jere wanted nothing more than to find peace and solace in Wren's arms for hours, but the peace didn't last long. He managed the ever-quickening pace at the clinic, wishing it would all go away. If there were riots now, Jere wondered what would happen in the upcoming weeks. More riots? More demonstrations? His faith in the Hojer police department wasn't strong enough to believe that they would have this under control.

"It's just temporary," Wren told him, trying to be comforting. "It will calm down once the SRA is officially passed. Once the demonstrations are over, it will be better."

"Better for who?" Jere asked. "Sure as hell not for Arae. Or the others. Wren, did you hear him? Paltrek? There was a *pile* of bodies. How many makes up a pile, do you think? Four? Five? Twenty—I don't even know how to begin to process this!"

Wren held him tight. "I don't know, and it doesn't matter. Obviously, none of them were in a good situation anyway; otherwise, this never would have happened. No master or mistress who is kind to a slave is going to do a thing like this just to prove a point."

"It's my fault," Jere insisted. "I brought this thing here. I was the one who pushed for it, who spearheaded it. If I had never started this bullshit—"

Wren silenced him with a kiss. "Think of the alternatives, Jere. Would you really want things to stay the way they were?"

"I don't want things to be the way they are now."

"This will stop," Wren reminded him. "The law will go into effect, the police will control it. This is temporary. What the laws were like before? Those problems were always a risk. What happened to Isis last year, what happened to me after the speed train accident? Being taken for evaluation? None of those things will *ever* happen again."

Jere nodded, still not entirely convinced.

"We both saw the massive number of healers and doctors out there — this is spreading. This is just the start. You helped to change things, to make things better for slaves. For us. It's becoming a national trend. All the reasons that you gave at the press conferences? Those weren't lies, Jere, and you know it. You were telling people the truth. Hell, you were protecting some of their rights to have slaves and treat them as they wanted, without audits like we faced. The people who are fighting this so hard... their slaves would have ended up like this anyway. Maybe not all on the same day, but that's how they would have ended up."

Jere shook his head, still haunted by the image of Arae's body, and the imagined image of a pile of similarly destroyed bodies. "Maybe they would have sold them or something," he muttered.

"What, to get a new one?"

It was a cold thought, but Jere knew it was true. He hated to think about it, but it was true. "They'll just get new ones now," he pointed out.

"Not before the SRA goes into effect tomorrow," Wren reminded him. "And besides, I wouldn't be surprised if a number of them got arrested. Not for what they did to their slaves tonight, that was unfortunately legal, but for the fights and destruction they caused. You saw it, just like I did. Those things aren't legal here, and they can carry hefty fines and even jail time."

"That's why Paltrek and his father went to drag Annika away," Jere realized. She had always been a monster, but having one of their esteemed family members put in jail like a commoner was unacceptable.

"The ones who died... it's over for them," Wren said gently, rubbing his hand up and down against Jere's back. "They don't have to suffer or fight anymore."

"Because they're dead."

"That's not always the worst thing," Wren reminded him. "Sometimes staying here with a terrible master is far worse than dying."

Jere pondered it for a moment. Wren knew that firsthand, and he knew how terrible it was to live in this state in general. Was it selfish of him to want Wren to continue living here? Leaving wasn't safe, but was staying any safer? The threats, the violence — this SRA was supposed to make things better, not worse. He had done this to keep Wren safe, but was he going to be in more danger? Jere was terrified that it was backfiring, and all he could do was cuddle with Wren and hope it got better.

Even that was ruined soon.

A noisy crowd could be heard, ever-so-faint, approaching the clinic. Jere glanced at Wren, hoping that he had just been hearing things.

"I guess the healers are burned out," Wren suggested.

"Or injured," Jere contributed, reluctantly rising to his feet.

Shaken, he made his way to the front entrance of the clinic, finding a small group of rather exhausted looking healers in front of him. A few had small cuts and bruises, most likely from being caught in the crossfire, but nothing more.

"They're bringing a few of the injured back here for treatment," one of them informed him. "There were a lot of injuries."

"I'm sorry, I..." Jere stammered. A part of him knew he should have been there. His medical ethics demanded that he help, that he heal the unwell, and his community ethics demanded it as well. Some of the people of Hojer weren't that bad; enough of them had cast their support in favor of the SRA encouraging the lawmakers to pass it. These were his neighbors, his regular patients, and he had abandoned them when they really needed him.

"Nobody expected you to be there," another of the healers pointed out. "You're more of a target than any of us are, and we figured it would be best for you to be available afterwards. Someone needs to heal us up, right?"

Jere managed to force a smile at that. It was true; while they could certainly heal one another, having someone on reserve to clean up the last vestiges of the mess had its appeal.

His clinic was suddenly filled with others like him, other healers. They made their way to exam rooms, where they tended to one another, and where Jere healed them. It was strange being around others with his same gift. He hadn't had this opportunity since he had been employed in Sonova. He missed it, the collegial nature, the jokes, the way that they knew exactly how draining and rewarding psychic healing could be. These were his people, and he was so often distanced from them.

Wren came out, perfectly polite and attentive. It still frustrated Jere, because even now, among his own kind, Wren wasn't accepted. He never would be in a slave state like Arona. Sure, these people were nice to him, nicer than most, at least, but they still saw him as something to be used and exploited. He had no doubt that they would treat their own slaves decently, but they would still treat them as slaves. Jere longed for home.

The healers' injuries were patched up pretty quickly, a little psychic healing and some traditional methods doing wonders. As they were healed, the remainder of those injured from the demonstration were carried to the clinic, mostly by slaves, although a few free people helped out as well when it was their loved one being brought in to be healed.

Jere quickly grew exhausted, dealing with all of this work at once. It was Wren who noticed, coming up behind him and carefully taking his hand.

"Go get Isis," Wren suggested. "You're letting them bleed you dry."

"She's upset," Jere protested. Isis was his usual energy source, not to mention another set of hands, but Jere didn't want to bother her. She was upset enough from seeing Arae, and he wanted to spare her the rest of the night.

"Go calm her down, and then siphon some energy from her," Wren persisted. "That's her job around here. She won't mind, and if you take enough, she'll probably sleep. I'm sure she has no plans of doing that now."

Jere nodded, seeing Wren's logic. He planted a quick kiss on Wren's lips before leaving, and if the healer who happened to be walking by was surprised, he didn't say anything.

Jere knocked on Isis's door, surprised when she got up and let him in.

"I was wondering when you'd be in here trying to do your vampire thing."

Jere smiled at the term. He really did feel like that; although the process of taking energy wasn't exactly like a fictional vampire sucking blood, it was close.

"Can I come in, or do you want to be in the clinic?"

Isis shrugged. "Do you need me in the clinic? I sure as hell don't want to be in there, but if you need the help, I guess that's what I'm here for."

Jere smiled at her offer. "Wren and I are managing pretty well. Like we used to."

"Yeah, except now you have a willing energy donor. I'd rather stay in here if you don't mind. There are so many people out there, a lot of healers. I swear, if one of them touches me, tries to steal my energy..." she shook her head. "Can we please just stay in here?"

Jere smiled, coming in and sitting on the edge of her bed. He would never allow someone to do such a thing, and he was pretty sure she knew that as well as he did, but it wasn't a completely illogical fear. Healers from a slave state would likely think nothing of such an action, although he assumed they would at least ask his permission, first. They asked to use his other tools and supplies.

She sat facing him, and he waited while she calmed herself and nodded before reaching out to put a hand on her face, lightly cupping around the back of her head. It was a good position to facilitate the energy transfer, and they did it often enough that it had stopped being too strange.

She let him in easily, and he connected to her psychic energy, turning the flow to himself. It was like a water faucet, except in reverse. He could feel himself filling up as she was drained, and he could feel her growing weaker and more tired with every minute that passed.

It was a short process. Not even ten minutes passed before Jere felt almost completely recharged. He pulled back, giving Isis her space, and watching in thinly veiled amusement as she shook off his touch like a dog would shake off water.

"No, you didn't hurt me, and no, I'll never get used to that," she declared, smiling at him. She knew Jere had experienced it himself, he had told her about how they used to practice on each other in medical school. It was a strange feeling.

"Are you sure you don't need anything else from me tonight?" she asked, looking instantly exhausted.

Jere shook his head. "Wren and I can manage. Plus we've got healers from all over. They can help, in exchange for the free healing they're getting. Are you gonna be okay?"

"Yeah," Isis said. "I've been through worse. Tell Wren I want something big and good for breakfast tomorrow."

Jere laughed at that. "I'll pass the message along. Thanks."

He returned to the clinic, leaving Isis to rest. He was glad he no longer had to worry about her the way he used to.

The night ran long. People kept wandering in, and Jere treated them accordingly. The out-of-town healers did their part, taking turns resting in empty exam rooms and eating the quick, simple meal Wren prepared to keep everyone well-nourished. Jere was reminded of his training days in the emergency rooms in Sonova, and was struck by a pang of loneliness. Still, this had to be a good sign. He had support, he had community... even the patients who were clearly opposed to the SRA were polite enough. Hojer needed him and he was here to stay. At least for a while.

By the following day, reinforcement police officers had been called in from other towns, and the number of riots dropped sharply to zero. If people were still killing their slaves, they were disposing of the bodies discreetly. Once the SRA was officially signed into law, the act was a crime, punishable by a considerable fine, up to a year in prison, and education on the proper keeping of slaves in a peaceful community. Nobody was testing that law out yet, but Jere was certain that it would come.

Paltrek and Dane left the following day. Paltrek was hung-over, Dane was still miserably depressed, but they had each other. Paltrek insisted that he had his hand around Dane because he was wobbly and needed his slave to support him, but Jere could see the way that it was Dane leaning into Paltrek, not the other way around, and he could see the way Paltrek squeezed him and promised him that everything would be getting better. Some things would never get better; Dane would never get his sister back. Monsters like Annika would continue to torment and abuse. Jere doubted he would be immune. Maybe the death threats would continue to come, sometimes thinly veiled in letters, sometimes in the forms of rocks through windows.

Jere was glad the SRA had passed, and that he had been a part of it. He had always done what he could for Wren and Isis at home, but he was their master. As a free person, he was the one with the power to change more than just how they ran things in private. He hated the role, but it gave him some leverage that he could use to his benefit. He might not be able to convince Wren to stay with him, and he would never force him to stay in a place like this forever, but while they were both here, it was his duty to make it as comfortable as possible. He had neglected those duties long enough; no matter how badly things had ended for others, he felt relief knowing that Wren and Isis would both benefit from the provisions of the SRA he had helped pass.

When he was summoned to meet with President Clemente again, he wasn't surprised. He went alone, figuring that Wren and Isis could use some time to catch up, anyway. The police slave still guarded the door, and Jere felt confident that his home, property, and family were safe.

"Thank you for supporting the SRA," Jere said as he entered the president's office. "It went over well. I hope your position as president is solidified for a while to come."

President Clemente nodded. "It is. I'm just trying to work out what happens next."

Jere was curious as to what his role was going to be in this process, but he didn't bother to ask. The man sitting in front of him clearly had the power to make things happen; Jere was just along for the ride, now.

"Now that the Slave Control, Regulation, and Enforcement Agency has been replaced with the Slave Regulation Board, and now that slaves must be treated in human health clinics, we need someone to serve as the director of our Slave Health Agency. That person will oversee the provision of healthcare to slaves across the state, including reviewing care, verifying that facilities are compliant, and performing state-mandated health screenings on slaves."

Jere nodded, fully agreeing. He hoped that person would be better suited for the job than Arnsdale was, but he had his doubts about anyone from a slave state. While the healers were in support of the new regulations, they still viewed slaves as far less than human.

"You'll be receiving a pay raise, and if you need additional assistants, we can provide them or provide you with the funds to purchase them," President Clemente continued. "You'll need to complete some additional trainings for slave-related issues. After all, our director needs to know how to perform sale evaluations."

Jere paused for a moment. "I'm flattered, sir, but I'm not sure I'm the right candidate for the job."

The president shrugged dismissively. "Once you sign it, your contract is indefinite. As a free man, you are always able to leave the state and void the contract. Don't forget that I pulled some significant favors to help you out recently. If I believe you are no longer a trustworthy associate, I may change my mind, and your assets may be seized again."

Jere felt his throat tightening. This bastard was threatening Wren, and he was barely trying to hide it.

"Dr. Peters, you are the person I want in this position. You were the one who brought the SRA to life, and unlike Ms. Arnsdale, I am completely confident that you and I will work well together in the future. I need that. So do you. So, are you interested?"

"I don't really have a choice, do I?"

"You always have a choice, Dr. Peters. The question is whether you can live with the choices you made."

Jere was quiet. He had hurt this man's daughter in ways that he should have been ashamed of. If this was the consequence, he was getting off fairly lightly. He'd want to do worse to Arnsdale if he ever got the chance, for what she did to Isis and Wren. "All right. I accept."

President Clemente smiled. "I'm glad we could come to an agreement. I foresee you having a long and happy life in Hojer."

Chapter 38
Decisions

Wren was pleased by how quickly things went back to normal, as if Hojer could ever be considered normal. What was left of the couches had been dragged outside and carted away by a team of slaves that worked for the city. Wren had picked out the new furniture from a catalogue he got at one of the stores, and a team of strength-gifted slaves would be delivering it later today. Once the house was put back together, he would feel more at home.

He knew that Hojer should feel normal to him, but living with Jere had changed him. He knew that the three of them were as normal as they were going to get. A slave, in love with his master, a master, in love with his slave, and yet another slave, their adopted little sister who was quickly turning from a damaged girl into a rather companionable young woman.

He and Isis enjoyed some downtime in the clinic for the first time in days. Jere had just finished sapping her of her energy, and she was working on food and Crucial Care to rebuild her strength.

"Aren't you glad that it's me instead of you who gets to do this?" she teased Wren.

"I have to admit that I am. I used to hate it when my old master would take my energy like that."

Isis smiled back at him. "I don't really mind it that much. Which I guess is good, seeing as it's pretty much an everyday thing, now."

There had been an increase in the number of slaves they were treating in the clinic. Just making the option available last year had opened the doors to many more patients; now that it was mandated that slaves be treated by human healers, the numbers were swelling.

Jere was even in contact with the local veterinarian, getting regular referrals from the most reluctant of slaveowners who still insisted on trying to get their slaves healed "on the side."

"It's busy," Wren agreed. "Hell, just keeping up with the front desk and all the records is a challenge, now."

Isis laughed. "Yeah, and you have a speed gift. And the other one. Still can't believe you kept that a secret. Jerk."

Wren smiled at her. Now that she knew, everything seemed easier. She was part of their family, after all. She deserved to know. And it was far easier to explain how the coffee was always kept warm without anyone needing to reheat it.

"It wouldn't be okay here without you," Isis blurted out, looking embarrassed the moment the words left her mouth. "We'd be too busy and stuff. I can't do what you do. The front desk, the people. I don't like to be alone with them. I can barely manage it when Jere is with me, and that's because he doesn't make me talk to them or do stuff for them. If you left, we'd have to get someone else, another slave or something, and I don't like other slaves, either. I don't like anybody else but you and Jere, and sometimes Kieran and Imelda. I don't want Jere to be all sad and moping all the time, and I don't want to try and explain how things work to some new person, and I don't want you to go."

Wren was silent, considering her words. He had come to his decision already, mostly, anyway, but he hadn't told either Isis or Jere, because he wasn't completely sure, and he wanted to wait for the right time.

"And I'll be really unhealthy, because neither me or Jere will make food, and we'll just eat toast and cookies and coffee all the time. And I'll miss you."

"Really?" Wren was a little surprised by the confession. He knew Isis didn't hate him like she used to, or fear him, but he thought she'd be okay if he just disappeared.

"You're from here. All the things that Jere doesn't get, you do, and you don't bitch all the time about how you want things to be different. You know how to deal with things the way that they are. And when Jere has his stupid whiny bitch moments and gets all depressed, you're the one who always cheers him up. He needs you, and so do I. I know it's not fair, and I know I don't even have any right to ask you this, but I don't want you to go."

Wren caved. He was going to tell Jere first, when he told him about the job offer letters, but he was waiting for the right moment, and the right moment presented itself with Isis first. "I'm not going anywhere."

"Just because I asked you?" Isis replied, in disbelief.

"Well, no," Wren admitted. "I've been thinking about it. I sort of made up my mind a few days ago, at least, for the most part. I want to stay, for now."

"Did you even tell Jere, yet?"

Wren shook his head. "Nope. Let the bastard stew for keeping us in the dark."

Isis giggled at that thought. "That's not really why you're doing it, though, is it?"

"No. I just wanted to be sure, completely sure, and I wanted to wait for the right time."

"So you picked a break at the clinic?" Isis said, giving him a skeptical look. "No offense, but you need to wait for a better 'right time' with Jere. He's going to want to be all happy and celebrate and kiss you and shit. This will make his fucking day."

"I know," Wren agreed, sharing a conspiratorial smile with her. "That's why I wanted to wait."

Isis looked proud. "Thanks for telling me. You should tell Jere tonight. I'll disappear after dinner, and you guys can have the house to do... whatever it is that you used to do after dinner, before you got me. Probably something super mushy and sweet."

Wren smiled, because she was completely correct in that assumption. The cuddling and kissing they used to do every night could absolutely be described as "super mushy and sweet."

"Thank you. It will mean a lot to both of us."

Isis shrugged. "No problem. You guys do a lot for me. The least I can do is let you have some time alone. If we ever all move to Sonova together, we have to have separate places to live, but like, next door to each other. That way, you guys can do your thing, and I can still be close, but not really in the same place."

Wren smiled at that thought. It was weird to think of moving to Sonova ever, much less as the three of them. He didn't know if it would ever be possible, but he figured that if Isis could consider it, he could as well. He wouldn't even mind having her nearby. In fact, he might even enjoy it sometimes.

The rest of the day passed quickly, and Wren contemplated all the possible ways in which he could deliver the good news to Jere.

As promised, Isis cleared out immediately after dinner, smiling and saying that she was still a little tired from the energy transfer. As usual, Jere was too busy trying to take care of her to have any clue what was going on, and she practically had to shove him away, insisting that she was just really tired, and that she really, really didn't need anything.

When she was gone, and Jere had stopped fussing over that fact, Wren took him and pulled him by the hand to the couch where they had spent so much time together. Well, not this exact couch. This was the new one, one of the two replacements that the insurance had provided. This one wasn't as soft or comfortable as the old one yet, and it still had some breaking in to be done. It was bigger, though, which made it that much more fun to cuddle up on.

"I have some things I need to tell you," Wren said, trying to look happy and hopeful instead of worried.

It didn't work. Jere's face fell immediately.

"Jere, I'm not—"

"I know," Jere said, shaking his head. "I know, you need to go, for your own sake. I won't take it personally, I mean, after what happened after the riots, with Arae, and I've been an asshole, and—"

Wren cut him off, pinning him against the back of the couch with a hard, passionate kiss. Jere was confused at first; at least, if the fact that his lips still moved in a desperate attempt to keep talking was any indication. Wren tried not to laugh at the utter ridiculousness of it, because that would spoil his plan to kiss Jere into silence.

Eventually, it worked, and he pulled away, smiling.

"I'm not leaving. Not anytime soon, anyway. I thought about it, and I want to stay with you."

Jere gave him a puzzled look. "But... but I thought you said you wanted to go, to be free?"

Wren laughed, pulling Jere into his arms. "Yes. But not as much as I want to stay with you."

"I'm not holding you back, am I?"

"Absolutely not," Wren assured him. "It's not *just* you. It's you, it's Isis, it's the work we have here, it's the SRA passing and all the things that might come after it. I have a life here, Jere. Do you even get how important that is?"

"Of course I do," Jere insisted. "I get it, community ties, and purpose, and—"

Wren placed a finger on his lips. "Shut up before I kiss you quiet again. Slaves don't have lives. They exist for their master, they work, they serve a purpose. They don't have hopes, or dreams, or futures. They just do whatever they need to survive, and that's pretty much the best that they can hope for."

"Okay..." Jere said, not quite getting it.

"I need to show you something," Wren said, quiet. He pulled out the job offer telegraphs that he had stashed since he received them weeks ago. He handed them to Jere, and he cuddled into his side, waiting as he read them.

Jere was quiet for a moment, studying them. "Wow, these took a long time to get here. They should have just sent them by mail. I guess the telegraph office really was busy with—"

"Jere, I've had these for almost two weeks," Wren interrupted. He couldn't look Jere in the face, so he settled for resting against his chest, instead. He waited for the response, and was pleasantly surprised to feel Jere's hand gently stroking through his hair.

"I'm guessing you didn't just forget them?" Jere said quietly.

Wren shook his head. His tongue suddenly felt stiff; at the thought of Jere leaving, he couldn't move, couldn't speak. As hot as he usually was, he felt frozen.

"Well, I think we did agree that you'd be better at hiding it than me," Jere pointed out. "Or is this payback for the months I kept you waiting?"

Wren shook his head again. He felt so low. Everything he had criticized in Jere, he had done exactly the same. "I'm sorry," he whispered.

Jere leaned down, kissing Wren lightly on the forehead. "I'm not angry. I am absolutely the last person in the world who should be angry. And I'm not going anywhere."

Wren breathed a sigh of relief, but he couldn't bring himself to look up just yet. He didn't want to see the disappointment in Jere's face; not because Wren had hidden the job offers, and not because Jere was choosing Wren over Sonova. "I should have shown you before telling you I was staying. It wasn't fair this way. I just wanted to be able to explain why I have to stay."

"Do you think I could see that beautiful face of yours while you explain it?" Jere suggested.

It was a suggestion, but the part of Wren that had loved Jere for years heard it as a plea, and the part of Wren that had been a slave for years heard it as an order. Reluctantly, he sat up, glancing up cautiously at Jere, waiting for the disappointment to crush him.

Jere was smiling softly, patiently. He didn't demand that Wren speak right away, he just waited.

"I got those when I came back from the evaluation," Wren admitted. "The thought of being apart from you, really apart, for a long time, or forever... it was like losing a part of my own body. I just froze, and I realized why you didn't tell me for so long, and I realized how scary it would be, how it would ruin everything we've worked so hard for, and I realized that I didn't want to make that decision and make you suffer by leaving, and I didn't want you to have to make it either. I thought you kept it from me because you were treating me like a slave. You kept it from me because you couldn't imagine a future without me, and that was how I felt when I saw that. You've always said you'd stay, always, no matter what, but I liked the option. I liked the plan to escape, because I've always needed a plan to escape. Whether it's death, or avoidance, or sex, or whatever, I want that choice, and the chance to cross the border? It was there. I never really wanted to go—I wanted the fantasy of going."

"Isn't it usually you who teases me about living in a fantasy world?" Jere asked, smiling. He ran a hand up and down Wren's arm, calming and comforting him.

"I felt so betrayed. I'm sorry I made you feel that way."

Jere shook his head. "You didn't, love."

"Don't just say that to make me feel better."

"Come on, at least I didn't have to hear it from Kieran while you were out of town," Jere teased, drawing the tiniest of smiles from Wren. "You told me once, back when we were getting ready for the certification, that collars aren't as nice when you can't take them off."

Wren nodded, failing to make the connection.

"No matter what I choose in life, no matter where I go, what I do, whatever, I get to choose that," Jere admitted. "You don't. I would move the fucking earth to give it to you, but ultimately, for as long as you remain in Hojer, or if you get caught trying to leave, you're a slave. Even if you escaped the border, you would still be a slave if you ever came back. You would never get the chance to travel freely, you'd never know what it was like to grow up in a place that didn't routinely torture children and enslave half the population. I like to play pretend, to act like everything is normal. I like to be able to take that collar off, and I do, even when it leaves you behind. I try to think of you not just as a free man, but as someone who grew up like I did—in a non-slave-state. I can feel more secure with you, because if I really want to keep you here, I can. That's not true both ways. And just because I pretend that doesn't exist, doesn't mean it's not true."

Wren nodded, amazed that Jere was finally reaching this conclusion. For so long, he had insisted that they were equal, that Wren had power... Wren had always been aware that everything he had was because Jere allowed it.

"I will never leave you," Jere said quietly. "Not for Sonova, not for more money, not because of anything. I won't ask you to make the same promise. You don't need to bear that responsibility. As a slave, you have enough. It's my responsibility; you just do what's best for you, I'll follow. If that means leaving at some point, we'll work with it. If it means staying and avoiding shitty political messes, I'll happily become a recluse. If it means making Hojer our home and continuing to change it, we can do that, too. We're on that path already. I will make my life wherever you make yours."

"I have a life with you," Wren admitted. "I look forward to seeing you every day. I look forward to seeing you after work even though we work *together*. I like that I can be here for Isis when you don't get things, because no matter how long you've been here, you'll always

be an outlander, and you'll never be a slave. I like the stupid con-
spiracies we plot out with Kieran, and the political things, no matter
how horrible they end up. I like them, because they're all things that
I choose, and they're things that are important to me. I like knowing
that some of our patients are starting to treat their slaves a little bit
better. I even liked seeing Paltrek and his terrible attempt to comfort
Dane. I like all of these things, because they're our life. Both of us.
And right now, that's more important than being free."

"You could have things in Sonova, too," Jere pointed out.

"I couldn't have you. Not for a while, and honestly... I don't
want Sonova. It was easy for Isis. It's safe, she's content, no need to
change things. I like to think I'm a little more secure than that, but
honestly, I don't want the change, either. I've spent my whole life
struggling and fighting and scared. I don't want to do it anymore. I
want to stay here with you. This SRA is making things better. I don't
want to leave just yet."

Jere gave him a hopeful smile. "You really mean it? You're not
going to resent me for keeping you here, right?"

Wren grinned, pulling Jere in for another kiss. "Like you resented me for keeping you here for the past two years? Look, I wanted
time to think about it, because I was so fucking angry at you when I
found out you were keeping it a secret from me. I wanted the choice,
and I wanted you to give it to me without a fight. I didn't realize
how threatening that choice could be. But the more I thought about
it... the choice is nice, but what I really want is to stay."

"That's a relief," Jere admitted. He smiled at Wren a little bit.
"When I met with President Clemente yesterday, it wasn't just so he
could tell me that he wants me to be the new director of the Slave
Health Agency. It was so he could tell me that he's basically hijack-
ing my life. He knows what I did to his daughter, and I think he
knows there's something special about you. He's made it clear that
my position is no longer voluntary. I stay, or you and Isis are at risk.
I didn't tell you because I didn't want to pressure you either way."

"So you're stuck here as well as I am?" Wren realized.

"Pretty much. Is it strange that I don't mind?"

Wren shook his head. "Maybe one day, we'll all be ready to
move on, but that's not anytime soon. Especially with shitty success

rates like that program has."

Jere even laughed at that one. "Kieran was so proud of them," he pointed out.

"Kieran has never set foot inside of a training facility," Wren replied.

Chapter 39
Marking

It was quiet for a moment. Wren held Jere close, loving the familiar feeling of just cuddling with him. It brought back memories of those first few weeks when they started their relationship, the tentative touches, kissing, exploring each other in the way that new lovers did.

"I'm so happy you're staying," Jere confessed, his voice barely above a whisper. "I was scared that you were really going to leave. And if you ever get job offers or something for me again—keep them. Although, I might send the one from Sonova to my mum, just to make her laugh. I tried so hard to get into that hospital when I was first out of medical school."

"I'm pretty happy you're staying, too," Wren poked fun at him. "Although, if you threaten to abandon Hojer without telling me about it first again, I'll tie you up and beat you."

"Promise?" Jere challenged, a playful look on his face. "That sounds like a pretty good night to me."

Wren laughed, tossing him lightly against the arm of the couch and kissing him roughly, his hand snaking its way down between them to cup Jere's cock, pleased when he made him gasp.

"Oh, look what I found," Wren teased. Jere thrust up against him. "You know, we haven't broken this couch in very well, yet."

Jere's eyes lit up at the suggestion. "That is a damn shame," he agreed, rocking his body against Wren's.

They kissed for a while, slowly, with nothing to rush them. After a while, Wren's hands came up under Jere's shirt, slowly sliding it up and away, exposing his chest for Wren to explore. He worked his tongue, teeth, and lips over Jere's skin, biting here and there, licking little circles with his tongue, faster and faster, until all that could be seen was a pink circle. Jere's hands worked over Wren's back, caressing and stroking the skin he had touched so many times before. Wren thought it had never felt better. After a while he shifted slightly, helping Jere to slip his shirt over his head. He breathed deeply as Jere touched him as well. He reached for Jere's pants, unbuttoning them quickly and starting to slide them down before Jere stopped him.

"Shouldn't we move this to the bedroom?" Jere suggested.

Wren shook his head. "Breaking in the new couch, remember?" he teased. At Jere's doubtful look, he explained further. "Isis was kind enough to offer us the house for the night. That's why she went to bed early. She wanted to let us celebrate with 'mushy sweet stuff' as she put it."

"She knows already?" Jere said, surprised. From the look on his face, he might have even been a little hurt to be the last to know.

Wren smiled, cupping Jere's face in his hand. "I didn't plan on telling her first; I was going to tell you both at the same time. But we were talking in the clinic today, and it just sort of popped out. So we planned this out for tonight. So you and I could celebrate."

Jere smiled. "I guess I had it coming. Not so fun to be the one on the other side of the plotting."

Wren laughed, resuming where he left off with Jere, sliding his pants down his long legs and tossing them aside. "That wasn't my purpose, but I'll admit, it does have a bit of justice to it. I didn't tell her about the job offers. Something told me you'd stay if I stayed, and I wouldn't worry her about it. Like she said, she doesn't care as long as she's here with us. The two of you are a lot alike in that respect."

"We're simple. You're the complex one. Skilled, talented...."

"Would you like to see some of those talents in action?" Wren suggested.

Jere smiled, nodding as Wren's hands pulled his legs apart, reaching for Jere's cock and grabbing it possessively. It was getting harder and harder with each stroke. Gracefully, Wren bent down, taking the length into his mouth quickly, sucking and swallowing like he couldn't get enough. Jere gasped, clutching at Wren's shoulders, holding on as though he was going to fall off of the world

Wren responded by sucking more forcefully, eagerly taking Jere deeper and deeper. Blowjobs had never been his favorite thing, but he had grown to enjoy them with Jere. Wren could relax, which made him far less likely to gag and choke, and he trusted Jere to be patient and careful with him. Making Jere lose all sense of control and dignity and hearing him beg for more helped as well.

It wasn't long before he had Jere at that point, and the fact that he was playing with Jere's ass while sucking his cock helped. He had no specific purpose in mind, he just knew that Jere loved the feeling of his ass being touched, kneaded, fingered, caressed, and he loved doing it. He never thought he would feel possessive over another person's body, but he did with Jere's. He touched it like he owned it, pleased when it responded exactly how he wanted it to. He loved Jere's body.

"You're the only one I've ever enjoyed touching," Wren admitted. "Or being touched by. I don't know how I lived for so long without knowing what it was like to feel this way."

"Me either," Jere agreed, touching Wren wherever he could reach — his shoulders, his hair, his face, his hands when they strayed up. "I've enjoyed it plenty of times before, but what I feel for you goes so far beyond that."

Wren sat up, fished a bottle of lube out of his pocket, thankful that he had come prepared, and started unfastening his own pants. He moved slowly on purpose, knowing Jere liked to watch.

Jere surprised him, sitting up and covering Wren's hands with his own. "Let me?" he asked.

Wren nodded, smiling as Jere made quick work of the fastening and eased his pants down, sliding them over his hips with so much care and gentleness that Wren felt like he was being worshipped. It was yet another thing that other people had done in the past to hurt, but Jere did so flawlessly. It was odd that such a simple act could make him feel this way, but it did, and he loved Jere that much more for it.

Soon, they were both naked and it was Jere's turn to service Wren. Jere's style so much different than Wren's; he helped Wren to lean back, positioning him carefully and making sure he was comfortable, smiling before dipping down to his cock, a slow, intentional movement that had Wren shuddering. Wren hadn't planned for this, but he loved it, and he knew Jere did as well, and he would never turn him down. As Jere worked his cock, Wren let one hand roam, finding Jere's head and wrapping his fingers in his hair, pulling him down in the way that turned them both on. In between sucking, Jere pulled off occasionally, turning his attention to Wren's ass, licking and kissing the sensitive skin there, dipping his tongue inside, only to come back for more of his cock.

Too soon, Wren was pushing Jere away, telling him to stop. "You're wonderful, but I have something else planned," he insisted, reaching for the lube again. He handed it to Jere.

"I just wanted to get you started," Jere pointed out, taking the lube. He started to reach behind himself.

"No," Wren said, catching his arm. "I want you inside of me. I want to ride you. But I want you to get me ready. You do it... it's so much hotter the way you do it."

Jere smiled, looking completely thrilled with the idea. He poured some lube in his hands and slowly worked it all over Wren's ass, inside of him, over his cock. Wren felt himself opening for Jere immediately, the soft, insistent fingers spreading him without being too demanding or uncomfortable. Jere had always known how to make his body do the most wonderful things.

When Wren was far past the point of being ready, he put a hand on Jere's shoulder, pushing lightly to signal him to stop. Jere came up, a proud smile on his face, and kissed Wren again before leaning back to where he had been, needing no further instructions.

Wren was on him instantly, his speed gift taking him from one side of the couch to the other in just seconds. His lips locked with Jere's for a moment as he maneuvered them both, finding the perfect place for their legs and hips, lining himself up with Jere's cock. He sat up, seeking the right angle, and slowly eased himself down, throwing his head back in pleasure as he felt Jere filling him. It was a wonderful, familiar feeling that he had grown to love. As he settled himself onto Jere's cock, he felt his temperature rising. It felt so good to express that part of himself, to use his gift to increase his pleasure and Jere's. He leaned back, adjusting the angle, and felt the tops of Jere's legs, brushing heat over them for just a moment.

Jere lay beneath him, reaching up to stroke his hands lightly over Wren's thighs. He reached back to feel the top of his ass, then around to the front again to take his cock. He held it in his hands and stroked it, slowly at first, then he built up speed as Wren started to work himself up and down on Jere's cock, faster and faster. Wren bit down on his lower lip to keep from crying out. Wren knew that the bedroom that he and Jere shared was soundproofed, but he wasn't too certain about the rest of the house. There was a naughty element to enjoying themselves in what had become a public area, and that added to Wren's excitement. He kept riding Jere until he felt himself about to come, thrusting to take him deeper and to drive his cock in and out of Jere's hands, which somehow always managed to be exactly where he needed them to be.

He covered Jere's hands with one of his own, warming it enough that he could feel the heat on his own cock. Jere shuddered underneath of him, the warmth turning him on even more.

"Do it again," Jere mumbled. "Mark me. Burn me. I want your handprints on my chest tomorrow."

Wren had to hold back to keep himself from coming at that request. "Like before?" he asked, adjusting himself so he could still work up and down on Jere's cock while placing his hands on Jere's chest. It was, fortunately, a convenient position.

"More," Jere challenged, a needy smile on his face. "I want it to last."

"It will hurt," Wren cautioned, feeling the heat spread through his hands. It was amazing how it came out; the same white-hot flames that had ignited paper and clothing and buildings could be toned down so easily, used for someone he cared about so much.

"Good," Jere replied.

"Tell me when to stop," Wren cautioned, raising the temperature in his hands as gradually as possible, feeling Jere's skin warm underneath. As it did, Jere gasped, struggling to hold himself still, but failing. He twisted and bucked, each movement sending waves of pleasure through Wren's body.

"Stop when you want to," Jere mumbled, arching his back and

pressing firmly against Wren's hands with his chest. "I trust you."

Once again, Wren felt his body trying to come, and he willed it away. He needed to be more focused, more concerned with Jere's safety, more in control. He kept increasing the heat, little by little, until he was sure it would leave marks for many, many days without blistering. Instead of removing his hands, he focused on the temperature once more, bringing it back down gently, stopping the burn right where he wanted it.

Finally, he shifted positions, leaning down so he could kiss Jere, muffling the sounds that he wanted to make. The new position was good; Jere's cock hit him in places it hadn't before, and Wren came quickly, moaning as he continued to kiss Jere, shaking as his orgasm almost overwhelmed him. The motions set Jere off as well, and Wren smiled as he heard Jere struggle to stay quiet, thrusting into him a few more times before he came.

They lay there, spent, naked, and messy with come. Wren was utterly content.

"I like the new couch," he decided.

"Me too," Jere agreed.

Wren considered it. "I think I like being anywhere that you are."

Jere didn't even take a moment to think before replying. "I know I do."

Author's Notes

Inherent Cost had a long development period. It started as a few simple scenes that didn't fit into *Inherent Risk*, and slowly I realized that these characters had more of a story to tell. Wren and Jere's love for one another had been firmly established in my world, but I wondered what would happen when this relationship was put to the test of a cruel outside world. More than any other book in this series, this one reflects the real world: how do we react in the face of disease? Where do politics and public safety intersect? Where do privacy and personal rights fit into the greater good?

Expanding beyond the safety of Wren and Jere's home and clinic brought with it a unique set of challenges. As their world expanded, so did mine, and the process of figuring out how to structure governments, how to handle exploitation, and how to do it all while sharing a sexy, romantic story brought a number of challenges. Fortunately, the stellar team at ForbiddenFiction (especially Rylan Hunter and James L. Wolf) was there to help make this happen! I am so pleased to see this little book "grow up" into something that is moving, exciting, and still hot as hell.

As the conclusion of the trilogy, this is the end of Wren and Jere's story... for now. I am currently working on some other ideas set in the same world, and I have no doubts that we will be seeing these two again.

—Alicia Cameron

About the Author

Alicia Cameron has been making up stories since before she can remember. After discovering erotica during a high school banned books project, she never really turned back. She lives in Denver, Colorado with a tiny dog and rabbit who conspire regularly to distract her from doing anything productive. By day she works in the mental health field and is passionate about youth rights and welfare. In her spare time, she enjoys traveling, glitter, and punk rock concerts.

ForbiddenFiction works by Alicia Cameron

Inherent Gifts Series

Inherent Gifts
Inherent Risk
Inherent Cost

Short Stories

Cuts so Deep
Dangerous Steps
In Other Hands
Jingle Boy
Twisted Gifts
Party Favors
Hot Rain
Lessons Learned

Demoted Series

Subjection
Sedition
Succession

Short Stories

Bethel's Brothel
Call It Even
For Science

Inherent Gifts

The Fall made the world a better place. The collapse of the old society and the struggle for survival in its ruins gave humanity a fresh start. The deaths of so many clarified things, it required the survivors to focus on what was really important. And the rise of those preternaturally gifted in mind and body allowed humanity to rebuild the world without completely returning to the toxic old ways.

Jere is a young doctor with a gift for psychic healing. Unable to find work in his native Sonova, he takes over an old friend's small-town medical practice after the friend's death in a mysterious fire.

Hojer is as different a place from Sonova as Jere could imagine. In Arona, the nation-state of which Hojer is a part, the physically gifted are enslaved, owned by psychic masters who ruthlessly punish any disobedience.

Wren is the slave whom Jere inherited along with the medical practice. Burned in the fire and broken by a lifetime of cruelty, Wren wants only to serve and be ignored.

Jere had never imagined that he would own a slave. He'd certainly never thought he'd fall in love with one. But in Hojer, where simple kindness to a slave is forbidden, loving Wren could be the end for both of them.

About the Publisher

ForbiddenFiction.com is a publisher devoted to writing that breaks the boundaries of original erotic fiction. Our stories combine intense sexuality with quality writing. Stories at ForbiddenFiction.com not only arouse readers through sensations, but also engage them emotionally and mentally through storytelling as well-crafted as the sex is hot.

ForbiddenFiction.com is also designed to be a social reading environment. You'll have fun even if just reading the latest post each day, yet you will have the chance for so much more. Readers and authors can be part of ongoing discussions of specific works and individual authors as well as more general topics.

Sign up for a FREE Membership today at ForbiddenFiction.com.